PRIME STOCK

THE STOCK SQUAD

MEL A ROWE

Also by Mel A ROWE

ELSIE CREEK SERIES:
The Art of Dust
Diamond in the Dust
Caked in Dust
Xmas Dust
Muster in the Dust
Rolled in Dust
Written in Dust
Doctoring Dust
Buffalo Dust

OASIS OF THE OUTBACK DUOLOGY:
The Station, Volume One
The Station, Volume Two

THE STOCKMEN SERIES:
Stockman's Sandstorm
Stockman's Stowaway
Stockman's Stormcloud
Stockman's Showdown

THE STOCK SQUAD:
Rough Stock
Cold Stock
Wild Stock
Prime Stock

STANDALONE STORIES:
Avoiding the Pity Party
Unplanned Party
The Football Whisperer
Winter's Walk
Run Beautiful Run
The Sister Trip
Forget Forever

Receive exclusive insights, and news on upcoming releases by joining:
https://melarowe.com/newsletter/

COPYRIGHT

This book is written in Australian English.

PRIME STOCK: *Refers to elite livestock with superior genetics and high market worth.*

Zero

2½ years ago

They say you only fall in love once.

They never say how much it hurts.

Love. It sucks.

And when you lose it, like really lose it—and all other forms of love—you end up in a place where footsteps echo down a concrete corridor, where chains clink and guards keep that wary step back.

The air in here is always cold and damp, like the walls were bleeding out every secret ever locked behind them. And someone like Finn Wilde? He was just another ghost in a Victorian relic that reeked of regret, cheap bleach, and old stone.

Finn never reacted to the sights and sounds in this hellhole. He'd just watch everyone like the apex predator he had fought to become. That's why they left him alone. Everyone knew not to mess with the inmate in cell twenty-three.

Even handcuffed and shackled like a dog, you'd know he was trouble.

The guy who got no visitors. Got no calls.

And friends? Ha.

The only one who'd bothered about Finn was the ex. From the other side of the country, she'd send the odd letter and regularly top up his canteen account to buy rations—instant coffee, toothpaste, a chocolate bar now and then.

Truth was, he didn't need anything or anyone anymore.

What he did need was the sun on his back, dust on his boots. The scents of horse sweat, saddle leather, wide skies and open paddocks. Not this. Not concrete, chains, and flickering lights that buzzed like blowflies over a carcass.

The guard in front led the way, with two behind. They never spoke to Finn. They kept their distance like they were handling a loaded weapon, as they walked him into the interview room — the one they kept for special guests.

Not that it was that special. Just a large, reinforced cage, without cameras, yet closed in enough for the guards to jump him, if needed.

Inside, there was a table, two chairs, and the visitor. Andrew *Drew* Bannon.

Now there was a ghost from the past.

'That won't be necessary, guard, you can uncuff him.' Drew stood from the table. In a neat suit, tie done up proper, with his short hair greyer than Finn remembered.

'But, Commissioner—'

'Say what now?' Finn arched an eyebrow at Drew, looking all official. A long way from the officer who used to wear scuffed boots and swear at broken printers in the old cop shop that was barely standing in the sticks.

The guard hesitated.

But Drew nodded again.

With a clink of chain, the cuffs came off.

Finn rubbed his wrists. Didn't sit. Didn't speak.

Drew then smiled like they were old mates catching up over a beer. 'Still not much of a talker, eh?'

Finn shrugged.

'You look well.'

Finn glanced at the ceiling light buzzing overhead. 'Place agrees with me.'

That earned a laugh.

Drew dragged out a chair and sat down, motioning for Finn to do the same. 'I've got a job for you.'

Finn didn't move.

Drew smiled. 'You always did prefer to stand.'

Finn still said nothing.

Drew rested his elbows on the table and folded his hands as if in prayer. A closed folder lay in front of him. 'So, you belted up your OIC. No one's arguing that. But, if it had been me, and someone had blocked my wife's messages while my boy was dying...' Drew peered around, and his voice dropped, 'I might've done worse.'

You'd think after eighteen months it wouldn't hurt. But it sure as hell made Finn bitter. This place was good at letting old wounds fester deep into your bones, twisting that bitterness into a heavy numbness that meant nothing surprised him anymore. Not since they'd buried his boy without him.

Drew slid a folder across the table. 'There is a way out of this, Finn. As the Federal Agricultural Commissioner —'

Finn let out a low whistle. 'Who'd you kill for that job?'

Drew chuckled, adjusting that fancy tie. 'Some days, I feel like the job is killing me.'

'It suits you.' The guy always had that politician's touch of speaking in circles and rarely giving a straight answer. 'What do you want, Drew?'

'I'm trying to set up a federal stock squad.' Drew tapped on the file. 'And I want you to run it.'

He tilted his head at Drew. 'From in here?'

'No, because I got you a pardon.' Drew pushed the paperwork across the table. 'This is your *get-out-of-jail-free* card.'

'Nothing is for free.' Finn knew that. 'And I don't work for suits.'

Drew smiled like he'd been expecting that. 'You won't be. But I remembered when you were a kid who'd brought down that string of stock thieves and helped me through the paperwork. You were what...'

'Sixteen.' It's why he wanted to be a cop. And how Drew had ended up being his mentor, through the bad and the downright ugliness that life kept piling up on him.

'I'm not a cop anymore.' Finn didn't believe in justice

either—not anymore. Not after what they'd done to him. So why the hell was Drew offering him a badge now?

Drew leaned back, nodding like he'd expected that question, too. 'But you're a man who knows what's right, in a world that keeps getting it wrong. That's enough.'

Finn remained silent. He didn't do speeches.

'Listen, son, I'm giving you a shot to do something real, out there…' He pointed to the high windows, so heavy with grime it effectively blocked out the world.

'I need your help, Finn. These farmers, they're already doing it tough. And when their livestock, their livelihood, goes missing no one cares. I can show you the figures of how rare it is for anyone to catch those thieves. And I want you to help them.'

Drew leaned forward, his forearms resting on the table. 'You'll answer directly to me. There will be no other brass breathing down your neck. Just you and the land, doing what you were born to do. You're a born stockman who thinks like a cop, which is a rarity these days. And we both know you never back down from a fight. So, this is your shot, Finn, to build something that matters.'

Finn stared at him, not saying a word.

This time, Drew didn't fill the silence. He just waited.

And, finally, Finn asked, 'Where?'

One

Present Day—Elsie Creek, Northern Territory

Taryn Hayes stepped off the tiny plane with her large suitcase, her chunky workbag, and the unshakable feeling that the sun had a personal vendetta against her. Especially when the heat hit like a wall that was thick, dry, and horrifically hostile.

She adjusted her sunglasses, scanning the bare patch of asphalt they called an airport. They didn't even have a terminal.

But it had an uninterrupted view of the surrounding outback, and a cranky old man in a pair of grease-stained grey coveralls, squinting at her like a geriatric Popeye having a bad day.

'Taxi?' she asked.

'Where d'ya think you landed, eh? New York?'

'How about some directions—'

'I'm not your tour guide, lady. I don't do tourists.'

'I'm trying to get to Elsie Creek Police Station.'

He barked a laugh. 'Foot falcon it is, then.'

'Huh?'

'You're hoofin' it. Road's that way. Unless you can climb a fence. The cop shop's there.' He pointed across the tarmac to where a cluster of buildings sat.

There was a gigantic red cross covering the roof of what she assumed was the hospital. A painted Dalmatian, cocking its leg at a red fire hydrant, lived on another roof. The building next to it, had a masked burglar carrying a sack held back by a very muscular arm, in what could only be described as a comic book scene that covered the entire roof. 'What is that?'

'Strong arm of the law.'

'That's the police station?'

'Yeah, it's good advertising, I reckon. The Sarge put floodlights on it so you can see it for miles.'

'He paid for that painting on the roof?'

'Nah. It just showed up one day, like all the other roofs that got painted in town. Didn't you see it from the sky?'

'I was looking out the other side of the plane.'

'Tourists. Just what this world needs, more bloody tourists.' He rolled his eyes, wiping his hands on his small hand towel, the same colour as his coveralls.

'I'm not here as a tourist, but to work at the police station.' She pointed to the building.

'Well, then, you'll have to take the long way round, won't ya? Coz no one walks on my airstrip, especially tourists in a city suit asking twenty-thousand questions.' He grumbled, disappearing around the side of a plane.

With a silent curse, Taryn grabbed the handle of her suitcase and trudged forward. Her heels immediately sank into the red dirt. It didn't take much for the blisters to start forming where the powdery dirt created friction inside her shoes, and that was before she'd even hit the main road.

And then she saw it.

A water buffalo.

Not just any buffalo…

This one had flowers and ribbons twisted through his horns like he was off to a wedding. Someone had scrawled SUPERMARKET SPECIAL: 50% OFF BAKED BEANS & BULK BOG ROLLS in white chalk across his black coat.

Taryn froze, unsure what the protocol was for approaching water buffaloes.

He snorted at her, only to turn around, ribbons fluttering in the breeze as he strolled past the sign:

Welcome to Elsie Creek

Behind her, the highway stretched out like a long strip of liquorice left to roast under the sun and disappear on the horizon. The odd dusty ute or two shifted ahead on the haze of heat that shimmered to distort the town.

Twin railway lines ran alongside the road in perfect unison, making up the boundary line for the stockyards. Although empty now, the yards were a ghost town of chaotic rails and troughs, bigger than the small outback town that was home to the Federal Stock Squad.

The wheels of her suitcase struggled on the road, her heels faring just as badly, as she kept walking the airport's outer perimeter. Along a highway that had no cars.

Suddenly, the ground shook beneath her heels like an earth tremor, as a deep rumble swelled to a roar. Taryn turned, eyes wide, heart in her throat, as a wall of red dust exploded skyward, led by a mountain of metal hurtling straight toward her.

It was a truck. Technically. But nothing like the semi-trailers she'd seen back in the city. This thing was a monster—three trailers long, and full of diesel fury.

It thundered past her, sending the wind to slap at her sideways, as a fresh wave of red dirt blasted into her hair, down the collar of her blouse, even into her bra. Leaving her neatly pressed suit streaked in outback grime, to look like she'd just wrestled a dust devil and lost.

'Seriously!'

Dusting off what she could—although the red dirt seemed part of her DNA now—Taryn resumed dragging her suitcase in a one-woman wrestling match against dirt, rubble, and a supposed road.

On the corner stood a cluster of sun-bleached signs that pointed this way and that: *Hospital, Park Rangers, Aged Care*— *The Lodge, The First Responders…*

On the right, stood the quaintest firehouse she'd ever seen. It looked like a dollhouse. Now she understood why the cartoon of a Dalmatian, mid-pee on a fire hydrant, was painted on its roof. Even if it was utterly ridiculous, it did give a certain quaint charm and unique character to the building.

So the other painted roofs she'd seen from the air—a cracked spanner, a vintage 50s styled woman in curlers, a snail racing with envelopes in its mouth, and the Mad Hatter's tea party—had her curious to see which business matched which painted roof.

When a puff of warm breath hit the back of her neck.

Slowly—*very slowly*—she turned around.

A *really big* buffalo stared at her. Ribbons tangled around one horn, and a daisy stuck to his ear, with the supermarket specials smeared in chalk across one side. His big black shiny nose sniffed at her neck, her ear, her hair.

It was enough for Taryn's breath to catch somewhere between a scream and a prayer.

If she moved, would he chase her?

If she moved too fast, would he jab her?

Even though the ribbons and flowers made him look friendly, that didn't change the fact his wide horns could skewer a watermelon without breaking a sweat.

But there were no cars, and no one to help her. Just her suitcase, and a walking billboard made out of a buffalo with the body of a tank and the manners of a Labrador.

She eyed the police station just down the street—so close.

'Alright, buddy,' she whispered, as if negotiating with a hostile hostage taker. 'I'm going to walk. Slowly. And respectfully. And you can just keep on advertising that toilet paper special like a good boy.'

She stepped sideways, one inch at a time, with her eyes locked on the buffalo.

He just watched her through long black lashes, tail swooshing with ribbons, as one ear flicked away a fly.

'Okay now, we're doing this…' Closing her eyes, Taryn turned her back on the beast, and resumed dragging her suitcase while walking on nails, ready to run at the first sign of attack.

Clip-clop. Clip-clop.

He was right behind her shoulder, breathing heavily in a way that was going to give her nightmares for a week.

How did he sneak up on her like this?

And who in their right mind allowed a water buffalo to roam the streets?

Almost there.

The *Police* sign glowed like a beacon of hope ahead. The car park held a sleek patrol car.

One step onto the bitumen. Then another.

The buffalo followed.

She didn't dare look back. Not now.

Just a few more steps and she'd be safe—or at least indoors and out of this scorching heat.

But as she neared the entrance, her reflection in the glass doors stopped her in her tracks. There she was, a walking dust storm in a suit, hair like a bird's nest as if coming off a big booze-bender… and behind her, a buffalo.

How did she end up like a tourist in a wildlife documentary gone wrong? When it was meant to be a simple trek to the office.

All she needed now was a David Attenborough voiceover: *Here we see the unsuspecting city woman moments before she realises she's wildly out of her depth…*

Finally, she reached the entrance, the door slid back, and the cool air hit her in a wave.

But the buffalo kept on coming.

'*Out, Cecil!* You know the rules.' The Aboriginal officer behind the high counter clapped her hands. The buffalo huffed, as he walked backwards out the doors, which thankfully slid shut.

Taryn could breathe again.

'So, you've met Cecil.'

'I'm assuming that's the creature with flowers on his horns?'

'Water buffalo. Big sook. Cecil wouldn't hurt a fly, unless

you try to shoot him, that is.'

'Naturally…' WTF!

The police officer, with perfectly groomed eyebrows and long lashes, blinked once. Twice. 'Can I help you?'

Taryn straightened her suit, wincing at the gritty rub of dust that was like sandpaper beneath her shirt, sticking to every patch of sweat. She smoothed her hair—or tried to—dislodging a fresh sprinkle of red dust that rained down around her shoes like confetti at a very unfortunate wedding.

Not exactly the impression she'd been aiming for. Still, Taryn lifted her chin, cleared her throat, and announced, 'Good morning. I'm looking for a Sergeant Finn Wilde.'

'And you are?'

'Oh, um…' She rummaged through her workbag, sending up a puff of red dust like she'd just upended a chalkboard eraser. 'I'm a federal investigator…' She dragged out her laminated ID card with the flair of someone trying to pretend she hadn't just face-planted into the outback. 'Here for the Stock Squad.' She gave a tight smile.

The receptionist's name badge read Tanisha, the letters for *Aboriginal Community Police Officer* half-obscured by fun stickers of tiny glittery cactuses and cocktail glasses. It gave the impression of someone cheerful. Yet, the receptionist's gaze raked over Taryn like she was scanning a barcode.

'Heard you were coming.' Like a queen ruling her kingdom from behind the front counter, Tanisha buzzed her through the security door.

To the right, a door marked OIC sat half-open, revealing a uniformed officer deep in a phone call. On the left, a large table—cluttered with half-read magazines, a closed laptop, and a chair buried under a landslide of folders—bridged the space between the back of the reception desk and a cramped kitchenette.

'Down the hall, on the right. Finn's there.' Then, Tanisha smirked. 'Don't worry. He only bites when provoked.'

'Well, okay then…' Taryn nodded. Although in desperate need of a hairbrush and an industrial dust buster, she marched down the hallway with her heels clicking sharply on the worn lino.

The cool air did little to hide the scent of dust, coffee, and whatever secrets old paperwork held onto after decades in a filing cabinet.

She tugged her suitcase behind her, wincing at the soft *thud thud* of its uneven wheels, half-convinced she was leaving a Hansel-and-Gretel trail of red dust.

When she reached the door it was slightly ajar. Stuck to it was a plain printout that read:

STOCK SQUAD

Beneath it, someone had scrawled in pen:

THE BATCAVE: Enter at your own risk.

Taryn brushed down her suit again—though at this point it was more symbolic than effective. But she was aiming for composed. Polished. Government-grade. Professional.

Even if it had taken the better part of two days with a flight that took her the long way around, that included three cities, and a questionable vending machine sandwich to get to the tiny tropical city of Darwin—where she'd landed just after midnight, bleary-eyed and questioning her life choices. Then five hours in a plastic airport chair with all the ergonomic charm of a cattle crate, until the mail plane took off at dawn.

What followed was a six-hour rollercoaster ride across the outback skies. Bouncing through turbulence, along with numerous take-offs and landings where the pilot chucked parcels out the door like Santa wearing a hi-vis vest, boots, and denim cut-off shorts.

By the time they landed in Elsie Creek, she was exhausted, fried, and sweating through clothes that used to be clean. Just to stare at a door marked *Batcave.*

She pushed the door open.

Inside the long rectangular room, whiteboards lined the

walls on the right, crowded with photos, scribbled notes, and red string, that looked more like a murder board than a mission plan. Large maps were spread across a table big enough for a family reunion. On the left were assorted desks. One desk held a graveyard of drone parts. Another, a V8 engine manual. A third sported cowboy spurs, a whip, and—naturally—dust.

And there he was.

Finn Wilde.

Or so she assumed, as he was the only one in the office.

Yet the man filled the room. With shirtsleeves rolled up, his tattooed forearms flexed as he adjusted something metallic on a workbench, while half-reading a file that seemed small in his heavily inked hands. Yet he seemed quiet. Intent.

She opened her mouth—

And immediately wished she'd rehearsed this bit.

He didn't look up as his muscular neck corded with tension, while working calmly, like the rest of the world didn't exist. Another sliver of ink peeked from beneath his collar, no doubt curling down his shoulder where there had to be more bad-arse tattoos. Effectively giving him the presence of someone who didn't need to announce authority—it just rolled off him in waves. Quiet. Controlled. Coiled. That if danger walked in, it'd regret it quick smart and look for the nearest exit.

'You the Fed?' His deep voice was rough as gravel and not at all surprised.

Taryn straightened her shoulders. Come on, she'd dealt with worse. 'Yes. I'm Taryn Hayes. I'm here to—'

'Audit. Assess. And tear us down.' He dropped the folder he'd been reading. 'Yeah, we got the memo.'

She stepped forward, holding out a hand.

He didn't take it. Just gave her a once-over. 'You look hot.'

'Excuse me?'

'It's thirty-nine degrees in the shade today. Why are you wearing a woollen blazer?'

Taryn straightened her shoulders, ignoring the heat rushing to her cheeks. 'I'm here in an official capacity, Sergeant. I'd prefer to keep this professional.'

'So would I.' He walked past her to the filing cabinet that looked like it had survived a flood. 'You'll find we don't pander much to Canberra types around here.'

'I'm not a type. I'm a federal investigator operating under ministerial directive with full review authority —'

'Good for you.' Finn didn't even look up as he rummaged through the files.

Her jaw tightened. 'What is that supposed to mean?'

Finn finally turned to face her, his dark eyes cold and unreadable. 'It means I've got cattle going missing, a tracker in the scrub, and half my team spread across two hundred k's of dust. So if you're here to flex a badge, do it quick. I've got better things to do with my time.'

At the filing cabinet, he grabbed a manila folder and dropped it on the empty desk. 'There are your review requests. The interviews have been pencilled in for the days squad members are around. We run mobile, so don't expect everyone in the same room. And try not to get in the way when we are. Be nice to the Territory cops, as we share this station's space as their guests. And whatever you do, don't tick off Tanisha at the front counter, or she'll make your life a living hell.'

Taryn nodded, even if most of that had flown straight past her. Because Finn Wilde had crossed the room. And with every step, her brain had lost its signal to apply any logic.

Finn moved like a man used to handling trouble, one who didn't need backup. Tattoos shifted over tanned skin and hard muscle, disappearing into sleeves rolled just high enough to be distracting. With a lazy flick, he popped open the small fridge and grabbed a water bottle, making the veins and muscles shift under his inked skin like a living warning label.

He was *everything* her mother had warned her about.

Tall. Brooding. Built like a threat. Probably smelled like the fuel from lots of bad choices—along with a double load of female-attracting pheromones.

'Where are you going?' Honestly, she wasn't sure if she wanted the answer.

He paused in the doorway. 'Back to work. You want to audit us? Start with your list of requests. Constable Montrose put it together, talk to her if you want more. She's our paperwork queen.'

'You're just leaving me here?'

'I'm not here to hold your hand.'

She scowled at him.

And yet his eyes glistened with a hint of amusement.

The prick.

'Email me a memo of what you want. Or better yet, send it by courier pigeon and I might actually read it.' And just like that, he was gone.

No goodbye. Just an exit so abrupt it left her blinking in the vacuum he'd left behind.

Taryn was pretty sure she wanted to throttle him. Still gripping her laminated ID with the folded official memo tucked behind it, that was practically an in-house warrant granting her access to all areas.

The only other sound in the room came from the squeak of a fan struggling to rotate the air in the corner.

Taryn turned in a slow circle. Left alone in the Batcave with a suitcase full of wrinkled suits and a truckload of bureaucratic determination. Finn Wilde wasn't the first hostile to walk away from her during an audit, and he wouldn't be the last.

She crossed to the desk he'd clearly meant for her, considering it was the only one not buried under gear, maps, or stockwhips and spurs. Another desk held a PC, but it was so military precise with its layout of pens, Post-it notes, and other stationery items, she didn't dare upset the meticulous feng shui layout.

The small fridge hummed more enthusiastically than the outdated fan as she yanked the door open. Snatching up a water bottle, she downed half of it like she'd just crawled in from the Simpson Desert.

With a long breath, she pulled out her notepad, flipped it open… and froze.

Tucked into the inner pocket, a photo stared back at her. Her cousin, smiling beside her, like sisters sharing a joke.

Justice wasn't abstract. It was a job—and this job was personal. And if shutting down this so-called Stock Squad was the only way to get that justice?

Then so be it.

Two

Finn let the back door of the police station swing shut behind him with a solid thud. The unforgiving Territory sun pressed down, baking the gravel underfoot. Beyond the meshed fence and token barbed wire, which made up the police station's small compound, the town's airstrip shimmered like a mirage.

Mickey, the airport mechanic, was out there in his oil-streaked coveralls, playing valet with his over-sized golf buggy as he towed a light plane toward the hangar like it was a fancy sports car.

Word of the Fed's arrival had blown through town faster than a dry-season bushfire. And Mickey, with his hate for tourists, would have given Taryn Hayes the full *tour of nothing* as the grouchy welcoming committee. He'd, no doubt, made the Fed walk the long way around the airstrip just to make an entrance — suitcase, blazer, heels and all.

Finn smirked faintly.

She'd handled it, though. Didn't crack. Even looking like she'd just rolled out of a wind tunnel, she still stood her ground with voice steady, and chin high.

Taryn hadn't said much, but he'd seen enough to know she wasn't just here to tick boxes and shuffle reports — and she definitely wasn't here to help.

Which made her dangerous.

And — *inconveniently* — interesting.

But he had better things to do than babysit a bureaucrat.

Lydia and Brodie were waiting. And if they were right, Red was slipping stolen stock through the yards again.

He climbed into the troopy. The V8 engine rumbled to life,

rough but reliable.

On the road, he spotted Cecil, the town's unofficial mascot and full-time traffic hazard, munching weeds by the roadside like he owned the place. Finn slowed down to pass him.

Only in Elsie Creek would they have a reduced speed sign for a water buffalo. And only Cecil would be the one to ignore the road rules.

He shook his head, smirking to himself. *Bloody town.* Elsie Creek did something to a person. It took in the rough, the worn-out, the ones with nowhere else to go, and gave them something like a home in the dust.

Sure, it had its fair share of sticky beakers and serial gossipers, but it also had something rarer—real rural spirit. The kind where everyone knew everyone but still gave you space. And when things went belly up, you wouldn't find a faster helping hand in the country.

Finn would never say it, but this town was different. Special.

This nowhere postcode? It was his—for now, at least.

The road out of town may be long, flat, and empty with a heated shimmering haze that met clear skies. But out here, there were no office doors to hide behind. No spin. No distractions in a land that remembered. And for those who didn't respect it, the outback had a way of biting you back.

He rolled the window down, letting the hot wind whip through. It didn't cool anything, but it cleared his head.

Taryn Hayes.

She was sharp. He'd give her that. She talked like she had the weight of the law behind her. And probably did. But she didn't know this place or the people. She had no clue what the squad had already sacrificed just to be here.

He'd let her poke around, but he didn't owe her any explanations, and he had no desire to be anywhere near her.

What sucked was that he had to. Didn't mean he had to be nice about it.

Finn didn't trust in justice anymore. Results drove him now, because if he wanted the Stock Squad to be permanent, he had to prove it mattered. And now he had to convince a stranger in a suit that this rough patch of country, and the people guarding it, were worth the fight.

That was the mission.

When Drew had first mentioned the audit, it hadn't sat right. *'Just part of the process of making it permanent. Every government department gets audited,'* he'd said.

But it was what Drew *didn't say* that Finn heard louder. And that was the Fed, currently taking up space in his office, had the power to shut them down. *For good!*

With the town fading behind him, Finn turned right, crossed the railway tracks, and hit the red dirt roads that made up most of the Territory. To his left, a small church sat on the hill, its graveyard tucked beside it, the place the locals always said *had the best view of the outback.*

He turned again, using the back roads to the stockyards back lots where the sheds sat half-hidden in the dried long-grass. The old ag yard was mostly abandoned now, just rusty fencing wire and busted drums baking in the sun.

Lydia, the stockyard's manager, chose this place. She wasn't comfortable being seen with Finn in the office anymore. Not now they were investigating her husband, Grady *Red* Galloway — the Stock Agent.

Finn parked behind a stack of empty lick tubs and killed the engine. He peered around. No one was in sight.

Good.

He ducked through the side gate, his boots crunching quietly on the gravel. The back shed's dented door was halfway open.

Inside, the air was stale and thick with grease and old hay, but the temperature had dropped considerably.

Lydia sat on an upturned milk crate, clipboard in hand, sunglasses perched on the brim of her stockman's hat. Calm on the surface, and worried like hell underneath.

Young Brodie leaned against a ride-on mower, arms folded, cap pulled low over his eyes. His jeans had more patches than denim, and the soles of his boots looked ready to part ways with the rest. But he had that lean, hungry look—like he'd do whatever it took just to be counted, and to do the right thing.

Finn recognised that in Brodie. Not just the attitude, but the weight behind the kid's actions, reminding him of a younger version of himself—before life got complicated. Long before he'd learned that sometimes the people you trusted most were the ones who left the deepest scars.

'Sorry I'm late. Had company,' Finn muttered as he stepped into the shed. 'The Fed's landed.'

'Aren't you a fed, too?' Brodie brows lifted.

A fair question. One Finn still hadn't made peace with—not with his criminal record.

Lydia looked up, calm as ever. 'I heard you're being audited?'

'Yeah. My first one.' Happy anniversary to the Stock Squad. Well, since he'd set up shop in this town and started tapping on some shoulders to create a unique team.

'I get audited all the time from different departments. All I do is give them a coffee, bring in a camping table and chair for their desk, and show them the files.'

'That's what I did. Kind of.' He didn't make people coffee. 'Anyway, is there a reason you wanted to see me? Not that I'm complaining. I'm half tempted to help Brodie muck out the stalls than head back to the office—not with the Fed sitting in my seat.'

Brodie chuckled under his cap as Lydia handed Finn a clipboard.

'What am I looking at?' Finn flipped through the notes that held columns with tag numbers, weights, breeds, and dates.

'Red's pattern.' Lydia's voice wavered, as if strained.

'We cracked the code.' Brodie grinned, brushing the dust off his dirty shirt. It was nowhere near the amount of dust Finn had seen on Taryn's suit.

'What code?'

'Brodie's been watching what's coming off the trucks,'

explained Lydia. 'Then I've been comparing that with what Red logs into our stockyards. And it's not matching up. Explain to Finn how.' She gave Brodie an encouraging nod.

'The mob that gets loaded at the stations is all legit. I've had a few of the stockmen take a video that they'll DM me, to get ready for their feed and water, and they'll warn me if any of the beasts are cranky. Keeps the customers happy.' Brodie scrolled open his phone. 'That's what I tell 'em, anyway. But then I use that video as a comparison. See...' Brodie played a video of white-coated Brahman being loaded onto a road train. 'This lot was being loaded in the rear trailer at Tinderflats Station.'

Finn nodded at the boy, who shouldn't be working undercover, but he wanted to do the right thing. 'Go on.'

'Well, this is that same trailer unloading in the yards a few hours later...' Brodie played another video. 'It's a different load. Older, mixed breed. Half of them shouldn't even be in the saleyard.'

Finn frowned at the video. 'Can you forward this to me?' Pity none of this was useable in a court, but it was enough to have his team scan for brands and tags.

'Done.' Brodie tapped away on his phone. He'd come a long way for a kid who could hardly read. The countless scars from cigarette burns were buried beneath the tan and dust, like old sins the sun couldn't bleach out.

'Any idea where the swapped cattle came from?'

Lydia leaned forward, her lips tight with worry. 'We think the good cattle are getting offloaded somewhere—a paddock, a holding yard, we don't know yet. Then the dodgy ones are loaded up and delivered into this stockyard like nothing happened. There's no change to the number of stock received, where Red signs off on the original paperwork that gets dropped into my in-tray like normal.' Lydia tapped on the paperwork to show a name.

Finn looked up, frowning. 'SW?'

'We've noticed from the last few SW Rural Contracting shipments that the stock is below par. That's why Brodie started getting the stockmen to film their loads.'

Finn frowned. *SW Rural Contracting* should've been shut down when his team had successfully closed their smuggling way station at Dixby Downs. He wasn't going to forget he'd almost lost one of his team on that *Wild Stock Case.*

'Wasn't that Sawyer Dixby's business?' And he'd been buried, twice. Yet they still weren't sure if the first time had been an accident.

'I think they've just set up shop somewhere else,' said Lydia, with Brodie nodding beside her.

'At least we know where to start.' Finn flicked over the paperwork, making a list of cattle station names. From there, he could work out the stock routes and the truck drivers.

Finn glanced up. 'Are you still okay about doing this, Lydia?' The poor woman. While she'd been instrumental as his informant, she was in a tricky situation with Red.

'It's always been a pet hate of mine, ever since someone stole stock from my father's farm, where we all felt that loss as kids. So, yeah, I'm still in. Just don't ask me to watch Red get arrested. I can't. And I won't testify in court against my husband. But I'll give you the paperwork and I'll tell you what we see.' She slid her arm protectively around Brodie's shoulders like a mother. 'We'll help how we can, quietly. But I can't and I won't risk Brodie.'

'But—' Brodie butted in.

'No.' Her grip tightened around Brodie's shoulders. 'We've fought too hard to keep you safe from your parents. You're doing well with your lessons. You're about to get your driver's licence and your first car. Once that happens, Cowboy Craig said he'll give you a job at Dustfire, helping him out between Train Days. Or you can work anywhere you want. You've got a bright future ahead of you, Brodie.'

'D'ya reckon Red knows?' Again, Brodie scuffed his boot in the dirt.

Finn didn't waste words. And he wasn't good with the soft ones either.

'Yeah,' he said, brutally blunt as always. 'Red's smart

enough to know someone's watching. But he's not spooked.' Which made Red cocky or more intelligent than they'd realised. Either way, it made him dangerous.

'Is that because Red thinks he's covered, huh?' Brodie squinted up at Finn.

'Yeah. Because he thinks Lydia would never betray him.'

'My husband is watching me.' Lydia clutched her hands together as if trying to contain the worry. 'Red now keeps all his paperwork locked in his ute, instead of leaving it on the kitchen table. And he's asking me questions like he's checking to see what I know.'

'That'd be tense.'

'It is. And I've lived with that man for thirty-three years. We know how to read each other. And I've been honest with him, too, Finn.'

Finn's jaw ticked.

'I've told Red something is wrong at the yards, ever since Amara's horse got stolen—that the whole town knows about. But Red also knows how much it upset me that someone would do that to us in the yards. It hurts me more to know he's behind it.' The heartbreak of the situation weighed heavily on her shoulders. 'But I know my husband would never physically hurt me.'

'But if he thinks he's cornered…' The prick would react like any other criminal. Finn had seen it plenty of times—when pushed too far, people often hurt the ones they loved.

He looked to Brodie. 'From here on out, we move carefully, yeah? No shortcuts or taking *any* unnecessary risks. Just act normal, but keep your eyes and ears open, and call me if you need me.'

'Got it, Boss.' Brodie nodded, wearing the cheesy grin of a fearless teenager.

Finn then faced Lydia. 'I'm sorry, Lydia, that you're in this position. But we are going to get Red. I have to. We both know people's livelihoods are on the line. The stockyard's reputation is, too. It isn't just a yard, it's the beating heart of this town.'

Finn raked his nails through his hair. 'I know that stock comes from families who've battled drought, fires, floods, and skyrocketing interest rates—who have so little, yet give everything to keep their cattle alive. That includes the stockmen who chose this life. The men and women who'll carry a newborn calf across their saddle, bottle-feed it through the night, to maybe fight off wild dogs and scrub bulls just to give it a chance.' He looked between the two of them. 'So, no—I'm not walking away from this. Not when it's *that* work being stolen.'

Three

The office door creaked open, alerting Taryn to someone entering the Batcave.

'You're still here?' It was Finn's deep gravelly drawl.

She lifted her heavy head like she was gracing the schmuck with her presence. 'Wow, great to see you too, Sergeant. You just missed a thrilling hour of me reading cattle transfer permits, dissecting fuel dockets, and decoding coffee-stained invoices from someone named *Cowboy Craig*. Real edge-of-your-seat stuff.' She nodded at the paperwork spread across the table that had taken hours to arrange into some sort of logical order.

'Careful. That coffee-stained invoice probably saved a hundred head last month.' Finn stepped into the room with a presence of an unseen power. 'And here I thought you'd be halfway back to Canberra by now.'

'Tempting.' And so were those tattooed forearms and how the office lights hit just right. 'But someone's got to make sure this squad isn't running on barbecue sauce and dodgy branding irons.'

He grunted, clearly amused. 'Come on. Pub's waiting. You're staying there, remember?'

'Do I have a choice?'

'Not unless you like sleeping in a cell.'

'Fine.' Taryn slid her notebook and laptop into her workbag, then gathered her suitcase and her suit jacket. 'But if this is some hazing, just know that I've lived through basic drills and a Christmas lunch with six colonels and a rogue goat.'

Finn shot her a sideways glance, the corner of his mouth twitching like he didn't want to smile. 'Six colonels and a goat? For lunch or…?'

Taryn realised too late how that had sounded. 'Not on the menu,' she blurted out. 'Though Uncle Ray tried to smoke it once—'

'What? The goat? Or the colonels?'

She narrowed her eyes at the cretin having fun at her expense. 'Let's just say the goat survived. Uncle Ray's eyebrows, not so much. Turns out the most stubborn one always wins, and it's rarely the one in uniform.'

Finn's smirk deepened, all dangerously calm as he stepped closer—close enough that the heat rolling off him rivalled the Territory sun. He grabbed her suitcase like it weighed nothing, then leaned in, just enough for her to *feel* the low rasp of his voice brush intimately over her ear and the skin of her neck. 'Good to know, Fed,' he murmured. 'I can see you're going to be trouble.'

Then he walked away, leaving her standing there with a racing pulse and no comeback. Which was rare.

Worse, she was left with no choice but to follow him down the dark corridor to head for the light outside.

The large troop carrier waited like a dust-coated beast. Beefy tyres, with a bull bar that looked like it had won more fights than Finn.

He opened the back and effortlessly tossed her suitcase inside.

While she struggled to lift her workbag, then hiked up the hem of her fitted skirt just enough to clamber into the passenger seat.

As she clipped on her seat belt, the scents hit her—red dust, sun-warmed leather, and *him*.

The kind of scent no department store could ever sell. Tough, unpolished, and unbothered. Solid as a boulder and twice as immovable, along with a double dose of raw testosterone, that should've been bottled and labelled as: *Unapologetic Masculinity*—*The Finn Edition.*

As he started the monster truck, she glanced at the airport and noticed the back gate, directly to the tarmac, where that grey-overalled old man was whizzing around in an oversized golf cart.

'That arsehole.'

'Who?'

'There's a gate.'

'So, the gate is the arsehole?'

'No. I mean, I could've used that gate and skipped the whole outback trek where I had the pleasure of a heavy-breathing buffalo on my heels, walking kilometres in a blazer, choking on dust—thanks to a passing truck on steroids—after I got snubbed by that airport mechanic who probably just needs glasses to fix his suspicious squint.' She pointed at the man who'd made her walk, waving at them through the fence.

Finn nodded at the guy. 'Mickey's got standards. Obviously, you didn't meet 'em. And Cecil probably liked your perfume.'

She laughed before she could stop herself as Finn drove out of the yard.

On the map, the town appeared like a speck swallowed by the outback. Google hadn't offered much either, just a vague dot in the middle of nowhere.

Curiosity had Taryn sitting a little taller as they rolled along the main street, lined with low shopfronts on either side. There was an assortment of stores, a small supermarket, a post office next to a craft shop, and a hardware store that looked more like a big shed with a drive-thru feed store sign out front.

There was even a zebra crossing waiting patiently for pedestrians that didn't materialise.

At the far end came the real centrepiece: a two-storey pub that rose above everything else, like a king's castle.

'What makes Elsie Creek a town?' she asked, breaking the silence. 'Why build here?'

Finn kept his eyes on the road like he was talking to the town itself. 'Originally, it was just a piss stop on the rail line.'

'Excuse me?'

'A place to stretch your legs before heading further into nowhere. Then the Yanks came through in the war and set up camp for a bit.' Finn rested his hand loosely on the steering wheel as he nodded at the railway station on the left. 'With the railway, the cattle stations shifted their stock routes to meet the train, to feed the Army during the war. Soon, the stockyards were built, and the trains kept coming. Beef headed east and south, and the exports go north to Darwin Harbour.'

'Didn't peg you for a tour guide, Sergeant.' Through her passenger window, the town seemed small, weathered, and a little stubborn-looking—like it had refused to disappear.

But there was something about it. A sense of place, surrounded by all this space. Maybe it was the stockyards, or the way the shops faced the road like old friends. Maybe it was the way people waved at each other, even if they didn't stop. She couldn't help but admire it.

The troopy rolled to a stop out front of the pub.

Finn cut the engine and nodded at the building that seemed to tower over the town. 'The pub is run by Samantha. The locals call her God.'

'Is that a nickname or a spiritual warning?' Taryn raised an eyebrow.

Finn smirked. 'Bit of both. She controls the only cold beer for five hundred k's. And you never get between a stockman and his beer.'

He leaned on the steering wheel, his voice low and matter-of-fact. 'Samantha was born in that pub. It was built by her great-grandmother—the original Elsie, the town was named after. And she might just be the youngest publican in the country.'

'Why so young?'

'Her dad got sick. Rumour has it, she was running the place before she even got her driver's licence or was legally allowed to drink. But she's whip smart for business and politics.'

'Why are you so invested in the publican's story? Do you do that with the shopkeepers too?'

'The woman has power in this town. Not that you'd know it to look at her. But she's well respected. So, if you value a roof over your head, and don't fancy your swag tossed into the scrub, play nice.' Finn climbed out and went to the back of the troopy. He slung her suitcase over one shoulder like it was filled with feathers, and grabbed her workbag before she could protest.

'Seriously, I can carry—'

'And I can do it without breaking a heel.'

'Rude much,' she muttered, only to be surprised when he held the door open for her.

'Ladies first.'

Through the glass door, the whoosh of cool air and the scents of ale greeted her. A rustic long bar ran along the left side, and the back wall of windows led to a beer garden and pool tables. On the right, stood clusters of tables and chairs, while ceiling fans spun with zero enthusiasm.

Yet it felt like she'd entered the Northern Territory's version of Parliament House. There was no mistaking it. This was where decisions got made. Where reputations were built—or torn down with a single round of beer and a raised brow.

This small town pub was exactly what she'd expected, with its wall of glass door fridges behind the long bar, the brass rail running along the bottom, and bar mats advertising beer brands covering the top.

Behind the counter, a woman with a full sleeve of tattoos and black lipstick, wiped down the bar with the casual air of someone who'd break noses and not spill her drink while doing it. Her leather vest looked like it belonged in a biker's bar. Was that the boss?

The tattooed warrior nodded at Finn, who replied with a curt nod. Without a word she flipped over a glass and started pouring a beer.

At the far end of the bar, an elderly man, wearing

suspenders and a felt fedora, was perched on a stool. Beside him, leaning against the bar, was a young woman, wearing jeans and a simple T-shirt, her blonde hair pulled into a no-fuss ponytail. Pretty. And surprisingly young.

That had to be her. God.

Finn dropped Taryn's bags by the side door and nodded at the woman with the ponytail. 'Samantha. Billy…' Finn dug around in his pocket, dropped some cash on the bar, and scooped up the beer glass. 'Thanks, Mean-Rene.'

'Figured you'd drag the Fed in, eventually.' Mean-Rene wiped her hands on a towel, blatantly sizing up Taryn like she was a slab of meat at the butcher's.

Sooo… *Everyone* in this town knew Taryn's business.

Finn didn't bother with an introduction—and he'd clearly perfected the art of letting the silence do the heavy lifting.

'You must be Taryn.' The blonde with steady eyes watched her carefully.

Taryn smiled, grateful someone was offering her any kind of warmth. 'You must be God.'

'Anyone who's lived in the outback and drinks hard enough reckons they've seen God at least once in their life.' She pushed off the bar and walked over, extending a hand. Her grip was firm, like someone used to shaking hands with men. 'I'm Samantha. Welcome to Elsie Creek.'

From behind the counter, the biker-bartender gave a grunt. 'Is she staying long? Or do I poke the possums in the ceiling for that night-long ambience?'

'Mean-Rene,' Samantha said lightly, not even glancing back. 'Play nice.'

Mean-Rene rolled her eyes and muttered something about *bloody bureaucrats with handbags and zero sense.*

'You'll have to forgive Rene,' Samantha said smoothly. 'She's all bark and slightly less bite these days.'

Taryn raised an eyebrow. 'That's comforting.'

At the far end of the bar, the man in suspenders and the fedora raised his glass in greeting. 'G'day.'

'That's Billy,' Samantha added. 'Our yardie, bouncer,

counsellor, and local card shark.'

Not exactly the typical nightclub bouncer Taryn was used to, Billy, who had to be pushing eighty, looked more like a retired jazz singer. Wearing a mischievous kind of grin of someone who knew all the rules and how to break them.

'Heard you met my brother, Mickey. Made you walk the long paddock, huh? Blighter, he is,' Billy said with that mischievous grin.

That arsehole. Did Mickey brag about it?

She glared at Finn, who just smirked behind his beer, leaning his elbow against the counter like he'd been there all day.

'Listen, luv,' called out Billy, 'if you need someone to show you the ropes, I'm happy to do it. Price of a beer will do me.'

'You're cheap,' muttered Mean-Rene.

'I'll buy you the beer, Billy, just for the gossip.' Taryn hoped her sass would pass for charm. 'But, do you think I'll survive a walk around town with a local legend in a fedora? What'll the locals say, *you* being seen with *me*, the Fed?'

Billy barked a laugh. 'Oh, I like this one.' Tipping his hat to her in an old-fashioned gentlemanly manner.

Even Mean-Rene cracked the ghost of a smirk from her post behind the bar.

Taryn took that as a small win.

Samantha reached behind the bar and grabbed a room key from the hook-board, then tossed it to Finn. 'The officer has room four.'

'Billy's been up there patching the bathroom floorboards. Mostly solid now,' piped in Mean-Rene.

'Only fell through once,' Billy added helpfully.

Were they for real? Or teasing her?

Samantha ignored them, keeping a measured calm as if trying to read beneath Taryn's skin. 'You've got a week, yeah?'

'Two.'

Finn groaned, dropping his head as if to drown his sorrows in his beer.

'Good. Unpack, remember to keep hydrated if you're not used to our climate, and don't poke Karma. But he doesn't mind the company.'

'Karma?' Taryn asked.

Samantha nodded at the beer garden door, where a sign hung crookedly above it:

KARMA BITES. DON'T FEED THE PET.

'He's a three-legged rescued saltie,' Billy chimed in. 'Locals love him, especially on betting days when we feed him.'

'You have a crocodile in the beer garden?'

'This is Elsie Creek, luv. It is croc country. So don't go swimmin' anywhere, unless you wanna be croc bait.'

'Naturally.' WTF? 'So you have a pool?'

'Only for Karma,' replied Samantha. 'Just so you know, we don't do breakfast anymore. You'll find that across the road at the train station's food van. It opens at dawn. Brilliant coffee, you won't be disappointed.'

'Coffee's good.'

'You can also help yourself to the coffee and tea in the dining room at any time. We do lunch and dinner, but the chef has strict hours. And trust me, you don't want to upset the chef.'

'And it's not some veganese-vegetarian menu of muck either,' declared Billy. 'This is cattle country, girlie. You'll get your steak the way it comes. *And* you'll like it.'

'Ask for almond milk,' Mean-Rene cut in, 'and I'll show you what I can do with a shovel.'

'Good to know. I'll keep my dietary preferences… shovel safe, shall I?' Was Taryn going to survive her stay?

Samantha chuckled softly with Billy, but it was the grunt of approval from Mean-Rene that made her breathe easier.

Finn finished the last of his beer, set the glass down, scooped up her suitcase, and jerked his head toward the side door. 'Let's go, Fed, before Billy offers turndown service and

Rene puts you to work.'

Taryn followed him into a narrow corridor that stretched out under pressed tin ceilings, lined with worn floorboards that creaked in protest under Finn's heavy boots. The office sat on the right, as the unmistakable scent of frying onions and searing meat drifted from the kitchen at the end of the hall.

It was enough to have her stomach growl like it had a life of its own.

To the left, the dining room sat with wooden tables polished by decades of elbow wear. A coffee pot simmered on the sideboard, near the simple chalkboard menu.

But her attention drifted… elsewhere.

Finn was ahead of her, ascending the narrow staircase two steps at a time. Broad shoulders, rolled sleeves, and a backside that really didn't deserve to look that good.

Not that she noticed. Much.

Taryn cleared her throat and kept her eyes firmly on the banister, like a professional.

But still…

It was right there, in her face. How could she not peek?

Finn stopped at the top, dropped her suitcase, and nodded toward the room. 'You're in here. Fresh sheets, working fan, fridge stocked with bottled water. I'd recommend sleeping with earplugs on some nights, especially Train Days and Fridays.'

'Naturally.' Did she ask what Train Days were?

'Did Tanisha give you the security card to get into the office?' Finn handed over the keys, his warm, rough fingers brushing hers fleetingly.

It shouldn't have made her breath catch. But it did.

The touch was nothing. A second. Barely a whisper of skin on skin. And yet her pulse betrayed her, anyway.

'Um… Yeah.' What were they talking about?

'Get some rest, Fed.' He stepped back from her. 'Big day tomorrow. Wouldn't want exhaustion clouding your judgement any more than it already has.'

Taryn blinked. Did he just—

'Charming!' She clutched the key to stop herself from launching it at his retreating back. 'I'll pencil that in, between taking a nap and defending your career, shall I?'

But Finn was already halfway down the stairs, leaving her standing in the hallway to wrestle with the dangerous fluttering in her chest, along with the rising storm of her own frustration.

Arrogant. Condescending. Impossible. Male.

Completely detached. Completely infuriating.

And somehow—*unfairly*—attractive from every angle.

How was that even possible?

Add in a truckload of hostility towards her, just for doing her job, and it was shaping up to be one hell of a long fortnight.

Four

T he sun hadn't fully risen when Taryn stepped out of the pub with her workbag over her shoulder, ready to get on with it.

'Morning, Miss.' Billy tapped his hat brim in a charming salute, falling into step beside her as they crossed the road, becoming her unofficial chaperone. He waved at nearly everyone they passed, introducing her with a cheerful volume and zero shame, 'This here's the Fed—don't hold it against her.'

It helped. A little.

Pfft, who was she kidding?

It was clear everyone already knew who she was as she made her way to the brightly lit food van at the train station. With the stockyards stretched out behind it, the food van was a busy place at this hour, where the stockmen gave her a wide berth. And the station owners, seated at the outdoor tables, sent glares her way like warning shots.

Even if the whole town saw her as the enemy, she was used to it. The side eye and the suspicion came with her job. Besides, she wasn't here to make friends—she was here for justice.

But to make peace at the office, she loaded up on warm lamingtons and bush-spiced sausage rolls and headed for the Batcave. Because today she started the interviews.

First, she had to get past Cecil…

Nibbling on the fire station's perfect green lawn, the town's walking billboard was dressed in blue ribbons and a tasteful display of assorted paper flowers. Today's announcement scrawled across his black sides was:

Cecil raised his enormous head. The ribbons fluttered around his wide horns as he sniffed the air. But then his whole body shifted to face her, effectively blocking her path, showing off the impressive flower display he wore like a crown. He'd be perfect for weddings.

'What are we doing, Cecil?' Eyeing him warily, she took a slow step sideways. 'I'm not a good dancer…'

Again, Taryn crab-walked away, trying not to spill her coffee and pastries, while maintaining some dignity.

But now her heels were coated in red dust, again, and the pastry bags had started to sag from the heat—but she was still on a mission to make it to the office.

Tanisha wasn't in yet, her receptionist's desk held photos of some cats, assorted glitter in tiny plastic jars, and a cactus mug that said *Don't Be a Prick*.

Taryn set the pastry box down on the large table near Tanisha's workstation and scribbled out a sticky note:

Thought the team might be hungry,
Taryn.

She headed down the hallway, hearing David Attenborough narrate her approach in that hushed, reverent tone usually reserved for nesting sea turtles: *And here, the lone female ventures into the heart of unfamiliar territory—a space referred to by locals as the Batcave. A curious habitat, eerily still at dawn. Biding its time to attack this unsuspecting female…*

Taryn rolled her eyes.

Heaven help her, if anyone ever heard the inside of her head, she'd be sent on a permanent vacation.

At her temporary desk, she dropped her workbag and opened one of the pastry bags to prepare a small plate for the first interview.

She glanced at the clock. Right on time.

With a plate in one hand, her laptop and notebook in the other, Taryn made her way to the interrogation room—armed with caffeine, carbs, and the misguided hope that sugar-coated diplomacy might coax a few honest answers from her first contestant.

Inside the interrogation room, Constable Amara Montrose was already seated with a simple tablet on the table.

Not lounging. Not waiting. But *positioned*. With her back straight, arms just as straight on either side of her tablet, and as crisp as the ironed creases in her shirt. Her expression unreadable, but the clear message radiating from every inch of her regulation-perfect posture screamed: *this is my turf*.

Taryn offered a polite nod. 'Constable Montrose. Thanks for making the time to see me today.'

'It was on the memo I wrote.'

'Right. Of course.' Taryn set the plate of pastries down between them as a peace offering.

Amara glanced at the plate. But made no move to take anything.

'Just thought I'd bring something, to keep things casual.' Taryn offered a smile. 'We're just having a conversation.'

Amara said nothing.

Taryn sat across from her, flipping open her notebook. 'You've been with the Stock Squad since its creation, correct?'

'Nearly. Finn worked alone for about six months, but I was the first to team up with him. It'll be eighteen months now.'

'And before that, you were with the Northern Territory Police?'

'No. South Australian Police. I'm on secondment while working with Finn—at least until the Stock Squad is made permanent.' The *t* at the end of permanent was very pronounced.

'Transferred by choice?'

'Yes.'

Taryn lifted her pen and waited for more.

But Amara just held her stare and said nothing as the pastries sat untouched between them.

Of course, Constable Montrose would be like Finn, who'd mastered the skill of saying nothing. Amara was his shadow, the eager apprentice to the wizard.

But this wasn't Taryn's first interview, or her first investigation.

Again, Taryn clicked her pen. 'So how did you become part of the Stock Squad? Did you apply for the job? Do up a resume? Have a board interview?'

Amara stifled a laugh. 'No. Nothing like that. I had to beg.'

'Excuse me?'

'I'd overheard someone talking about Finn starting a federal stock squad in the station. He was in Adelaide, getting permission to visit the existing set-ups down south to gather intelligence. Look for the holes. The gaps.'

A faint smile tugged at the corner of Amara's mouth, her full lips were the kind botox lovers could only dream of. 'No one had heard of Finn Wilde. He was just some federal badge carrier—'

'Is that what we're calling Feds these days?' Taryn raised an eyebrow, having been called a Fed since she'd landed here.

'Back then, it meant someone who didn't belong.' Amara then gave a quick shrug. 'Funny, I guess I wear the same badge now.' She didn't take it back—but the edge in her tone softened. Just slightly. 'Are you really a federal police officer? Exactly what is your rank?'

Taryn met her gaze. 'I'm a Senior Federal Agent, with the Financial Crimes Unit, on ministerial secondment. I've got a badge and a gun I rarely use these days, since my job mostly involves asking annoying questions that'll ruin most people's day.'

Amara raised an eyebrow. 'Do you outrank Finn?'

'Technically, we're on equal footing. Except Finn leads the squad, and I get to decide if it survives.' Taryn took a slow sip of her coffee. 'Think of me as the accountability officer... with the nuclear button.'

Amara said nothing, but something in her eyes flickered. Not fear, not exactly. More like recalibration.

Taryn had seen that look before.

The moment someone realised you weren't just passing through—you were the one with the power to blow it all up.

'So, where were we?'

Amara re-straightened her posture. 'Finn came through the police stables. Don't ask me why, but that's where I was posted.'

Taryn waited, pen still.

'He wasn't hiring. Wasn't even building a team yet. But I offered to help. Figured if he was collecting data, he'd need someone to turn it into something useful. So I helped him collate the stock theft stats, cross-referenced locations, livestock types, and transit routes. All the stuff you'd need for a case study.'

'For the Commissioner?'

Amara nodded. 'Finn was trying to create a proposal to prove why they needed to invest in a federal stock squad to assist the various state police departments. To help bridge that gap, especially since livestock is regularly transported interstate or overseas. I just made sure it didn't look like a pile of scribbles in a notebook.'

'This was while you were working for the equestrian division in Adelaide?' Taryn had done her homework on paper, but she needed to see beyond the data to learn about the players in this game.

'I was nothing more than a uniformed stablehand, who was going nowhere there. But I know how to do paperwork.' Amara sighed as if letting her guard down. 'I had to chase Finn for the job. I even volunteered to work without pay.'

'Why?'

'Because I wanted in. It's why I joined the police in the first place—to get those who steal livestock... But Finn wasn't interested, he didn't want a female on the team. Said he needed a stockman with the same skills I had for paperwork.

But I showed him I could be all that and more.'

'So, he's against women —'

'Not like that.' Amara frowned. 'Finn said we'd be on the road. And we started mobile, with no base or station, just Finn's troopy. Carting a couple of duffel bags, his laptop, my tablet and a satphone. We'd use Finn's gas cooker for coffee in the mornings, while rolling up our swags, towing his two Harleys in the trailer. We worked out of borrowed rooms in whatever police station would have us. Most of the time it was in roadhouses, or empty small-town stockyards. Once we camped in an empty horse float to escape the rain.'

Taryn raised an eyebrow.

Amara shrugged.

'So, how did you end up at Elsie Creek?' Taryn asked.

Amara paused, the nostalgia perhaps softening her pose. 'I didn't even know this town existed until Finn told me we were heading here. It was my first time in the Northern Territory, too. But he'd been called in over some stolen stock at Elsie Creek Station...' she trailed off, brow furrowing. 'Huh. I only just realised it was Bree who called him. That's why we hauled interstate, taking turns to drive nonstop, except for fuel and food, to get here in record time, too.'

Taryn lifted her head. 'Who called?'

'Bree. Finn's ex-wife. She's a blacksmith, who runs the local stock brand register. But back then she'd been accused of cattle theft by the station owners, the Riggs brothers, and Finn came to help.'

Taryn made a note. 'Did he now?' Her voice was level, but internally — *ah, hello*... Ex-wife. Cattle theft. A road trip for justice.

How noble.

'Sounds like a personal call,' she added casually.

'Finn didn't see it that way. Because the stock theft — it was a big one. And it mattered.' Amara leaned closer, the excitement in her voice. 'We're talking eighty head worth close to a million dollars. Prime stock, tied to an illegal fighting pit that Finn and Marcus shut down in one hit. It was a big enough win for Finn to take back to the Commissioner to ask for a bigger team and a permanent posting. Here...' She patted the table. 'At Elsie Creek.'

'Why here?' Was it the ex-wife, perhaps? Especially if Finn had hauled butt to the other side of the country like that.

'The Northern Territory Police don't have a stock squad — though they should. Cattle is the second biggest industry out here, after mining. And Elsie Creek is the heart of it, with the stockyards just across the road making it a prominent position to have as our home base.' Amara pointed in the direction of the yards. 'Plus, the people in this place made it possible. They're happy to have us here, and they'll help if you're here for the *right* reasons.' Amara's look was sharp enough to draw blood.

There it was. The territorial warning wrapped in rural diplomacy.

Taryn offered a cool smile. 'And your position? Surely it came with a set of duties?'

'No.' Amara shook her head. 'The job evolves all the time. There are no set duties and no set hours. Sure, there may be long days from sunset to sunrise, but seeing it stretch over the outback is... special.' She sighed again, this time with her posture softening. 'Knowing I've done the paperwork to send that prized stolen stallion home makes it all worth it.' Amara's mouth curved slightly to surprise Taryn.

'You know he called you his paperwork queen?'

Amara blinked a few times, shifting in her seat. 'He did?'

'High praise, coming from a guy like Finn.'

Amara leaned back, arms crossing just slightly. 'Finn never says much. And he thinks on the move. Even when he can't move, he'll follow the lines on a map like he's moving to think. But when he shares his plan... it counts. Finn does great work. He's tough, fair, precise and I've learned a lot from him these past eighteen months. Even though the Stock Squad has only been officially running for a year, I hope it continues to serve in the long-term future.'

Constable Amara Montrose wasn't just loyal, she was

earned loyalty. A young officer with a quiet strength. Smart. Focused. And clearly capable of corralling more than just paperwork. The constable loved her job and respected her boss by the bucketloads—and that was rare.

Taryn clicked her pen closed, sitting back. 'One last question.'

Amara tilted her head as if ready for the worst.

Taryn pulled out a crumpled set of fuel dockets, held together by a rogue paperclip that may have been made from fencing wire. 'Any chance the paperwork queen can help me decipher these?' She slid them across the table. 'Someone labelled one just: *Fuel for the Hellhound*. And this one: *snacks and sand for the rodeo tanks.*'

Amara smiled, for real this time. 'That'd be Cowboy Craig. He likes to play on words.'

Five

Craig Callahan didn't knock.

But he had Taryn's attention the second he strolled into the interrogation room, like it was the back verandah of a cattle station, complete with dust on his jeans. Deeply suntanned, he had his shirtsleeves rolled to the elbows. His champion rodeo buckle caught the light, drawing attention to places no self-respecting federal investigator should be looking.

He dropped into the chair opposite, tipping back his white cowboy hat in a way that cleverly haloed his sun-kissed curls, sky-blue eyes, and a smile so white it practically needed a licence to shine.

Well audit me sideways! This was Craig Callahan?

Cowboy. Rodeo champion. And a walking HR violation in boots.

Taryn cleared her throat, forcibly reminding herself she was here to audit. Not ogle.

The plate of pastries she'd laid out twenty minutes ago were disappearing fast as he chewed the last bite of something decadently flaky.

'Hope that wasn't reserved.'

'Please, help yourself.' She flipped through the pages of her notebook.

'Already did.' He cleaned off the plate, then leaned back in his chair, legs wide, in an easy posture, as if this wasn't an interview but more of a smoko break.

Taryn kept her voice neutral. 'Craig Callahan, you're not a sworn officer.'

'Never said I was.'

'But you work with the Stock Squad?'

'Part time. Consultant, Finn calls it. But I'm just a stockman. A ringer. I'm a rodeo champion, too.'

Of course, he'd draw attention to that big belt buckle. And those thick thighs wrapped in denim like sin and saddle dust.

Taryn didn't look.

Okay—she glanced. Purely for audit accuracy.

She scribbled something in her notebook just to keep her hands busy, although she had no idea what. Hopefully something like: *Focus. Not thighs.*

Cowboy Craig leaned back in his chair, throwing her a wink. 'You writing all that down, or just doodling my name with hearts around it?'

'Neither. I was underlining delusions of grandeur, but thanks for the visual.' She clicked her pen. Twice. Just to make a point.

Craig chuckled like she'd only confirmed his suspicions. 'I'm also a livestock inspector, and the export quarantine manager for livestock, up in Darwin. And I track hooves, cars, trucks, or whatever needs following.'

'Well, that makes sense.'

'What does? That Finn hired me for my charm and that I know my way around a paddock puppy or two?'

Taryn arched an eyebrow as she flipped to the next page like she understood what he'd just said about paddock whatsits. 'How long have you known Finn?'

'We worked together as young stockmen out at Elsie Creek Station.'

'Elsie Creek Station?' *Again.*

'Back then, it was owned by Darcy—long before Finn married Bree—when Charlie was training us to be stockmen.' His face fell, like a wave of grief had washed over him.

'That long, eh?' Taryn raised an eyebrow.

'Enough to be a friend for life.'

'So how did you end up working for Finn after so long?'

'Bree.'

'The ex-wife?'

Craig nodded. 'I'd been injured and Bree came out home —
'

She quickly referred to her notes. 'That'd be Dustfire Holdings?'

'Yeah, that's our pocket of paradise.' He even gave a wistful sigh.

'So how did Dustfire end up as the quarantine station for the squad?' Taryn tapped the edge of her notepad.

Craig casually shrugged. 'We had the land, the infrastructure, fenced yards, with plenty of watering points, but no stock back then. Bree knew what Finn was chasing — tight fences, isolation, room to hold stock safely. And like I said, I ran the quarantine export yards, so I knew what was required.'

Taryn raised an eyebrow again. 'So, Bree, Finn's ex-wife, got you in? And she's your… wife?'

'Nah.' Craig smirked. 'Bree and I've been mates since we were kids. She's like a sister to me. My wife, my bee queen,' he said with a goofy grin, as he gazed down at his wedding ring, '… is Izzy. She's a lawyer, and ten times smarter than all of us combined. You'll meet her soon enough. I wrote her interview time down on the board at home. She forgets things because her brain moves superfast.'

Oh, Taryn was looking forward to meeting Isobel Callahan. She just had to play the game for now. 'That still sounds like a close connection with Bree to get the job with Finn, while also giving you the quarantine station contract without putting it out for tender. Convenient, wouldn't you say?'

Craig straightened a little in his chair, the grin dimming a fraction. 'Do you think by being hand-picked by Finn, I'm given preferential treatment?'

'I think the lines blur easily in a town like this.'

'That's a fair point. But you see, Finn needed help. He needed someone with what he called a specialised expertise.'

'And you had that?'

'It's what Finn called it.' Craig gave a shrug. 'You see, the first case out the gate was the *Rough Stock Case.'*

'The what stock?'

'Rodeo bulls. Trained for the *rough stock* category. You know, bucking bulls.'

'Right.'

'Well, one of the top bulls and a bunch of his male calves went missing.' Craig double tapped on the table as if making a point. 'That's when we first learned about the Stock Agent. Turned out they'd stolen more than just bulls—they were after DNA. Sperm. Embryos. All sorts of genetic material that got cryogenically sealed into these canisters that could last for years. No need to move a branded bull anymore when you can export the bloodline in your carry-on. And that first lot?' He gave a low whistle. 'Breeder's gold mine it was. The Stock Agent knew exactly what he wanted out of that rough stock.'

Taryn paused, pen hovering. 'Who is the Stock Agent?'

Craig smirked. 'Talk to Finn. I'm not sure what I can say about the cases. Confidentiality, you know. My wife told me to say that. She's our lawyer.'

Taryn narrowed her eyes at Craig, who apparently was well and truly lawyered up—personally and professionally. She also knew a legal dead end when she hit one.

Taryn flipped her notebook closed with a soft snap. 'Last question then. Just for curiosity's sake.'

'Shoot.'

She slid one of the fuel dockets across the table. 'Why do you need sand for rodeo tanks? Is that about water tanks? Or is that about some hellhound thingy?'

Craig grinned like he'd been waiting for that one. 'The Hellhound is Porter's bush buggy—built like a bull catcher, goes like hell and it's good on fuel. Great for tracking, like we did on the manhunt for the missing overseer in the Wild Stock Case. Ah...' He paused.

'I get it. Talk to Finn about that case.'

Craig grinned.

'Your wife taught you well.'

'I'm gonna tell her you said that. It'll prove to her I

actually listen to what she says.' His charming grin and boyish chuckle made her smile softly.

He tapped the dockets with a calloused finger. 'And the sand for the tank? That's for the rodeo bulls. It keeps them calm, where they'll play like it's a big sandpit. Others will lie down on it like dogs sunbaking at the beach.'

'Wait—bulls lie down?'

Craig chuckled. 'Only when they're spoiled rotten. Or homesick,' he said, glancing at his watch, 'like me.' He pushed back from the table, tapped the brim of his hat, and left behind nothing but crumbs on the plate.

Taryn sat back in her chair with her pen tapping against her notepad. That made two interviews that only created more questions than answers. But what worried her more was how many members of the Stock Squad had Isobel Callahan counselled not to talk?

Six

Finn should've known the Fed would still be here. Still feeling the sun baking the back of his neck, and with his shirt stuck to his spine with sweat, when all he wanted was a cold drink and ten minutes in his own bloody office without a battle.

Instead—there she was.

Taryn Hayes.

Stationed at his desk like she owned it, with files spread in front of her, highlighter uncapped, picking through the bones of his life like a bureaucratic crow.

Finn turned around and headed back the way he'd come. No way in hell was he dealing with that.

'Sergeant Wilde?' Her heels click-clacked behind him. '*Wait!*'

His jaw clenched as he punched through the back door. He didn't stop.

'You signed for feed and fencing supplies two weeks ago, but the receipts don't match the delivery records.' Taryn chased him down, waving a folder like it was a weapon. 'There's a discrepancy.'

Figures she'd find something he'd missed.

'I'm working.' His boots crunched on the gravel as he headed for his troopy. 'Ask Craig or Amara.'

'I did. They said you handled the order.'

He stopped and finally faced her, leaving only the afternoon heat to shimmer between them.

Her blouse clung to her collarbones, with her hair twisted in that sharp, neat knot. Those eyes—goddamn them—still watching, still dissecting him like she was three moves ahead.

'Are you always this persistent?' He hated that she was here with the power to kill the whole damn squad, and not a hint of a smile to soften the blow.

'Only when things don't add up.'

Finn dragged a hand down his face. *Of all the days…*

But then he caught it—that scent. Subtle. Clean. Not perfume. Not out here. Something softer. Citrus maybe. And like skin after a hot shower.

His brain refused to name it.

His body, unfortunately, had no problem recognising it.

And how it curled around him like smoke, messing with his focus, making him stupid. Noticing the strands of hair that had slipped from her neat little knot, curling against her neck like they didn't care about the rules either.

He stepped back, as if distance might cure the stupidity.

But it didn't.

'You want the paperwork?' His voice was rougher than he liked. 'It's at the feed store. We've got an account there. I'm sure they'll print off what you need.'

'Where?'

Don't do it.

Why should he play nice with *her*? The sharp-eyed woman with a government badge and heels, sent to dissect his squad like a butcher.

Since when did the devil come wrapped in a package like her?

He exhaled through his nose. Hard.

'I'll drop you off. Less chance you'll get lost.' Dammit. He hadn't meant to say that but now it was too late to take it back.

You'd think the drive would be short…

Not with Little Miss Perfect, perched in the passenger seat like the upholstery might catch on fire. Her eyes on the road, and that notebook balanced neatly on her lap like it held state secrets.

He didn't look. Not directly.

He didn't trust himself to.

But again, that *scent*. Soft, clean, and shower fresh. There was citrus and something else, like vanilla blossom, maybe. It was the kind of scent that didn't belong out here, not with the bulldust and sunbaked leather. Yet, it wound through the troopy like it owned the space.

She flipped a page in her notebook, pen tapping thoughtfully, not looking at him as she spoke. 'Are you always this quiet, or is it just when you're cornered?'

'Nope,' he grunted. 'Just tolerating the company… barely.' He shot her a sideways glance. 'Figured the quicker I got rid of you, the quicker I could breathe again.'

'You offered to drive me.'

'Yeah, well, I was raised right. Unfortunately.' Why did he have to be the good guy? Especially with the enemy.

She hummed under her breath. Some smug little sound that slid under his skin like a thorn.

'You know,' she said, flicking through that notebook, 'for someone so allergic to being questioned, you're not half bad at dancing around the answers.'

'Must be all that time behind bars. Real educational.'

It was no secret he'd done time, but it shut her up.

For about three seconds.

'Are you going to throw that at me every time I ask a question?'

'Only if you keep pretending like you don't already know the answers to your questions.'

That earned him a look, one that shouldn't have made his chest tighten.

But it did.

Did he dare dig for details? Get under her skin and see what made her crack?

Challenge accepted.

'Have you ever worked out bush before?' he asked, with just enough weight in his voice to sound interested. Just enough bait to test the waters.

She glanced out the passenger window to the stockyards, nestled on the other side of the railway line. 'Plenty of times.

On my grandfather's wheat belt farm.'

'Wheat belts aren't anywhere near the Territory.'

'No, but it taught me where to stand when a crush of sheep come barrelling through a gate.'

'Bet you stayed neat and tidy, and got no dirt on you. Scar-free.'

'Is that why you're so heavily tattooed?' Her voice, and that stare, were cold enough to frost the inside of the cab. 'To hide your scars?'

Everyone had a story behind their tatts. That was a given. Only one person knew his story.

'Careful,' he said, low and dangerous. 'You keep digging like that. You might not like what you find.'

'That's the thing about audits... They uncover *everything*.'

Oof—she was good. She'd taken his little game of digging, and somehow she'd turned the spade and shoved it straight through his armour.

His jaw locked, a muscle twitching as his hands tightened on the wheel. He should've kept his mouth shut and made her walk to chase her silly receipts.

And she sure as hell shouldn't be wearing skirts like that. Not with those long, toned legs, smooth in all the wrong ways, where the image was now lodged in his brain like a burr under a saddle. Especially after she'd hitched that tight little pencil skirt up just enough to climb into his troopy. Only to sit beside him like a devil's trap full of temptation, all sharp tongue and stubborn pride, with her scent curling through the cab.

Of all the women to send into his world, it had to be this one. Smart. Cold. Gorgeous. Built like trouble, dressed like sin, and carrying a government lanyard instead of her badge. Same rank, sure—but she outranked him in every damn way that mattered.

The silence hung heavy in the air. He was used to the silence, but few liked it.

All the while that damned scent of hers still lingered.

Thankfully he pulled up out front of the feed store, the

gravel popping beneath the tyres as he shoved the troopy into park.

He kept his hand on the gearstick. 'Next time, wear jeans and boots.'

'Excuse me?'

'If you want people to talk to you, dress like the locals. You'll blend in better. Why would anyone want to talk to you when you look like a tax auditor in that skirt and heels?'

Her brows lifted. 'And you look like a bad attitude in boots.'

That pulled the corner of his mouth. Just a twitch. Not a smile.

Definitely not.

'Careful, some people might bite, if you keep sassing like that.'

'Uh-huh.' Taryn reached for the door, then hitched her skirt just enough to climb out.

Dammit. He tried to keep his eyes on the wheel.

Tried.

Then she looked back at him over her shoulder and smiled.

Here it comes. She was one of *those* women—one who had to have the last word. Just like the ex-wife.

'If they bite,' she said with a sinful smile, 'I'll just bite back… *harder.*'

The door slammed.

He didn't breathe for a full second.

Bloody hell.

He stared at the dash, the muscle in his jaw ticking so hard it hurt, as her heels clicked on the gravel. He didn't watch her go. But he sure as hell felt every step like a hot iron pressed into his chest.

She was trouble. The kind that was already slicing too close to the things he'd buried deep.

He threw the vehicle into gear and rolled away without looking back.

He needed to stay the hell away from her.

Only problem was… he didn't want to.

Seven

Taryn tugged the cuffs of her new jeans down over her stiff new boots—which had nothing to do with that smug, square-jawed prick and his whole *ditch the heels* comment.

She was here to audit a rural squad, not walk a fashion house's runway. It wasn't like she was about to throw on a flannel shirt and fake a nasally Aussie drawl. That was for childhood farm days, when her hair never saw a straightener and dirt under the nails was just a part of lunch.

Her new wardrobe selection was just a strategy. Camouflage. A smart move to blend in, to win trust, and gather intel.

It most certainly wasn't *his* idea. Absolutely not.

And if she kept telling herself that enough times, she might start believing it.

She wiped down her auditor's shirt with crisp precision, checked her hair was still neatly pinned, make-up on point. Still her. Still in control.

Yet Finn still took up unnecessary space in her head. The way he looked at her. The way he didn't. And the way his jaw had clenched when she'd tossed that line about biting back.

Finn Wilde was *everything* she couldn't stand. Cocky. Closed-off. Infuriatingly hot in that sun-scorched, inked-up, ex-con kind of way.

Bringing down his squad was what she'd been ordered to do, and she'd do it cleanly, professionally, and by the book.

The hostility she was getting wasn't new either. She was used to being considered the enemy, usually because those she dealt with were villains themselves. And the angrier they got, the more they treated her like the enemy, the clearer it was that she was doing her job right.

But this time... the job felt different. Less like justice, and somehow more like she was betraying the good guys. But her boss wouldn't send her here if there wasn't an issue, and it was her job to push past the niceties for their secrets.

In between shopping for new clothes, she'd picked up a few tips thanks to the pub's yardie, Billy, and the Outback Mafia—four card-playing retirees who hung out at the hardware store and handed out gossip like currency.

One of them warned her about her next interviewee. Another offered her a tango lesson, complete with a wink and tips on how to handle the town's wandering water buffalo. They were the ones who told her to wear boots and jeans—*not* Finn—pointing her toward the feed store that was part of the hardware store, which sold clothes, hats, and animal feed, with farmers driving through, filling the back of their utes with bags of chicken feed, and large slabs of dog food.

While she was in the change room trying on jeans, Speedy—the fast-talking cashier with a softball glove strapped to her hand—was out front yakking nonstop. Something about her softball team, the Stock Squad, and a dozen people Taryn had never heard of, all while tracking down her missing receipts. But the gossip was good.

So, after that visit with the locals, and a few strategic purchases, she was better prepared to tackle her time at Elsie Creek.

She started the morning off by carrying a bunch of chrysanthemums to greet Cecil. It really was the sweetest thing hand feeding a buffalo, with the manners of a labrador.

She'd then slid a catnip growing kit onto Tanisha's desk for her feisty felines. The label promised *Happy Cats, Happy Humans*, so it was worth the gamble. Hoping her strategy, was enough of a bribery-type gift to raise eyebrows the right way, in what Taryn liked to call diplomacy.

And now she was ready to interview the next member of the Stock Squad.

Stone Kipp.

Who was ten minutes late.

When he finally showed up, there was no apology. No excuse. Just a gust of hot air, filled with pure ego, as Stone Kipp strolled into the interview room, with the swagger of someone who thought he was the Stock Squad's rock star.

'Alright, what do I call you?' He dropped into the chair opposite her. 'Hayes? Fed? Destroyer of Dreams?'

Taryn looked up from her notes. 'I respond to ma'am if you're scared.'

Stone grinned. 'Nah. Scared is not in my vocabulary.'

'That explains the job of hugging it out with crocodiles.'

'And the helicopter. And the beer deliveries. And the time I accidentally airlifted a goat.'

'Is that in the records?'

'If it gets me a pay rise, sure.'

She clicked her pen and flipped to his file—or rather, the thin collection of invoices and loose paperwork that passed for it. 'You weren't officially interviewed for this position.'

'That's because I wasn't officially hired. Finn tapped me on the shoulder and shouted me a beer at the pub and asked if I liked chaos. I said, only if it comes with altitude.' He leaned forward and tapped on the table. 'That's *al*-titude, not *at*-titude.'

'Shame,' she said, not looking up from her notes. 'You seem overqualified for one and tragically burdened by the other.'

Stone let out a low whistle. 'Well, hell, don't you have some claws? I like that. Romy will love that, too.'

'Romy has my sympathy.'

'She doesn't need it. She gets to fly with me.'

'So, she's your co-pilot and therapist?'

'Romy is my *everything* and all the above.' Stone grinned widely, like he was winning a game she didn't even know she was playing.

'So, you weren't officially interviewed for this position, and you're not on the payroll either?' She glanced down at the receipts. 'Yet you carry a federal badge, as a consultant who invoices for airtime and fuel?'

'Correct. And I make damn sure those invoices are inflated.' Another wink.

She went to press further—

But he cut her off, eyes sharpening just slightly, his tone serious. 'I also log heat signatures, irregular flight paths, road train activity, and land access patterns across fifty square k's, every time I'm in the bird.' But then he leaned back, tapped on the table wearing that cocky grin again. 'You know, when I'm not playing part-time crocodile wrangler and full-time sweetheart, wrestling crocodiles, or delivering beer.'

'Is that what you do for fun?'

'That's what I do for love, lady. Crocodile conservation. Protecting land, stock, and the odd people rescue or two. Oh, and I moonlight as a tour guide for my lady—Romy's filming a documentary. We're inseparable.'

'A documentary about you and your helicopter?'

'Nah. The crocs.'

Taryn paused, her pen hovering over her notes. 'Right. Because nothing says romance like a cold-blooded predator with better skin than you.'

'Don't be jealous. She's got great teeth, too.'

Who was he talking about now? 'Did Finn hire you for the comedic comebacks?'

Stone grinned wider. 'Finn knows talent when he sees it.'

'So you'd know what he does for fun, too?'

Stone didn't miss a beat. 'Polishes his handcuffs and stares off into the outback horizon. It's very broody. You'd love it.'

She chuckled. 'Shall we add that to the file notes: Sergeant Wilde also enjoys long walks on the crime scene and emotionally repressing things.'

Stone laughed as he slapped the tabletop like he was applauding her. 'I heard you were sharp. And yet you got done by Mickey—which means we share the same enemy.'

'Who?'

Stone crossed his arms and rested them against the table.

'Mickey, *the master of all things mechanical*. The airport mechanic who runs the town's airstrip like its Area 51.'

'Grey hair, grey overalls, has that Popeye squint.'

'The one with the God complex. Smells like WD-40 and old grudges. I heard he made you walk the long way around the airport.'

She gave a sharp snort. 'What did Mickey do to you?'

'Won't let me land my chopper on his airstrip.' Stone pointed to the back wall in the direction of the airport. 'That old fart said there's only one heliport, and that's for hospital emergencies only.'

'Did you ignore him?' Because Stone seemed the type.

Stone tried not to grin. 'I may have attempted a stealth landing on the tarmac once.'

'Let me guess, Mickey blocked you with that big golf buggy of his.'

'Worse. That grumpy prick towed my chopper away. *Towed it!*'

'I'd believe it. I'm just surprised he didn't weigh it down with a dozen chains padlocked to his tall radio tower.'

'Don't give him any ideas.'

'So, where do you park your chopper now?'

'Behind the pub.'

'Ah, right. Hence the beer runs.' That made sense, but she wasn't going to ask about the goat. However, they were momentarily united in mutual Mickey-induced trauma.

This could work.

Before she could steer him back on topic for answers, Stone cut in —

'Let me guess, you want to know about Bastion. The tech?'

She kept her cool, taking notes, letting Stone do the talking. 'The tech…'

'Big Daddy says I was cleared of that death.'

'Who?'

'The Commissioner. Finn's boss.'

'Big Daddy?' Taryn tried not to laugh. After having met the Commissioner a few times, she doubted someone like

Drew Bannon would appreciate the nickname.

Stone winked at her, but the cheeky shine wasn't there. 'I have to thank Romy and her drone footage. It proved it wasn't my fault in cinematic clarity. Bastion didn't off himself over a sad story—he was terrified.' Stone sighed, scratching beneath his chin. 'No surprise, really. Dane Carter died in prison. And then that Renzo had that little *accident* down south not long after we cracked the *Rough Stock* case. So when we started digging during the *Cold Stock* case, Bastion panicked and took a swim with the salties... Like I've said before, and I'll keep saying it, all roads lead back to Everlight Energy Solutions.'

Her pen froze mid-scratch.

Everlight.

The name she'd been waiting to hear.

But before she could pounce, Stone smiled innocently and leaned back in his chair. 'Anyway, Finn knows what can and can't be said on the record. He doesn't need Izzy to lawyer-up. The man practically wrote the confidentiality clause himself.'

'So now you're stonewalling?'

'I prefer evasive excellence. Sounds sexier.'

'How did you get involved with the squad again?'

'Told you already, front bar at the pub.'

'That's not how recruitment works. There should have been a tender for the use of your helicopter.'

'Not where Finn's concerned. He doesn't give a damn about resumes or red tape. He hires by gut instinct. He looks for loyalty, and people who won't flinch when it hits the fan. Lucky for you, we've got all that in spades. And we play to win.'

That made her sit back, because it was true. Every member so far had been extremely effective and fiercely loyal to Finn, even though the hiring methods had been wildly unconventional.

Still, there was one anomaly with Stone.

'So why are all your invoices from this air service

company? Are you employed by them? Like Amara is tied to the South Australia Police.'

Stone's grin widened as he leaned in, resting his elbows on the table. 'Because I own it. I'm the CEO.'

'You're… what?'

'Self-funded, self-employed, semi-retired, whatever. I could live in Bali and drink cocktails all day, if I wanted. Instead, I get to fly with my lady at my side, while protecting my patch of paradise, keeping one foot in the fight.'

'This isn't a job for you.'

'Nope. It's a calling.' He even sighed at the ceiling, like he was expecting applause—or some sort of divine intervention from the patron saint of BS.

She studied him for a moment. Sure, he was ruggedly handsome, but under all the swagger, the winks, and the cheekiness, there was something serious about Stone Kipp.

And for the first time, Taryn saw the pattern not just in the people, but in the purpose.

Finn hadn't just built a squad. He'd somehow built a cause.

But she still didn't trust him.

Eight

The short and sharp session with Stone had left Taryn with two pages of scribbles, half a headache, and the unmistakable sense that the Stock Squad wasn't just cobbled together—it had been carefully curated by Finn. The so-called mastermind.

And yet none of this matched her orders.

She'd been sent to audit a waste of government funding. Specifically told to *tear it apart with a fine-tooth something-or-other.*

The briefing had painted a picture of unqualified misfits, paying their mates to gallop around the outback like cowboys with badges. No resumes. No job descriptions. Not even proper job titles for half the roles, let alone documentation for bizarre purchases like sand for rodeo bulls to roll in.

It was utter, unapologetic chaos.

And somehow… it was working. The case files—those few she had access to— proved that.

She hadn't even interviewed the full team yet, and she was a long way off from finishing her investigation—but maybe, just maybe, Finn Wilde actually knew what he was doing.

In dire need of coffee, Taryn headed back to the front desk area, expecting the usual silent treatment, but Tanisha offered her a nod and—was that—a *smile.*

'Thank you for the catnip kit,' she said, swinging her legs from her high stool to match the front reception counter. 'You've bought some civility. For now.'

Taryn grinned. Diplomacy and bribery still worked.

She was halfway through making herself a terrible instant coffee when another police officer strolled in. Utility belt slung over one shoulder, NT Police shirt unbuttoned and flapping, with his hair windswept as if he'd driven through a cyclone and enjoyed it.

He pulled off his sunglasses and squinted at her like she'd grown a second head. 'Hello. And who might you be?' He was polite, even.

'That's the Fed touching our kettle,' Tanisha answered.

'Is that a problem?' Or did Taryn need to add coffee to her list, to steer clear of their kitchenette?

'Only if you break it. Or leave the milk out. Then we'll all have to suffer one of Tanisha's scoldings.' The man grinned. Big and easy.

He dumped his police belt down with a thud onto the large table and nodded at her cup. 'Are you making it that strong on purpose? Late night? Or is the coffee trying to help you fight something?'

'It's fine-*ish*.' Oops, she'd forgotten how many spoons of coffee she'd put into the cup.

'Sure it is.' The senior constable reached past her and gently tugged the spoon free from her hand like he was disarming her. 'Sit down, Fed, and I'll make you one that doesn't taste like regret.'

'You're offering to make me a coffee?'

'Why not? You're not *my* enemy.' He shrugged, plucking up a fresh mug for himself, and Tanisha's prickly cactus cup, then went about making coffee for everyone. 'I've still got my job. Still got a station to work out of. And I get you're just doing your job, but it doesn't mean we can't have caffeine and some civil conversation when working in the same space, right?'

Tanisha spun around in her high stool, her immaculately groomed eyebrows arching, with her claws quietly retracting.

'Who are you?'

'Senior Constable Porter,' he added, grabbing the milk. 'NT Police. I live here. Well, not *here* here. Just... you know. Around.'

The interaction was so normal. Without any of the clipped

silences or side-eye looks as if she'd kicked someone's dog on the way in.

'Federal Investigator Taryn Hayes.'

'Nice to meet you, Taryn.' Porter shook her hand, then handed over a cup of actual coffee, not just muddy water. 'You'll want that. Especially if your next interview is with Stone. Bloke's a menace.'

'Already survived him. Barely.'

'Then you've earned it.' Porter dragged out a chair before the silent laptop that occupied the far end of the large table, lifted the laptop lid and sipped on his coffee while giving Taryn an inviting nod to sit.

Did she dare?

She did.

'I've been told that you're the man to ask about the Hellhound. I found some receipts,' she said, cradling her cup. 'Exactly what is the Hellhound?'

Porter grinned. 'It's a four-wheel-drive-converted beach buggy that looks like a Frankenstein's version of a Mad Max movie escapee. Built it myself—ex-speedway junkie.'

'You raced?'

'Junior Champion many times. But these days, the Hellhound's more of a bush-bashing speed machine I use for hunting ferals. And those receipts were for a manhunt while on that *Wild Stock* case.'

'So you work for the NT Police, stationed at Elsie Creek, but help the Federal Stock Squad?'

'Sure. When they need me. Prison transfers. Manhunts. Bit of backup. Sarge, there,' he said, pointing to the OIC's closed door, 'he'll loan me out—especially if something's gone bush. I do some tracking. Nothing like Cowboy Craig, who's a master at it. But after wearing out three patrol vehicles, I do know the roads in this region.'

'And the Hellhound?'

'Can go places no patrol ute can. Here, I've got a picture...' Porter thumbed through a few images on his phone. 'There's the hell on wheels.'

It was a beast. The Hellhound looked like it had been forged in a thunderstorm. Caked in red dust, on oversized tyres, with welded mesh for a bull bar that'd definitely hit things on purpose. Racing seats, roll bars, lots of spotlights, and aerials that reached skyward like antennae on a monster-eating creature that could sniff out trouble from a kilometre away. And fast.

But leaning against the side of it, in dusty boots, was Constable Amara Montrose. Her stockman's hat tipped low, her hair down, and laughing. Relaxed. And herself.

Porter stood beside her, holding her hand, sharing a laugh with her in the kind of unguarded moment that didn't need explaining. They were a young couple sharing a moment together, and were deeply in love.

Taryn said nothing.

Porter just took the phone and shared a soft smile at the photo lighting up his screen. 'She keeps up with me, even when the Hellhound doesn't.'

'How big an area do you patrol, if you've worn out three patrol vehicles?' She'd seen the hefty ute parked in the back. It was nothing like the simple police vans she'd seen in the city. Porter's police vehicle was a big four-wheel-drive ute with a cage, winches, beefy tyres, rows of spotlights, and a solid bull bar, heavily kitted for the outback.

Porter dug around his pile of files occupying the nearby chair and pulled out a heavily creased map. He spread it across the desk like he was rolling out a blueprint. 'This area...' He drew a circle on the map. 'It's what this station, NT Police, cover. My patrol area. It's big enough to get lost in twice, huh?'

Her eyes widened. 'That landmass is over a third the size of Victoria.'

'But then...' Porter flipped the map over and tapped a broader area that dwarfed the first map. 'That's the area Finn's team covers. All these cattle stations that run from the north, west, and east.'

She blinked a few times as if ridding some grit in her eyes.

He was talking about Northern Australia. 'That's got to be —'

'A hundred times bigger than our area.' Porter nodded. 'And we've got how many cops trained in livestock crime out here?'

She didn't answer.

Ported did. 'Two. Four, if you count the part-timers. I'd say the Stock Squad's running lean, wouldn't you?'

She stared at the map, gripping onto her coffee mug. No one had put it that plainly before. The sheer scale. The overwhelming odds. And yet they kept showing up.

Before she could ask another question, the back door slammed shut, followed by a set of heavy boots that came down the corridor, heading for the coffee.

It was Finn Wilde, complete with dust in his wake.

He stopped. Then narrowed his eyes, which were full of heat, on her.

He said nothing. Just turned and barged straight into the OIC's office —

And slammed the door behind him.

'I think the big man likes you.' Porter casually sipped his coffee as he eyed the door that Finn had just slammed. 'What do you reckon, Tanisha?'

'Please…' Tanisha over-dramatically rolled her eyes. 'That was a full-blown *I like you, but I'm emotionally constipated about it* door slam. That man right there,' she said, pointing at the closed door with one of her dangerously long fingernails, 'needs glitter, a double cocktail, and a big bear hug.' Tanisha then winked as if she'd just dropped the juiciest gossip of the day.

Porter laughed so easily, fist-bumping Tanisha, while casually keeping Taryn involved, like she belonged.

How was Taryn meant to audit this?

Not when Finn's silent storm had somehow stirred up an in-house scandal.

Nine

The door slam echoed like gunfire through the station. Followed by Tanisha and Porter's laughter.

Bloody Fed, making friends with Tanisha and Porter like she belonged here.

Marcus casually glanced up from his desk, mug in hand. 'Did that door offend you, Wilde?'

'It was open.'

'Mm. So was the front gate last week. We didn't slam that.' He sipped his coffee. 'You here to hide, throw a tantrum, or talk stock routes?'

Finn dropped into the visitor's chair with a grunt. 'What do you know about the Spinifex Highway?'

Marcus straightened slightly, his police uniform barely containing the bulky mass of muscle that came from brutal, disciplined effort—the kind that'd make even the hardest of prisoners, the ones who'd hog the barbells in the yard, nod with respect. 'Just that it's a little red vein of hell. Why?'

'Young Brodie was sent a video of cattle loading at Tinderflats Station.' Finn played the footage on his phone. 'That road train, supposedly carrying the same load of cattle, turns up at the stockyards with a different load of breathing assets. They'd been swapped out somewhere under the radar.'

'And you think they're doing it along the Spinifex Highway?'

Finn nodded, pulling the map from his pocket and spreading it over Marcus's cluttered desk. 'It's happening somewhere in this region…' He tapped on the map. 'It's central to half a dozen western stations, with plenty of space for two trucks to swap out a trailer load of fats. It also wouldn't be too hard to stash a stockyard somewhere in the scrub, to draft out the prime stock in that area either.'

'Any idea which stations are involved? Or stockmen?'

'That's the problem. Station owners might be double dipping, but I'm betting its contractors.' Finn started folding up his map. 'SW Rural Contracting. Ever heard of them?'

Marcus shook his head. 'A lot of stations hire contractors these days. Mustering crews, fencing, transport teams—it's cheaper than staffing full time.'

'Makes the paper trail messier. And I'm guessing some of the stockmen might be complicit.'

'Or they're being leaned on, hoping to cover their debts. A lot of cattle stations these days are fighting a mortgage, sky-rocketing diesel costs, and the risk of a corporate takeover.'

'And if they're corporate-owned stations, who's to say their staff aren't turning a blind eye?' Finn slid the map back into his back pocket. 'But Spinifex does have a long, unbroken stretch of red dirt and no cattle fences.' The perfect cover.

'And you think it links to the smuggling ring?'

'Yeah.' Finn leaned back in the chair, grinding his teeth.

'How can you be so sure?'

'Because Red is the one signing off on the paperwork. And only the locals know the Spinifex Highway exists. It's not on any GPS or any other official stock route planner. But it's how they're sneaking cattle across without going near a weighing station or a stock inspector.'

Marcus gave a low whistle. 'So, they're running stolen stock down a ghost road, backed by real paperwork.'

'Exactly. It looks legit, because on the books, it is. But the genetics don't match because the prime stock is being swapped out before they hit the yards.'

Marcus glanced up at the ceiling for a moment, as if letting all this news settle. 'Red may be smart, but he'd need someone bankrolling his operation. Someone who'd put in the collateral.'

'I agree. You heard Sawyer telling us someone is pulling

the strings. Red's a local mover, he knows where to send a truckload of beef, maybe grease a few palms at the yards. But cryogenic stock for DNA cloning? Crocodile eggs and hatchlings. Banteng and polo horses. That's way above Red's pay grade. We're talking about someone who knows how to ship shadows across international borders without leaving prints.' Creating an enormous threat to the entire industry.

'Are you going to tell the Fed?'

Finn's jaw ticked.

'Thought not.' Marcus shuffled some files across his desk. 'Audits are common.'

'But this isn't your common audit.' Finn moved towards the door, only to pause like it might bite him. He didn't want to find *her* sitting out there, winning over Tanisha and Porter, sipping their coffee like she'd always belonged.

'We're here if you need us. Just tell me what you want.'

'Thanks.' He gave Marcus a nod. 'I'm planning a sting soon and will be running surveillance all week out at Spinifex.'

Marcus leaned back in his chair behind that desk drowning in paperwork. 'And this has nothing to do with the auditor sitting beside my station's kitchen bench?'

Finn didn't answer.

'Uh-huh.' Marcus smirked. 'FYI, I overheard Porter talking to your auditor about the Hellhound, something about fuel invoices. She knows he's NT Police, and your local backup. Not Stock Squad, but he's close enough when you need another badge to make your arrests official.'

Porter was more help than Finn cared to admit. Between the Hellhound, his tracking skills, local knowledge and outback cop experience that came with an NT Police badge, Porter filled the gaps Finn couldn't always cover.

Only Amara and Finn had the authority to make arrests and file the paperwork—at least until Stone finished his courses. Izzy was doing a great job of pushing her husband, Craig, into doing his as well—even if the cowboy kept feigning that paperwork gave him hives.

On the other side of the door, he heard Tanisha's laugh, loud and unbothered, like it was just another cocktail party with friends, filled with juicy gossip.

And then Taryn's laugh that was so much lighter.

It shouldn't have made the hairs on his neck stand up. But it did.

Bloody Fed.

Not because she was in his way.

But because she was already under his skin.

Ten

The next morning, Taryn paused outside the Batcave, her workbag over her shoulder, her coffee and breakfast in hand, as a familiar voice echoed from inside the large room.

Amara's.

'That's good to hear, Constable. I appreciate the update,' came an authoritative male voice over a speaker. It was the kind of smooth voice designed to reassure a crowd, where every syllable was deliberate and polished to the point of feeling rehearsed. Like someone used to giving speeches or press briefings, not orders.

Taryn's spine stiffened. She knew that voice.

Commissioner Andrew Bannon.

'I'd appreciate it if you could monitor the team, and Finn, for me,' he said. 'I trust you'll raise anything if it looks off?'

'But—'

'Any concerns, you come straight to me, Constable. Don't wait. Understood?'

'Yes, Commissioner.'

The video call ended with a faint beep.

Taryn waited a beat, then pushed the door open like she hadn't overheard them.

Amara, rising from her desk with her trusty tablet in hand, stiffened.

'Morning.' Taryn offered a polite smile. 'Would it be okay to use this big table instead of the interrogation room? The Batcave feels more appropriate today. Less hostile.'

Amara gave a half-smile. 'Romy will appreciate that.'

Taryn began setting up the table, and casually dropped,

'Commissioner Bannon rarely calls constables directly. Especially not during an active audit. That's... unusual.'

Amara squeezed her tablet tighter. 'I—he...' She cleared her throat. 'The Commissioner just wanted an update.'

'Then he should ask the superior officer directly,' Taryn said, keeping her tone light. 'They're the ones paid to carry the responsibility.'

Amara chewed on her bottom lip, clearly caught in the middle of something. 'I agree. But...' She shrugged, full of unease. 'The Commissioner asked me, like it was a direct order.'

Taryn saw it then—the tightrope of blurred lines that poor Amara was walking. Still new to the job, torn between the chain of command, and her loyalty to the man who'd built this squad from nothing.

Thanks to her parents, Taryn was well-schooled about ranks, especially the power and danger of command. A Federal Commissioner had no business placing that kind of weight on the constable's shoulders.

'You should let Finn know. He is your OIC. With a team this small, the chain of command matters—*especially* during an audit.' She waved her hand over the piles of files she'd been trudging her way through.

Amara pressed her lips tight. Then finally, quietly, she said, 'I will.'

'You're not in trouble, Amara. I'm only saying this as a friendly warning, female officer to female officer. When someone that high up goes around your OIC to pressure you for information... it's not just bending the rules—it's putting you in the firing line.'

Amara's frown flickered, full of uncertainty.

'My mother's in the military. And she always says the higher the rank, the heavier the consequences if things go sideways—especially when the chain of command isn't followed... Guess who takes the hit when something leaks or paperwork doesn't line up? Not the Commissioner. The constable who answered a call she shouldn't have.'

Amara swallowed hard.

'I don't mean to harp on about protocols, when I know you see me as the bad guy. I get it.' But Taryn was hoping Amara understood the gravity of the situation and the potential risks. 'But I believe in protocols because they were created to protect *you*. All of you, from being manipulated.' And the Commissioner knew better.

Enough said, Taryn gave the young officer a soft smile, then went over her notes for this morning's interview.

Yet, Amara lingered by the door. 'Porter mentioned he spoke with you yesterday... Something about glitter cannons and cocktails?'

Taryn grinned. 'Tanisha was telling us how she's making glitter cannons to surprise her friend Felix for their next cocktail party, but her cats keep setting them off. And how Stone did that one time... She's a force of nature that woman is.'

Amara smiled at that. 'It took me weeks to figure out whether Tanisha was joking or testing me. Turns out it was both. And Stone, well...'

Taryn gave a knowing smirk. She'd witnessed Stone teasing Amara like an annoying big brother. But underneath the cheek and charm was some healthy respect, too. It was just that Stone's way of showing it was loud. 'One day, you're gonna stop curtsying and actually bite back with the boys, Amara. I just hope I'm around to bring the popcorn.' And she'd be cheering for the Tiny Titan from the sidelines too.

Taryn had grown up around lots of men like that—the uniforms, the banter, and the hierarchy. Luckily, her mum had taught her how to hold her ground with a smile and a spine. The constable was still learning, but she'd get there.

Amara glanced toward the doorway, then back again. 'How are you going at the pub?'

Taryn shrugged. 'The staff seem like nice people.'

'They really are. The chef used to have Michelin stars in his restaurant in Europe, and you can taste it in his meals. But don't order breakfast or talk to him before midday. He's a real grouch...'

'Duly noted. Any other tips?'

'Samantha is a lot more switched on than any of us realise, but she won't interfere. Billy's great for gossip and as a chaperone should you ever want to sit at the front bar. And Mean-Rene, she's a mother of four boys, who's really a sweetheart under all that black leather and ink.'

'Four boys?'

'I know, right?' Amara playfully rolled her eyes, the grin friendlier now. 'Did they tease you about poking the possums in the roof for the night-time ambience?'

Taryn laughed as she nodded. 'Did you stay there, too?

'A lot longer that I should have. Living out of a suitcase, assuming that this was all temporary.' Amara glanced around the office. 'Eventually, it wears you down. This place... it doesn't open up easily to strangers. The locals take their time to see if you're a good fit for them. Finn knew that. That's why he got Craig and Stone involved, to get an *in* with the station owners, the stockmen, and the rest of the locals. And it worked. Showing them he wasn't here to judge or interfere but to help... But it was Porter who helped me see that there's more to this place than just a job—along with a big lesson on teamwork. Porter is big on teamwork.'

'I noticed.' And she'd noticed how much Amara loved her job, the team, and her partner.

'Porter not only showed me this town's incredible depths of community spirit, but he also helped me find... *home.*' The smile was adorable, full, wide and beautiful as she shared a nod, then left the room.

But the word *home* landed heavier than Amara probably meant it to, shifting something inside Taryn's chest. A word that still felt intangible, like a dream she used to have when she'd stay at her grandfather's for the summer, chasing shade on his old verandah, sipping sodas and swapping girlish secrets with her cousin—when they were still alive.

Everywhere else had just been a posting. Just another military base on another rotation to not settle into a home.

Only her grandfather's had been the place that felt constant.

Taryn tucked the thought away, to sort out her notes, just as the Batcave door swung open and in walked Romy.

Stronger and shorter than expected, wearing a big friendly smile while lugging a heavy camera case over one shoulder. Dressed in cargo pants and hiking boots, Romy looked like she'd just stepped off the set of a wildlife documentary.

David Attenborough, eat your heart out.

'Morning,' she chirped. 'You must be the one poking around all our secrets. I've been warned.'

Taryn raised an eyebrow. 'Warned?'

Romy grinned, stepping around the table. 'Stone said not to flirt, unless I'm getting tasered. Izzy said not to overshare. And Amara just gave me *a look* that could be interpreted in so many ways—knowing my luck, all wrong. As for Finn? He just grunted and walked off muttering something about not bleeding on the carpet. So naturally, I came to talk.' Romy set down her case with a thud, then offered a hand. 'Romy Radford. Consultant-slash-drone-wrangler, so says Stone, but mostly I'm a wildlife videographer. And you are?'

'Taryn Hayes.'

'Lovely to meet you. Do you prefer Taryn, Hayes, or just *the Fed*?'

'Taryn's fine,' she replied, half-smiling at the newcomer.

Romy casually flopped into a chair like she owned it. 'Great. So, the short version is, I came up here to film a documentary about crocodiles, met Stone, and accidentally helped the team crack the *Cold Stock Case* by using my drone.'

'Cold stock?'

'Crocodiles. Hatchlings and eggs—over a hundred. Huge scandal. Big bucks. French fashion houses. Family legacies. Generational drama.' Romy waved her arms wide, eyes sparkling, with an excited energy that was addictive. 'As much as I was ticked off that I couldn't use any of my drone footage at the time for my own films, and we're talking incredible cinematic imagery gone, all because Finn made me sign an NDA. But he did pay for the footage—'

'I've got the invoices.' Taryn tapped the paperwork resting on the table.

'So you'll know that I'm technically a consultant. Whenever Finn calls, I follow Stone.' Romy leaned in, all conspiratorial. 'The camera *loves* Stone.'

Did Romy just purr?

'Anyway, we're on the hunt to explore the mysterious Spinifex Highway, so I can't stay long. Like I said, I mostly film wildlife documentaries when not helping Finn, and I cannot wait to do one on the banteng. Especially after that last bust, when Amara got lost with Porter and nearly died with that super expensive stolen horse, which ended up shutting down their illegal way station and recovering all that wild stock.'

Taryn blinked. 'What?'

Did the woman even breathe?

'Oh, wait. Was I supposed to tell you that? Izzy mentioned confidentiality.' Romy tapped her chin. 'Stone said not to give away too many company secrets.' She winced. 'Oops.'

Taryn blinked again. Once. Twice.

'You'll need to talk to Finn for the details.'

'Naturally,' Taryn murmured.

Romy beamed.

Interview over.

Eleven

The aircon in the world's smallest supermarket rattled like it was one loose screw away from retirement. It was annoying as hell. Finn grabbed a few tins of baked beans, tossed them into his basket beside the jerky and chips, and turned down an aisle—only to pull up short.

There she was… Taryn Hayes. Bent at the waist, reading a jar label like it had personally offended her, with a few curls slipping from her hair tie.

And she was in jeans.

Damn! It was worse than those skirts.

No skin, no flash of thigh. Just denim stretched in all the right places, hugging her curves like the damn fabric had fallen in love with her.

He ground his jaw.

Jeans and boots should have made her less distracting than tight pencil skirts and heels that made up her suit. They didn't. If anything, they made his brain short-circuit harder. He just couldn't stop tilting his head, picturing his hand on those hips.

She straightened suddenly and caught him.

There was a flicker of recognition. A pause.

Then came the frost.

Oh, boy, was it frosty.

'Get a good look, Sergeant?' Her spine snapped straighter.

'Just wondering how denim survives that much attitude.'

She arched a brow. 'Funny. I was wondering the same thing about testosterone.'

The corner of his mouth might've twitched—hard to say. 'You following me now, Fed?'

'Don't flatter yourself, Sergeant. If I wanted to tail someone with the emotional range of a stapler and poor snack choices, I'd go audit a vending machine.'

He should've been insulted. Hell, part of him was, sure. The other part—the stupid part—wanted to laugh and keep that comment in the memory banks for later.

A stapler? Really?

He clenched his jaw, glancing up at the flickering fluorescent lights in the hope of some divine intervention.

Of course, she had to be smart. A woman who'd leave bruises with her words.

And the worst part?

He liked it.

Idiot.

Since when did he let anyone get in his head like this? Let alone a Fed, with a file on his life, and a mouth that could cut steel?

Let's not focus on the mouth. Hell. NO.

But he let his eyes drag over her half-filled shopping basket—then lower. Following the walk. The sway of her hips. Those legs, wrapped in denim like a Christmas gift he had no business wanting to unwrap.

And yet, some traitorous part of him wanted to unzip that gift. Then drag that denim down, slowly. To feel her gasp against his mouth, all fire, fury and friction, until the only thing sharp between them was the edge of want.

He stepped back—both mentally and physically—trying to shove the entire image from his brain before it did something reckless to his self-control.

'Finn! You're back!'

That voice was like getting slapped in the face with some ringer's old boot that had been roasting in an outback sun all day.

'I'm so glad you're visiting.' That singsong voice belonged to Amelia, the manager. She moved like a perfume-soaked freight train, her arms loaded with wedding magazines marked with way too many colour-coded tags.

His eye twitched from the approaching torture.

'I saved you that jar of pickled onions your team likes—oh!' Her eyes latched onto Taryn. Sizing her up like a cattle judge at the Royal Darwin Show. 'Is this *her*?'

Finn didn't think, only reacted, as he stepped in close to place his hand on the small of Taryn's back. It was only meant to be a light touch. Something casual.

Yet, it felt familiar.

Enough to fight the urge to slide his fingers into those back pockets that cupped her backside beautifully. But then he'd cop an elbow to the face, when right now he needed her help. 'This is Taryn.'

That's all he said.

'That's me.' Taryn didn't even blink.

Amelia's smile froze, staring at them with hope dying in her baby-doll blue eyes—the kind that belonged on creepy porcelain dolls. 'So… You two are… *together*?'

Finn let his fingers curl around Taryn's hip, bringing her so much closer to his side. 'Yep,' he said. 'Together.'

Taryn gave him a look that read: *You owe me for this.*

She then smiled at the bouncy blonde and leaned her head against his shoulder like they did it every damned day. There, her warm and citrusy scent filled his lungs, doing a damn fine job of scrambling his thoughts.

But then she playfully stroked his chest. Right over the sternum, like she had every right to touch him, igniting something deep in his gut. Stirring up the kind of instinct that lived deep in the bones of a man who hadn't been touched in too damn long.

'Almost a year now,' she said, tossing it out like a grenade. 'He's very punctual. Excellent with paperwork. The man truly is gifted at filling holes.'

Finn coughed.

'That's… really nice.' Amelia's screechy voice was way too cheerful. 'I didn't know you liked anyone, Finn.'

'I didn't,' he muttered.

'He does now.' Taryn nudged him playfully with her

elbow, but it was a sharp stab in the side, making him hold her tighter.

For a second, their eyes locked in a way that was too damn hot to be a lie.

Finn's jaw tightened, fingers flexing slightly where they rested against her hip. And damn if she didn't just lean in closer.

Shit.

'If you're together…' Amelia squeaked in a way that scratched down his spine like a rusty nail. 'Why the two baskets?'

Again, Taryn came to the rescue. 'We're competitive. First one to the checkout wins. And I count calories, he doesn't.'

Amelia's eyes widened. 'Riiight.'

Nope, they were losing this battle.

Again, Taryn rested her hand against his chest, right over his heartbeat—which picked a helluva time to speed up.

'He cheats in our games,' she murmured.

Finn arched an eyebrow at her. 'I'm not a cheating man, babe. Never have been. Never will be.'

'No,' Taryn agreed, still smiling sweetly at Amelia, her voice like warm honey. 'But you do try to distract me in the condiments aisle, hoping I won't chase down the missing sauces. You know, the ones that make the dishes so much healthier, which you're avoiding.'

Finn's mouth twitched. How did she turn her job of chasing down his invoices and paperwork into sauces and dishes?

But it worked on the bouncy blonde. Amelia's smile strained at the edges to become a sneer. 'Well, that's… nice.'

'You have no idea,' Taryn purred—low, velvety.

Aimed straight at him, it unstitched something deep in his chest.

Helpless to stop himself, his hand tightened at her hip, drawing her closer, that her body melded so wrongly against him in all the right ways.

'Careful, Fed.' Finn dipped his head close enough for his

voice to brush the delicate skin just under her ear. 'You keep talking like that, and I might forget where we are…' Or that they were faking.

He watched the goosebumps prickle along her arm, hearing that subtle hitch in her breath. And then she shifted, just slightly, allowing her shirt's collar to part, giving him a spectacular view. A hint of lace. A tease of cleavage.

Finn's pulse kicked hard.

Oh, he was in deep. And drowning. Taryn may be playing her part—but he was starting to forget the rules of engagement.

'Well…' Amelia hugged her colour-tagged wedding magazines like a life raft. 'You two make a very surprising couple.' She turned and disappeared down the next aisle fast.

Taryn stepped away, brushing his hand off like it had burned her. 'You owe me.'

Finn tried to forget the look on Taryn's face. Or how his hand still remembered the feel of her.

They walked in silence to the counter, as Finn felt the heat crawl under his collar with one undeniable truth: it hadn't felt fake. Not for a second.

His basket hit the bench with a quiet thud. He could only stand there like a damn statue. Watching her. Wanting her. And not saying a word.

'I'll need to speak with Bree next,' Taryn said casually, as if talking about the weather, while the cashier packed his groceries.

What the—

She'd just dropped it.

The bomb.

Right there, between the flavoured milk and the chocolate. Like it meant nothing.

His spine went stiff. 'No.'

'Bree runs the local brand registry. And there's an invoice for her services for a brand consult. It's relevant.'

'No,' he growled. 'It's not happening.'

'She's also the reason Craig's part of your team, and how

you found your quarantine station. Oh, and that first job you had before you set up shop here in this little town of trouble, was all from Bree's phone call from Elsie Creek Station.' She folded her arms, looking at him all cool, calm and in control. Like she hadn't just ripped the steel door off the vault he'd welded shut as the barrier between his work and personal life.

How the hell did she know all that?

Finn's jaw locked while glaring at her with heat. She wasn't just auditing paper trails, she was piecing together the things she shouldn't have known.

She'd make a bloody good detective — for the right reasons. Shame she was here for all the wrong ones.

And dragging Bree into this? That was a line he would not cross.

'You're playing with fire, Fed.' His voice dropped low and dangerous. 'That woman bends steel for a living. You dig too deep, and she'll hand you your clipboard in pieces before she sends you sprinting across the tarmac to catch your flight back to Canberra. Do not mess with Bree.'

Taryn gave one of those annoying, casual shrugs of someone completely unfazed. 'This audit includes every consultant, Finn. Which now includes her.'

He stepped closer, tension rippling through him like a live wire. 'Bree is out of bounds. Find another angle to dig the screws in.'

'Why? When it looks like I've found the *right* spot to dig, eh, Sergeant.' Her voice had that cool edge to it. But her eyes didn't flinch. Not even a stutter. And the scary part was she wasn't backing off either.

He dropped a wad of cash onto the counter and snatched up his bag. 'No. And that's my final answer.'

Twelve

Most mornings, Taryn had stood shoulder to shoulder with the locals at the train station's food van. She was still an outsider, even in boots and jeans, but she'd started earning polite nods now. They'd tip their stockman's hat, and offer that polite wave to let her step ahead of them with a mumbled *ladies first*.

A pleasant change from the city where it was *every man for himself*, where people spent their time staring at their phones, and ignoring the noisy world. Here, they chatted, bartered and bantered while waiting in line for coffee, as if in a forgotten time, before mobile phones and social media were invented.

Only this morning, Taryn didn't go to the police station and claim her space in the Batcave. This morning, she'd reserved a table far enough away from anyone to overhear and set down her workbag and waited.

A sun-faded red ute rumbled around the edge of the green, belonging to Cowboy Craig. It pulled up in the same usual unhurried way he'd walked the corridors of the police station. Then he elaborately opened the passenger door as if for a queen.

There she was. Isobel Callahan—Izzy—wearing snappy suspenders that accentuated her posture. In pinstriped trousers and a white shirt, the picture of a big-city lawyer.

Holding her hand, Craig leaned down and kissed the back of it like a gentleman in love.

Aww. Taryn sighed.

Izzy beamed at her husband as he muttered something in her ear. She laughed, kissed his cheek, then made her way across the lawn.

'Hope I'm not late? Craig had to stop and say *hi* to three dogs and a horse on the way here.'

'All good, I—'

'I don't drink coffee,' Izzy cut in, 'but if you've ordered a peppermint tea, you've already won me over.' She took a seat opposite Taryn.

Taryn grinned as she pushed a cup across the table. 'Peppermint and ginger with a dollop of honey. I believe it's your homegrown honey, too.'

Izzy lit up. 'Oh, you did your homework. I like that.'

Then came the pause, as if waiting to see who'd make the first move.

Taryn was predicting Izzy would speak first. Having learned all she could about the reputation and habits of the top-notch criminal lawyer with quirks, because this was the interview Taryn had been waiting for.

'Do you want to talk about cattle and the weather? Or something really interesting?' Izzy swirled her cup like it might reveal their secrets in the tea leaves.

'How about, are you missing life as a big-city lawyer?'

'Hell, no.' Izzy gave a theatrical sigh. 'It's quieter. Fewer death threats. Even though it's mostly wills and property law, there's still plenty of drama. Plus I'm about to have a cooking class with Bree. We're canning my first harvest of tomatoes. Pro-tip: don't empty the whole packet of seeds on a windy day, thinking it'll never work. I have tomatoes growing everywhere like weeds.'

'From high courtrooms to canning tomatoes,' Taryn said with a soft smile. 'That's quite the pivot.'

Izzy shrugged lightly. 'Turns out, growing and harvesting your own produce is oddly satisfying. No one's ever tried to bribe me with zucchinis. But eggs are becoming quite the commodity of currency, of late.'

Taryn leaned in with curiosity. 'Don't you miss it at all? The rush, the wins, the pressure?'

'Some days. That thrill of chasing down the answers, to

then sort it all into a neat box, sure. But I don't miss who I was.' Izzy sighed, glancing around the train station. 'Craig taught me that different isn't always bad. And I needed stillness, to make the time to stare at the stars, and I needed...*here*.'

Izzy sat back, her tea forgotten, to study Taryn again — like really study her.

Taryn should have read that as a warning.

'You know, you're not the only one who does her homework.'

Taryn blinked. 'Excuse me?'

'Your mother's a high-ranking officer. Only one step off from becoming a judge for... what do they call it officially? Judge Advocate General? Not the Americanised JAG, like your everyday military lawyer, but the *real* deal — the highest judicial officer in uniform.' She paused. 'Or do you just call it JAG?'

'I grew up calling it JAG. Less of a mouthful.'

'Either way, your mother is a woman well-known for being methodical, and by the book. But also unafraid to challenge protocol when justice requires it.'

Another pause.

Taryn wasn't sure whether to fill it.

'Your father works in intelligence, not sure which department, but cybersecurity is his forte, with career postings to various embassies across the globe. Rarely photographed. Rarely quoted.' She looked directly at Taryn. 'A very private strategist.'

Taryn held her gaze, letting Izzy say her piece.

'So, with your mother's military discipline and your father's analytical mind, you were raised sharp, emotionally restrained, and rule focused. Moving from one military base to another, getting an elite education — especially when stationed with the embassy — only added to it. It gave you the skills to quickly climb the ladder in federal investigations. In particular, high-value corporate fraud, the white-collar crimes, with a high conviction rate. You deserve a lot more than your gazetted wage as a reward.'

Izzy leaned forward, her voice dropping as if sharing some secret. 'Rumour has it you're being groomed to run your own division and already have that office with a view.'

Izzy sat back, her eyes wandering over Taryn's clothing. 'And yet here you are, in boots and jeans. Auditing the Stock Squad's books, which a first-year grad or a half-decent clerk could handle. In a town that most people couldn't even find without a paper map.'

Well, audit me sideways and ruffle through all my inner files, why don't you?

And the worst part?

Izzy wasn't wrong.

Taryn had spent a lifetime staying two steps ahead—out-thinking, outworking, and outlasting the competitors, office politics, and the bad guys. But somehow, in less than a minute, Isobel Callahan had laid out her entire life, without any theatrics or malice.

This wasn't just a lawyer casually sipping peppermint tea and thinking about canning tomatoes. This was the woman who'd once faced down a kidnapping and turned it into a federal case file so airtight it should have made headlines. Where most of Izzy's cases did end up. So, of course, she saw it all.

But then something else clicked. 'You told them.'

Izzy's smile didn't fade. 'Told who, what?'

'Finn. Amara. Craig. Stone. That's why they've been on the defensive ever since I got here. You told them—'

'That they don't send someone like you just to dig through receipts in the middle of nowhere,' Izzy finished, calm as ever.

Taryn shared a dry laugh. 'You're right.'

'So why did they send you out here?'

Taryn sat back. 'I have my orders.'

'No, it's more than that...' Izzy tilted her head at Taryn as if seeing straight through her. 'It's Everlight. That's the big fish that got you out of bed.'

Izzy shared a slight curve of a smile that had Taryn panicking. What else did Izzy see?

'You like him, don't you?'

'Who?'

'Finn.'

'*What*? Where did that come from?'

'Craig said Finn's been weird lately. Slamming doors and avoiding the Batcave. He also told me there's this tension between you two.'

It was rare for Taryn's conversations to get flipped on its head like this, especially since she was supposed to be asking all the questions. 'I don't—'

'Like him?' Izzy arched a brow. 'Come now, Taryn, you're a well-seasoned federal investigator. You know better than to answer a yes-or-no question that fast.'

Taryn opened her mouth, then closed it again. She hated how warm her face felt right now.

'It's not a crime, you know.' Izzy leaned back, wearing a satisfied expression. 'But if you're planning to tear down the house, while falling for the man who built it… Well, that's a very complicated manoeuvre. Don't you think?'

Taryn cleared her throat, desperate to get this conversation under control. 'Everlight is the real game plan for being here. For the fraud and all those manipulated grants that were dressed up as clean energy. Where you and the Stock Squad presented a case that pointed to a major prosecution—until it all just disappeared.'

Izzy's smile faded. 'Were charges ever laid?'

'No.' Taryn held her gaze. 'Nothing.'

'What?' Izzy's face paled. 'Drew—'

'Passed it to an investigative department. The paper trail from his office is there. But after that… No press release. No court filings. No trial. When, by rights, the Stock Squad should've been recognised for their part. You especially, Izzy. What you uncovered about Everlight, and the millions you saved the government, you should've received a medal.'

'Is that flattery, Agent Hayes?'

'No. It's a fact. And it's partly why I'm here.' Yet, Taryn couldn't reveal everything. 'You're the reason I flew up here. Just to speak to you.'

Izzy lifted her chin. 'Ah, so the truth is finally revealed.'

'I've read the file, what's left of it, as most of it's been heavily redacted. But I got my hands on an older copy that has your name in there. You were doing searches on shell companies, following the paper trail, trying to find Everlight's owner. Did you?'

'No. I found a legal firm with no clients. A trust linked to a registered lobbyist who hadn't paid tax in a decade. And a bunch of bankrupt companies that shouldn't have been trading.' Izzy tapped her fingers against her teacup. 'I could find the properties that Everlight had bought and, like you, went through their receipts and found they were faking their solar farms. They were using the land protestors to stall the building phase—yet they had phoney contractor bills for construction and installation of massive solar panels.'

'But there weren't any?'

'No. They were empty parcels of land, with just a shed, a sign, and a few solar panels creating just enough power for the shed, like an onsite construction manager's office. The rest were nothing more than ghost towns.' Izzy fiddled with her paper cup, as the frustration laced her voice.

Taryn stayed quiet.

'You know, they killed my assistant. Meghan… I've had other assistants who couldn't keep up or got frustrated with how my brain works, because it gets demanding or scattered when I crash. But not her. Meghan had this way of grounding me, like nothing rattled her.' Izzy smiled faintly, the kind that held more grief than joy. 'She'd laugh so easily and had this gift for finding fun. Even when we were stuck in these underground archive rooms, rifling through paper, with dust on our skirts, you could hear her laugh echo between the compactus shelves…' Izzy frowned, shuffling in her seat. 'You know, I never felt Meghan got the justice she deserved, not after what happened to her.'

'I have to ask… how did your assistant die?'

Izzy looked up slowly, a small frown forming. 'That's in the report.'

Taryn shook her head. 'Not anymore. As I said before, the file's been redacted. Her name's gone. And the state police file was pulled, too.'

Izzy blinked like she'd been slapped. 'They pulled all of it?'

'Everything. No court documents. No arrest logs. No mention of your kidnapping, or the guys who did it.'

'Dane Carter and Renzo.' Izzy shivered at the names.

Now we're getting somewhere. 'All I've got is lines of black ink, done by someone who went to great lengths to hide the truth.' Taryn sighed heavily. 'It's been frustrating. The closed doors and continuous setbacks, made it feel like I'm taking one step forward and ten steps back.' Taryn leaned in a little closer, her voice quieter. 'I've had to be careful. One misstep, and the wrong people will start to take notice of what I'm doing.'

'So you're not just here to tick boxes.'

'No. And yes.' Taryn held her gaze. 'I'm hoping you've kept a copy of the original case files, or will let me look at any notes you may have, so I can start putting the pieces together.'

'You want to find out who owns Everlight?'

Taryn nodded.

'It's dangerous.'

Taryn wasn't going to state the obvious to spook the woman on the other side of the table, who was already weighing up the pros and cons in the blink of an eye.

Izzy took another sip of her tea, straightened out her napkin, then grabbed a few more from the square metal napkin holder. She then laid them all out in a neat line across the table, as if filing her thoughts into order.

It wasn't promising.

The cons—like *life in danger again*—were winning.

'I've got an untraceable laptop my father built for me, to follow trails that don't want to be found. And he's only a call away if I need that extra push for deeper research. He's very good at finding ghosts.' She hoped, with fingers and toes crossed, that Izzy would come to the party.

But Izzy refolded the napkins, one by one, stacking them neatly back to their original state.

Taryn's pulse kicked.

No. That wasn't good. That looked like a retreat.

Taryn couldn't afford to walk away with nothing. She needed to push on a weak spot, so she asked again, 'How did your assistant, Meghan, die?'

Izzy let out a quick breath as if she'd been sucker-punched.

It had Taryn regretting that question.

'Meghan was murdered just before lunchtime, in a public car park next to a government building where I'd been collecting company reports and research results. I remember it was full of security cameras, but all of them were non-operational.'

For real? 'Go on, what did you see?'

'Renzo pulled up in a vehicle behind our work car. He then got out, smiling, and stabbed her. Before she'd hit the floor, he came after me. But I ran.' Izzy stared at her hands in her lap. 'I still feel guilty for not being able to help her, you know. And now you're telling me poor Meghan's death doesn't even exist in the case file?'

Taryn nodded as she tenderly put her hand on Izzy's. 'But you can help her now. You can help me give Meghan the justice she deserves.'

'How?'

'Help me find out who owns Everlight Energy Solutions.'

Thirteen

Finn ripped open the station's back door, his boots hitting the floor hard. Every step down the hallway carried three things: fury, betrayal, and the sting from his last phone call.

It had been from Craig, who was fuming over the possibility of Izzy being dragged back into the crosshairs. All because of Taryn Hayes.

Then, Amara, his by-the-book, most loyal officer, told him Drew had been calling her directly. And it was Taryn who'd pushed her to admit it to Finn.

Somehow, that woman hadn't just gotten under *his* skin—she was working her way through his entire team.

He reached the door to the Batcave and ripped it open.

Taryn looked up from her laptop, calm as anything.

He slapped the manila folder he was carrying onto her desk. 'You're digging into Everlight, yeah?'

And there was that poker face. She didn't even flinch.

Of course she didn't.

Finn stood there, his pulse raging hotter than the road outside. 'SW Rural Contracting. If you're so set on chasing Everlight's ghost, start there.'

He turned to walk out.

'No.' The word cut through the air, sharp and fast.

He stopped. 'No?' Was she asking for a fight?

'I need answers, too.' She walked around the desk, with fire in her eyes. 'I see what you're doing. You've been ghosting me in some lame attempt to avoid my questions.'

He narrowed his eyes at her. 'You're the one who came into this town swinging an axe, and now you're surprised no one's rolling out the welcome mat?'

'I'm not here to be liked. I'm here to do my job. And now you're expecting me to follow your lead? I'm not your lapdog, Sergeant.' She crossed her arms in defiance. 'If you want me to dig, you have to give me something first.'

'This *is* me giving you something,' he growled, tapping the file. 'Don't mistake cooperation for consent to my intel, not when you're walking through my team, making my people question me.'

'Am I? Or have they always been questioning you? Maybe I'm just the one who's game enough to say it out loud.'

Didn't that hit like a fist to the guts.

'So, what's it gonna be?' Taryn stood toe to toe with him. 'Are you going to answer my questions, or keep on avoiding me?'

Careful what you wish for, sweetheart.

'You want answers? Fine. Grab your workbag and get in the troopy. And no complaints.' He stormed down the corridor and back out into the heat before he changed his mind.

Sliding into the driver's seat, slipping on the seatbelt, he had the engine idling as his fingers drummed with impatience on the steering wheel. He'd give her two minutes and then he'd leave.

But then Taryn walked out of the station, her bulky workbag over her shoulder, gripping that notebook like it held state secrets. He definitely wanted to read it now.

She might think this exhibition was all about giving her answers, but his plan was all about keeping his enemy closer, to find out why someone like her was out here. And that file he'd thrown at her was a test, not just of her skill for finding information either, but how good she was at reading between the lines.

But her expression caught him off guard, and how her jaw was set to war mode. This time, there was no skirt to hitch as she climbed inside. Just boots, jeans, and a takeaway coffee cup she held with her teeth, slamming the car door, to sit there pretty as could be.

She clicked on her seatbelt. 'Where are we going?'

Finn put the troopy in gear, and with his eyes on the horizon he said, 'The Spinifex Highway.'

Fourteen

Inside the troopy, Taryn's jaw was clenched so tight her molars ached, as she glared through the windscreen.

The silence between her and Finn was thick enough to bottle. She'd pushed him too far this time, but dammit, she was here for answers, and if Craig had already filled him in, then there was no point beating around the bush. It's why she'd gotten on this hell ride.

She glanced around the interior of the rugged, boxy wagon that could easily seat eight adults. Rugged enough to go anywhere in this county, its immense interior space had plenty of room to hold a rolled swag, a battered gas cooker wedged between a jerry can and a tangled camp chair, with an esky tucked into the corner beside a duffel bag. It wasn't tidy, but it was efficient and prepped to disappear at a moment's notice.

He still didn't look at her. Just shifted gears and took some back track, with tyres crunching over sunbaked gravel. A small church stood on the hill on one side, with the stockyards taking up space on the other, when his phone buzzed on the dash.

He glanced at it, and something in his posture changed. 'We're taking a detour. I've got to meet someone. Keep your mouth shut.'

'That's charming.'

'Wouldn't take you if it wasn't urgent,' he muttered. 'Or I could sit you under a tree—'

'Are you meeting an informant?'

He gave a grunt. 'Something like that.'

'I get it. I'll play nice.' Taking a stranger to meet an

informant was an enormous risk, and she knew enough to not interfere. But it also cleared the air to form a truce.

The troopy veered off the main road, and down a narrow track, where the land became a complex sprawl of timber rails and iron gates.

It was the backdoor to the stockyards.

The heavy aroma of cattle manure, blended with rusted metal and diesel oil coming from an outgoing beastly road train, churning up the dry soil with a roar.

Red dust clung to everything. The sides of sheds that hoarded hay, and wooden posts sagging under the weight of time and too many seasons.

And the cattle—hundreds of them—were putting on a full vocal performance.

One let out a deep, throaty bellow.

Another joined in from somewhere across the yards, slightly off-key.

Then a third chimed in, and suddenly it was all happening, sounding like a choir rehearsal on the wrong end of a pub night—all full of baritone bravado and no conductor.

She stared out the window, lips twitching despite herself. Half of her brain still bristled with anger. The other half?

Well, that part was waiting to see if Mr Personality beside her would suddenly break into some gruff stockman's solo.

The thought was so absurd it made her grin flicker.

Finn shot her a sideways glance. 'What's your problem?'

'I was just wondering,' she said, oh so innocently, 'do stockmen really sing lullabies to settle the cattle? Or is that only on special occasions?'

His look was pure stone.

'Riiight… So, what's your go-to? Bit of Slim Dusty? Or are you more of a Dolly man?'

He said nothing. Naturally.

'So,' she said, resting her elbow against the passenger window. 'Do you do music?'

He still didn't answer.

'Or do you just sit in silence while the show tunes play in

your head?'

That earned her the smallest twitch of his mouth. Not a smile—never a smile—but something.

They pulled up behind a rusting fence panel that blocked them from the yards, as a shadow darted from the edge of a shed. It was a teenager, tall, with wiry limbs, running straight to Finn's open window.

'Hey, Brodie. What's up?'

The boy paused spotting Taryn.

'Ignore her. I do.'

Charming. Not. But she'd promised to behave, even biting her tongue to stop the backchat.

'Yeah, okay…' The boy wiped the sweat and dirt from his face with the sleeve of his even dirtier shirt. 'Red's sniffing around and I mean bad.'

'How bad?'

'He's checkin' Lydia's phone, Finn. Like all the time.' The boy's voice was filled with worry, as if he was talking about his mother. 'I heard them arguing in the office just before. I don't think she's safe.'

Taryn leaned slightly forward to get a good look at Brodie. He was thin and covered in dust, like it was part of his skin and suntan. But there were burn marks—pale scars that barely blended against tanned skin. Some on his neck, too.

Her stomach twisted as she recognised them. *Cigarette burns.*

Finn's voice, which always had that hard edge, had softened. 'You did the right thing telling me, Brodie.' He even tapped the boy's shoulder in reassurance. 'I won't let anything happen to her. Not on my watch.'

Even though the boy nodded, he still looked worried.

Hold on. Why was a kid, this young, Finn's informant?

Especially when he barely looked old enough to drive, let alone be dragged into a backdoor op for the Stock Squad. Sure, teens gave statements all the time—but this wasn't a witness. This was a source. And Finn was treating him like a seasoned CI.

Finn shifted in his seat, effectively blocking her view. 'Look, I've told Lydia that if she needs an out, or if she's worried about anything, she can come to my place or the station. I mean it. Lydia knows this already.'

Brodie's shoulders eased a fraction, as he took a deep breath.

'You don't need to do this, Brodie. I won't risk you or Lydia. That was the deal.' She could tell from his voice that Finn didn't just say that to cover his arse because Taryn was in the car, he *meant* it.

Who was this man?

Not the prick she'd been sparring with since the day she'd landed, but someone who also had a backbone and was full of quiet loyalty. It was unexpected.

'Yeah, I know. But what they're doing is wrong.' Brodie's spine straightened as if filling with courage as he leaned in closer, so much surer of himself. 'But the reason I called you is that I'd just overheard Red talking on the phone about the trucks. SW trucks. He mentioned Billycan Corner. You know it?'

SW—SW Rural Contracting? She squeezed the file Finn had slapped on her desk, as her mind rushed to fill in the blanks on this conversation.

Finn gave a single nod. 'Yeah. I know it.'

'They've got a truck coming in. Early hours, I reckon. To meet the train.' Brodie tapped the side of his temple. 'I know their pattern now.'

'What's that?'

'They come in on the rush, when the last trucks race to get loaded to meet the train.'

'Hoping you'll be too busy to notice the switch.'

'Yeah… It's that or early dawn, hoping we're too wrecked from pulling an all-nighter unloading and feeding cattle, because we all know the train's deadline and it waits for no man on Train Day.' The kid jerked his chin back over his shoulder.

Taryn twisted in her seat. *Train Day.*

She'd heard that somehow Train Day made this sleepy outback town come alive. Billy, from the pub, had warned her when he'd escorted her across the road for breakfast at the food van: *'Hope you're not expecting any sleep the next two nights, luv. It's Train Day tomorrow.'*

Now she understood why…

A line of road trains—massive, rumbling beasts—snaked around the edge of the yards, stretching along the highway like a steel-backed convoy. Some were parked, others were crawling in, with stock mewling from inside the double-decked trailers, as dust curled through the air like smoke.

But it wasn't just trucks and cattle.

There were horses tied up under lean-tos, along with cattle dogs ready to muster, as drovers passed around battered mugs, and kids darted between the rails under their watchful eyes.

Retired stockmen sat along the fence line in wheelchairs or walkers, wearing their old stockman hats and sun-faded shirts, watching the action like it was a footy final. Some shouted advice. Others just smiled and nodded at an old mate or two.

Much younger men and women moved through the yards, some nervous, while they were being guided by quiet murmurs and sharp whistles from the older hands.

Altogether, there was a rhythm to it—even if it was rough, dust-choked, and loud, it still held an unspoken elegance to it, like a song every person here knew by heart.

Taryn had never expected this. Not the scale. Or the chaos.

Most of all, not *the heart*.

It was as if the town itself was breathing, and the lungs of it were right here, in these stockyards on Train Day.

Now she understood why they defended it so fiercely. Why Finn was fighting so hard. And why a kid like Brodie would risk himself to protect it.

She just wasn't sure who they were defending it from.

'They'll be flat out until midnight,' Brodie told Finn. 'I'll be up all night, for sure.'

She glanced at Brodie—so young, so tired, like he'd already lived three lives.

Then her gaze shifted to Finn, who hadn't said a word.

But she could feel it now, the weight of what they were all about, and what they were trying to stop. Because in all this dust and movement and noise… no one would notice the switch of one single cow or twenty, where each beast easily came in at two grand a head.

Finn patted the kid's shoulder not just like a mate, but more like a big brother. 'You've done good, mate. Now keep your head down and call me if there's any trouble. If you can't reach me, hide at my place or go straight to the station. Got it.'

'She'll be right, mate.' Brodie grinned so wide his teeth were a bright white against the dirt.

'Just tell me you've got it, Brodie. Or you'll be giving me ulcers.'

'Yeah, yeah. A man your age, that's bound to happen.' The boy chuckled before slipping back into the stockyards like a ghost in dirt, dust and denim.

Taryn watched him go, as the questions built in her chest. 'Who was—'

'Not now.' Finn shot off a text to his team, catching the words: *…timeline moved forward. We're a go.* He then tossed his phone on the dash, shifted gears and steered them back onto the road.

There wasn't any anger in his voice. But something in the way he gripped the steering wheel told her he wasn't shutting her out—he was holding himself in. He was worried for the boy, and this other woman, Lydia.

Taryn sat back, her pulse thudding annoyingly out of sync, like a warning she should've listened to.

But she ignored it, as she'd just seen something she wasn't meant to—a glimpse of who the real Finn Wilde was behind the scowl.

And that, somehow, made detaching herself from this case so much harder.

Fifteen

The tyres hummed against the bitumen before it gave way to gravel. The familiar crunch of dirt under the wheels, with gravel pinging against the underbelly before it got tossed around like confetti, was normally a sign for Finn to breathe.

But today it just wasn't doing its magic, not with the Fed taking up space on his passenger seat.

They were maybe thirty k's out of town, and she still hadn't said a word since he'd told her to zip it.

Good.

He didn't want words. He wanted space to think, to clear his head before he did something stupid—like slam the brakes and demand to know what the hell was she doing getting into his team's heads.

But his thoughts weren't just on her. They were on Lydia. And on Brodie, the kid wearing old burns and even older eyes.

Finn went over the conversation again. He'd said the right things, offered the safe house, the station, the fallback plan—but was it enough? If Red was escalating, would Lydia ask for help?

He should've pushed harder.

He should've—

Finn exhaled through his nose, keeping his jaw locked tight.

At least the intel was solid. He'd suspected a load was coming through soon, but now Brodie had given him what he didn't have—*a timeframe.*

Tomorrow morning. Ten sharp. That was when the last

truck was allowed through the stockyard's boom gates, when the yards were closed to focus purely on loading the train.

With a quick text message to the team to get into position, they had one night—tonight—to plan the sting, and pray Red didn't sniff them coming.

And Taryn?

She shouldn't have been there, hogging his passenger seat.

He hated that she'd seen Brodie, forcing him to trust her. It was a risk he hadn't meant to take. But the worst part?

He wasn't sure if he regretted it.

Taryn sat beside him, flicking through the file he'd slapped on her desk earlier. Her pen tapped the side of her notebook, with her legs braced as the troopy hit a dip and rumbled on.

She didn't ask for aircon, only rolled down her window, and tightened that bun in her hair. There was no whine about the heat or the corrugations, as she scribbled something down, flipped a page, and kept on reading.

He hated how much he respected that.

Finally, she spoke.

'SW Rural Contracting,' she muttered, still scanning the file. 'Ten pages of government-approved dribble that says exactly nothing. You have to give me more,' she said flatly. 'Unless your plan was to drag me out as a seat warmer to play I-spy on your BS? I'll get out now and send you a copy of my report from Canberra.'

Figures she'd be thorough. But damn her for being right.

She closed the file with a snap. 'You knew there was nothing in that folder.'

'Didn't say it'd have answers. Just said it was a place to start.'

'It's not enough,' she shot back. 'Not with your record and that pardon.'

There it was, that bloody pardon. His get-out-of-jail card that had branded him for life with that one question: *How the hell did he get that?*

'Spare me the dance, sweetheart. We both know you were sent out here to shut us down—so don't pretend otherwise.'

His grip on the steering wheel was so tight he might just break the old girl.

'Fine. I was sent here to shut you down.' No fluff. No lead-in. Just clean truth.

'Why?' He wasn't ready to let the squad go. Not now. Not when they were this close to nailing the Stock Agent. And hell, people needed them out here. Surely, they'd proven that by now.

'No one greenlights a pardon for a violent crim, then hands him a badge and a healthy budget, to run some outback cowboy show. Not with your history. Looking at it from the outside, it reads like a stitched-up back-woods fairy tale with blood on the pages.'

She wasn't wrong.

That's what stung the most, he'd bled between the pages of his own story for too long to believe in any fairytale bulldust and their happily-ever-afters.

'And now that you're here?' The question left his mouth before he could stop it, when he should've been asking himself why her opinion mattered—the woman sent to tear his team apart.

'I get it,' she sighed. 'Sort of… I'm looking at this from the outside, and things like that stockyard,' she added, tossing her thumb behind her, 'helps to build a picture. But I need more. And not drip-fed junk, either. My patience is running thin, and I'm on a deadline, with my flight to Canberra already booked. Right now, I've got enough to shut this whole thing down.' She wasn't bluffing either.

Damn.

'How? Based on what?'

'The paperwork you gave me was just on your expenses. Besides the official reports on the system, you've never told me about your cases, your processes, and your wins. Nothing. All you've shown me is just a lot of money being spent on overpriced cow—'

His glare cut her off.

But the damage was done. She'd seen enough to make the

Stock Squad disappear—and he'd handed her the bloody matchbook to light that fire!

That wasn't what he'd planned, when he'd been doing his best to avoid her.

Of course he hadn't explained the wins, the lives changed, the family farms they'd helped, and the numbers in the stock recovered. All he'd done was toss her breadcrumbs in the paperwork like that was enough.

And yet she'd chosen not to pull the plug.

Instead, she'd climbed into his passenger seat chasing answers.

Hold on…

'There's more to this,' he hissed. 'You wouldn't have dragged this audit out for nearly two weeks unless something else was pushing you.' Whatever it was, it wasn't orders. And it sure as hell wasn't some fascination over paperwork. 'Nah, this is personal. I can smell it. Has been since day one. This isn't just a job for you—it's revenge. Or justice. Or both.'

She didn't deny it.

But she didn't look at him either.

'With your skill set, you could've wrapped this up in two days. Paperwork, interviews signed off, done. But you didn't. You dug deeper. Booked yourself in for two weeks at the pub, then dragged it out these past nine days, poking around in places that had nothing to do with funding or resource allocation. You didn't need to talk to half my team. But you did.'

Taryn's jaw twitched as she flicked open her notebook.

There was definitely more to this. He could see it. 'You said you needed to understand the early casework—our very first case, the one that involved Everlight Energy.'

'I told Izzy I wanted to know who was behind Everlight.'

'Sure. But there were certain questions you kept asking Izzy. And trust me, she replayed that whole conversation back to me, word for word. It's one of her skills.'

Oh, yeah, he had her attention now, even though she'd been staring at the same page on her notebook for a while now.

Steering them down the dirt road, he kept her in his periphery reading the shift in her posture, and the way she controlled her breathing.

He was close. Damn close.

'I asked Izzy why she bothered talking to you at all. She told me you reminded her of someone. Said you cared about what happened to her assistant. What was her name?'

Taryn's tapping pen went deadly still against her notebook. She didn't look up. And she didn't breathe. Only for half a second.

Finn still clocked it.

A tell. The tiniest chink in her armour.

He dug deeper, flipping through his memory like it was an old filing cabinet. Something Izzy had said about her assistant, who'd helped her trace that paper trail through various department registries, trying to uncover Everlight's owners.

'Meghan,' he muttered. 'Meghan Forrester. That was her name.'

Taryn's knuckles went white around the notebook sitting in her lap.

'It wasn't just a tactic, was it? Saying you wanted justice for the assistant—that wasn't just to tug on Izzy's heartstrings. Was it?'

She didn't answer.

'You're not here for policy. Or for your office. You're here for *her*.'

The silence dragged on, as if she were asking herself: *how the hell did he just figure that out*? It's what he'd do if in her situation.

'Who was she?'

'She was my cousin. Meghan…'

He could hear the way she'd said the name it hurt.

'Go on. You want answers from me, then you go first.' He wasn't sure she would, but he kept driving, giving her the space.

'Fine...' She huffed, clutching that folder and notebook to her chest like they could shield her from feeling anything.

But he saw it—that crack in her armour exposing a layer of vulnerability, right there beneath the edge. And damn it if it didn't catch him off guard. He wasn't supposed to care. Wasn't supposed to notice the way she gripped that folder like it was her last defence.

He told himself it didn't matter. After all, he'd spent years spotting weaknesses just to use them to his advantage.

But with her?

She was flipping the rulebook on him in ways he hadn't even begun to comprehend. Because that kind of hurt—you couldn't fake.

The only problem was it made it matter to him.

'We grew up together, that Meghan was more like a sister than a cousin. As a military brat, my family moved around frequently, so friends, well... Besides my parents, Meghan was the only constant in a life built on goodbyes. We spent most summers together on my grandfather's farm. She may have been a few years younger, but she was there for me...'

He'd be damned if he let that little line slip past him: *a life built on goodbyes*.

She said it like it was nothing, and yet it explained everything. Like why she kept her distance to not get attached. And why nothing rattled her, not even the open hostility from the people around her since she'd arrived in town. Because if you already had an exit plan, why bother unpacking your suitcase in the first place?

'Meghan was murdered for helping Izzy uncover something no one wanted found. And someone has made sure it stayed that way.'

Finn's jaw ticked. 'You're not blaming Izzy for that.'

'No. Not at all.' She shook her head. 'Meghan was excited to be part of Izzy's work and digging for new leads. She even left me a message, asking for advice, for my help—'

Holy hell.

Hope suddenly flared in his chest.

Help. Actual *help* from someone who may just shift some of the weight he'd been carrying solo for too damn long.

Only her expression killed all that hope just as fast.

'By the time I got her message… she was dead.'

Finn flinched.

To control himself, his fingers curled tighter around the steering wheel as his throat locked up like his body had heard something it couldn't forget.

Because he knew.

God help him, he knew.

He'd *missed his message*, too.

Liam had called. His little boy. Late at night. Voice thin and tired, barely more than a whisper on the machine that said, *'I love you, Daddy. It's okay. I get it.'*

Finn never got the chance to call his boy back.

Then, finding all his messages had been blocked: the ones from Bree, from the doctors, Drew, even his old sergeant from Queensland—all of them had been held up by a chain of command more interested in headlines than humanity.

By the time they'd reached him, he'd already lost everything that mattered in gut-wrenching order of...

His son. His wife. His career. His freedom.

That was the crack that broke the rest of him. The moment the wires snapped, and the mask fell off. What was left wasn't a cop, it wasn't even a man. It was just pain, walking.

What made it worse was he never got to say goodbye. Or to even say he was sorry.

It's why he came back to Elsie Creek, to watch over this town. And why he always slowed down when he drove past the town's dusty church, which stood on the hill, where they said the graveyard had the best views of the outback.

He drove past it more than he needed to...

Because his son was buried here.

And that was reason enough for him to stay.

The silence in the troopy thickened like heat off the bonnet. The gravel crunched beneath the tyres as they headed towards the Spinifex Highway.

Finn exhaled heavily, as if he had to drag it up from somewhere deep just to breathe, while fighting against all that pain of his past.

Thing is, she was sitting right beside him, sharing the same breathing space, and didn't even realise they shared the same pain from the exact same thing.

But he could see it now.

He understood.

That moment no one ever talked about—hell, he couldn't explain it—but there was something about losing someone like that. *Missing that call.* The message. And that moment it tilted your world on its axis.

It did something to you. Twisted grief into guilt, then guilt into fuel. Where you then tucked away the pain and turned it into purpose.

And here they were, enemies who had somehow formed a kind of de-facto trauma bond on steroids.

He'd turned it into rage—while she was chasing justice.

'That's why you told Izzy your father would back you up,' he said. 'It wasn't a bluff. He's Meghan's uncle.'

Taryn gave a tight nod. 'He'll do whatever he can to help… unofficially. My mother, too.'

Damn. A federal intelligence analyst and a JAG officer with reach. Talk about wildcards. No wonder Taryn walked like she had classified clearance in her back pocket.

That was a helluva combination to have in the family, that was more than just a family motivated by shared grief. It was deep government wiring. The kind that could reroute careers and bury bodies if needed. It was also a golden ticket into places very few people had access.

He looked at her again. Like really looked.

Taryn Hayes wasn't here to chase numbers or headlines.

She was chasing ghosts.

Just like him.

'Your laptop… Izzy says it's off-grid and encrypted? Specialised hardware?' He tried not to get his hopes up. But, come on, in Taryn's hands… That'd be like someone handing him a custom Harley after years of pushing a busted bike uphill. If it were true.

But then she nodded.

It was enough to have him raking his hand through his hair, trying to put a lid on that too-good-to-trust-it feeling.

'I'm here to dig up the truth. And if there's something in your files that can help—'

She never got a chance to finish, as Finn pulled the troopy off to the side of the dirt road, stopping on a low ridge where the late afternoon sun was dragging its belly across the scrub like golden fire.

He reached beneath his seat and dragged out a battered folder wrapped in a rubber band, thick with handwritten notes, dog-eared pages, and dropped it onto her lap before he could change his mind. 'Then let's find out what they buried. Together.'

Before he could get the car back on the road, she'd cracked it open. Flicking through his notes, maps, drawings and clippings from articles with enough red ink to bleed the truth out of each piece of paper.

Her eyebrows rose at the circles, arrows, and what looked like a drawing of a livestock truck with angry eyebrows. 'Amara mentioned she had to decode your chicken scratch scribbles for the Commissioner? What was that—two years ago?'

'Yeah. That was the first one.'

She grinned, and surprisingly so did he, enough for the heaviness to lift, just a fraction, but in the right direction.

'What you have there is every hole I found in the livestock industry from transport through to quarantine and exports, mapped out in a nice and neat little dossier, we call the *Gaps File*.'

Taryn muttered, 'Simple. Easy to remember.'

'Yeah, up all night thinking up that title,' Finn deadpanned.

Another short grin, but this time there was some excitement flaring in her eyes.

The engine droned on as she read the file that had lived in this troopy longer than some of his shirts had lasted. It held notes from truck-stop conversations. Cattle yard whispers. Rumours from roadhouse staff. Things Amara had once called *circumstantial garbage*—until some of it turned out to be real.

He kept his eyes on the road, but he could feel her flipping through it as if reading him. In a way, she was. Because every page, every scrawled note or underline was a confession in ink.

He hadn't built a case. He'd built a map. A trail that uncovered all the holes in a system so flawed that someone could drive a convoy of stolen livestock trucks straight through them—and had.

But would she see it?

So, he drove and waited. Hating how Taryn's opinion mattered. Because if she didn't see something in it, if she thought it was useless, then maybe he'd just spent the last two years chasing ghosts.

Taryn flicked through the last few pages of the bulky file. 'You've mapped out a field manual of every flaw in the livestock industry's supply chain—from farm gate to freight terminal.' She then held up a crumpled napkin, covered in Finn's rough scrawl. 'Even if some of it's written on pub napkins.'

Finn grunted. 'Was the only thing I had on hand.'

She shook her head with the faintest curve on her lips. Just enough to show she wasn't laughing at him, but more as an acceptance of his methods.

Then her expression shifted as she slowly flipped the paperwork back to the beginning again, then smoothed a hand over the coffee-stained, dog-eared cover.

'You didn't just find the cracks,' she said. 'You saw where the system fails. Where oversight becomes an opportunity for the wrong people.' She paused, with only the engine humming to fill the silence. 'What matters, Finn, is that you saw what no one else was willing to face. That it was broken.

And more importantly, *why* that matters.'

It was the first time anyone had said it like that. How she had seen it, not as a list of failures, but as something that mattered. And coming from the woman sent to shut him down—that meant more than he cared to admit.

Sixteen

Taryn stared down at the Gaps File. A file with no colour-coded tabs or index. Just page after page of rough notes, brand sketches, names half-scribbled in the margins, and arrows looping between export laws and real-world logistics, like Finn had been trying to map chaos itself.

And somehow, it made sense.

This wasn't just data. It was insight full of uncomfortable truths. Collected by someone who understood the land, who listened to the people, and gave a damn—all in brutal black ink.

She flicked through pages of hand-drawn maps of interstate stockyards, trucking routes, rail hubs. Dates. Times. Company names. Stock route patterns. Everything from feedstock to fencing wire. Nationwide.

She gave him a side glance. Silently driving, with that jaw set like he'd rather chew gravel than ask if she understood what he'd handed her.

He didn't ask her questions, as if he knew she was still sorting through the colossal mess of fragments, trying to force them into a timeline that made logical sense.

She wanted answers, and he'd delivered—just not how she'd expected it.

What she'd give for a whiteboard, a stack of markers and a jug of coffee, with a big do-not-disturb sign on the office door. Given her current transit status of red dirt and a sunset stretching across the sky, give her a patch of flat ground and a few decent rocks, just enough to pin the puzzle into place would be a start.

She glanced over. 'You logged all this by yourself?'

Finn's eyes didn't leave the road. 'Didn't have much of a team back then. Amara—'

'The Tiny Titan,' Taryn muttered.

Finn paused. 'Hmph…' He even gave a slight nod. 'Yeah. I can see her running the show one day. Romy's brilliant with her drones and camerawork, perfect for surveillance, and she's learning comms. Craig and Stone have their individual skills that are a big help, while avoiding paperwork like the plague.'

She huffed. *Typical.*

'Porter helps when he can. He knows all the backroads better than most, and I fully trust him to handle himself… He's not on the books—but I've asked. Reckons he likes doing his Territory patrols, as a revhead, but he still shows up as part of the team in all the ways that matter. And Izzy, she's our legal counsel when I need it, of the best kind.'

'I imagine she would be.' But together, his team of misfits, with their unique blend of qualifications, had worked wonders on the many cases they'd had, so far. The official files told her a story, the paint-by-numbers kind she'd read a thousand times in every other crime report. But what she held in her hands now? She'd never fully understood the full weight of their work—until now.

As the tyres hummed, her side mirror caught the thick plume of red dust behind them, curling in the wind like ghouls over a graveyard, trying to rebury the secrets of the outback. And how the landscape stretched on, sunburnt and blistered from baking under that sun for a millennium.

Yet even in its harshness, there was a wild beauty to it all…

She sighed at the distance, where the land rose in folds and rolled like waves. A land dotted with pale ghost gums, that arched like dancers frozen in mid-twirl, their white trunks such a stark contrast against the ochre dust. Spinifex clustered like messy curls, catching specks of gold in the sunlight. While termite mounds stood tall and defiant, like something ancient guarding secrets she hadn't yet earned the right to know.

Here, the road unravelled like a red ribbon, its heat shimmer dancing towards a horizon they always seemed to be chasing. And above them, that colossally big sky that was so impossibly beautiful, it felt like the ocean had tipped the world on its head.

Altogether, it was like driving through a painting that hadn't quite dried yet. With its colours too loud, seeping into everything like it owned the horizon and everything in between.

She hadn't expected to feel so drawn to the dust and harsh sunshine, as if daring her to look deeper. To see what lay beneath the legends, the stories, and the whispers taunting her to find her own path.

And how loud that emptiness became when all you had were your own thoughts that were suddenly so clear to find the answers.

'These patterns you found,' she said, 'you were hunting something.'

His hands tightened on the wheel. 'I was hunting for answers. Didn't realise how close I got until it was too late.'

'How so?'

'I thought I had time with Dane Carter, who'd first mentioned the Stock Agent. But they got to him first. Renzo admitted to Izzy that he worked for Everlight, but didn't name names.'

'Renzo was the one who murdered Meghan?' Her cousin.

Saying it out loud, hearing it bounce off the Troopy's windscreen, hit her differently.

But his pause... that only made it worse, like he knew how personal it was for her.

'And?' She pushed for more. She had to.

'You already know Izzy saw it happen right in front of her.' He gritted his teeth, steering them along a road of hazy heat. Filled with so much tension it practically rolled across his heavily inked knuckles as he gripped the steering wheel.

'Renzo could've killed Izzy, instead he kidnapped her to find out what she knew about Everlight.'

'Everlight is the key…' But she still didn't have that file copy from Izzy, and with Finn's angry protectiveness over Izzy, this Gaps File might just be the compromise.

But if he kept this much paperwork…

Maybe she'd been asking the *wrong* person the *right* questions.

Turning back to the file, she dragged out her notebook, and started cross-referencing dates, the connections he hadn't known he'd made, and the doors he'd unknowingly opened.

'Let me get this straight… The *Rough Stock* case. Your team's first case. That was all about genetics, DNA, sperm, embryos. Cryogenics. All done on prized rodeo stock. With two suspects dead. And on Everlight property.'

Finn nodded and kept driving in silence.

She then read on, digesting his notes, as the fragments from her interviews with his team helped fill in the puzzle.

'Then, between all of the other jobs, a few months later you have the *Cold Stock* case. Stolen crocodiles, where you find the mystery vet-technician who took the DNA, sperm, and eggs from the Rough Stock case. Only, Bastion chose to die in fear of his life.'

Again, he nodded.

And she took more notes.

'Then the *Wild Stock* case.' With her notebook balanced against her belly, she flicked through his extensive file of notes, wishing she had a desk, or even a slab of wood, to work off. But she pushed through, digging for information to form some sort of preliminary conclusion. 'The deserted cattle station, Dixby Downs, was illegally being used as a way station?'

'Stockmen call them spelling yards,' Finn cut in. 'Somewhere to rest the mob, swap 'em out, feed 'em up before they disappear again.'

'So the perfect place to switch prime stock,' she said. 'And to collect and store genetic material—sperm, embryos,

DNA—harvested from stolen polo and equestrian champions.'

'That bust included wild buffalo and a mob of banteng that are on the endangered list,' he piped in, resting his wrist on top of the steering wheel, somewhat relaxing, while she felt the strain deepen across her shoulders, the more she dug into the Gaps File.

It was certainly living up to its name, filling in the gaps of what she'd learned in conversation, interviews, and research.

'The missing overseer—Seery, Sawyer Dixby—revealed the identity of the mysterious Stock Agent, as Red...' She dug through the paperwork.

'Grady *Red* Galloway. He's married to Lydia, who manages the stockyards.'

'And she's your informant, along with young Brodie.'

He nodded.

Great, now she was getting somewhere. 'According to your notes, Sawyer told you that someone else was behind it. Someone above Red?'

'Has to be,' Finn replied. 'We thought SW Rural Contracting was Sawyer's company. But Red's still swapping out prime stock, and signing off on the paperwork, right beside SW.'

'SW Rural Contracting.' Taryn's gaze sharpened. 'Which is why you want me to look into this company?' She gathered it all together and rested the file and her notebook on her lap. 'You're hoping it connects to Everlight?' The company that had her cousin murdered, Izzy kidnapped, and stole millions in government grants.

'I know it does. I just don't know how.'

She looked at the man who'd finally stopped avoiding her to share some answers. Only now they were both chasing the same company, just from different angles, and for different reasons. She might not fully trust him, but she did say, with clear conviction, 'I believe you.'

Seventeen

Finn pulled up to the ridge, with the engine low. Among the open scrub, with a skyline smeared with a deep burnt gold, as the Spinifex Highway stretched like a scar across the earth.

It wasn't a real highway. Hell, it wasn't even on any map. But out here?

It was a wild vein of lawlessness that ran straight through the heart of the outback, which only the locals used. A simple dirt track, that was the road you took when you didn't want questions asked.

It was the road to take when your truck was too heavy and your paperwork was too light, and the weighbridge too close for comfort. Or when you had one too many at the pub and needed to avoid the police, to get back to the station before sun-up.

First created by the cameleers as an outback supply route, the infamous Spinifex Highway was where things fell off the back of one truck and into the tray of another. Where cash changed hands without receipts, and a handshake sealed the kind of deal that never made it to a ledger.

It was a place where a circle of utes lit up bare-knuckle brawls between stockmen, drawing a crowd, while in the car park, there was a roaring trade of bootlegged gear like some outlaw outback bazaar.

And Finn had been watching it for days, with the Gaps File in his lap.

But today he no longer held the Gaps File, Taryn Hayes did. Gripping onto it like it was a newborn as she climbed out of his passenger seat.

She stared at his set-up—two chairs, an old gas cooker, the battered esky—and gave him a look like he'd just offered her a bed of nails.

'You didn't say we were camping,' she said, dragging out her hefty workbag.

'Can't you see this is rural hospitality at its finest?' He dusted off the chairs, ready to watch another sunset bleed out across the scrub while watching over that red dirt road below.

The plan was to listen for the hum of engines beneath the wind, with eyes scanning for dust plumes rising like smoke signals.

SW Contracting's shipment was due to roll through soon—but from which station? And when?

He glanced at his watch. The team were due within the hour.

Then he turned his gaze to the land that stretched wide, free from the world of concrete boxes and artificial light. Just saltbush and shadows that grew, as the scent of dry spinifex cooled beneath a sky so wide it felt like the heavens were just in reach.

He still loved that. The taste of freedom. The silence. With the sun on his skin and no one else around—and knew how rare it was.

But now Taryn was here, gripping onto the Gaps File like she owned it, which meant she was about to do his head in with questions.

Surprisingly, she didn't speak. Just dropped into the nearest camp chair and dragged over his esky like she was setting up shop. No thanks. No pleasantries. Just a whack of the file on the esky lid and the soft flick of paper, along with the scratch of her pen.

He fiddled at the back of his troopy, waiting, hoping her questions were smart enough to create new leads.

Izzy said Taryn had the kind of mind that could see things others missed, like a crocodile overlooked in floodwaters. Smart. Patient. With the kind of bite that didn't need to show their teeth until it was far too late.

But trusting her? That was a whole other thing.

Taryn flipped through the pages and started sorting the paperwork into neat piles across the esky lid like it was a table. Then she found a few flat rocks, a bare patch of dirt and laid out the rest like she was building a damn war map.

Finn wasn't sure whether to feel violated or impressed. It was like inviting someone over for a visit, only for the woman to suddenly decide to move in and rearrange his bloody house.

'Are you planning to interrogate me, or just rearrange my notes?' He was hoping for something out of her, not this silence.

She flicked him a look over the top of a printout. 'That depends. Are you planning on answering anything? Or are you going to just glare at me like I've touched your laundry?'

Finn huffed. 'You're the one nesting.'

'Organisation is not nesting. And this isn't a filing system, it's a scrapbook of conflicting witness statements, with chicken scratches in the margins, and pick-the-date roulette. You've got three versions of the same report, with six different times. If this goes to court, it'll burn on contact, or make my stapler run screaming into witness protection.'

He watched her for a moment longer. Sharp eyes and steady hands with the kind of brain that didn't need noise to function—just patterns.

Damn Izzy for being right. Again. Because Taryn held the power to shut him down. Not just the squad—but *him*.

Finn grabbed his billy. He needed to do something while Taryn continued to tear through the Gaps File, sorting papers into neat little piles held under more rocks.

He could offer to help or give her a tarp to lay over the dirt, but her focus told him to not interfere. So, instead, he lit his single-flame burner—an old tin thing that had seen more country than most blokes in the burbs.

Beside it, his dented thermos sat like an old soldier. He'd hurled it at a runaway thief once, outside a roadhouse, and cracked the bastard clean in the temple. Still kept it, even with the dent, because it'd hold heat for days.

The water hissed and steam curled up as he emptied the coffee grounds into the billy. The stuff was so strong it looked like floor shavings mixed with gunpowder, set to brew a round of bullets. They'd need it if they were going to pull an all-nighter.

Finn put the coffee down for her. He'd actually made someone a coffee. And that never happened. 'You're welcome, by the way,' he muttered.

'For what?'

'The hill. The view. The coffee. The tactical genius system in my folder of—'

'Sticky notes, highlighters and the odd roadhouse napkin or five, do not make a system.' She took a sip. Then peered inside her cup with a wince. '*Sheesh!* This coffee tastes like a sour pool of poor life choices.' She gave him a sideways look. 'What'd you brew this with? Floor shavings and a dash of vintage gunpowder? You know, it should come with a warning label: *Do not ingest if you ever want to sleep again.*'

'Just drink it. Builds character.'

She grinned, with a sweet spark lighting up her eyes, as she took another sip, and put her cup down on the ground beside her chair. 'But I will thank you for the hill.'

'Huh?'

'I know what a good stake-out spot looks like.' She nodded at their view. 'High ground, clear view, with fallback options and only two entry points. It's almost charming.'

He grunted. 'Charming. Right.'

She smirked. 'What, you want praise? A round of applause? Wait, I can download something off the internet. Put it on a loop, to really boost morale.'

'I wanted quiet.'

'And yet, here we are.' She took another sip of coffee, tucking a stray strand of hair behind one dainty ear, and leaned closer to the pile of paperwork now surrounding the esky.

But the way the sunset cast a fine shade of gold across her

face, did wonders in highlighting her smooth skin.

Her sleeves were rolled up, with a pen gently held between her slender fingers, belonging to a woman with brains and the nerve to sit in his space like it was hers.

It should've ticked him off more.

But it didn't.

Which wasn't right.

'You could've stayed in the office,' he said finally. 'No one forced you out here.'

She met his stare with steady eyes. 'Says the man who's been avoiding me for days to sneak off to solve the world's problems with a deck chair and a billy can.'

'It's a camp chair,' he muttered.

'It's a habit,' she shot back. 'You, playing the lone wolf all the time.'

He gave a huff as he dropped heavily into his own camp chair. 'Are you always this bossy in other people's camps?'

'You always this territorial over your paperwork?' The paperwork she was busily cross-referencing like she'd been doing it for years, as if his operation now belonged to her, pinning each pile with a rock for a paperweight.

He frowned over the lip of his cup. Her comebacks, her insistence on having the last word, were doing his head in.

'You don't play well with others, do you?'

'I play just fine. I just don't like being handled.' He sipped his coffee. It was bitter, rough, but also too strong, too hot. Just like her.

'Who said you were being handled? When I'm just reorganising your intelligence.'

He huffed again. Not a laugh. Not a growl. Just something caught between the two. 'Do you always have to have the last word?'

'Only when I'm right.'

They shared a smirk.

Damn.

What followed was the bliss of silence as they sipped their coffee, watching the last of the sun's globe slip off the edge and bleed into the big blue to look like it had caught on fire.

The hum of cicadas picked up. A few crickets and other critters began their night song, as the breeze stirred across the open plains, cool enough to make the coffee worth it.

And still—he felt her beside him. Too close. But the thing is, she wasn't just seeing his world, she was starting to understand it, too.

He cleared his throat. 'So go on then. Ask your questions.'

She sighed, with her coffee mug balanced on her knee. 'Alright… What aren't you telling me, Finn?'

He held her gaze for a beat. The dying light had dipped low enough to throw something of a soft spotlight across her face. It'd be gorgeous if she didn't look at him like a suspect.

'You want answers? Start with the questions that don't come from some auditor's template.'

She arched an eyebrow. 'Then give me the right ones.'

'You think that's how this works?' He barked a humourless laugh. 'You walk in, grab the files, sort through my stuff like you've got clearance to my head, and I'm just gonna hand it all over?'

'Don't flatter yourself,' she snapped, putting her coffee mug down. 'I'm not interested in your head. I'm interested in the truth.'

'Same thing, isn't it? You want intel, context, motive. You want the *why* behind the paperwork? And that lives here.' He tapped his temple. 'Not in some notebook.'

Taryn shoved back her chair and stood, holding up the file like a weapon. 'You think I'm just here for the paperwork?'

'Aren't you?' he snapped.

'God, you really don't get it.' She threw the file onto the chair. 'You hand me a jigsaw with missing pieces, then bite when I try to see the bigger picture.'

'You weren't meant to see any of it.' When he'd meant to control the flow of information.

'Too late.'

She stepped in. So did he. Not that he remembered getting to his feet, it happened that fast.

'You don't get to control this, Finn.'

'Neither do you.'

Their breath tangled. Fury. Frustration. The kind that scorches deeper than either of them wanted to admit.

'You drive me insane.' Her voice cut like a razor's edge.

'Good. Means we're even.'

And then it happened —

He didn't mean to move.

And there was no plan. No permission. Just heat and hunger.

Where suddenly, this wasn't a stake-out anymore. It was the start of something a whole lot messier.

One second, she was glaring at him like she wanted to gut him with her pen, the next —

He was right there.

Over the line.

Finn had crossed it without thinking. Without planning to. And without permission.

And in the next breath his mouth was on hers, hard and hot, in a kiss that told her there was nothing careful about it.

It wasn't even polite.

It was the kind of kiss that shoved everything else aside, like swiping a tabletop clear of paperwork, while ignoring the reasons why they weren't supposed to want this. Why they were bouncing heat off each other with enough sparks to start a bushfire. Matching words and wits, making him want her in ways he should never want someone again.

But she didn't pull away. Hell, she dragged him closer, her fingers curling into his shirt like she'd tear through the fabric to get to his bare chest.

Their kiss... It wasn't soft. It wasn't sweet. Just two stubborn forces smashing together, trying to crush whatever the hell this tension was building between them since the first time she'd challenged him. The glares, the snaps, the snarls, and slammed doors, to keep them circling, only to clash with lips and tongues thirsting for that taste.

To hell with it, he kissed her until she whimpered, until

his pulse pounded through his veins. In a kiss where clothes were suddenly too tight, too hot, with the need for her nails to scratch across his skin. And that scent, that crazy combination of outback sunset and *her* was driving him off that ledge.

He was one step away from dragging her to his swag, while bunching her shirt in one fist and stripping down those jeans to make her moan his name. All in the name of control that had long left the building.

God, he wanted to watch her fall apart. Wanted to feel it. Own it. Growl through it.

His body hardened, dragging her closer.

And then—

They broke apart.

Breathing hard, she stared at him. 'Was that supposed to shut me up?'

He wiped his mouth with the back of his hand. 'Did it?'

She scoffed. Picked up her pen from the dirt. 'Not even close.'

But he was close enough to feel the heat off her skin, and to see the pulse kick at her throat.

They didn't speak.

Only the sounds of their breaths slowly settling, as the sting of that kiss lay raw on his lips, with her taste on his tongue, that he'd never forget.

Then the radio crackled.

'Hey, Bossman?' Stone's voice cut through, with the sound of a helicopter in the background. 'Romy and I are on our way.'

Finn moved to the troopy and reached for the handset like nothing had happened. Like he hadn't just nearly devoured the federal investigator in front of him.

'Switch to the secure channel, Stone.' Finn changed channels. Waited a beat, then said: 'Go ahead, Stone.'

'Romy and I are inbound. We're going to set up on the western ridge, like you suggested. Do you want me to run a flyover on the way through, or go wide?'

'Wide. Don't want to spook them. What's Romy doing?'

'Calibrating her drone for night vision. While I'm in charge of snacks and hillside setting. Almost sounds romantic for a stake-out, huh.'

Hmph.

Taryn wiped a hand over her mouth, gulped down her coffee and dragged her chair closer to the paperwork as if redrawing that line in the dirt, as if distance might cool their blood.

'Copy that. Radio if you have news, and stick to the secure channel from here on out.' He set the radio back down on the troopy's dashboard with a click, grabbing the handheld radio.

Scooping up his binoculars, he turned to the east and spotted Porter's police ute towing the trailer that held the Hellhound. 'Good. Amara and Porter are inbound. Craig will come in at four in the morning, because he's not leaving Izzy alone.' He tossed a glare at Taryn, tucking her back into the mindset of *the enemy*, never mind that he'd just kissed her.

Taryn ignored him, flicking through the pages like she hadn't just returned that kiss like a woman full of fire, now behaving colder than steel as she sorted out his life's work with surgical precision.

Finn keyed the radio, needing to get his head back in the game, too. 'Listen up, you lot. Keep your lights off before settling into position, and that includes torches. Out here, beams travel like Min Min lights. And forget starting a campfire, or you'll have every stockman within a hundred k's watching the ridge for bushfires.' He glanced at the dry scrub, brittle as old bones. A tinderbox full of fuel. 'Keep your eyes on the road. Report anything out of the ordinary.'

Amara and Romy responded, as their partners were either flying or driving them into position for the night.

At the back of his troopy, Finn dug around in his kit and pulled out the spare headlamp, flicking it on to the red filter. He handed it to Taryn, who was busy with her outback office set-up with rocks for paperweights, and red dust for carpet. Good thing he had no markers, or she'd use the side of the troopy as her whiteboard.

She took the torch with a nod. Flicked it on, and adjusted the headband, and went right back to reading like nothing had happened.

He grabbed his radio, binoculars, his mug of killer coffee, and set his chair a few paces away—close enough to keep her in reach, but far enough to keep the line clear.

Looking down at the road below, he scanned the area. Stone and Romy were covering the west. Amara and Porter had the east. Craig would swing in from the north. Finn had the south.

Four points of a compass, where all roads led to one place—Billycan Corner, the heart of the Spinifex Highway, and the black marketeers' backyard.

It was going to be a long night.

Eighteen

The first road train's plume of dust that rose to greet the dawn was the giveaway, with the second one coming from the opposite direction. It had Finn muttering a low command into the radio. 'Up and at 'em, team.'

It was time.

Taryn crouched by her workbag and dragged out what her dad called *the Kevlar's kiss*. Her armour.

Not your standard-issue ballistic beast like the one Finn was sliding on. Hers was custom-made, lightweight, and reinforced in all the right places. She wasn't sure if it came from her mother's old military unit, sourced off-grid—or from her father's world of classified procurements and black-budget favours.

Either way, it was a gift from two parents who believed in safety through preparation, and who had the contacts to provide it.

She slipped it on, the weight settling more like a memory.

The holster came next. Sleek. Balanced. Also a gift for her side-arm, that she clipped into place—a Sig Sauer P320, just like the one her Uncle Ray, a Lieutenant Colonel in the SAS, had taught her to field strip blindfolded at fifteen.

'Most kids got fairy bread and pool parties,' she muttered. 'I got babysitters who ran toy box threat assessments and intel rundowns on my closet layout, like we were breaching top-secret clearances that came with sniper drills and ten ways to disarm a teddy bear using a pen.'

Behind her, she could feel Finn watching.

'Figures…' Finn just gave her that look. The quiet one.

She squeezed back her smile.

'Remind me not to tick you off with a ballpoint lying around.' Giving her a slow nod, as if a little impressed.

Nah. This was Finn. The man with the emotions of a granite boulder, chiselled to block out anything like surprise.

Although, he'd been just as surprised as she was at *that kiss.*

Nope, not gonna go there.

She clipped her badge to the front of her vest. Not the lanyard. Not the ID card. Her actual federal police badge, that she rarely flashed around these days, but it had made her parents so proud at graduation. Where, for once, her mum hadn't worn the uniform that commanded attention, and her father was just a nerd in glasses. Just parents from the burbs.

Taryn snapped the vest shut. If she was in—she was all in.

And she was *not* thinking about that kiss.

The one that left a heat simmering low in her belly, as a sweet-tasting static skated across her tongue. A kiss that was so dangerous and oh so deliciously wrong, it lingered under her skin, like a secret she wasn't ready to admit.

Nope. She was definitely not thinking about that kiss.

Focus, Hayes.

Nothing killed a moment like a full-blown tactical op and the mental monologue of David Attenborough in her head: *And here, we observe the elusive Northern Territory Stock Squad's bossy male in his natural environment.*

Note the careful way he moves—silent, focused, dangerous. See how he secures the rear of his troopy, his posture radiating pure alpha-cop energy. And how these creatures are solitary by nature, deeply territorial, and known to grunt when irritated as a substitute for most words in the English language.

She smirked.

Finn glanced back over his shoulder. 'I can feel the sass vibrating off you from thirty paces, like a heatwave, Fed.'

She arched a brow. 'What? Are you suddenly an alien with mind-reading powers now?'

'Nope. Just been around long enough to spot trouble when it's smirking in my direction.' He slammed the troopy's rear door shut.

'Touché,' she muttered, grabbing her workbag with the Gaps File tucked in next to her laptop, and climbed into the passenger seat.

The troopy made a slow descent to avoid stirring the dust on the hill and warn the incoming trucks they were there.

In position, it idled behind a low ridge, its engine a hum beneath the brisk morning breeze.

Taryn gripped the tablet she shared with Finn, watching the drone feed stabilise from ghostly shapes into high-def clarity against dawn's dusty haze. 'Stunning vision.'

Two road trains on a lonely dirt road, a kilometre away from Billycan Corner. One road train was pulling in. The other already parked and waiting.

The incoming roadtrain, which Finn called a triple, was a massive truck dragging three trailers. Each tall trailer held two decks of cattle, and altogether, it carried over a hundred head—maybe more.

It stopped, the driver jumped out to unhitch the back trailer, then drove forward to get into position.

They were only switching the back trailer.

Fast. And efficient.

Dust curled around the massive tyres like red smoke as the rear trailer clicked into place behind the big rig. Too quick for paperwork to be checked and signed. And too big a deal to be a simple oversight.

The location didn't help, either. A simple dirt road that Google couldn't find, but it was now on Finn's map. A road that led to a sunbaked four-way dirt crossroad made of old shortcuts, surrounded by scrub and dry hills. It was the perfect place for things to fall off the back of a truck, with no one around to ask questions.

Inside the troopy, the air was thick with dust, tension... and Finn.

Taryn tried not to notice the way his broad shoulders bunched beneath that worn shirt, or how his muscles flexed as he leaned over the steering wheel. It only made her follow the ink etched down his corded forearms, all the way to the tattoos gift-wrapping his strong capable hands. It was so distractingly hot, yet so wrong… in the best possible way, that it was both impossible and unforgettable.

Even the way he frowned had no right being that attractive.

Come on, Hayes. You're here to investigate misconduct by this guy, not mentally undress him.

She shifted in her seat.

This was not the time. Never would be a better time. Blaming the thrill of the sting that made her blood rise.

Which was kind of ironic, really… Here she was, sent to shut them down, and now shoulder to shoulder with the man she was meant to report on. Getting a buzz from his killer coffee and getting flashbacks from that kiss, that she was never going to mention again. Ever.

But it wasn't just him getting under her skin. It was the realisation that she was starting to bend her own rules, just to keep playing whatever complex game they'd built between them. All under the neat excuse of justice.

Somewhere along the line, her professional audit had slipped into the *personal* side of things. There the emotional columns weren't balancing, and she was starting to lose track of which rules were his—and which ones she'd quietly rewritten for him, just to see where this arrest would take them.

Romy's voice came over the comms: *'Target confirmed. Trailer swap in progress. Illegal transfer caught on camera. And I even remembered the time stamps, this time.'* Romy gave a slight giggle, as if enjoying the game.

On-screen, both drivers had jumped out and moved fast between the trucks and trailers, as if they'd done it a dozen times.

Taryn nodded at the small screen. 'All I see is a simple trailer shuffle. Hardly seems like an arrest-worthy offence.'

'You really think they're playing musical road trains for fun?' grumbled Finn.

'Hey, we both know I'm a city-bred Fed. So this is your chance to enlighten me.'

'Okay… If there's no weighbridge, no inspector, or paperwork? Then it's not legal.' He pointed at the tablet's screen. 'Out here, cattle are currency. You swap a B-double on a backroad with no one watching, and it's a duffer's dream. Doesn't matter if they're branded—without a paper trail, it's like they never changed hands.'

He nodded at the screen. 'That trailer alone could be worth a quarter of a million, if it's prime stock. And they're looking at over fourteen years, minimum, if we catch 'em moving it like this. More if the paperwork's forged. And if they're repeat offenders… well, you know the drill.' He nodded at her shiny Federal police badge.

Didn't that smug little look of his have some kick to it. Not only had it been a while since she'd been on a sting like this, but she was behaving like a rookie.

Come on, I know the drill.

She shifted in the passenger seat, the bulk of her Kevlar vest digging into her ribs. So, it had been a while since she'd worn one of these. And it'd been longer since she'd watched a crime unfold in real time, instead of dissecting it from behind a desk scouring spreadsheets.

Here there were no heels, skirt and blazer that made up the suit. And no neck-swinging, laminated lanyard.

Just boots, dust, and a front-row seat to a cattle theft sting, beside a man who smelled like coffee and vengeance and intoxicatingly *him*.

No, not him—*this*.

She used to love this part, the exciting minutes before the take-down. The hand on her gun holster, as the door was getting kicked down.

As a kid, she'd spent hours training to tactically breach her toy cupboard, rescuing Barbie from yet another hostage situation, orchestrated by her plush warlord teddy. Her military babysitters were tough taskmasters with their drills—but her parents had been so proud.

Just your average suburban household, where dinnertime conversation meant decoding missions they legally weren't allowed to discuss, in between conspiracy theories shared with the same enthusiasm as who spotted a sale at the supermarket.

No wonder she could follow the tangled threads of Finn's Gaps File without flinching. And no wonder she wasn't scared, riding shotgun with the outback's grumpiest beefcake.

She wasn't new to this. She'd just been wearing the wrong shoes.

Finn gripped the radio's mic. 'Stone, track the single-trailer truck, once it rolls, to see where it goes. Stay out of view. The rest of us will take the triple. Romy, I'll need your drone on us for the bust, and on comms.'

'Copy that, Bossman.' Stone replied for both him and Romy as the sound of a helicopter came to life in the background. 'Birds are in the air.'

'Amara and Stone have been teaching Romy to monitor the truckie's airwaves,' Finn explained with his eyes on the screen. 'If the driver gets spooked and calls it in, we'll hear it.'

'Can we jam it? Short-range, just enough to stop him raising an alarm?'

Finn nodded. 'Briefly. Stone rigged a signal disruptor onto Romy's drone. It's got limited range, but it should buy us enough time if it goes sideways. Romy's been putting in some serious time on her skills. She can record a baby croc hatching from fifty metres and still catch the wind in the grass. Sound tech is becoming another one of her superpowers, that really helps this team.'

Taryn gave a short nod. 'You forgot the part where Izzy says video and audio are the best kind of evidence.' So did the courts.

Finn's mouth twitched as if to stop the smile as he keyed the mic again. 'Craig? Park that horse truck near the north bend, inbound to Elsie Creek Stockyards. But keep the engine running and that shortcut in your sights.'

'Righto,' Craig replied.

'Porter, take the Hellhound east. If he bolts, he'll head toward that ridgeline. Box him in, but don't engage unless I say.'

'Copy that.'

'Amara, sit quiet in the police ute on the west. If this goes sideways, you light him up.'

'You want me to spook him or cut him off, sir?'

'No lights and sirens, just make the police ute visible as if Porter's doing one of his usual patrols.'

The radio clicked off.

Taryn watched as the dust started billowing out from behind the tyres of the two trucks, announcing the trailer swap was completed.

No way... Her eyes widened at the screen, at that thing that wasn't just a truck. It was a beastly metal serpent three trailers long, loaded with cattle and momentum. No wonder they called it a road train... that was what—120 tonnes?

Even empty, those things could chew up a patrol vehicle without flinching.

It'd be like bringing a knife to a gunfight.

And here she was, tucked into the passenger seat, as Finn stealthily drove them closer to Billycan Corner, preparing to take on a road-born behemoth.

The radio hissed, then Romy's voice cut in: 'We've got comms. Triple trailer is checking in—*Clean swap, ETA forty to the stockyards,* his words. No questions asked. First truck says he's *homebound. Just running late.*'

'Which means they're used to this routine,' Finn muttered, as he started down the hill. 'Swap, split, and no one blinks.'

Taryn watched it unfold on the tablet feed...

The drone filmed the long road train gaining speed like it knew the road well.

Ahead, the red dirt road stretched wide, but the five-way intersection narrowed into the perfect choke point.

They were close enough to hear the truck lower its gears as it approached the intersection.

From the south end, Finn was sneaking up on the thing,

using the road train's thick dust cloud for cover, that was like a rolling, red wall that swallowed them whole.

Visibility: zero.

Control: definitely not hers.

She reached for the hail-Mary bar on the dash, fingers locking tight, the other braced on the grab handle above the door—because clearly, this troopy came fitted for trauma.

She didn't flinch. Didn't panic.

Just let Finn drive blind at highway speed, through thick walls of churning red dust and God-knows-what, like he did it between breakfast and his first strong black.

Lord help her, she might actually be enjoying this, as the adrenaline flooded her system like a drug.

'So,' she called over the roar of the engine, 'is this the part where I'm meant to scream, or sign a liability waiver?'

Finn didn't take his eyes off the road—if there even was one. 'Just hang on and don't start preaching like some back-seat driver.'

'Preaching? Trust me, if I was preaching, you'd be getting a whole PowerPoint presentation, including footnotes!'

He snorted. 'Always gotta have the last word, don't you?'

'Occupational hazard.'

Alert the fun-police, Finn Wilde was grinning now. Gone was the usual grim set to his jaw, instead something wild and alive shifted the corners of his mouth. He *loved* this part, she could feel it in the way he drove. Controlled chaos, weaponised with loads of confidence. It was hot.

And… yeah. She *loved* it too. Not him.

No, pfft.

The rush. The maddening pace of running in blind behind a massive beast of metal, churning up the countryside.

What did *that* say about her?

Probably nothing good.

Except maybe… she'd just met her match in the ink-covered muscular male with a bad attitude, who was absolutely nothing like she'd wished for—yet somehow, was exactly what she needed.

Not that she would ever admit that to herself.

The truck was massive up close. A steel leviathan on wheels, belching heat and rolling thunder like drums of war, as blinding swirls of dust spiralled in its wake. Her eyes were glued to the tablet's screen, just to see where they were going.

But Finn pushed the troopy, building speed until they burst through the thick wall of red dust—and finally, the back trailer came into view. That's when he pulled out to overtake, the engine roaring as stones and grit kicked up like the troopy was stuck in a hailstorm.

'Got a plan for this Sunday drive?' she called over the engine.

'The driver will either ignore us… or he already knows.' Finn's jaw flexed, his grip tightening on the wheel as the troopy, which didn't even look like a cop car, tore through the dust with its headlights on.

But they were closing in on Billycan Corner.

'Well, what are you waiting for?' Taryn shot back, like *she* was in charge now.

'Bugger it.' Finn slapped a blue light onto the roof.

'He knows now,' Taryn muttered, lips curling into a grin.

He flicked the siren on.

And just for a moment, he glanced at her, dust in his hair, adrenaline in his veins. Their eyes met.

'Game on.' Finn then hit the radio. 'GO!' he barked out to his team.

The radio crackled, followed by a harsh male voice, loaded with panic. *'I've got company—cop lights at Billycan Corner.'*

What made it worse was the truck revved louder as if changing into higher gears.

'He's not stopping.'

'Romy?' Finn snapped out over the radio, 'you jamming?'

'The UHF band, but for only a kilometre,' she said. *'They'll think it's a drop-out or a dead zone. But we can't hold it long.'*

The land around Billycan Corner opened up with sirens wailing. Amara hit the lights on the police wagon right at the intersection just as the road train bore down.

The shock enough for the truck to jerk hard—too fast.

Finn punched the accelerator, and the troopy launched forward. '*Porter, cut east!*'

'*Already on it!*' The roar came as the Hellhound launched over the ridge with dirt flying, engine snarling, blue lights blazing from the roll bar sitting above his gun rack, looking like something out of a Mad Max fever dream.

Taryn blinked at the small tablet screen. *That was a cop car?*

Porter, in full NT Police uniform, was behind the wheel, calm as anything, like flanking a runaway road train on a bush highway was just another Tuesday patrol.

He didn't even try to stop the truck—just distract and redirect, drawing its attention with the subtlety of a battering ram—effectively cutting off the truck.

Outback policing, apparently. Taryn shook her head, half in disbelief, half in admiration. She'd never underestimate an NT cop again, especially one who'd worn out three patrol wagons as part of his day job.

But the truck fishtailed. Just for a moment, as if trying to make a choice on which track to take.

They'd blocked off three roads at Billycan Corner. All that was left was one tiny gap of a wallaby track and the road that Craig had blocked with his horse truck.

The road train hit the wallaby track.

'Come on.' Finn gunned it, and the troopy roared in response with pure steel and stubbornness on wheels.

The road train hogged the entire wallaby track with its massive tyres chewing the dirt.

That left Finn with only one option…

Off-road.

Taryn gritted her teeth, and held on tight, as the troopy ploughed through the scrub, as the bull bar smashed through saplings like they were matchsticks. A cloud of powdery red exploded as they obliterated a termite mound, with the impact rattling up her spine.

Yet Finn kept the truck pinned to their left, shadowing it through choppy ditches and pig ruts.

The wheel juddered in his grip. The chassis groaned and the V8 engine howled with every jolt. But Finn looked like he was *born* for this. Focused. Fierce.

She wasn't sure if this was bravery or madness—but either way, she was into it. Right seat. Right team. Wrong terrain. And loving every second of it.

The drone's footage showed the Hellhound was doing the same on the other side of the truck, with Amara in the police ute closing in from the rear.

'Amara, Porter,' barked out Finn on the radio, 'keep the pressure on. Craig, you know what to do, take that shortcut *now*. And we'll let the driver think he's choosing the paddock over prison.' Finn pushed the troopy to roar down the sides of the road train, a double-decker wall of cattle so close, Taryn could reach out and touch it.

Ahead, from nowhere, Craig's horse truck suddenly appeared like a wall of steel—parked sideways near the curve, effectively narrowing the path.

The driver saw it.

He braked.

The rig skidded.

One of its trailer's jack-knifed dangerously close to wiping out the troopy, as dust exploded from beneath it.

The entire metal beast groaned—a deep, grinding scream of torque and steel—as the cattle bawled, with panic rippling through its trailers.

When, finally, it shuddered to a stop.

Finn brought the troopy to a halt, dust swirling around them in hot, blinding clouds.

Taryn shoved the door open, badge and gun already out, adrenaline surging, as she raced for the truck driver's door. 'DRIVER, OUT OF THE TRUCK NOW! HANDS WHERE I CAN SEE THEM!'

For a second, nothing happened as the dust fell like a curtain to reveal the sky.

Then the cab door cracked open.

A sweaty male in his early forties lifted his hands. 'What's going on, officer? I'm just making a delivery.'

'You're under arrest for livestock theft, dangerous driving, and endangering livestock. And that's just the start of our list of charges.' Taryn's tone was as cool as stone.

'What are you gonna do?' Finn's voice was gruff as he climbed out of the troopy—all six-foot-something and bad attitude with a badge. 'Play cowboy? Or play nice for the lady?'

Ooh. He called her a lady now.

The driver shoved his hands into the air.

With cuffs in hand, the way Finn slammed the troopy door practically shouted: *Try something. I dare you.*

Still, she kept her aim steady while he cuffed the driver, neither of them needing to speak. They had it covered, like they'd done this a hundred times.

The only difference was, this time... they weren't just covering each other's backs. They were playing to win. *Together.*

The driver glanced between them, frowning. 'She with you?'

Finn didn't miss a beat. 'Yeah,' he said, tightening the flexi-cuffs. 'She's with me.'

A simple answer. Just three words: *She's with me*—were loaded as hell, like a sucker punch to her heart.

With him. Not under him. Not against him. But *with* him.

Taryn arched a brow, holstering her weapon. 'Careful, sergeant. You keep saying it like that and people might get the wrong idea.'

'You saying it's wrong?' he muttered, while still patting the guy down.

She held his gaze for a heartbeat too long. 'I'm saying I still want the last word.'

'Wouldn't expect anything less.' He gave her a sly wink.

Her pulse gave the briefest traitorous kick.

She ignored it.

Well, she tried to... Not react and just play the Fed, like a good little professional.

Down the road, Craig pulled in beside Porter's beastly buggy, as Romy's drone did a wide sweep overhead. That thin, high-pitched buzz cut through the air like a mozzie, recording *everything*.

'In a few days, once the dust settles from this bust, we might have to buy the Fed a beer and tell tall stories,' Stone's voice drawled over comms.

Porter's voice chimed in next, over the speakers: 'Long as she's buying the second round.'

Taryn smirked, shaking her head as Finn handed her the driver's wallet. Their fingers brushed, just for a second, but it lingered.

And when their fingers brushed, just for a second, it lingered.

'Good work,' he muttered.

It was tough to not smile at him.

Then he dragged the driver towards the police ute, his tone all tough-guy-official again. 'Amara and Porter, check over the truck and trailers. Craig, do a headcount on the cattle. Check their condition to see if we need a vet.' He then keyed the radio, glancing up at the drone buzzing overhead. 'Stone, Romy, you know what to do, play ghost.'

Finn paused, holding the driver like a ragdoll, halfway to the police ute, and glanced back at Taryn. 'Fed, the truck cab is yours. Paperwork. Keys, phone, radio logs. I want it all.'

And just like that, she was in.

Nineteen

The local police station's interview room wasn't much, just a metal table and two chairs in the kind of space meant to squeeze out the truth by sheer discomfort. The same place the Fed had extracted information from Finn's team these past ten days, in the place he'd been trying to avoid.

Arms folded, and jaw tight, Finn leaned against the open doorframe, still in his police vest with the radio on low to listen out for the others. He didn't do interrogation rooms, he'd rather get confessions from the back of police vans, or at the scene of an arrest. Call it a kickback from his days of living in a 6x4 concrete block with window views of nothing but bars and bullies in orange jumpsuits.

At the table sat the busted truck driver. His wrists were still zip-tied behind his back, with sweat soaking his shirt collar.

And sitting opposite?

The Fed. Taryn Hayes. Clipboard in hand, posture sharp enough to cut steel—like she ran the AFP's entire interrogation unit.

Especially in that vest of hers.

Tactical. Tailored. And way too polished for the Territory.

And somehow, on her, it worked wonders on his pulse.

Not only was the woman gifted at always having the last word—she was now running point.

Didn't help that Finn had no team left in town, either. Craig and Amara had taken the truck and cattle to the quarantine station to meet the vet to check the animals' condition after that jack-knife. There, they'd do a check on cattle brands and stock against the so-called paperwork. Porter, towing the Hellhound behind his patrol ute, had to meet his own sergeant for an NT Police job. While Stone and Romy were in the air, stealthily following that other truck.

Which left him with either Tanisha, from the front counter, to talk about glitter cannons, cocktails and cats… Or *her*. The Fed.

He hadn't agreed. Not out loud.

But he'd stepped aside. And *let* her.

Which might've been the most dangerous thing he'd done all day.

Taryn pressed the button on the video recorder, its red light blinking, making sure to hold eye contact with the suspect as she spoke. 'For the record, this interview is being recorded under caution. What you say can be used as evidence and may be admissible in court. And unlike telemarketers—this *won't* be used for training purposes.'

Then she took her seat opposite the driver, keeping her voice smooth as syrup and clicked her pen. 'First, let's do the cocktail party niceties, shall we, and confirm your name and address…'

And damn if she didn't pull it off, delicately peeling back the guy's defensive layers without him even realising it.

No bluff. No stutter. Just steel in a silk shirt, jeans and boots.

Finn stayed quiet, occasionally shifting his weight in the open doorway, careful to never cross that threshold, with his boots creaking on the old tile. But giving enough of a death glare to make the driver swallow nails and let the beads of sweat trickle down his face.

He'd done interviews alone before. Maybe hundreds. But something about watching her do it—on *his* turf, with *his* suspect—felt like the beginning of something neither of them were ready to admit.

The driver cracked fast, sweat pouring down his temples, nerves twitching, and stuttering through every answer, like it was his first time in such a situation.

And it may be, just from the basic research they had: Darren Tooley. Forty-two. Long-haul truckie out of Katherine. Married, two kids, with a mortgage hanging over him like a dust cloud. No criminal record.

Desperate? Maybe.

Dangerous? Not likely.

But someone had his leash, and Finn wanted to know who was holding it. And he was letting her do the talking.

Taryn didn't raise her voice. Didn't lean in. She just kept pressing calmly with the preliminary questions—but, damn, if it wasn't the sexiest thing he'd seen her do all day.

'Who gave you the order for the trailer swap?' she asked.

'The other driver, didn't get a name.'

'Seriously?' She raised an eyebrow at Tooley.

'Bob. Okay?'

'Bob who?'

'Bob. Y'know Two-bob Bob.' Tooley shrugged.

Taryn tilted her head. 'Two-bob Bob? What—couldn't he score an upgrade to Fifty-cent Frank?'

Finn sniffed to stop the smirk.

It was enough for her to reset with a click of her pen. 'So, you've driven for this Bob before?'

Tooley sucked in his bottom lip as he hesitated.

But Taryn just waited patiently.

It was Finn who sniffed with impatience.

'I've got kids and a mortgage...'

'I'll make a note of that.' She flicked a page, as if she were making up a list of plus and minuses, that if the driver gave her enough pluses, he'd win some lucky door prize. But she never actually said it, just implied it, giving the driver enough hope.

Oh, she was good.

'So...' she said with that buttery voice, followed by that click of the pen. 'You work for Two-bob Bob. How?'

'Said he'd call when he needed a job, like all my other customers do. I'm just the truck driver.'

'How many times have you done this for Bob?'

'A coupla times. Always in the early hours, just before Train Day's cut-off time.'

'Where do you come from?'

'All over.' Tooley shrugged. 'It's muster season, so I'll take whatever driving contracts I can this time of year.'

'I meant, where and when do you meet this guy, Bob?'

'Depends. Today it was one click south of Billycan Corner. Once it was at this makeshift holding yard just outside of Tinderflats, just twenty clicks shy, along the Spinifex Highway. Another, down that old Ridgeback Road that links out toward the Black River mouth.'

Finn's brow lifted. 'Where the old cattle barge used to load?'

Tooley gave a series of nervous nods. 'I overheard Bob's mate natter on about flying some boxes out from the airfield tucked behind the old quarry from here on out. Swear one of 'em cannisters was smoking, had this misty appearance to it like dry ice gets.'

Cryogenic canisters. Did Taryn realise the importance of this?

Finn clocked the way Taryn didn't react outwardly, but he caught the flicker of interest.

Please ask the right questions, Fed.

Her pen barely made a sound, but every tick was like a clock, winding tighter. 'So how big were these things, the canisters?'

Tooley squinted, unable to lift his hands from the flex cuffs. 'Um...'

Taryn moved without hesitation, tugging a cutter from her fancy police vest and sliced through Tooley's plastic restraints. 'Don't even think about walking out of here,' she said lightly, 'not with a six-foot wall of law blocking the only exit.'

Finn didn't move. Didn't need to.

She flashed Tooley a grin. 'And trust me, you don't want to try your luck with him.' She sat back in her seat, swapping the tool for the pen and clipboard. 'So, where were we? The cannisters…'

Tooley held his hands apart, roughly just over half a metre. 'They were silver. Cylinder-shaped things.'

Taryn tilted her head at the distance of his hands as if seeing it differently. 'So, like a gym junkie's water bottle on steroids? Made of metal, about five litres. The bulky ones you know they're never going to drink, but carry to look good.'

Finn didn't move from the doorway, fighting the twitch of an eye roll trying to break free.

Tooley gave a vague nod. 'Kinda, I guess. To me, they look like them welder's gas bottles. Only much smaller. And shinier. They had these weird nozzles and labels all over 'em.'

Taryn nodded slowly. 'Do you think those canisters could hold biological material? Semen? Embryos?'

Tooley's eyes went wide. 'Like… bull semen?'

'Or high-end embryos. Rare prime stock.' She clicked her pen.

'I never looked or asked.' He gave an awkward shrug. 'But they paid me triple for that run straight to the export yards in Darwin. Didn't think much of it at the time—just saw a bunch of boxes tucked under the tray that held them shiny canisters. They looked expensive.'

'Cryogenic-grade canisters can burn you. It's all about liquid nitrogen. And that's instant frostbite.'

Tooley swallowed hard. 'Yeah, there was this smoky mist coming off 'em. Cold, not hot. Didn't know they were there, you know. I only stopped because the back trailer started knocking like it'd dropped an axle. Pulled over on the side of the Spinifex Highway, and had a look, and found them loose, rattling around under the tray.'

Finn watched the bloke scratch at his neck, guilt sweating through the bravado.

'I called Bob,' Tooley went on. 'Told him something had come loose. He turned up not long after and helped me get the new boxes out of the ute and repack everything. Told me not to touch the bottles or I'd lose a few fingers. Said we'd get it sorted. And we did. I guess…'

Tooley hesitated as he frowned at the grains that made up the tabletop as if remembering that day. 'Then Bob handed me a bonus on the spot. Cash. Said to buy the missus some flowers and take her out somewhere fancy. I figured...' He shrugged, looking up to face Taryn. 'It was hazard pay. And to not ask any questions, so I didn't, and just drove as planned.'

'What kind of boxes?'

Tooley rubbed his palms down his thighs. 'They were just boxes. Plain cardboard with brown tape. Didn't pay much attention, except they were light enough to lift.'

'Like a shoe box?'

'Nah, more like the size of them boxes you get for nappies or load up your groceries in.'

'Did they have any labels or addresses on them?'

'Just something like *Conference Pack—NT Tourism* with a bunch of flags on the side. Thought they were full of brochures or tourist junk. You know, the kind you chuck in a bin at a servo.'

Finn didn't know what part had her hooked, as much as he was, waiting to see which thread she'd pull through to unravel.

'Where do those boxes go?' she asked Tooley.

'They used to stash them under the trailer, but the heat melted the glue on the tape. That's when I heard Bob talking on the phone to someone about meeting the plane for future pickups. Don't ask me where.' Tooley shook his head. 'I haven't got a clue. And most cattle stations have airstrips, you know.'

Finn scowled. Out here, airstrips were like ballpoint pens—everywhere until you needed one. But finding the right one? That was like chasing a single grain of sand across a sunburnt outback.

'So, do you know who's behind it?' she asked.

'No idea.' Tooley shrugged. 'Look, I'm just a truck driver.'

'Surely you must have seen more.' Again, she flicked over a page, that pros and cons page, the one that promised his golden ticket to freedom—and yet she'd never promised anything.

'Well, I mean, there's Bob. And there's this other guy, a stock agent. He's got this long red beard, goes by the name of Red. Shows up, checks the brands, makes sure it's the right mob. Always disappears fast after he signs something with Bob.' And Tooley flinched.

It was a small twitch in the jaw, followed by a quick shift in his seat—but it was there.

Finn's pulse ticked harder.

Was Bob SW? The initials scrawled next to Red's on half the dodgy paperwork, and waybills. Would Taryn realise this?

She was calm. Controlled. Playing the good cop like it was second nature.

Finn kept quiet, even if he was itching to tell her—*Use the photos, Fed…*

She'd spent all night in his troopy, having turned it into a makeshift photo studio. Making him toss a tarp over the top to block out all light, while she took happy snaps of every page of his Gaps File, to create a digital file, effectively getting to know every name and every face in this operation.

If ESP was real, this was it. *Come on, Fed… ask him if it's Red.*

'Last question, Tooley, and I need you to be honest with me, okay?' She even smiled at the guy, like they were old mates, as she scrolled through her phone.

Meanwhile, Finn had to fight the urge to reach across the table and shake the answer out of the guy—*if* it was the question he hoped she was about to ask.

She then held up her phone's screen to Tooley. 'Can you confirm that this is Red?'

There was a pause.

Tooley narrowed his eyes at the screen, then nodded.

'Can you answer yes or no, please. You know for the…' She smiled sweetly at the camera, like they were shooting home movies or something, holding up her camera to capture the photo on film.

Tooley swallowed a few times before squeaking out, 'Yes. Um, that's Red.'

'So, can you confirm that you saw Red personally inspect the stock, the same stock you and Bob had switched out with your trailer-swap routine, and that he signed off on the paperwork?'

Tooley hesitated, licking his lips as a bead of sweat trickled down his cheek.

Come on, say it.

Taryn clicked her pen. Once. Twice. A third time. Like this annoying countdown, but it made Tooley nervous.

'Okay…' Tooley shuffled in his seat. 'Yes. A few loads back, we'd just swapped the trailers over, and Red came by, checked over both truck loads, and gave Bob the new paperwork for me to deliver to the stockyards.'

And there it was.

The sentence that cracked the whole case wide open.

On video.

Taryn didn't gloat. She didn't so much as blink.

But Finn caught the flicker in her eyes. That spark.

He met it with a look of his own, with a breath of a nod. *Damn, lady. You nailed it.*

Tooley kept talking, none the wiser.

And they let him.

Because sometimes, the biggest wins came within the quietest moments.

And both he and the Fed got that—like how they got each other. No big gestures. No fanfare. Just a look that said all that needed to be said. And that was rare.

'For the record,' stuttered out Tooley, 'I'm just a truck driver. I don't look at stock, I don't do the paperwork. All I do is check the weight's right, and the trailers are in good nick, because it's my trade. I just deliver the paperwork, and whatever they put on board, that's their deal.'

'But you knew they were stealing stock? Swapping out the original prime stock for different stock.'

Tooley leaned back, sighing so heavily his shoulders

slumped over, as if finally realising the implications of his actions. 'I just saw it that the cattle stations were still getting paid for their livestock. Not—'

'Stealing?'

Taryn closed the file, her forearms resting on the table as she looked the driver dead in the eye. 'We're done for now. You will be processed and held pending federal charges. And if you continue to cooperate, we'll put bail on the table where you might go home to your wife sooner than you think.' She then leaned in, only this time her voice was cold. 'But if you run—now that I've got your prints, ID, and a digital facial scan—we'll find you faster than you can hitch your trailer.'

The driver swallowed hard.

Finn didn't need to say a word. But he was coming back, with a plan just for Tooley.

Taryn stopped the video recording and walked out, clicking her pen like she'd just wrapped up a boardroom pitch.

He closed the door behind her, leaving Tooley to sweat it out for a bit longer.

But damn, it felt good to finally be moving in the right direction.

And the way Taryn had asked all the right questions? That had his mind reeling, even as they walked the hallway, side by side.

Then she said under her breath, 'You know, Izzy said you had the vibe of someone who'd run a drug cartel.'

Finn snorted.

'Do you ever get tired of being intimidating for a living?'

'Nope.' And for the second time that day, he almost smiled.

'You're welcome, you know.'

He wasn't about to give her a pat on the back, not when he could give her something better—exactly what she wanted. 'There's more to the Gaps File. And I've got a copy of the prosecution's case file Izzy helped build on Everlight. The names, dates, patterns, everything to do with Everlight

Energy Solutions and your cousin's murder.'

She stopped walking. 'Where?'

'At the house. I kept a copy because I never trusted paperwork in the hands of the Feds.'

She arched an eyebrow at him—the very picture of said Fed, in boots, badge, and sass.

'Come by tonight. We can use the spare room's walls, instead of using rocks as paperweights. Oh, and you can bring dinner. The food fairy hasn't been around lately, so you're it.'

She blinked as if caught off guard, just for a second.

And for once?

No comeback or any biting last word.

Hell, he'd take that as a win.

Twenty

The old wagon coughed a lungful of black smoke as it lumbered to a rolling stop under the lone gum tree. The *should've-been-retired* police wagon's sun-faded decals peeled like sunburnt skin, and the aircon had given up somewhere back near the turnoff. Not that Taryn could blame it when she was considering the same.

Still, she was here, even if the wagon groaned and creaked in protest as she shut the driver's door.

Freshly showered and changed, with dinner bags in one hand, she tucked a small box under her arm containing enough stationery supplies to start her own store. Finn's mud map was tucked into her back pocket, complete with a note: *Key's under the busted tail-light. Don't cut yourself.*

Typical.

Finn's place was tucked away, about twenty minutes from town. It was a low-slung house on stumps, shaded by old gum trees and wrapped in silence.

A Harley staunchly sat under the verandah, its polished chrome sparkling. Amara had mentioned, during her interview, that Finn had two that he'd dragged in a trailer behind the troopy in their cross-country tour of the livestock industry. So where was the second motorbike?

She climbed the steps, the dinner bags rustling.

The note had said busted tail-light. But there were two cracked specimens, who'd retired to front door guard duty, as Finn's form of pot plants or garden gnomes.

She picked the left light. Checked underneath, and there it was: a key, tucked in behind a rusted bracket.

The front door opened with a sigh. Inside, she found the

second Harley, dead centre of the living room, in mid-repair on a tarp. Grease-stained rags kept it company, along with an assortment of tools lined up with military precision, and a single lamp bent over the engine like a spotlight gone to sleep.

Piled against the other wall was a stack of vinyl records, beside a record player. There was no couch. Not even a TV. With nothing on the walls but faded paint.

In the other corner stood a group of rolled maps.

Figured, he had a thing for maps. When Finn had maps clustered in the troopy, or covering the large round table in the Batcave, and now, here, lined up like fat toilet rolls. Although some looked ancient.

But the rest of the place was completely clutter-free.

Of course he lived like this, without distractions or junk. Just engines, records, and maps, as if plotting his exit.

In the kitchen, the battered round table looked handmade, like someone had taken a chainsaw to a slab of timber and called it done. The three chairs didn't match—all different heights, all equally sun-warped. Probably left out as rubbish that he'd dragged through the red dirt on the back of the Harley to make their home here.

There were no appliances, not even a microwave or a toaster clogged up the kitchen benches. Only a battered kettle beside the gas stove.

The fridge, though—that was new. Huge, too. A beast of stainless steel that held water bottles, tomato sauce, a half-loaf of bread, and meat in the freezer. That was it.

'Figures,' she mumbled in her worst Finn impression. 'Food fairy's day off, huh?'

The pantry held even less. Besides his tins of killer coffee that could be used as motor fuel, there was lots of salt, cracked pepper, and a surprising selection of herbs and spices. Even more surprising was the neat row of homemade preserved goods, the old-school kind. Mango, beets, beans, chutney, and something suspiciously pink.

And all of the labels were neatly written. Most definitely

feminine.

Her eyebrows lifted.

So there really was a food fairy. Who probably wore slippers and an apron that said, *Bless This Mess*.

The jars reminded her of her grandfather's farm. Mornings with porridge and bottled peaches she'd helped pick with her cousin over summer, back when things had still made sense.

But she wasn't here to psychoanalyse Finn. Or judge the kitchen. Or figure out why someone who lived like this still had room for canned fruit.

She was here to work.

Down the hall, she found two doors—took a guess and kicked one open with the side of her boot.

An enormous bed with black sheets stood centre stage. One pillow dented, the other untouched. A few duffel bags were stacked like deployment gear ready to roll. Another half-unzipped pack had clothes spilling out.

She backed out fast.

Definitely not the spare room.

'Other door,' came Finn's rough voice behind her.

Where the hell did he come from?

Finn leaned his shoulder against the hallway wall like he'd been there the whole time.

You'd think she'd be used to how he looked by now—all six-foot something, bristling with ink, muscles, and attitude— that still made her pulse jump.

'Spare room's yours.' Finn pushed the other door open and flicked on the light.

She squeezed by him in the narrow hall. So—*so* incredibly close as he stared down at her like she meant nothing.

She told herself it was fine. They were professionals. And this hallway was like being crammed into a lift with strangers. And he was just a man with a Harley in his living room, a bed with black sheets, and enough red flags to start his own parade.

The spare room had bare walls, of course, and one window. That was it. Perfect for what she needed.

She dropped the file box on the floor, and started unpacking like his presence, and the fact that they were alone, didn't bother her.

Finn didn't cross the threshold. He just stood there with one shoulder against the doorjamb. One foot in and one foot out, as if between enter and exit.

She'd noticed that earlier, the way he'd hovered outside the interrogation room. Like he was always mapping his exits, even in his own house.

Was he like this because of her? Or was it something he just did?

Taryn got busy, laying out the first page that trembled slightly in her fingers, as flashbacks of him kissing her senseless had left her second-guessing everything. And with him, blocking the door should she want to run, only made it worse.

'Need anything?' he asked.

'Just tape. And maybe a whiteboard, if you've got one stashed behind your Harley shrine.'

Finn gave a small huff.

He still didn't step into the room.

Instead, he grabbed a large plastic tub. Lifted the lid and passed her a roll of tape, and a battered clipboard.

'Thanks.' She got to work and taped up the first few sheets that made up Tooley's statement.

She sorted through the freight schedules and stock route maps as the start of her web. But it felt lopsided. Fragmented. She needed a second set of eyes.

'Do you want to help or just lurk?'

His brow lifted. 'You're the one running point.'

'I am. Which means I get to delegate.' She handed him a stack of papers without touching him.

He stepped in. Quietly. Like the floor might give out, or the ghosts might speak.

Funny how he could chase down a road train, or lean against the public bar like he owned it, but still paused like this—like walking into his own spare room was something he had to earn. Was it a prison rule he hadn't shaken, or just... Finn? With her?

It was awkward at first, but soon they settled into a rhythm—her taping up evidence, him sorting out freight manifests. The two of them dancing around each other in the room like they'd rehearsed it.

He didn't ask questions, just got to work grouping statements and manifests, laying it out like they already saw the pattern beneath the mess.

She taped another stock route to the wall and tried not to watch him. She knew she'd have to sort through this lot, before he gave her the missing file, the one about Everlight. It's what she'd do in his situation.

Taryn reached over to stick another stock route map higher on the wall and cursed under her breath.

Finn glanced up. 'Need a boost?'

'You were given height for a reason. Don't waste it.' She held up the tape to him.

His mouth twitched just enough to hint at a smile he wasn't letting her see. But those sinful eyes of his were calm. Along with a heat she was getting dangerously good at interpreting.

He took the page from her, their fingers brushing for just a second, but it was enough to scramble something under her skin.

He stepped in closer. She didn't move. Not because she was frozen, but because if she shifted now, she might do something stupid.

Like breathe.

Finn taped the page to the wall, dead centre, of course. His arm brushed hers as he stepped back, leaving her nerves sparking like they'd just shorted out over a freight manifest.

Fantastic. So now red dirt and spreadsheet crimes were her kink.

Come on, this was about paperwork. Ink. Pages. And where pushing pins into the wall was like playing voodoo dolls for bad guys.

Yet somehow, she was having a full-body crisis over the proximity of a man who smelled like spice and poor decisions—the kind you knew better than to want but wanted to taste anyway.

Either she was losing it, or this was karma for pretending she could kiss Finn Wilde and go back to being professionally unaffected.

She just needed a minute.

Or a hose.

She cleared her throat. 'Here's another one to pin to the wall.'

Pin to the wall.

Brilliant.

Her traitorous brain instantly replayed that phrase, with Finn pinning *her* to the wall. Legs around his waist. Mouth on his. As if they'd skipped every logical step between banter and good manners.

Wait! Had she said that out loud?

The silence dragged long enough to make her question reality.

Finn just looked at her. Like he was receiving signals she didn't mean to send, in some bent-out-of-shape, primitive form of Morse code. The kind only cavemen and men like Finn Wilde could read.

Fantastic. Now she was fluent in horny cavewoman now.

The air between them wasn't normal anymore, it was more like it was waiting to catch fire.

She cleared her throat. 'I said the page. For the wall. Paperwork.'

Nope. That wasn't even close to what she had said because, frankly, she'd forgotten everything but Finn.

She risked a glance.

Finn had remained still, yet the air in the room had shifted a few degrees warmer. Especially when his gaze slid over her, slow and intense in a quiet look that was anything but casual.

And then, because Finn Wilde was infuriatingly unreadable and probably evil incarnate in at least three doctrines, he said, 'Right. Paperwork.'

She handed him the page.

Again, the brush of fingers, while he kept that neutral expression. Like she tried to do…

Well, she hoped she did.

Yet the tension thrummed between them like a pulled wire, stretched and waiting to snap.

She turned back to the wall like it was the only safe place in the house, while her regretful list of *what not to say to Finn Wilde* grew.

Her eye caught the record player in the lounge. 'You do realise those records are supposed to be played, and not get treated like vintage drink coasters?'

'Touch my vinyls and I'll tell Tanisha you chipped her cactus cup.'

She stared him down. 'You do realise that only makes me want to do it more, right?'

'My house. My music. My rules.'

She arched a brow. 'Give me five minutes and a Bluetooth speaker, and I'll have this place pumping with something that'll make your eyebrows fall off and have the troopy cry.'

'I bet you could,' he muttered, sorting another stack of paperwork.

She grinned, reaching for her workbag.

'Save it, Fed.' Dropping his wad of papers on the floor in a neat stack, he left the room.

Soon there was a soft click, a low crackle of static, then the unmistakable sound of a needle hitting vinyl.

The first chords rolled in—slow, smoky, deliberate.

Chris Stapleton's *Tennessee Whiskey*.

Of course, he'd own something country. While it was doubtful she had anything close to the country music genre on her playlists.

But she knew this song.

'Tennessee Whiskey, huh?' She peeled back a strip of tape, then lined up a manifest with more force than necessary.

Finn's voice came low behind her. 'Didn't think you'd

know it.'

'I won't admit it in public.' She shrugged, keeping her focus on the wall they were filling up like a jigsaw puzzle that had no shape. 'This song is a regular in military bars. Like an unofficial anthem for deployment nights, as that last slow song before goodbye. You hear it enough, it sticks… That if someone starts slow dancing, you know their plane leaves at dawn.'

She hadn't meant to say that much, but it spilled out anyway. 'Never saw much point in getting attached to people or places when we were always leaving.' She knew the drill. Her hellos always came with a ready-packed goodbye, where the in-between time was just waiting for the next rotation.

She could feel Finn watching her. He didn't offer to change the music. And she didn't ask. But that song did its job of making her remember her purpose.

She was doing this for answers—for her family.

So they kept moving through the paperwork. Her dodging the crate stack, him ducking under the red string she'd strung across one wall, as the music became more upbeat as different records were played. They bumped shoulders, passed pens, clipped pages, and kept at it. All their conversations were about the job, with a clear goal now in sight.

The paperwork spread like wallpaper made into something between a scrappy paper quilt and a conspiracy web masquerading as decor.

They were halfway into colour-coding connections when a knock on the front door broke through the rhythm.

'*Finn?*'

Finn straightened as the front door opened.

'*Finn, you around, luv?*'

That didn't sound like a cop calling. Was this Finn's food fairy?

Twenty-one

*L*ydia.

Finn slipped out of the room fast, with Taryn giving him a look. They both knew no one was supposed to see that wall. That was the whole point of doing it here, away from the station and prying eyes, and the possibility of something making it back to Red.

Also, this place was the safe house, should things go wrong for Lydia and Brodie. And with Lydia showing up unannounced meant something was wrong.

He scanned over Lydia's posture, checking for any wounds. Catching the tension in her jaw, and the way she clutched her bag to her chest like a lifeline.

There was no sign of Brodie.

'Everything alright?'

Lydia didn't answer right away, just peered over his shoulder towards the hallway. 'Are you alone?'

'No. Taryn Hayes. The federal investigator.' He shifted his stance, blocking Lydia's view of the spare room. 'She's here helping with a case.'

Lydia's brow lifted. 'Brodie said he saw her yesterday, in the passenger seat of your troopy. Is this the Fed who came to shut you down? Is she helping now?'

'Looks that way.' He rubbed the back of his neck, still not making heads or tails of it, but it was working in ways he'd never expected. 'Just no one really knows about it. So, I'd appreciate it if…'

'I get it.' Lydia casually swatted at the air between them. 'Like no one knows I'm here.'

Behind him, the door creaked open. Of course, Taryn

stepped out, calm as you please. 'I'm making coffee. Who wants one?' She held up the kettle, like this was her kitchen. 'I promise it'll be an improvement on Finn's—his brews are so strong the spoon wants to run away with the cracked mug.'

Lydia gave a surprised laugh. 'That'd be good, thanks.' She headed for the table, only to pause on the other side of the kitchen bench. 'Lydia Galloway.' She offered a hand to Taryn. 'I'm the clerk at the Elsie Creek Stockyards.'

Taryn shifted two mugs into one hand to shake with the other. 'Taryn Hayes. I rearrange paperwork and occasionally tick off Stock Squad agents, especially their leader.'

Lydia grinned, clearly amused.

'Not wrong,' mumbled Finn, but it was seamless—Taryn filling the mugs, Finn dragging out chairs, Lydia settling down.

'Alright,' Finn said, wrapping his hand around the steaming mug of coffee, which was better than his mud. 'Talk to me. What's wrong?'

Lydia took a slow sip of coffee, like she was buying time, her eyes darting to Taryn.

'Don't worry about the Fed, I'll end up telling her anyway.' Which was true. And it wasn't the first time he'd worked with a partner, it'd just been a while. 'So, shoot.'

'Red's been on edge all week... Today was the worst, on account of a truck that didn't show up this morning.' She glanced between Finn and Taryn. 'Tooley was the driver. He's a regular, who is very reliable. He runs the route from Tinderflats Station, like he's done for over a year, and normally arrives before first light. But today, he didn't.'

'How do you know it's missing?' Taryn asked.

'The paperwork was lodged in advance, and Tooley radioed Brodie to have the yards prepped to unload that truck. Only, Tooley never arrived.' Lydia paused, tapping the side of her mug. 'And out here, when a triple-deck of cattle doesn't turn up, people take notice. We're talking hundreds of thousands of dollars of stock. I always send out a few stockmen to check the truck didn't get bogged, or worse.' She looked directly at Finn. 'But this truck... It's *gone* gone. And I haven't been able to reach Tooley on the radio, or on the phone, all day.'

Finn and Taryn exchanged a look.

The bush telegraph hadn't caught up yet. Which meant no one knew the Stock Squad had pulled the truck over and arrested Tooley at dawn.

Did that mean Lydia was here for confirmation? Or she already knew and was waiting for Finn to say something he couldn't.

Finn leaned back, toying with the handle of his coffee mug. 'You know I can't comment on active cases, Lydia.'

Lydia gave a small nod, the kind that said she'd expected that answer.

'What did Red do?'

'Red has been circling the stockyards all day. Hassling poor Brodie with demands, in such a foul mood—and now this. Red's gotten...' Lydia exhaled, long and tired. '...worse.'

'How bad?' His voice dipped lower. He wanted names. Times. Heads to smack.

But then, he felt it.

A soft pressure against his leg.

Barely there. Yet, it surprisingly grounded him.

It was Taryn.

She didn't say a word as she sipped from her mug. Didn't look at him. Just that gentle pressure of her leg against his as a reminder to stay calm, and to listen first.

Lydia's fingers trembled as she fiddled with the handle of her mug. 'At home, Red's been walking around at night like he's checking for ghosts. Then I found him flicking through loading dockets in my office—ones that had nothing to do with him. And then he had a go at me when I asked what he was doing.'

Finn's jaw clenched. 'He'd better not—'

Again, there was that gentle press against his leg, but this time Taryn leaned over and placed a hand on Lydia's. Only for Lydia to grip it like a lifeline.

'What was it about?' Taryn asked gently.

'Red said the numbers don't match. That there's stock unaccounted for.' Lydia paused. 'He's right. But he's blaming Brodie. Mocking him for his writing again. Saying he scrawls like a child and calling that poor boy useless.'

A protective fire built inside Finn over a kid who'd already been through hell and didn't need this. 'Do you think Red is going to use Brodie as a patsy for the missing stock, and put it down to clerical error?'

'I hope not. Brodie's just a boy. It's not his fault what his parents did to him.' Lydia's voice wavered. 'He's come so far. Izzy's been helping him, giving him tricks and tips to improve his reading and writing—and he's trying so hard. He really is… I don't want Red pushing him. Brodie doesn't need to carry the weight of that.'

And Finn was just another selfish bastard who'd added to that pressure, too.

Idiot.

Taryn squeezed Lydia's hand again. 'Hey, you shouldn't have to carry it on your own, either.'

Lydia shared a soft look of someone who'd played their part of being strong for everyone else and was tired. 'Some days, I wish I could build Brodie a flat at home. I'd happily let him take the guest room, if Red would only agree. Because he's…' she trailed off. 'Brodie is like a son to me, and I'd do anything for that boy.'

Taryn pulled a small notebook from her back pocket. Ripped out a page and wrote a number on it. 'That's direct to me. If Finn's out of range, or off chasing a lead, and you need backup, or just a chat—use it.'

Lydia took the slip of paper, as if it meant more than just digits, and laid it on the table. 'You're only in town for a few more days, right?'

'That's what the paperwork says,' Taryn replied. 'But let's just say I don't mind staying a little longer if the company's decent.'

That earned a small, tired smile from Lydia.

'Finn watched Taryn stepping into that space beside him like she belonged. Saying what he wouldn't. Or couldn't. Like she was his balance, like they were starting to find that place… And then the reminder that she was leaving.

'You know where the spare key is,' he said bluntly. 'You're welcome, anytime. Brodie, too. The food fairy hasn't made a drop in a while, so you might have to bring your own tucker. But I don't want you sleeping in that house if it's not safe.'

Lydia offered him a tight smile, as her hand wrapped tightly around the mug. 'Thanks, Finn. But that's my home. I also know Red's moods better than anyone, and I know he won't hurt me. He's just blowing off steam.'

Taryn said nothing, but Finn could feel her reading between the lines like he did: *was Lydia truly safe with Red?*

Lydia put her cup back on the table. 'I know why Red is upset. I just don't know what he's doing it for.'

Finn exchanged a glance with Taryn. *The motive.*

'No talk of a holiday? Land? House? Anything out of the ordinary?' Taryn asked for the both of them.

Lydia shook her head. 'Not a word. And trust me, I'd notice.'

Finn frowned. 'Then what's the play?'

Tooley had a mortgage and kids as a reason to drive that truck.

But Red?

'If it's not for the house,' he said, 'or a trip, or for some stud farm and herd out in the hills, then what the hell is he doing it for?'

'What if it's all of that?' said Taryn. 'And none of it.'

Lydia frowned. 'Excuse me?'

'Men like Red… They've seen the shift in the industry, and in the way people talk to them. One day they're the backbone of a town. Next, they're being replaced with tablets, QR tags, or direct connection to clients via the internet.'

'Progress,' Finn grunted like it was an ugly word, that even had Lydia nodding.

'I bet he started it for you,' Taryn continued. 'Something

good, like an early retirement plan. Maybe for that extra security over the mortgage. But now, Red's probably in so deep, he can't get out.' She then sat higher in her chair. 'And maybe the idea of you finding out, or if you were to look at him differently for doing this... That might be what's eating him alive.'

Lydia's mouth pressed into a line. She didn't deny it.

'Shame makes people do stupid things...' Taryn said under her breath, but it was loud enough.

Lydia looked away, as if feeling that shame for her husband. 'No, he's not like that. Red has always looked out for me, since I was eighteen. He fights for the people he loves.'

Finn didn't interrupt her. But he watched the crack form. The protectiveness and loyalty Lydia carried for her husband was falling the way the first rain washes the caked-on dust from buildings and vehicles, to reveal the colours you forgot were underneath the dust.

She'd been holding on so tightly. But now?

Finn could see it—the truth was bleeding through now.

'He just... gets overwhelmed sometimes,' Lydia whispered. 'Red doesn't like change. He struggles with the way the industry's shifting. Feeling like he's unheard.'

Taryn shifted slightly as if to speak—but this time, Finn was the one who pressed a knee gently against hers to hold her back.

He knew what she was thinking.

'Shame makes people do stupid things.' He'd seen it before. In the prison yards, where men circled like well-behaved dogs, with their heads down and their rage tucked behind their teeth. Shame took the wheel, until fear took over to drive them somewhere they never thought they'd go.

'And fear's the worst of the lot,' he hissed. 'It doesn't stop until there's no way back from the brink. Only the fall.' And Finn was gunning for Red's arrest to ensure he'd fall. Families had been hurt, and people had died under Red's command as the thieving Stock Agent.

Lydia stiffened her posture, the shade darkening the rings under her eyes. 'No. He's not like that. He's not.'

Denial.

Finn felt that old splinter under the skin.

The way his mother used to say everything's fine, while the bruises faded, and the excuses stacked up. How his father sat on the porch cradling his whisky like silence was a virtue. Both parents, grown-ups, living with a lie. Pretending a man—or men—weren't capable of something terrible, especially when you loved them.

Denial… It was just the devil dressed in a Sunday hat.

Taryn pushed the slip of paper closer to Lydia. 'Still, if Red crosses a line, even just with words, you call me. You don't have to carry this alone. Not anymore.'

Lydia slipped the note into her pocket, then fiddled with the wedding ring on her finger as if contemplating her next move. The silence didn't last long. 'He's back on the road. Said he had to follow up on a missing trailer with Bob, or Rob, or something.'

Bob. The man with the burner phone. The lead from Tooley.

Finn stood. 'Time to meet up with Stone and Romy. House is yours, Fed.'

Taryn frowned at him. 'You haven't checked in with them yet?'

'Of course I have.' He frowned at her for butting in. As if he'd leave his team out on surveillance without checking on their welfare. 'Besides, Stone knows to call if it turns sideways.' They all did. That's why he'd chosen them as his team because he didn't need to babysit them to do the job they all loved.

'I'll walk Lydia out.' Taryn then passed him a brown paper bag. 'Your dinner.' She gave a small shrug. 'It's okay, I'm used to eating alone.'

Like he was.

Strangely, he'd been looking forward to sharing a meal with her. Not because he was lonely, as he'd long made peace with solitude, but because he wanted to hear her thoughts over the Gaps File and this case.

He'd also wanted to simply sit across from her and share that space and not have to explain a damn thing.

But she'd gone back to the dining room, and the silence filled in behind her like it always did. And he had a job to do.

Twenty-two

Finn sat in the troopy with the driver's door open, scoffing down the last of the dinner Taryn had brought, which tasted better than anything he'd cooked in months. Pity he didn't get to share it with her.

Forking in another bite, he kept his eyes on the scrublands filled with burnt gold and growing shadows as the sun began to dip.

Porter had named this place Campdog's Scratch. With a sandstone rise that stood just off the floodplain, it was flat enough for a chopper, and too remote for tourists or phone towers. Making it a decent meeting point that you'd only find if someone showed you how to get here. Perfect as that place between somewhere and nowhere, while he went over his plan, again…

While Taryn had snooped around his house earlier, Finn had let Tooley out on bail as bait. On the condition Tooley make a phone call and told Bob he'd been busted. Which he did, right in front of Finn.

And with Lydia showing up, telling him Red was on the road, it confirmed the plan was working.

The bonus was figuring out Red's motivation, thanks to Taryn. It hadn't been as straightforward as Finn had first thought.

Red wasn't just a stock agent, when he came from a line of blokes who'd learned the trade the old way. Not in a classroom, but out in the yards, apprenticed under a man who'd learned the same way before him. It was a job passed down like a saddle or a name, where you earned your stripes through hard muster seasons, while forging long-term relationships.

Now all of that was being replaced by technology. Along with the rules that were constantly changing, as the industry kept shifting, that somewhere in that shuffle Red had lost his grip on the status he'd spent a lifetime earning.

So Red did what bitter men, overstuffed with pride, often did when the system no longer made room for them—he'd found a way to milk it.

The real kicker?

Finn, who'd come from that same world, saw the irony for what it was. Red, who'd regularly rage against progress in the pub like it was a personal insult, was now using it to steal from the industry he'd once protected. Doing it through genetic smuggling techniques to create a modern version of cattle theft.

To Finn, it wasn't progress. It was the same old crime just dressed in better clothes.

He finished his dinner, and wiped his mouth with the paper napkin Taryn had folded with ridiculous neatness. Then tossed the empty container onto the passenger floor, just as a low beat of wind shifted the trees, as the sound came thick and rhythmic.

The chopper.

Finn stepped out of the troopy and rolled his shoulders. Time to work.

The helicopter came in low and fast, whipping the treetops and flattening the spinifex like it had something to prove. Typical Stone, too much flair, with just enough control to get away with it.

Finn squinted into the grit as the skids hit the dried-up floodplain. The moment the blades slowed enough to not lose a hat, the door swung open.

Stone jumped down, headset still on, carrying a bag in hand. Grinning like a kid as he adjusted the coiled lead from his headphones to tuck it into his shirt pocket.

Romy remained seated in the chopper, giving Finn a short wave through the windshield, then turned back to her screen that manned the drone. Good.

Finn nodded to Stone, then motioned toward the troopy's hood where his maps were spread out, anchored by spare water bottles and half a brick. It reminded him of Taryn's use of rocks and dirt to put his paperwork in place.

That woman. It was enough for the grin to curl for just a second.

'What did you find?'

'We followed that truck to the old quarry. They're all set up here.' Stone pointed to a spot on the map.

Finn scanned over the map as Tooley's voice echoed in the back of his mind from today's interrogation: ...*flying the boxes out from the airfield tucked behind the old quarry...*

He'd added it to his mental notes, as he hadn't had time to follow up on it. But now, it lined up just right. The quarry wasn't just a stop—it was more. And Finn wanted to know everything going on at that place. 'Get any motion cams set up there?'

'Only on the entrance ways.' Stone put the bag on the bonnet. 'Got more if you want.'

'Good. I want full surveillance on that place if we can.'

'Thought so. I've already got Romy's footage uploading to the cloud. She's clocked a pen of cattle, a demountable for an office, one ute, two trucks and a stack of fake livestock transport trailers.'

'How do you know they're fake?'

'None of the trailer numbers match any of the manifest logs with the trucking company. The Duchess taught me how to do the searches.' Stone grinned, proud of himself, and the fact that Amara had taught Stone anything made it sweeter.

'Which company are they using?'

'HHA.'

Highway Haulers Australia were huge and had the kind of loyalty you couldn't buy. They were one of those trusted brands in a field where clients didn't like change. Just like Red, who'd been the stock agent for the same cattle stations for decades.

'If they're all branded the same, that explains how the swapped trailers went undetected in the stockyard...' Finn's mind put the pieces into place. 'And that's why HHA hasn't called about the road train taking up space in Craig's yard. Red and his crew have been using those fake trucks, but on paper as SW contracting.'

It all made sense.

Finn tapped out a message on his phone, reminding Craig and Amara to check the VINs and any other identifying details on the road train in Craig's yard, then trace where it came from. If Porter was still at Dustfire, he'd pick up on any tampering, he was well trained to read those signs. And Amara would know exactly where to find them in the system.

Behind them, another engine approached. It was Amara's new patrol wagon clawing its way up the ridge.

'What's this?' Amara closed her car door and approached them. 'The Good, the Bad, and the Barely Groomed—live from Campdog's Scratch, starring the feral pilot as the Stock Squad's answer to *Mission Impossible*?'

'Keep talkin' like that, Duchess, and I'll make sure your next mission involves a seat on the chopper, with doors off while I take a nap.' Stone shot back, always grinning.

'Remind me why we let you two talk in public?' Finn grumbled over the map.

Amara tossed a cloth roll of GPS tags onto the bonnet. 'Here are the tags. You know, sir, we don't have the warrants for surv—'

'I know.' Finn wasn't annoyed at her, because that's why he had the black-and-white paperwork queen as part of his team, to remind him what they could and couldn't do.

Stone picked up the bag of vehicle tags, cracked the seal, and gave a theatrical sniff. 'Smells like new car and Montrose's attitude—sharp, expensive, and a little toxic.'

Amara didn't look up from her tablet. 'You'd know toxic, Stone. You exhale it.'

'Please, Duchess. I'm like an essential oil for fieldwork. A few drops of me and everyone's mood improves.'

She snorted. 'Only because you're not allowed to bring actual petrol fumes into meetings anymore.'

Stone leaned in with a grin. 'You're just jealous I smell like success.'

Finn cleared his throat sharply, like a teacher stepping between bickering teens. 'Can we get on with it?'

Stone grinned, lifting his boot to rest on the troopy's bull bar. 'So, what's the play, Bossman? Tag and run?'

Fin nodded. 'We'll go in after dark. Set up a few more cameras on the perimeter, and tag everything that moves — trucks, trailers, utes.'

'Maybe a few cocky cowboys, if they stand still long enough,' Stone added.

Amara said flatly, 'Shame you never stay still long enough to qualify.'

Finn sighed, rubbing his temples. Running this crew was like herding cats — with flamethrowers. 'Who's volunteering?' He had to ask.

'Only if it gets me hazard pay,' Stone said with a grin. 'Romy and I'll keep eyes from above.' He then tapped on the map. 'Watch that bend near the quarry. It's a blind spot behind the ridge. The place has got a few of them.'

Finn nodded as he studied the map. 'Stone, keep the bird low with that spotlight ready. Just close enough to blind anyone watching from the tree line, if we need it.'

'Done.' Stone nodded, adjusting his headset. 'Romy's going to use the thermal vision, it'll tell us who's getting curious in the compound.'

'Good. We stay quiet. No contact unless it's unavoidable.'

He looked to Amara, who was already loading trackers and small cameras into the pockets of her police vest.

'You and me, we'll tag the trucks, check the manifests, and get out. Quick and clean.'

Amara gave a firm nod. 'Yes, sir. I'll start on the west side.'

'Good, I'll go east, and we'll meet in the middle.' Finn started strapping on his own vest.

Of course, Stone took the silence as his cue to start tossing commentary around like confetti. 'You packing that granny holster again, Duchess? Or going rogue with a taser and some bad-boy attitude today?'

'You're one to talk,' Amara muttered, checking her side-arm. 'Pretty sure that camera you dropped on that last op ended up in a cow paddock.'

'Strategic placement,' Stone shot back. 'Cattle intelligence is underrated.'

'Right. Must be why that footage featured twenty minutes of a bull scratching its arse on a fence post.'

It had Finn glancing up from checking his side-arm, with one brow lifting. 'About time...' Even giving the young constable a quiet nod. If Taryn had been there, she'd grin and mutter something smug like, *Aww, the Tiny Titan finally grew claws.*

Stone's laugh was loud as he clapped Amara on the shoulder. 'Living with Porter is doing you some good, Duchess.'

Amara's smile was full of young love for Porter, with some self-pride too, as she slid the last of the trackers into her vest pocket.

The young constable had come a long way in a short time. Hell, Finn could see her running the Stock Squad one day — if Taryn didn't shut it down.

He exhaled slowly, the dry bush air catching at the back of his throat, thinking of Taryn still at his house, alone, buried in the Gaps File. Which is where he wanted to be. Answering her curious questions, talking over what-ifs, digging deeper on the bigger picture.

But he couldn't bring the Fed out here. Not when he was about to bend the rules she was paid to uphold. 'Let's go.'

Twenty-three

Sunlight was gone. Not faded—but gone. Swallowed by the escarpment and the creeping hush of the outback after dusk. The perfect cover for Finn and Amara as they moved low along the fence line, boots soft in the dirt, the air thick with the scents of diesel, dry grass, and cattle.

Stone's chopper was using the shadows of the night sky to hide, but Romy's drone would be close.

The clearing ahead revealed a small set of portable stockyards with galvanised panels, freshly welded. The area was so new the wet season rust or cobwebs hadn't had a chance to settle in yet.

A water trough sat at one end, along with a fresh scatter of hay, its scent clinging to the breeze, where cattle shifted inside like calm shadows.

Finn stepped in close, careful not to startle them, and used his phone to take flash-less photos of their flanks—each marked with brands that he was pretty sure wouldn't match the paperwork, let alone their ear tags.

He zoomed in, snapped another grainy shot. He wasn't after quality like Romy's imagery, he just needed the basic outline.

One brand he recognised, belonging to a station three hundred kilometres east. More interestingly, several wore the Tinderflats Station brand. He tapped his mic. 'Amara. The cattle are tagged. Stolen stock confirmed. Got my images?'

'Yes, sir. We have enough to bust them, if we deny the camera's existence and just say it was a tip-off,' she murmured from the shadows.

'But we won't. Not yet.' Finn wasn't here for small wins—

he was after the one who signed the cheques. The ghost behind the cattle-dust curtain who never got their hands dirty.

Finn scanned the clearing beyond the trucks, and that's when he saw it. Just past the fence line, a slight shimmer warped on the horizon where the last of the day's heat rose finely over a flat, cleared airstrip.

On the other side, a demountable. A simple box with a door and a tin roof. No lights. But an antenna jutted from the flat roof.

This wasn't some simple bush loading point. It was a depot that made up a big part of the supply chain. And with the Stock Squad setting up their stealth surveillance, it didn't feel like he was breaking the rules to do it.

'Camera check, Romy?' Finn asked.

'Umm…' Romy meditated like some monk over the airwaves, where Finn was expecting some gong to go off. Fully aware Romy was still learning the radio lingo.

Stone's voice came over faintly in the background. 'Not a yoga class, hon, just say the thing and get off the air.'

'Right. Yeah, sorry. Um—Camera one, live… Two, live. Three and four… standby—okay, now they're live. Six to nine…' Romy sighed with relief. 'All cameras are operational.'

'Copy that,' Finn said. 'Can you give a count of how many vehicles and work crews? Someone must be babysitting this livestock.'

Again, Romy's voice came softly in the earpiece. 'Two livestock trucks. Six trailers. One single-cab LandCruiser ute. Besides the livestock, and you lot, the thermals are picking up on someone inside that demountable.'

Finn signalled to Amara, and they split.

He took the larger truck, moving like a shadow across the clearing. Amara curved toward the second trailer, her silhouette vanishing behind it.

Click.

The first tracker was set in place. He then peeled back the manifest folder tied to the frame and flipped through it.

A lot of it was blank. Or worse—deliberately vague.

He took a video of it from his phone. Then tapped his mic. 'Truck one's tagged. Manifest is dodgy.'

'Same here,' Amara whispered. 'Generic descriptions. No brand IDs. Not even a receiving station listed. You want me to tag the ute?'

'Do it. Then we pull out.'

'*Aw hell.* Bossman?' Stone's voice crackled over the comms, tight with tension. 'You've got a vehicle inbound. Moving fast. They just flicked on their headlights. They must've been running dark up the fence line. Bugger, I missed it.'

'It'd be doing that to avoid detection,' Finn muttered. 'Pull back, Constable. Now.'

'Too late,' came Amara's voice. 'I've got a visual. Headlights inbound.'

Romy's voice chimed in, quieter but urgent. 'How the hell did we miss that? We've got eyes on everything—'

'Not everything,' Stone's frustration bled through. 'They used the ridgeline. But you're right, I should've caught it.' And normally, he would've. Stone could spot a camouflaged crocodile in a swamp without blinking. He'd stew on this one for a while.

Finn didn't hand out praise, and he didn't do mollycoddling or back pats, but if Taryn were here, she'd say something like: *Even snipers blink, Stone.*

He muttered, almost an echo of her, 'It happens.'

Just enough for the team to take a breath without the fuss.

That woman was rubbing off on him.

But he shouldn't even be thinking about her, not as he got low behind the trailer, to watch a dual-cab LandCruiser rolling in. With a set of the mismatched tail-lights, it was far too clean for a station vehicle.

The engine cut. The driver's door opened.

It was Red. '*Bob, you in?*' He pressed on the car's horn to shatter the silence.

The demountable door swung open, spilling yellow light across the blackness as more spotlights lit up the scene. A second man, lean and fit, wearing a battered stockman's hat, and a loose, long-sleeved stockman's shirt, trotted down the steps in well-worn boots.

Bob.

He was younger than expected. Dirt under the nails, sliding a pack of rollies into the back pocket of his dusty jeans. His eyes were sharp as he glanced over the yarded cattle as he strode casually across the compound. But there was nothing casual about it at all, it was the look of a well-trained stockman who'd effortlessly read the shift in the herd just by the lean of the shadows.

Finn got down low and barely murmured over the mic, 'Hold position. And listen in.'

Amara ghosted into the shadows of the rear tyre of the last trailer. And Stone was radio silent, no doubt leaning over Romy's shoulder to watch from one of her many cameras.

Red's voice barked in the night air. 'You said the switch *was clean*. You said *no delays*.'

Bob shrugged, hooking his thumbs through the belt loops of his jeans. 'What do you want me to do? The truck is gone. The switch was made perfectly. Only a few minutes late, but it went down like clockwork. And we've got all those fresh beasts catching a snooze before we draft them. Besides, didn't you always say to be ready for losses? So, no biggie.'

'It's sloppy. And if this brings heat on me—'

'Heat's already on you, mate. They arrested Tooley. I warned you not to be near any changeovers with the drivers around.'

'Dammit.' Red dropped his head, his wide-brimmed hat casting shadows over his face, leaving only the long red bushman's beard visible. 'They gave him bail?'

'Yes,' Bob answered.

'Did we?' Amara murmured over the airwaves, watching from the shadows.

Finn confirmed. 'To make Red panic.' Bailing out Tooley hadn't been kindness, it had been bait. A way to make Red show up hot, to forget his carefully curated cover as a respected stock agent, to hopefully spill like a toddler throwing a tantrum.

And Red was fuming now — pacing, swearing, showing his cards. Exactly what Finn wanted.

Red stepped in closer to Bob. 'Does Tooley know this place?'

'No,' Bob said, steady. 'Just you and me, mate. We're the only locals who do. And the only others are Clancy and the pilot who fly in, load, and leave fast coz Clancy hates the heat. Come on, it's why we chose the quarry in the first place. No one comes out here.'

'Next time, no mistakes. Or I'll find someone who can follow instructions.'

'You reckon you've got that kind of pull?' Bob let out a chuckle. 'You're not running the show, mate. You're just another hand in the mob, same as me.'

Red's jaw clenched.

There it was. Red *wasn't* the top dog. He was just another one on the leash, like the others, and didn't like it. Finn hoped Romy got all that on her drone somewhere above them.

'Here's the paperwork. I want no mistakes, so check it now.' Red tugged the paperwork free from his ute and headed across the clearing, still arguing with Bob. Their voices fading as they stepped inside the demountable with the door open.

Finn shifted fast.

He could barely make out their faint voices through the thin tin walls and what floated out through the open door.

'Draft the cattle tomorrow,' ordered Red. 'Find another driver, someone clean. Then have the cryogenic canisters ready for the plane to do a quick land and go. And that'll be it for a bit.'

There it was. Their exit plan. Cattle and canisters. Freight and flight. The fallback route in case things got ugly. All the points Finn needed to work on to cut them off.

Bob dropped the paperwork on a desk by the door, near a simple camp bed set-up. 'Are you saying we're shutting up shop?'

Red trotted back down the stairs. 'They have our truck!'

'Yeah, so?' Bob followed him. 'Tooley won't say anything.'

'Of course he will. That's how he got bail. Finn Wilde would never have let Tooley walk unless it was bait.' Red started pacing. One hand wiped over his thick red beard, as if he could wipe away the mess.

'But Tooley doesn't know this depot exists. He's never been to the quarry, so we're safe—'

'But it's still exposure!' Red's voice cracked across the yard like a whip, silencing the low cattle murmurs.

Bob didn't flinch, but he took a wary step back.

With his eyes wild, chest heaving, mouth drawn tight, Red was unravelling, slamming his hand against the side of the ute. The sound rang out like gunfire in the stillness.

'Easy now…' Bob murmured, taking another step back as if dealing with a feral scrub bull.

'*Dammit!*' Red jabbed a finger toward the open yard. 'Finn's done this to me too many times now! Only now he's rattling the entire chain above me.' Red prowled in a tight circle, like a caged dog, hands on hips one second, tugging at his collar the next. His thoughts must have been in such a violent storm that his body couldn't contain them.

But then he stopped pacing. 'It was never meant to get this big. It was meant to…' Red trailed off, wiping down his beard as if to compose himself. 'We were particular about what we took. Just skim off the top and no one would notice. But they're noticing it now…'

Red started pacing again, batting at the bugs attracted to the spotlights that shone down upon them like some outback theatre, where Finn and Amara had ringside seats in the shadows, right alongside the cattle.

'Now I've got my name on the paperwork that is linked to that truck.' Red broke off, rubbing his forehead as if preparing for the mother of all migraines. 'She doesn't know. She can't know…'

There it was. That raw edge of fear surfacing beneath

Red's fury. More worried about Lydia finding out what he had been doing than Finn catching him. Just as Taryn and Finn had explained to Lydia earlier, how that mix of shame and fear was a potent combination if left uncontrolled.

Red spun around again, his voice full of authority, as if fighting for self-control. 'We move what we've got out of this yard. Then we shut it down.'

'Another panic shutdown?' Bob scoffed. 'Aw, come on.'

'Orders from above. That new fed's heading back to Canberra soon. Then we've got a month, max, to wait it out.'

Finn scowled with heat.

Were they talking about Taryn?

'Same as the banteng and horses, same as the crocs that the Stock Squad recovered,' snapped out Red. 'We lie low for a bit. Only this time we wait until that fed goes home and does up her report, and we get the all clear.'

'Pfft, you're just panicking.' Bob's laugh echoed into the night air.

Red spun around and took a step closer.

And another.

Stalking straight up to Bob to get right in his face. 'You think this is a joke?' Red's voice was low and barely restrained. 'You think I want to shut it down? Do you think I enjoy cleaning up after every stuff-up, every near miss, and every bloody delay?'

Bob held his ground—but his chin dipped as if a small retreat.

'You laugh again, and I swear I'll bury you in this quarry like you were nothing but dirt under my boots. *You know* what I'm *capable* of. You saw what I did to your cousin—and the dumb cops still haven't figured that one out.'

Finn froze, as his mind rushed. Who was Bob's cousin? And had Red just confessed to something like murder?

Then Red stepped back, his hands flexing like he wanted to hit something but didn't.

Finn held his breath behind the truck. Now he saw it. Not

just panic or shame, but the deadly kind of violence that filled prison cells.

But then a thought whispered effectively capturing Finn's attention, enough to make his heart squeeze…

They didn't just know Taryn was going back to Canberra—Red and his crew were counting on it!

Her presence, or exit, was now part of their plan. The excuse to pause their smuggling operation, just long enough for Taryn to report to Canberra on the job she'd been sent here to do—to assess the Stock Squad and decide in a month whether it stayed or shut down.

The same timeframe Red had just told Bob to stand down for.

No more Stock Squad. No more Finn.

The realisation hit like a fist to the ribs, leaving something hollow and sick in its place.

He'd been so focused on baiting Red, on making him crack by using Tooley as the tool, Finn hadn't seen the bigger play where he himself had been used as *the bait*.

He'd been fighting against Taryn from the start, guarding the squad, while treating her like a threat. All while Red and his master just stood back as Finn bulldozed through everything, like they knew he would.

They'd expected him to ignore the Fed, to never answer her questions, to piss her off so completely that of course she'd file a report that would bury the Stock Squad for good. Which is exactly what they wanted.

Finn clenched his jaw, the taste of bile and shame thick in his throat.

They'd played him like a green recruit.

And now they had a month to vanish, while Finn stood in the wreckage, looking like the fool who had helped shut down his own squad.

Had Taryn known?

Or had they played her, too?

That thought hit harder than the rest.

The man who'd spent most of his time avoiding her questions, was now itching to ask her the one question that could change everything: *Who sent you?*

Twenty-four

Finn closed the front door behind him with a quiet click. But nothing felt quiet. Not with his pulse hammering in his ears, and his teeth clenched so tight his jaw ached. He shouldn't have let her in. Not into his house. Not into his team. And not into his head.

She was the Fed.

The weapon they'd sent to gut his squad from the inside, the polite executioner in a smart suit. To shut him down.

And he'd let her get close.

Hell, he'd fought her, barked and bristled and shoved back. But he'd still let her in. Trusted her.

Dammit, he'd kissed her!

And now look where they were.

He strode down the hallway like a man ready to break something.

Who sent you? The words burned in his throat.

He wasn't just angry. He was furious at himself for thinking that she could be different. That maybe she understood him. And that maybe she gave a damn.

Light spilled from the spare room. He stepped in—

And stopped cold.

The air shifted and all that heated rage cracked. All at the sight of…Taryn. Asleep.

Curled up in front of the wall art she'd built with red string stretched from corner to corner, pinning photos, paperwork, and notes. She'd colour-coded connections, flagged key stations, brands, names, and dates. His Gaps File, which had once been a chaotic mess, was now mapped into an organised war plan, listing out facts and timelines.

And she'd done all that while he was gone.

But it wasn't the files that stopped him cold.

It was the photo.

Pinned to the wall apart from the web of notes and names, hung a photo he'd never seen before.

It was of a young woman, with curly brown hair, smiling like the world was a safe place. The caption beneath it was written by Taryn: *Meghan Forrester*.

For the first time, Finn put a face to the name of the young woman he'd only ever known as Izzy's assistant. The one who'd been brutally murdered, sending Izzy running for cover in Elsie Creek, long before Finn had even heard of Everlight Energy Solutions.

And just like that, everything shifted.

Taryn hadn't come to take the Stock Squad down. She'd come for Meghan.

No one, not even Red's crew or Taryn's boss, knew that. They all thought they were using her to shut down the squad, and for Finn to drive her out of town—just like they'd planned.

But Taryn Hayes was the wildcard they hadn't accounted for.

Hell, he hadn't accounted for her either.

And suddenly, he couldn't breathe.

She wasn't the weapon.

She was the one fighting beside him.

Not because someone told her to, but because she gave a damn. Because it mattered. Her true motive for being here, and why she was putting in all this effort, was for her cousin. She was chasing justice for her family. For blood.

And for a man who'd lost his family—that meant more than anything.

He dropped to a crouch beside her, all that fire in his chest now gone.

He didn't touch her, just looked at her. The ink smudge on her wrist. The crease between her brows, even as she slept, as if working behind those closed lids. The way she'd folded herself down like she didn't belong here, but had done everything to stay anyway, no matter how hard he'd pushed her.

The stubborn thing.

He reached out, gently brushing her soft hair from her face, her beauty making his throat tighten.

Even though she may have come to shut him down in the beginning—but now? Hiding behind her job for her own reasons… Who was using who?

'Who sent you?'

Did she even know the answer?

Carefully, he slid one arm beneath her knees, the other under her shoulders, and lifted her.

She stirred but didn't wake, releasing a soft breath against his collarbone, as her head fell against his chest like it belonged there.

Damn… He held her closer than he'd meant to.

Taryn Hayes. The woman who'd met him blow for blow with wit, sarcasm, and federal procedure, had never let him off the hook. His enemy, so soft in his arms, asleep, made something inside crack.

Sure, she was all sharp edges and stubborn pride in the daylight—but seeing her like this stirred something primal inside him. Something protective.

She shifted slightly in his arms, her nose brushing that place where his neck met his shoulder as if snuggling up to him.

If she'd been awake, she would've made a smart-arse comment, demanding he put her down.

But she wasn't.

Heaven help him—his body noticed.

Not in a way he could shake off. It wasn't lust or heat, but something deep beneath his skin, to settle there like it had always belonged.

His throat burned. His chest ached. Like he'd been holding a breath for years and hadn't realised it until now.

She may have come to tear down everything he'd built.

And yet, she was the only one who'd seen him for who he really was. The criminal under the badge, and the desperate fighter clinging onto something worth keeping in a life full of wrongs.

She snuggled up to him, asleep in his arms like *he was safe*. Like he was the thing *worth* trusting. And that—

That undid him

Where in that stillness as the world slept around him, he finally allowed himself to feel...

The shape of her in his arms. The warmth of her against his chest, where the strange, impossible peace of a man who'd spent years surrounded by chaos, was somehow left holding the calm he never knew he'd craved until now.

He carried her into his room, to the big bed that he'd made with fresh black sheets, and laid her down so gently, like she might vanish if he moved too fast.

He didn't linger.

And he didn't let himself touch her again.

He just stood there, arms burning with the memory, with his weary heart now thudding with life, somewhere beneath the armour he hadn't taken off in years.

Then he left her alone.

Twenty-five

Taryn woke to the distant clink of glass. For a moment, she just lay there, staring at the ceiling, confused by the softness beneath her.

Black sheets. In a room that was too quiet.

Finn's bed!

Her pulse ticked *hard*.

She was alone. And fully dressed.

Taryn swung her legs over the edge, the hardwood floor cool under her bare feet. The air smelled of citrus and something else… Tomatoes, basil and other herbs?

She followed it out of the room, hearing someone humming.

In the kitchen, a redhead stood barefoot at the bench by the sinks. Well, as close as she could get with that round belly, elbow-deep in a basket of fresh produce. Food filled jars lined the bench as she moved with practised ease, stacking things into the pantry like she belonged.

The woman looked up as she put some jars away. 'Morning,' she said, casually turning to slice a mango sitting on the counter, with an exceptionally sharp knife. 'Well, you don't look nearly as scary as Finn made you sound.'

'Who are you?'

'Bree.' The woman angled the knife expertly and sliced the mango onto a plate of other cut fruit.

'Finn's ex-wife.'

'Well, that depends on who you ask. Some days I'm just the town scandal with a Kombi van, or the anvil-bashing blacksmith having a bad hair day.'

'Right.' Oh, she was awake now.

'I know who you are, too. The Fed. Fresh from Canberra, sent out here to sniff out cronyism and burn down the cowboy outfit my ex-husband has built.'

Bree sliced into another mango with surgical precision, as her eyes flicked back to Taryn with lazy amusement. 'So, what's your story, buttons?'

Taryn tilted her head. 'What did you call me?'

'*Buttons*.' Bree didn't miss a beat. 'I heard you arrived in stiff collars and shiny shoes. All tightly stitched and highly strung. Besides,' she added, with a grin, 'we both know I'm gonna be pushing your buttons for sport. So, I may as well label the target.'

Taryn arched a brow. 'And if I push back?'

'Then we're gonna get along just fine.' Bree handed Taryn the bowl of sliced fruit and a coffee. 'And, if you're lucky, some man may show up and save you the trouble.'

'I don't need a man to save me.' But her stomach growled at the bowl of fragrant fruit and coffee that didn't smell like mud.

'Well, kudos to you, buttons,' Bree drawled. 'But just so we're clear, I didn't need one to save me either. I only got married because I needed someone to reach the top shelf.'

Taryn snorted on a mouthful of coffee to grin. 'Does your husband know you say that?'

'Of course he does. Ryder thinks it's romantic.' Bree grinned. 'Now sit and let that brain of yours wake up.'

'I'm awake.' But she was hungry.

The pineapple was so sweet it nearly rewired her tastebuds. Yet the flavour was pure summer—sunlight and sugar, dragging up memories she hadn't touched in years, from a time of bare feet on warm tiles. Her cousin's giggle matching her grandfather's laugh that echoed along the verandah, as the soft brush of a breeze carried the scents of cut grass and summer fruits ripening on trees.

Now, as a grown-up, she sat barefoot at Finn's plain table, the tiles beneath her toes warmed by the morning. Outside, the scrublands shimmered gold, bathed in that quiet hush of early light that made the whole world feel magical.

'This fruit is fabulous.' She glanced back at the kitchen bench full of assorted fruits and vegetables that Bree was packing away. 'Is this why Finn calls you the food fairy?'

'Can't have the man starve. And this way I get to check on him.' Bree unloaded another set of jars on the counter with a thud beside the beefy tomatoes, capsicums, and a loaf of bread. 'Don't worry, it's all organically grown. I've got more bloody zucchinis than I know what to do with. Might as well offload them before they form a union.'

Taryn rushed forward. 'Here, let me help—'

'Nope.' Bree waved her off from behind the kitchen counter as she lifted a cabbage from a box, filled with more fruit and vegetables. 'I ran away from home this morning purely because my husband, his brothers, and half the bloody station's stockmen, were following me around with pillows and teacups like I'm about to drop the royal heir. If one more man tries to tie my boots for me, I'm gonna set fire to a hay bale and blame it on the hormones.'

'Okay then...' Taryn backed away from the heavily pregnant woman. 'Izzy said she was having canning lessons with you.'

'That we did.' Bree popped the lid off a jar of chutney, gave it a sniff, and nodded like she'd just solved a crime. 'Can't beat your own recipe, and that little canning session made me realise how starved I am.'

'Huh?' When there was food everywhere.

'For news and gossip. Simple chatter on anything and everything that does not involve my pregnancy or baby talk.'

Bree then turned to face Taryn, setting the pickle jar down carefully. 'So tell me, buttons. Did you really come here for an audit? Or was it an excuse to escape the Canberra weather?'

Silence bloomed.

And for a second—just one—Taryn felt caught without her armour, facing a heavily pregnant woman who saw everything.

'Do you always interrogate barefoot?' A feeble attempt to

get the conversation back on track, but the redhead ruled the room. How was that possible?

Bree smirked. 'Only for those who need it.'

'And you're here to help Finn. Your ex?'

'I don't know where Finn is.' Bree shrugged, slicing more mango for herself. 'But I do know he'll panic when he learns that we're in the same room together, praying he'll still have a house left when the dust clears.'

A flicker of a grin crossed Taryn's face as she lifted her coffee. 'It might be smarter to start boarding up the windows for safety reasons first.'

Bree gave a bark of laughter as she pointed at Taryn with the mango knife. 'Careful, buttons. Keep that up and I might actually like you.'

Bree washed her mango-sticky hands in the sink, dried them on a tea towel, then rested one on her belly with a dramatic sigh. 'But because you aren't going to pander to me in my *delicate condition*—and honestly, who calls it delicate when I'm the size of a prize heifer trying to smuggle a bloody watermelon? I'm gonna let you have the floor. Ask what you want. But be quick, you've only got a few minutes before the cavalry arrives.'

Taryn peered out the window at the empty drive. There was no sign of Finn's troopy. But beside the old police wagon stood a surprisingly bright yellow vintage Kombi van. 'What cavalry?'

'You'll see soon enough. Oh, and this is the part where I promise to be brutally honest.' Bree smiled sweetly, tapping at her bare wrist. 'Tick-tock.'

Taryn leaned her hip against the counter. 'Alright. You found Cowboy Craig for Finn. You found the land for the Stock Squad's quarantine station. Did you also find Izzy to be their lawyer?'

'Einstein was my lawyer first, told Finn that.'

'And you found Stone?'

'Pebbles, yeah.'

'Do you say that to Stone's face?'

'Hello, *buttons*.'

Taryn should have frowned, instead she laughed.

'And to finish your next question—'

'Am I that obvious?'

Again, another one of those knowing grins as the redhead's green eyes sparkled. 'When Finn said he'd need a pilot, I told him Pebbles would be perfect for the job. Turned out I was right, huh?' Bree took a bite of sliced rockmelon.

'So, you run the local stock brand register?'

Bree rolled her eyes. 'Why ask questions when you already know the answers? You know my family has been making stock brands in this area for generations. Come on, you can do better than that. Dig deep, buttons.'

'Fine. Did you know about the Spinifex Highway?'

'I'm a long-time local. And every local knows that highway. Aren't you going to mention cronyism?' Bree shot back. 'Oh wait, I dropped that word already.'

Taryn's eyes flared. 'Why do you think that?'

'It's what I'd be thinking if I were in your shoes, even though I can't remember the last time I slipped on my own socks.' She peered over her enormous belly to wriggle her toes. 'Do you think it's too late for a pedicure?'

'Um… How far along are you?'

'I'm overdue. So says the doctor.'

'What do you mean?' The tingly sense of worry started creeping up her spine.

'Yep, any day now.' Bree patted her belly tenderly, while surprisingly calm. 'Keep going, we haven't got long to finish this conversation.'

'I heard a rumour…' Yet Taryn didn't want to say it.

'About Finn, huh?'

Taryn nodded.

'With you staying at the pub, you would've heard about Finn drinking a fair bit a while back. And if you were looking for reasons to shut them down, you would have zoned in on that.'

Of course she had. 'Is it true?'

'Finn has been through hell. But he does not drink alone. He may not talk to people when he drinks, like in the pub, but he'll only drink spirits when in the company of others.'

'Why?'

'His father drank alone and caused trouble, and Finn won't do that. Besides, you're in Finn's house. You're a nosy Fed, you would've noticed he's only got a few beers in the fridge, that's it.'

'But you just said you're here to check up on him, playing food fairy.'

'So Finn doesn't starve and keeps out of trouble.'

'I still don't get it. You're divorced, right?'

'Look, Finn may be my ex-husband, but I've known him for a very long time. He's still part of my family, and we trust each other.' She held eye contact with Taryn to make a point.

Then Bree glanced up at the empty drive through the window, as if waiting for someone. 'So which rumour do you want to know first?'

'That it was you who called Finn to Elsie Creek. You were accused of cattle rustling.'

'Correct.'

'And Finn stayed here for—'

'No. Not for me.' The redhead shook her head. 'That rumour is not true. But we're both here for the same reasons.'

Taryn didn't get it.

'Next question.'

But with her next question she hesitated. 'I don't know if I should…'

Bree waddled around the counter, hand on her lower back, the other on her baby bump. 'You're going to ask me if Finn went to prison because of our son?'

Taryn couldn't ask about that. Not when that same mother was about to give birth to another child.

'Fine, I'll answer it for you, chicken.' Bree even gave a smug grin that disappeared with her sigh. 'It's true. Four years ago, Finn and I lost our son, Liam.' Bree smiled softly down at her belly, but there was a touch of sadness dulling the shine in her eyes. 'And, yes, Finn was sentenced to two-and-a-half years for assault, and only served eighteen months before…'

'The pardon.' That Taryn had yet to ask about. 'Did Finn come straight back after his release?'

'No. He called me and told me he was free. And said if I ever needed him to call him.'

'Where did he go?'

'Finn needed a few months mustering in Queensland to clear his head and get as far away from anything brick for a while. He'd negotiated the break before starting the job, said he needed time to find his footing in the real world again. And yet, while out there mustering, he ends up catching these duffers, stealing a trailer load of prime stock. It re-triggered his old desire and got him motivated to start that road trip for research.'

Bree leaned her hip against the counter. 'You see, Finn has always wanted to be on a stock squad, back when he was a sixteen-year-old stockman who'd caught a string of cattle thieves. It's why Finn became a cop. It's the same for Amara, although her motivation is to do with horses. But they both have that inner drive for their dream job to do good. Do you know why you do what you do?'

Taryn used to, in a way that she'd feel it in her bones. Yet lately, it was only justice for Meghan that got her out of bed.

But then came the outback.

The heat and the endless red dust that stuck to her lashes and made her question every life choice by midday. The stake-outs with spectacular views of sunsets that were too gorgeous to be real. Chasing down road trains on dusty highways that didn't officially exist. Feeding a water buffalo on her morning walk to the office—like it was normal. Because here it was.

As for the office…

Honestly, she liked the Batcave and each one of its chaotic team members.

Stone, with his dry humour and smart mouth, made the

hours fly, literally. She never knew if he was flirting with the world or just rich-boy bored, but he was sharp, fun, and impossible to hate.

Then there was Cowboy Craig, with his old-school country charm, who made her think that maybe the cowboy cliché had some merit.

You then had Romy who saw everything through her camera, the way the dust danced on a sunbeam in the window like it was all part of a magical realm—reminding Taryn that perspective was a choice, all in the way you looked at things.

And Amara, the Tiny Titan, with all her rules and steel nerves to do right, was finally growing her wings. Taryn couldn't help but be a little proud to watch the constable develop every day.

Of course, she couldn't forget Tanisha. How she'd raise her cactus mug, complaining about another cake left on the large muster table, because the hospital staff were on diets again.

There were the casual conversations over coffee made by Porter, where even the OIC, Senior Sergeant Marcus Moore, made a show of quizzing her on some legalities and budgets for his own station.

And Finn…

Finn who grunted more than he spoke. The man who didn't trust easily, made mud for coffee, and preferred rolled maps than put faith in a GPS. The guy who'd checked under the hood of the old wagon, and put air in the tyres, before letting her drive it out of the police yard.

She was meant to shut Finn and the team down. All of it. Instead, she'd been standing shoulder to shoulder with him.

This place wasn't just changing how she worked. It was changing *how she felt* about the work. Suddenly, her job didn't look like justice anymore. It looked like paperwork that carried the expectation of ticking off KPIs. Following protocols designed by people who wouldn't even know that Elsie Creek existed, who weren't out for justice only results on a spreadsheet.

Bree watched with sharp green eyes and said softly, 'It gets in, doesn't it? The dust and the people who live here. But also the truth starts to reveal the story you didn't come looking for.'

Taryn didn't answer. Not when the ache in her chest said enough.

In the distance there was the unmistakable crunch of tyres on gravel coming down the drive.

It was the troopy.

'And here comes Mr Panic himself.' Bree rolled her eyes.

Finn's troopy skidded to a stop out front. The driver's door flung open before the engine had finished dying.

'*Bree!* What are you doing here?' Carrying a brown paper bag and a tray of takeaway coffees, Finn stormed inside like he expected to find a hostile hostage situation. His gaze snapped from the kitchen bench, to the Harley commanding space in the living room, then to Taryn standing beside Bree, like he was checking for damage. 'You're supposed to be resting.'

Bree rolled her eyes. 'I'm not a bonsai, Finn. I don't need constant misting.'

'You're overdue.'

'And so is your taste in music, but here we are.'

Finn turned to Taryn, wearing an expression that was caught between resignation and horror. 'You let her carry boxes?!'

'I was asleep. And she threatened to burn something and blame it on hormones.'

'That's true,' Bree said. 'You gonna offer me a chair, or do you want my water to break on your floor?'

'Here...' Finn shoved the coffees and food at Taryn to escort Bree to a chair. 'Sit. I can scrounge up a pillow. Water? Food?'

'Just show me that photo you couldn't send before the cavalry arrives.'

'Fine...' He scrolled open the phone and handed it to Bree.

Taryn had to peek over their shoulders. 'What is it?'

'I'll explain later.' Finn dismissed her, while hovering over Bree as if she was made of fragile crystal.

Bree zoomed in on the image on the phone's screen.

It was a picture of a young man in a stockman's hat, with the dust baked so deep into his tanned skin, it might've been holding him together. Nicotine-yellowed fingers curled around a smouldering, hand-rolled cigarette. Eyes a pale blue, almost grey, but full of that quiet, unsettling bush wisdom.

She could just hear David Attenborough narrating this himself: *Here we have the lesser-spotted Territory ringer—dust-covered, and unbothered. Watch closely as he blends seamlessly into the scrub, communicating only through nods, cattle movement, and the occasional grunt.*

He'd stand out in the city like a goat at a board meeting. But out here? He is camouflaged perfection.

'That's Bob.' Bree nodded at the phone's screen. 'Or as some like to call him, Two-bob Bob.'

Taryn frowned. Two-Bob Bob. Just like that truck driver Tooley had mentioned. 'Is that name for real?'

Bree gave a dry huff. 'It's his nickname, *buttons*.'

Taryn rolled her eyes while Finn shot her a questioning glance.

'His real name is Samuel Ward,' continued Bree. 'He's Seery's cousin, if I remember correctly.'

'As in Sawyer Dixby?' Finn asked.

Taryn had read the name. He'd been the missing overseer of Dixby Downs on the Wild Stock case.

Bree nodded. 'Bob was lead ringer, running muster crews out near Tinderflats Station. Quiet as a shadow, he is. Always looking like he'd just rolled out of the scrub. But don't let the looks fool you, he's good, too. Bob knows cattle like most men know their footy stats. I've seen him read a mob and tell you which heifer would throw a good calf, and which one would cause havoc going up the rails.'

'What else do you know about him?' Finn dragged a pillow from his swag and tucked it behind Bree's back.

She eased into the chair with a wince, one hand on her

baby bump. 'By rights, Bob should've made head stockman out at Tinderflats.'

Finn dragged over another chair, and lifted Bree's feet to rest. Then passed her a glass of water without her even asking.

And not once did Bree complain.

'Bit young to be a top hand, isn't he?' Taryn asked Bree.

'Believe me, Bob's got the skills. And it was promised to him.'

'Why?'

'Well, the owner of Tinderflats—the Colonel, who never served a day in the military in his life—liked to run Tinderflats like it was a battalion until he semi-retired.'

'And Bob was to get the job?' Finn asked Bree.

'That was until the Colonel's son came home, fresh from another failed business venture in Darwin. As a kid, the guy has zero stock sense and a chip on his shoulder the size of a rusty water tank. But word is, the Colonel gave him the job, hoping being head stockman would straighten him out. But now they've got long-time stockmen looking for work elsewhere, leaving Tinderflats to hustle for contractors.'

Stockmen that angry, overlooked, and ready to walk—it was the perfect conditions. Especially if the Colonel had handed the reins to someone unfit, because then Tinderflats Station wouldn't even know if their stock was missing.

'Do you know the name of the contractors?' Finn asked with that deep rumble.

'No. Why would I?'

And then it clicked. Bob, or Two-bob Bob, was Samuel Ward. SW. The initials on the dockets for stolen stock. SW Rural Contracting. Her fingers itched to do a search on her laptop.

Before Finn or Taryn could ask another question, an engine roared down the track.

A black, beastly ute, the top-of-the-range kind, slid to a halt with dust curling in waves behind it.

'And that,' Bree muttered with a sigh, as she dropped her

feet from the chair, 'would be the cavalry.'

Finn helped Bree to her feet. 'Did you tell him you were coming?'

Bree grinned.

'Great. So now I've got to deal with Ryder Riggs.'

Taryn was unsure whether to back up Finn or watch like a spectator with popcorn and beer. Luckily, her coffee was closer.

Bree's husband climbed out of his black ute, his boots hitting the dirt like the man was spoiling for a fight. Broad shoulders, thick arms, and a trimmed black beard that made him look like someone who'd chew through fence posts for breakfast. But all together, *wow!*

'BREE!'

'Are you going to be safe?' Taryn muttered to Finn.

Finn gave an eye roll that said *as if.*

A younger version—probably a brother, with the same good-looking genes—jumped out of the passenger side of Ryder's ute, looking equally concerned as he followed Ryder inside.

'There you are.' Bree sipped her water like she hadn't just staged a domestic escape. 'Took you long enough.'

'You ran away,' grumbled Ryder, his voice deep.

'I drove off. The Kombi can only go so fast. It's not exactly a tactical vehicle that's gonna break some land-speed record now, is it?'

The towering man of brawn and beard stalked past Taryn, to wrap his arms gently around Bree, while checking her over like a mechanic inspecting a beloved engine.

'You okay, babe?'

'Fine. I was just having a lovely banter session with Taryn here.' Bree angled her water glass toward her. 'Taryn, this is Ryder Riggs. And his brother, Ash.'

Taryn gave them a small nod. 'So you're the cavalry?'

'More like containment team,' Ash muttered under his breath with a grin.

Ryder didn't smile. He just grunted and assessed Taryn the way a bull might assess a new muster dog in the yard — curious, cautious, and not quite convinced she wasn't going to nip.

'What, no nicknames?' Taryn asked Bree.

'Cupcake and snowflake,' Bree said sweetly.

Taryn giggled, as Bree bumped shoulders with her like they'd known each other for a decade. While the men grunted in stereo and made for the counter, grabbing fruit and opening jars like Vikings raiding a settlement.

Taryn watched them for a moment, spotting the similarities between Ryder and Finn. She then leaned toward Bree and said quietly, 'You've got a type.'

Bree smirked. 'What can I say? I like my men big and emotionally repressed.'

Ryder swiped the Kombi keys off the kitchen bench and tossed them to Ash. 'Stash this somewhere she can't find it.'

'Oi, you can't hide my Kombi like it's an Easter egg,' complained Bree. 'It glows in the dark, you know.'

'That thing has no airbags and a god complex,' Ryder said, while gently steering his wife past the Harley in the lounge room, and towards the front door. 'But while we're in town, we'll visit the hospital and have the midwife check you out.'

'They got their dates wrong, not me.' Bree didn't fight him. Just grumbled about alpha males and public transportation as both Ryder and Finn helped her into Ryder's passenger seat with more care than a sacred artefact.

Bree leaned out the passenger window and waved at Taryn with a grin. 'Fun morning, buttons. Let's do it again the next time I decide to make a prison break and play food fairy.'

'Looking forward to it.'

'Oh, FYI, Finn does a mean barbecue. Don't let him fool you into thinking he's not domesticated.'

Finn groaned. Ryder sighed. Ash meanwhile looked like

he was considering an upgrade in his life insurance policy as he climbed into the Kombi.

As the black ute rumbled down the drive, with the *put-put-put* from the older, shockingly bright yellow van following, Taryn took a long breath as if a storm had passed.

Finn turned towards her, seriousness rolling off him like heat. 'We need to talk.'

And just like that, the storm rolled back in.

Twenty-six

The kitchen still smelled like mangoes and rockmelon, with his fridge overfull with more veggies than any man could eat on his own. 'Well, so much for bringing breakfast…'

Bree was gone. Ryder and Ash, too. But Taryn was still here, sitting at the table, sipping coffee from one of his cracked mugs while scrolling through her phone, like she'd always belonged in this house.

That unsettled him more than working out who SW was, and all the other intel Bree had delivered.

On his phone, he tapped a message out in the group chat Amara had set up:

> Quarry caretaker and SW suspect identified:
> Bob. Two-bob Bob. Real name—Samuel
> Ward. Sawyer Dixby's cousin.
> Amara—run background checks on Bob.
> Find a link to SW Rural Contracting. And the
> quarry's owners.
> Romy—pull images of the ute tyres from the
> quarry and Red's ute, too. Send to Craig and
> Porter to check if they match the mystery
> tracks from Seery's crime scene. The ones
> near his buried quad and body. Also, grab
> shots of cattle brands for the team to
> identify.
> Craig and Stone—head to Tinderflats with a
> photo of Bob. Confirm he's been working out
> there under SW Contracting and dig up

Sawyer *Seery* Dixby didn't just drive into that bulldust pit by accident. He knew that land too well. The coroner ruled it a fluke that the tyre on that quad blew out, causing Seery to lose control, getting pinned beneath the bike, and drown in that bulldust pit.

But it never sat right with Finn and the rest of his crew. Not with the mystery tyre tracks that ran straight across the path of Seery's quad. If he'd been panicking, looking over his shoulder, desperate to get away from Porter and Craig, who were racing after him in the Hellhound, he'd be looking for an exit.

If Seery saw a ute waiting, he would've gunned it in hope of a rescue. But instead, someone let him die. Maybe Red.

But Seery's ute was registered to SW Contracting—that had to be Bob's business. The same Bob who was running stolen stock out of the quarry, must've been running stolen stock off Dixby Downs Station—while his cousin, Seery, was busy digging holes to find the deeds to the place.

It was too much of a coincidence to ignore.

And in this game, every little breadcrumb mattered.

Finn stared at his phone as his team gave quick replies. That left him home alone with the Fed.

'You handled Bree.' Who really didn't like being handled by anyone. Ryder Riggs had his hands full, that's for sure.

Taryn didn't look up from her seat at the table, scrolling over her phone. 'She's one of a kind.'

'Yeah...' He didn't smile. Couldn't. Not yet. Because whatever this was between them still felt as dangerous as barbed wire. It had to be cut before it got twisted any tighter.

'Who sent you?' he asked.

She just looked up, calmly. 'My director sent me to audit the unit. That's the official version.'

'And the real one? Not the one about your cousin, I get that. But the speech your boss would've given you to sell this job.'

'Russ warned me it'd be a cowboy operation, while telling me about his fishing trips that involved crocodiles the size of sedans. Or was that a bathtub?' She shifted in her seat to face him. 'I came out here expecting a hillbilly mess. Instead, I found you, the team, and this town… All of it.'

He didn't move.

She then placed her phone down on the table. 'What's going on?'

'Last night, I set up surveillance in the quarry. Cameras. Drone feeds. Vehicle tags. With no warrants.'

'What sort of cameras?'

'Romy's specialised field cameras that she uses for her documentaries. That's where Bob's photo came from.' The real SW signing off on the paperwork the entire time.

Finn was pretty sure he'd walked past Bob dozens of times in the pub, and at the stockyards, looking like any other ringer. Hiding in plain sight.

'I'm telling you this because if this case blows up, I don't want you blind or burned because of me.'

'Are you saying you trust me?'

He hesitated. Had to. 'I want to trust you. But if you're still here to tear this squad down — and if you're just playing me — then say it now. Don't smile in my kitchen and stab the squad in the back later.'

She answered with nothing but silence and that steady stare.

'So, ask me anything,' he said. 'Question me over what you've set out in that spare room, and I'll tell you whatever you want, as I'm trying to trust you. I'll give you the file on your cousin, no strings attached. But here's the thing…' He shuffled his boots, crossing his arms tight over his chest. 'Last night, Red announced to Bob that they're stopping for a month because of you.'

She didn't even raise her eyebrows at that.

'They know you're here to stop me and my team. And they're waiting for you to shut us down.' He huffed with annoyance. 'Were they wrong?'

Taryn didn't blink or fidget, she just stood. 'The whole town knew I was coming, and they weren't wrong about my assignment. I came here to evaluate this team and give my honest report. And if the numbers didn't stack up? Your squad was on the chopping block, as it was only on a trial.'

Finn's jaw clenched.

She stepped closer. 'But I came here seeking justice for my cousin, and for the part of me that still believes this job means something... But what I found wasn't a mess. Even if the rules don't always apply the way they should, the job was getting done.'

'And you?' she added, with her eyes narrowing a little. 'You're not broken. Or some rogue cop. You're...' She breathed in heavily.

While he held his own, waiting for her judgement.

'You weren't the threat they warned me about, Finn. Instead, I found proof that someone like you could make this team matter, while also showing how it'd make a big difference to this region. I'll admit they didn't send me to help you, but to confirm their excuses for shutting you down.'

He dropped his head, with his shoulders suddenly weary. 'You weren't part of it?'

'No. My boss, Russ, told me to be fair, and he's a good guy. As to who put in the initial request for someone to come out here? I don't know. But I'll admit I was biased, thinking you'd let Everlight get away with murdering my cousin because of your incompetency.'

Finn scowled hard at that.

'I know now that you didn't,' she said, her hands raised as if to calm him down.

Surprisingly, it did.

'But after what you've told me, I believe I'm just a pawn in their game. Do you agree?'

He nodded. Just once. 'Last night, Red said he's shutting down for a month, hoping you'll send us packing. He's not cleaning up, he's just covering until your report is completed. That means we're close.' Closer than they'd ever been.

But they had to do this right and not go in guns blazing.

Even though they had enough to make arrests, Finn wanted everyone. He wanted to shut them down properly and not let them pop up somewhere else like they'd done, moving from Dixby Downs to the quarry, demonstrating how fluid their operation was. Who knows how many backup places they had in the outback—the place where secrets went to die.

He headed for the spare bedroom to face the wall of red string filled with file notes, places, dates, and names that she'd spent all night pulling into order. 'Now that you've gutted my Gaps File, do you think we can connect anything back to SW Rural Contracting, or the quarry, for leverage?' He pulled out the folder from the hallway cupboard, the one she'd been waiting for, and dropped it on her laptop. It was hers now.

Taryn moved beside him and stared down at the file. Surprisingly, she didn't touch it. 'You know I'm going to ask this, so I'll just say it—*Why?*'

'We need to find out who's bankrolling their operation. Someone has to have the funds for land, like the quarry, the utes, trailers, fuel and fencing. I've always thought that money came from Everlight's grants.'

'Really? How?'

'Izzy's research of Everlight showed me the pattern they had for buying those particular blocks of land—'

'Across the nation.' She shrugged. 'Go on.'

'They were all in prime livestock corridors,' he said. 'Our first case, the Rough Stock case, was on Everlight's property. It wasn't set up for a solar farm, but it had all the signs of being a way station for livestock.'

'Are you saying that Everlight was going to set up other way stations, like they did at Dixby Downs?'

Even though he could feel it, he just couldn't prove it, and with her skills and almost unlimited access to information, maybe—just maybe—Taryn could help him find those missing links.

'I know Red is the local source who finds the stock worth taking. SW—Bob—is the one who manages the cattle drafts and trucks like a muster crew. And now I have two extra names to add to that list.' He picked up a marker from the stationery box and wrote over the peeling wallpaper, the names: *Clancy* and the *Pilot.* Then in bold letters he wrote *the Top Dog* drawing a line back to *Everlight Energy Solutions.*

Taryn was quiet for a moment staring at him and not at the board. 'You're different when you're in the game.'

'Focused?'

'No, hopeful.'

He froze for half a second. Because hope was dangerous.

'Did you carry me to bed?'

'What?'

'Last night. I fell asleep under the wall. Did you carry me?'

His jaw ticked. 'You were half dead on your feet—'

'So that's a yes.'

'It was nothing.'

'Sure.' She walked towards him. 'Because you're real good at nothing, aren't you?'

She was so close he could see the flecks of blue in her eyes and the tiny scar on her lip that only showed when she smirked like that. 'What do you want from me, Finn?'

He didn't know how to answer that. Not without saying too much.

She stepped even closer. 'I've got questions about what's on that board. And about SW Rural Contracting, and where all of this leads. But right now?' she said, tilting her head in a way that did something to his self-control. 'I'm wondering if you kissed me last night when you put me to bed? Or if I dreamt it.'

Finn's breath caught.

He hadn't.

But he'd wanted to more than he'd even admit to himself. But she'd been asleep—and that was a line he'd never cross.

But now he was thinking about nothing else.

'No,' he said, with a rough voice. 'I didn't want it to be

something you missed. Or something I stole.'

Taryn's eyes softened, while the tension hummed between them like a live wire, as her fingers lightly brushed the side of his hand, to send a light spark scurrying across his skin.

'So, kiss me now,' she said. 'While I'm awake. While it's mine to remember.'

Finn didn't move as his pulse thundered. 'Taryn—'

'Don't think, Finn. Just do it, before we both say something dumb and start fighting again.'

He reached for her, one hand cradling the side of her face, his thumb brushing her cheekbone, the other hand sliding to her lower back like he'd known her body shape his entire life.

She leaned in at the same time, and their lips met.

The kiss wasn't hesitant. It wasn't shy, either. It was everything they'd been holding back, that was finally allowed to break free.

And when they pulled apart—just barely, for air—she didn't step back.

Neither did he.

They stayed there, foreheads brushing, breath mingling, long enough for him to know this wasn't a mistake or a distraction. This was like a beginning.

And for once in his life, he wasn't waiting for the fallout.

He was going to let himself *fall*.

Twenty-seven

His kiss had been filled with fire and patience that was as sexy a contradiction as the man himself. And now Finn looked at her like he didn't want to stop. Like he was trying to find some internal brake pedal and couldn't remember where it was.

The thing was, Taryn didn't want him to stop.

She stepped back, barely, just enough to grab his shirt at the hem and tug on it.

That did it.

Finn didn't lunge—he *claimed* her. One hand at her jaw, the other gripping her hip, as his lips met hers and he was walking her backwards out of the spare room with a steady, determined pace. She'd assumed the bedroom, but he went the other way, where every step back down the corridor was accompanied by a look as if he was asking permission.

But when she gave it—he took it like a man starved.

Her back hit the edge of the kitchen counter with a gasp, the cool timber grounding her as his mouth traced a path down her throat, his rough stubble scraping against her skin.

'Still with me?' he asked, his gravelly voice filled with want.

'Barely.'

He grinned against her collarbone. Then kissed lower.

Buttons popped. Not with finesse, but with *intent*. Peeling her open like a secret he'd waited too long to read.

His hands were big and warm, trailing heat across her ribs, around her waist, and up under her bra until her breath stuttered.

Taryn yanked up his shirt, pausing until his arms lifted,

then sent his black T-shirt to hit the floor.

He wasn't just fit. He was sculpted. Like his body had been forged in hard days and harder nights, where the ink told the story of his survival scars.

She ran her hands over him slowly, reverently, watching his eyes go dark.

'Taryn,' he warned.

'Hmm?'

'You keep touching me like that, and I won't stop.'

'Good.'

The kiss that followed was messier. Needier. All tongue and teeth, between moans she didn't recognise as her own.

Her jeans were gone before she noticed. One powerful arm lifted her, and slid her onto the bench, as fruit and vegetables were shoved aside with a grunt that rumbled through his chest and into hers.

'Comfortable?' he asked with a rough voice as he dropped to his knees.

She blinked. 'What—'

'Told you,' he murmured, with hands sliding up her thighs, spreading her slowly. 'No shortcuts. I want you to remember this. Every damn second.'

And then he showed her what he meant.

His mouth was relentless. His hands unforgiving. Making her forget what time was, when it felt like seconds now played into long hours as she came undone on his tongue, with her breath catching on his name like it was a prayer she'd never dared say until now.

When he stood again, her fingers fumbled at his belt, but he caught her wrists gently.

'You sure?'

She kissed him with heat and passion. Forgetting... Rules? What rules.

He thrust into her in one slow, devastating stroke, and her whole body arched—back, neck, and soul as she wrapped her arms around him, while internally stretching to accept him.

And it was so much better than good.

His hands gripped her arse, forcing her to hold his shoulders, and with her legs around his waist he started to move. Oh, lord, he was a devil doing devilish things to her. And how each thrust was a statement and each kiss a vow to eternal damnation of sizzling sin and fire.

His fingers firmly pressed against her bud as the tip of his dick stroked against that spot inside her, quickly leading her to implode.

But Finn didn't let up.

His hips didn't stop.

And his fingers kept rolling.

Sending jolts of pleasure through her, making her eyes water at the intensity of this moment. She barely had time to react—but felt *everything*.

His arm banded around her back, the giant body before her, while inside he flexed and thickened, that she could only marvel at how full he'd made her feel.

'You feel it too, don't you?' His deep ragged voice was against her ear with his hard length lined up in such a perfect way, where each stroke was unbuttoning her from the inside. 'This… the way you look while I'm with you right now,' he said on a pant, 'is purely criminal.'

Hot, horny, and smouldering was this man with his hard lines and impossibly broad shoulders, with biceps she'd love to sink her teeth into. And how he towered over her. Pure male, growly, bossy and broody, built with raw muscle and ink. Shifting his hips, his hands and his mouth pleasing her, giving her an image she'd never be able to scrub from her mind. And didn't want to. Ever.

'You're so soft,' he murmured against her skin. 'So damn soft. And warm.' He cupped her head and kissed her gently this time, all while trying to coax her back from one edge right through to another. Trying to tell her things through his touch that he would never say out loud, where lips moved slow and sensuous as their bodies found that perfect rhythm.

His muscular chest rose and fell, as his fingers moved of their own accord, exploring her folds while watching her fall apart around him. He was the master, making her body buck as he pressed, teased and taunted right at that one delicate spot, and she was nothing more than his puppet.

Instantly, her head fell back as the breath rushed out of her lungs. 'Yes,' she gasped. 'God, *yesss*...' The sensations collided as he overwhelmed her with his rhythm that only made her nerves sing.

His hands gripped her calves dragging her closer, then slid to her hips. There, he pulled her down deeper, eliciting a gasp as he moved with a level of assured madness, until there was nothing left between them but sweat, skin, and the sounds of two people finally—*finally*—giving in to each other.

Every part of her clenched. Her legs. Her body. Her hands in his hair, pulling him into her as the vibrations racked her body. His fingers lapped at her, effectively drawing out another orgasm so insanely, impossibly long that she could only look at him in awe as she exploded internally, while her cries echoed in the kitchen.

Bringing his lips down to her ear, he growled, 'You're going to do that again.'

Not like she had any choice.

His massive muscular frame owned this room and was doing a damned fine job of owning her, too.

One palm glided slowly up the inside of her leg, causing ripples to scurry through her body, which was already trembling with anticipation. His mouth crashed on hers, and she struggled to breathe but surrendered so willingly.

His strong arms lifted her to the edge where his movements became more authoritative, but his touch gentle.

And all she could do was shiver as she watched him take her.

Every roll and flex of his hips spoke of barely contained control. The emptiness when he drew back, the suffocating fullness when he re-entered her. That tip teasing her like a trigger from the inside. How his hands framed her face as their tongues tangled, and moans rolled. Losing herself with a want for his full body weight to pin her down, and to have him crave her the same way she needed him.

'I like you watching me take you.' His eyes, his fingers, and how he pumped into her were as if he was branding her, while overwhelming her with his unbridled masculinity. He wasn't smooth and shiny, he was rough, yet tender. His kind of beauty came with pain, and yet here he was busily pleasuring her.

His eyes were wild, and his jaw locked as his fingers dug their way into her hips, gripping harder. He buried himself in her and just like that—she came again, so unexpectedly she clenched around him with a cry she didn't muffle.

Full and moaning, she clawed at his hot inked skin to hold him closer as his thick length glided purposefully in and out of her, with his chest heaving.

But then his eyes rolled back, and he plunged deeper with swift, punishing thrusts. Growling in her ear, his body tensed as he slammed himself deep and released a guttural moan that rumbled from the depths of his chest.

It was the sexiest thing she'd ever heard.

He moved slowly to completely empty himself and then held her.

They panted, with their hearts pounding, trying to get some precious air into their lungs, while covered in perspiration.

She rested her forehead on his, still perched on that bench, her body buzzing and her heart… It wasn't just fluttering.

It was flying.

'So,' she whispered, breathless, 'no bed, huh?'

His gaze dragged over her body, then back up to share a mischievous smile she'd never seen before. Even his voice was lazy and deliciously wrecked. 'Didn't want you thinking this was anything ordinary.'

Her eyes drifted across his inked body to meet his dark hungry eyes. 'Nothing about you is ordinary.'

Twenty-eight

The front of Finn's house was nothing but a simple door and broken bike parts for decor.

But out the back?

Well, it was a whole new world…

There was a stone-edged firepit where the fire crackled low, with coals glowing red and gold like embers stolen from the sky. A well-used barbecue plate was rigged for the specially spiced meats Finn had thrown over the flames, sending out a scent that could summon gods, devils, and every hungry soul in between.

Bree had told Taryn that the man did a mean barbecue, but she'd never imagined how. Starting with the way Finn prepared the meat with his own secret blend of spices, then worked over the coals like it was a religion, to cook with dedication and style. It was the most masculine way for a man to cook.

She sipped her beer slowly, watching Finn move with his usual grace, tongs in hand, shirtless, with jeans low on his hips, allowing the ink and shadows to dance across his body with each flicker of the flames.

Behind him stretched an outback view that would take decades to dissect, where open plains stretched to meet rolling silhouettes of hills that got lost on the darkened horizon.

And above?

The stars didn't twinkle here. They burned like they had a secret to share, and a world to watch over.

She now understood what Izzy meant about needing time to stare at the stars, and out here, they were better than any movie.

'A few more minutes and we're good to go.' Finn nodded at the meat resting on the edge of the grill.

'Take your time. No one's rushing this.' Not with that view.

But he'd taken the meal to the next level. Barbecuing thick slices of pineapple and mango alongside skewers of colour and flavour: red onion, zucchini, cherry tomatoes, button mushrooms, corncobs, and bright red capsicum, brushed over with a buttery herby glaze. All courtesy of the food fairy. Altogether, it was like nature's candy on a stick.

'Oh, wow,' she said, licking her fingers. 'This is criminally good.'

'I'll take that as a compliment.'

They settled beside each other on the fallen logs near the fire, with knees bumping and eyes trained on the flames, to eat in comfortable silence.

With the meal over, she said what had been bothering her the most. 'I need to go back to the pub tonight.'

'Are you heading out early?'

'Not for a few more days. But I've got things there. Clothes … my pill.'

That made him look.

'I didn't exactly pack for an overnight stake-out followed by a… well, *you*.'

His lip twitched into that smouldering smirk.

'You are both a god and the devil of pleasure in bed, Finn Wilde. And I say that with the full exhaustion of a woman who forgot her contraceptive schedule because you fried my brain.'

'Didn't realise I had that much power.' But he unleashed a smile that made her heart skip.

'Take the ego boost while you can, cowboy.'

'I'm no cowboy.'

'And I'm still going back for the pill.'

Finn didn't argue, and he didn't offer to take her either. Which somehow made it worse.

She blurted out the next part, the adulting part of grown-up sex. 'We never talked about protection.'

'We didn't talk much at all. We didn't even finish sentences…'

There was another grin, this one they shared.

'But I'm clean. Last test was post-Queensland. Haven't been with anyone since.'

'Okay. Thanks for telling me. And me too…' Not that she going to admit it had been way too long—which might have explained her lack of sanity to rush the guy.

'You scared?'

'A little.' She barely nodded.

'Yeah. Me too.'

There was another stretch of silence, accompanied by the crackle of the campfire.

'Can I ask you something else?' she said, keeping her eyes on the coals.

He gave the smallest nod.

'How did you get the pardon from Commissioner Andrew Bannon?'

He turned his head slightly as if to study her.

'Feels like we're past secrets now,' she added. 'And that's the only official question I haven't asked. What is your connection to—'

'Drew?' Finn rubbed the back of his neck, as if fighting the tension creeping into his shoulders.

He stared at the fire for a few moments, then finally said, 'Were you ever in a police station at ten years old?'

'No. Military bases and embassies, sure.'

'Well, I was. So was Bree. It's how we all met.' His voice softened at her name. 'Bree's father had just killed her mother in their kitchen. And they were trying to work out where to send her. Me? My mum had just been raped, and the detectives were making her go through the mugshots. Only my old man was telling her to come home and pretend it never happened.'

Taryn's breath caught. She didn't move.

'I didn't remember him back when I was ten. I remember being there, sitting beside Bree who was just as shell-shocked and scared as I was, two kids not fully understanding what was going on at that age. But he remembered me. Drew.'

'The Commissioner?'

Finn nodded. 'Back then, Drew was fresh out of the police academy. First day on the job, with no clue what to do. So, he offered Bree and me both a soda and some chocolate while the grown-ups argued about their bad life decisions.'

He pulled long and hard on his beer as if swallowing his emotions. 'After that night, Mum forever lived in a valium stupor, even during the pregnancy. And Dad cradled his whisky, watching the weather from the front porch, flicking his cigarette butts in my direction.'

'Pregnancy?' *Oh no.* And the cigarette butts—what? She glanced over his heavily inked arms and hands.

'I had a baby sister,' Finn whispered, drawing her attention to his eyes, and the pain that made them darken.

He looked away. 'Took her years to get her tongue around Miri and called herself *Mi-wii*. Even longer to try Miriam—that always came out like Mi*w*iam.' A rough laugh escaped him. 'Damn cute kid she was, too.' He scraped a hand down his face. 'They say she killed herself, targeted by bullies for being different.'

Her gasp was quiet, but she felt his pain.

'My old man had refused to get her diagnosed, to see if they could help her, because he didn't think she was his kid. And Mum didn't want to admit she had an addiction that had affected Miri during the pregnancy. And maybe Miri, that poor kid, never stopped wondering if Dad was right, that she was the product of...'

Taryn gripped his hand, stunned by the blunt and yet brutal revelations. But the way he stared at the fire, he wasn't done.

'Three years after I first met Drew, there he was again. Same man. Same soda. I was thirteen, shirt torn, nose bloodied, and officially expelled from school. Bree sat beside me, not a scratch on her—except for the red handprint across her cheek.'

'What happened?'

'Some rich kid cracked a joke about my mum. By then, I understood what had happened to her. So did Bree. So she fired back a cracker about *his* mum and the pool guy. Turned out it was true, and he wasn't happy about it, so he hit her. And that's when I lost it.' He exhaled heavily with heat. 'I laid that prick out flat in the dorm hallway, where he curled in a ball screaming for his mummy.'

She now understood why Bree and Finn were tight. 'What happened?'

'Bree got suspended. I got expelled. But the prick who'd started it, his parents wanted to press charges. And that's when Drew showed up... Even back then, he was a smooth-talking politician-in-training, who talked them down, promising to get the two troublemakers out of town.' Finn even grinned for a fleeting second.

'Back then, Drew wasn't some fed, he was just a Queensland city cop who'd upset someone and got sent bush. But he had pull in the right places. Made a few calls. And got us into another school.'

'Your parents? Bree's—'

'We were bush kids. Back then, unless you had School of the Air and a generator that worked, you got shipped off interstate to boarding school.'

'Right.' That made sense.

'So while Bree and I waited for the bus to take us to our new school, there was Drew in his shiny police uniform, babysitting us. His pen tapping against a word puzzle book— one of those grids where you find words hidden in little squares, like he was trying to crack a case. But that day he put us on the bus, I remember him saying to me, *One day, when the world stops chewing you up, come find me.*'

Taryn's chest felt tight, the ache building behind her ribs. 'You did.'

'At sixteen. I'd stumbled onto a bunch of blokes stealing

cattle out in the sticks during a muster. They tried to cut me in, but I liked the boss and his family—and they stole that man's stock. So I dragged them to the local cop shop myself, in the cattle truck full of stolen beef. And there was Drew. His printer had jammed, and he was swearing at everything that wasn't nailed down, with another one of those half-finished word puzzle books on his desk.' Finn smiled faintly. 'Didn't need to remind him who I was. He hadn't forgotten the kid from his first day on the job. And from that moment on, he was on my back, telling me when I came of age and got sick of playing stockman, I should apply to the academy. So I did. Drew wrote the recommendation himself. Nicest thing anyone ever said about me—on paper, anyway.'

The fire crackled, popped and sparked to the stars, Taryn silently listened as he paused, cradling that beer stubby in two hands.

'But he did more than that… Drew not only backed my application, he also turned up to my graduation and stood right next to Bree, who I'd married by then. Told me I could be more than a statistic and was worth something. Which meant a lot back then.' He drank deep, as if needing that breather for the next part.

'Years later, when I was recruited for that undercover job, Drew warned me. Said the OIC had a bad rep, and being out-of-state, I wouldn't have the same backup. Drew told me he couldn't help if things went sideways. But I took the job anyway.'

'That was a big bust.'

'And that OIC still screwed me over. He blocked everything—including any messages—to make sure that bust stayed on track. My phone was full of messages from Bree, my old work partners, even Drew… and my *son*—that last message from my son…' He dropped his head as if weighed down by the burden.

Taryn's blinked as she sat taller. 'You missed the message?' She glanced up at him, eyes widening. 'You missed it, like I did from Meghan, before she was murdered.'

He met her eyes, and something unspoken passed between them. 'Yeah. I know…'

'That's why you gave me the file.' She remembered that moment in the car and how he'd looked at her like he understood her.

Only he had. Deeper than anyone had before.

Even now, Finn looked at her with that same steady gaze that read everything about her like lines on a page.

'You had that look, the one people wear when they're living with a ghost,' he said.

He was right.

Finn shifted, his gaze dropping to stare at the ground beneath his boots. 'It was Drew who got me the pardon,' he murmured. 'Said I'd earned a second chance to build something good. He'd remembered me as that sixteen-year-old, wanting to join the police just to be on the Stock Squad. So I built this squad. For him. For Bree. For what we all lost. But also for everyone in this region, and all those involved within the industry.'

With her heart full, and eyes stinging, Taryn tried not to let the weight of it pull her under.

She suddenly understood why he fought so hard. Why he couldn't stop. And why he owed Drew everything.

Lost in their thoughts for a while, she finally found her voice to say what she didn't want to say at all, 'I'm leaving in three days.'

'I know.'

'And I'm not asking you to say anything you don't mean. We both know what this is.'

Finn looked at her like he wanted to argue.

But didn't.

'You don't do goodbyes, right?' she asked.

'Not well. No.'

'Then let's not say it, because I'm used to leaving.' That's what happens when you're a military brat. You've already got one foot out the door, never getting close to anyone.

He didn't move for a moment. Just stared into the fire like

he was weighing up the pros and cons. 'So… we've got three days?'

Taryn lifted a brow. 'Are you calculating the hours now?'

'Not yet. But I figure we can use them.'

'How? Spend my time on surveillance and smuggler spreadsheets?'

'Worked last time.' He slid his arm over her shoulders, bringing her close to his side. 'And I think you should finish what you've started, with me… After all, Fed, you made the trek all the way out here for answers.'

'Finn, no one can know about us. Because if they did, it'd be seen as a conflict of interest. Everyone and everything would be compromised.'

'I know,' he murmured with heaviness in his deep voice.

She stood slowly, brushing off her jeans. The firelight painted him in red and gold and shadow—this man who wore silence like armour, looked at her like she'd slipped through its cracks.

He rose with her. Close now.

So close.

'Taryn.'

She turned into him like gravity wasn't a choice.

'But we'll know, and I'll never forget.' He kissed her slowly—and for once, it wasn't about heat or hunger. It was the preparation for a goodbye without saying it, even if part of her wanted to believe this could hold.

She knew how time, distance, and reality could strip even the best moments bare. That the second she stepped back into her office, it would all fade like a half-remembered dream. Where Finn might become nothing more than a name she whispered in the dark when the city got too loud. And already knew she would never forget him.

Twenty-nine

One month later—Canberra

The smell of bacon was the first betrayal.

Taryn had barely gotten the pan sizzling before her stomach flipped like it was having a bar fight in a tin can—and then she was sprinting.

The bathroom tiles were freezing against her knees. Her hair stuck to her cheeks. And she hated every second of it, hugging that toilet bowl as the waves of nausea washed over her.

But she loved bacon. Loved it like a comfort blanket.

And this? This wasn't just a dodgy flu brewing.

This was different.

It took her all day to build the courage to dare get an answer. Finding a chemist well away from work, so she wouldn't risk bumping into anyone she knew.

She had meant to take the damn thing home. But now, as she sat back, flushing the taste of bile, she glared at the test sitting on the edge of the sink.

Even if her body felt off in that subtle, traitorous way that she ignored until it screamed enough for her to stop dancing with denial. Blaming it on jet lag from her quick trips to Melbourne and Adelaide to catch up on her other cases. Work stress. Weather changes. Too much chilli with her tacos.

But now?

Now, the test stared back with clear blue lines...

Pregnant.

This was one of those moments where you wished you'd stayed in bed. Pulled the covers over your head and waited for a different version of reality to load. One without complications, or kisses from a man who looked at you like you were worth staying for.

But that was a month ago.

She dropped her head back against the cabinet and groaned. 'You've gotta be kidding me.'

Her parents would have a joint aneurysm. Not because she was pregnant—but because she hadn't cleared it with them first.

Her mother would treat it like an intel leak and demand a mission briefing, to assess, contain, deploy. There'd be a tactical support unit on standby, matching onesies in every size by lunchtime, and a baby-proofing protocol drafted with an airlift plan ready to go.

Her father, meanwhile, would sit in silence, pretending not to be terrified, while quietly running background checks on every male in the Northern Territory, cross-referencing satellite footage, and ordering a discreet sweep of Finn's federal file.

And the worst part?

She loved them for it. Because beneath the code names and contingency plans, they'd always shown up—every time it counted.

Taryn hadn't exactly planned for motherhood. Not like this.

She'd always figured it'd be a choice she'd make one day, on her own terms, when the world felt safe enough, or if she ever felt soft enough to let her guard down.

Not to complain, but she did *not* want to relive the kind of childhood she grew up with briefings and protocols, and being babysat by lieutenants sucking up to her parents, teaching her gun drills. She wanted something slower. Warmer.

Like summers with Meghan. And that pantry full of canned peaches and the smell of eucalyptus trees and grass. A place where shadows slowly danced across the back porch from dawn to dusk, where the backyard firepit became the place to share secrets and marshmallows. That's what Taryn had tucked away in the corner of her mind.

If ever. Maybe. Someday.

Yet, it always came back to Meghan. Her cousin. Her reason for everything, and her focus on this job.

Taryn hadn't stepped foot in Elsie Creek for career advancement. She'd gone there for Meghan. For answers about a young woman who'd started asking the right questions and ended up dead for it.

And so far?

The investigation had only raised more questions.

Everlight's trail had gone cold, files had vanished, testimonies were redacted, its digital footprint swept clean. Officially, it was dead.

Unofficially?

She didn't buy it.

SW Rural Contracting had seemed like the thread to pull. Everyone thought it was Sawyer Dixby's company, and then Samuel Ward's. The paperwork even pointed that way. But when she dug deeper, it was owned by another shell company…

Temp Roicks Pty Ltd.

A rural contractor for fencing and mustering jobs. Legit enough on paper. But it also owned the same quarry where Two-bob Bob had been babysitting the airstrip and the so-called office.

Whoever was behind it wasn't just smart. They were buried under layers of companies, paper-thin identities, with just the right level of misdirection.

But she was close. Taryn could feel it. They were all connected to each other, fake companies, stacked like a ladder—each one owning the next. Every time she dug deeper, another company name surfaced:

Merc Topski

Spick Metro Ltd

Priscom Tek

Corp Stimek

M.T. Spiker Co
Spertick Nominees
E. Mockstrip & Co
Plus a dozen more.

And at the very top of the food chain sat *Stokemir PC Inc.* An offshore entity, posing as an international parent company. No records. No office, or even registered owners. Just a name in the finest of fine print that you'd miss if you blinked.

And she'd blinked a few times, missing it completely, until the other day.

Taryn was just waiting on confirmation about that offshore company to see where the next breadcrumb would lead her. Hoping for that same someone who'd helped bury Meghan.

After burying the pregnancy test deep in the waste bin, she forced herself back to her office, dropping behind her desk, and opening the folder on her desktop.

Her office smelled like paper and jasmine, thanks to the scented candle she never lit, but luckily it didn't make her heave.

How she missed being able to open a window, to not hear congested traffic and screaming sirens, or people talking about nothing in their all-important rush to and from work.

Hard to believe it had only been six weeks since she'd first landed at Elsie Creek Airport—which wasn't really an airport at all, just a sunbaked airstrip run by a grey-haired grump named Mickey.

For their last encounter, he'd given her a proper serve, grumbling about *bloody tourists* and how the town wasn't some sightseeing stopover, all while chucking her bag into the belly of the mail plane with a grunt.

As the propellers spun to life, Tanisha waved at her from the back fence of the police station, which Taryn had dared to cross to catch her plane. No way was she going to walk the long way around again.

As for the rest of the Stock Squad, they were on the job, especially Finn, keeping up the pretence that Taryn was still their enemy and wasn't seen near her in public. Even though she'd been staying at his house for days.

She'd expected the radio silence when she left. They'd agreed on it during those last three days spent side by side in Finn's house, sleeping together, trading theories, maps, and whispered truths. Anything more would've risked everything: her report, her position, and the covert work she was doing—not just for Finn, but for Meghan.

If one person let slip that she'd been sleeping with the supposed enemy, the stock smugglers would bury their trail before the ink on her report dried, and the integrity of her work would be void. Goodbye promotion.

When she'd reached her hotel room in Darwin, at the start of her trek back to Canberra, she'd found a burner phone in the lining of her bag, along with a note in Finn's handwriting that simply said *Only use in emergencies.*

She recognised it as standard operating procedure, especially in offices like hers, where informants couldn't afford to be traced. A trick her boss, and her father, had taught her. But she'd never needed a burner before. Not until Finn.

Even then, they didn't talk. They didn't call. But every few days, without fail, the screen would light up with a single message: *Still breathing?* All in the simple style of Finn.

And every time, it punched her square in the chest.

Only for her to stare at the screen like a teenager, agonising over a reply that was smart but casual, guarded but warm. Because under all the strategy, the silence, the cloak-and-dagger subterfuge, they were still them. And she missed him more with every message.

But now she might possibly, accidentally, phantomly—be pregnant.

What was she supposed to do?

Admit to herself that her boobs had turned into hypersensitive traitors, protesting against her bras that were suddenly a smaller cup size? That she might be growing a brooding Finn clone, while the real one was out there playing enemies-to-lovers in reverse?

Come on. She'd done her research on Dr Google's web of wisdom, spurred on by a double dose of late-night panic attacks, to conclude that she couldn't be knocked up. Not when she'd always been particular about her contraception. Every time. Only for her body to have the audacity to hit the fertile on-switch and turn her ovaries into supercharged babymakers. Just. Like. That?!

There's no way she was even close to being ready to think about how *he'd* react—not when she was still trying to convince herself the whole thing was a false alarm brought on by stress, bad lighting, and one too many cheese toasties. And that her suddenly developed aversion to bacon, which made her want to cuddle the toilet bowl, was perfectly normal.

Denial was a perfectly valid coping strategy.

And right now, it was the only thing keeping her focused on the job, especially when there were so many others counting on her.

Finn and his team were still fighting to keep their squad alive, chasing cattle thieves through the outback's dust. Her family was still grieving for Meghan and needed some justice that no one else seemed willing to give them. And the poor townsfolk of Elsie Creek, who depended on the integrity of those stockyards, didn't even know they were being played by someone they trusted.

Taryn's department was trusting her to be impartial, thorough, and professional—even if she was strictly hypothetically, absolutely denial-fuelled, completely unconfirmed, half in love with the man she'd been sent to audit.

Taryn didn't have the luxury of spiralling.

Not now.

Not when the whole damn house of cards was ready to fall.

So she squared her shoulders, tied her hair into a no-nonsense knot, and turned back to the files. Her personal crisis could wait, because she had work to do.

She scrolled through the draft report on her screen for the umpteenth time, only this time the numbers seemed sharper against her headache.

Performance metrics. Compliance charts. Live export impacts. And the model for the Northern Territory Federal Stock Squad that Finn had been trialling.

The one that shouldn't have worked.

Only—it had.

Brilliantly.

In just under twelve months, while based out of Elsie Creek Police Station, the Stock Squad's case load had recovered over $16.4 million in stolen livestock and rural assets.

If it were a business, the cost-to-recovery profit ratio would've sent shareholders into a frenzy.

Yet this wasn't a business. This was a federal department.

And that was just part of the bigger picture...

Especially when some bureaucrat—who'd never left their air-conditioned office—had decided the Northern Territory Police could reduce their entire Stock Squad to, literally, a generic email address on a website.

That's it.

No team. No boots on the ground. Just an inbox somewhere in Darwin, collecting dust.

Not that she blamed the cops out there. After having spent time inside the Elsie Creek police station, Taryn could see they were pulling off miracles on a shoestring budget. These officers weren't underperforming. They were badly under-resourced, while trying to do a job in a sprawling playing field, so unique to the Northern Territory, it was incomprehensible to anyone who didn't live and breathe it.

Before the Stock Squad had set up camp in the Batcave, over 92% of reported stock thefts went nowhere. They became cold cases, scattered across the outback like cow-shaped tumbleweeds.

Now? They were closing nearly 70% of those cases, most within weeks, not years.

Stock theft reports across the Territory had jumped—not because livestock theft was suddenly trending, but because, for the first time in years, graziers were actually reporting thefts, because they believed someone might do something about it.

It was the kind of turnaround that made other departments twitchy. And made career bureaucrats whisper words like unsustainable and disruptive, like the nerdy kid in the playground whining because someone else figured out how to win their game.

The Northern Territory Government had ignored the problem for so long, they'd stopped even pretending to care. Which, considering how much the cattle industry propped up the Territory's economy, was either criminally negligent or impressively stupid.

Possibly both.

But what she did know was that Finn cared. Deeply. And that care had shaped the squad's focus into a design that was working.

And here was the kicker…

Even if she'd disliked him—bashing against his bullish, grumpy ass from day one—and even if they'd never kissed, or had never spent those three long, unforgettable days buried in files with shared silence and sizzling sex, she still would've come to the same conclusion, because the data didn't lie.

The Stock Squad was working.

Taryn leaned back in her chair, with the hum from the office lights suddenly too sharp. Three days. That's all it had been. Working side by side, sleeping within arm's reach. No arguments, no tension. Just ease. Like it had always been that way.

She wasn't ready to admit what that meant.

But her chest ached, like her heart already knew how much she missed him.

Focus, buttons.

Grinning to herself, she scrolled again, crosschecking the data. The NT had green ticks across the board. The other states had livestock losses. Big ones, too.

Her stomach tightened as town after town were listed in recently filed stock theft cases.

The names, however, rang a bell. Not because she'd worked them, but because she'd seen them on Finn's wall, and in a file. They'd been scribbled on butcher's paper, pinned beside freight routes and brand registers and even on the odd napkin or five.

They were straight from the *Gaps File.*

Had to be. Somehow?

She dug deeper through freight logs, ag reports, and obscure internal folders. Using the same instincts her father had taught her: go where no one else bothers to look.

And then she found it.

A memo. Buried in an archived state audit report on rural transport risk assessments. Nothing dramatic. Just a footnote, referencing a background source from a federal funding proposal: *Operational_Gaps_v2_bby_final.docx.*

That was Finn's file. The very first draft version. Meant only as context.

Finn had handed it over to Drew eighteen months ago. And Drew had used it, by the book, in his submission, to get funding for the trial.

Taryn had followed that paper trail herself. Tracking every step of the funding process, just like her job demanded on how the squad got their money, how they spent it, and whether it stacked up.

And it had.

The right departments, the right memos, the right signatures.

To Drew and Finn's credit, they'd followed the protocols perfectly.

There was no corruption. Just a desperate team trying to fix a broken system, which made this even more chilling.

Yet, someone else, somewhere along the long, bloated conga line of departments, policy units, funding panels, advisory boards, and god-knows-how-many think tanks that lacked actual brains, had taken Finn's roughly written draft of the Gaps File and twisted it into a goddamn playbook for organised theft!

Her chest locked. Her throat burned. As all the pieces clicked into place.

They'd used it, but not to fix the system. Based purely on the list of current interstate police reports of stolen stock, they'd taken Finn's file, and all his research, to exploit the system to escalate stock theft.

Her chest went still.

The nausea returned—not morning sickness this time, but the bitter, sharp edge of betrayal.

The data didn't lie.

She looked up when a voice carried down the corridor, and through her open office doorway.

It wasn't loud, but she'd heard it once in Elsie Creek police station. All smooth and polite while talking to Amara about Finn in the Batcave by video link.

Drew Bannon.

The Federal Agricultural Commissioner was in the building.

She sat higher and peered through the glass windows.

It was him. Drew. The one Stone called *Big Daddy*.

The Commissioner was a formidable figure, dressed in a tailored suit that fitted his tall frame perfectly. His sharp gaze assessed the surroundings with practised ease before glancing at his wristwatch while talking with her director, Russ Colgrave.

Why was Drew here?

She sat back, pressing two fingers to her temple. The lights felt brighter now.

Her boss walked in a minute later, oblivious to the storm still spinning behind her eyes.

'Taryn. Your draft's raised a few flags. It's been suggested it implies a lack of oversight. Commissioner Bannon wasn't exactly thrilled with the tone.' Russ flicked through a few pages of the report itself.

'The Federal Agricultural Commissioner read my preliminary report?' Of course, Drew would show an interest. After all, he was the one who'd backed the Stock Squad's creation to get the funding for this test case. On paper, he had every reason to watch the data roll in, waiting for proof it worked.

And now that she'd delivered exactly that, she had to ask, 'Was there a problem?'

Russ dropped onto her couch, like he did every time he came into her office. 'I think he was expecting something else. Is it because you only had six weeks? I know that's a hell of a turnaround—not the usual three months. Maybe something slipped? But then I thought, hey, I sent in a pit bull when a shih tzu would've done the trick.'

'Hold on…' She sat higher in her chair. 'Are you saying the Commissioner was the one who requested I be sent out there—knowing exactly what I do?'

She'd never have questioned it, not until Finn asked her to find out who'd sent her.

And now, after a month of chasing dead ends and clean paperwork, did she have her answer?

Russ gave a curt nod. 'Drew thought the NT would fold, as they had no infrastructure to carry them, and figured you'd come back with a list of failures.' He paused. 'Instead, you've given him a blueprint for the squad's permanency and expansion.'

Drew sent her to Elsie Creek? To tear down his own trial program, when it was working. That made no sense.

From his spot on the couch, Russ flipped through the folder. 'I think it's brilliant work, for what it's worth. What you've presented and what they've done up there? Solid. Smart. Field-ready.' He gave her a half-smile. 'And that's the reason why I keep saying you should take the promotion. You've got the receipts to show for it—same as this Stock Squad does. And the numbers don't lie.'

'Um, thanks, but I'm still considering it.' Taryn nodded slowly, as her mind ran at warp speed. What was the

Commissioner doing, sending her in to shut down his beloved Stock Squad? And why?

O-oh…

'Did you do any fishing while you were up there, in the Territory?'

'No. Sorry.' She glanced at her department-issued PC screen with its cursor blinking. Her fingers pushed the mouse to hover over the search bar, just beckoning her to type in those two words: *Andrew Bannon.*

But she knew better.

Drew had started his career as a cop to become a master government manipulator. A public official with the power of a politician, but without the inconvenience of needing votes to keep his job. Which meant if she typed his name on her office PC, there was a 99% chance it would trigger some internal flag—maybe even an automated alert that'd go straight to him.

That's how Meghan got caught.

And why Izzy almost didn't make it out alive.

Taryn fake-smiled at her boss, who was halfway into a yarn about fishing in the Territory, as she reached into her trusty workbag.

'When I was up north, they say you don't just catch barra, you race crocs for 'em.' Russ leaned back on her couch, hooking his bad leg over his other knee to rub the joint that had landed him a permanent desk job. 'I'd never seen anything like it. Big salties sunbaking on riverbanks like they were British backpackers on holiday, waiting on you to catch the fish so they could steal it from you. And some of them crocodiles were bigger than the boat we were in…'

'Really?' She nodded politely as her fingers brushed past her notebook until they closed around her encrypted laptop. The one her father had purpose-built for her, days after Meghan's funeral.

She killed the office wi-fi, then booted into her father's ghost-net protocol. And typed only a few words into the secure console:

Andrew Bannon + Meghan Forrester

The search was short and showed nothing, no red flags, because she'd already combed every file, every shared email trail, every whisper for a connection, for Meghan's name.

So why not try something new?

While her boss droned on about crocodiles the size of bathtubs, she keyed in:

Andrew Bannon + Renzo

Just the first name, since she had no last name for the man who'd murdered her cousin, all without any hope that it'd work. She even leaned back in her chair and listened to her boss. 'Did you eat that fish?'

'Eventually. The guys I went fishing with helped me cut it up, snap-freeze it, and I carried it home in my hand luggage.'

Taryn let out a soft laugh. 'You big game hunter, you.'

Russ chuckled. 'The customs copycats—those quarantine fellas at the airport—didn't love it. They thought I was smuggling in frozen dinosaurs when I landed back in Canberra.'

The spinner ticked.

Still digging.

Oh, she hated that thing now.

Her boss kept nattering from the couch about crocs sunbaking like retirees, and how small boats barely outrun them. She could recite this story by heart: *Crocodile story number seven.*

But this time, she couldn't laugh. Not with her own monster somewhere in the system. And the longer that spinning cursor of doom rolled like a beach ball that went nowhere, the deeper it was trolling for information, the more her patience frayed.

She should've called it, shut the lid and let the thread go cold.

But now the spinning thing had her hooked.

It was still searching.

By now, like all the other searches, it should have stopped cold.

Yet, it was still searching.

Then—

Three results pinged.

She clicked the first one.

The screen blinked and showed a plain document. No letterhead. No classification. Just some old metadata with the title:

> SEALED FILE – CLASSIFICATION:
> INTERNAL ONLY
> Authorised Access: Restricted
> Access Key: [DECRYPTED]
> Name: *Lorenzo Matteo Caruso*
> Alias: *Renzo*
> Age: *16*
> Referral: *Property crime – suspected rural theft syndicate*
> Outcome: *Referred to Qld Rural Work Initiative*
> Supervising Officer: *A. Bannon*
> Status: *Completed.*
> Notes sealed.

Taryn stared hard with a long, slow exhale caught halfway in her throat.

Finn's words whispered in her ear—*Drew was working in the old cop shop that was barely standing in the sticks*. Through Finn, she'd learned the Commissioner was a cop who'd sit at bus stops, doing word puzzles, while babysitting kids who'd been expelled from school.

Back then, it had sounded like nostalgia for a good guy.

Now it felt like a warning.

Taryn's heart thudded. Drew knew the man who'd killed

Meghan.

Her hands trembled as she grabbed her mouse.

Finally, she had the link, that thread she'd been chasing all along, the one that would unravel everything.

With her fingers flying, she tapped out a secure message to her father, attaching an encrypted copy of that file:

It's him, Dad. It's Andrew Bannon!

Even if the name felt radioactive now, she didn't hesitate to hit send.

And for the first time since Meghan's murder, she felt like justice wasn't just a dream. Drew, the man who'd sent her after Finn, was linked to Meghan's murderer. It was him, the Commissioner.

It had to be him.

He was the one who'd accessed Izzy's file on Everlight and her kidnapping first.

The first to receive Finn's Gaps File, submitted in good faith, and full of holes that Drew knew how to exploit.

Had he set Finn up to fail? To use him? Then tried to shut him down once he'd exposed too much, while using her to do it?

Her pulse roared in her ears.

She closed her laptop, slipping it back into her bag. Then sat straighter and locked her posture into the perfect picture of tranquillity.

Across from her, Russ was still going on about something about mud crabs with nippers so big they'd snip your big toe.

His phone alarm dinged, and he switched it off. 'Ah, right, that time already… It's my turn to pick the kids up from sports practice.' He pushed himself up from the couch.

'Russ? The Commissioner might be right. If there are inconsistencies, and if he wants me to dig deeper, I'll need to go back to the Territory and take another crack.'

'You think something's wrong with the data?'

Taryn smiled at her boss. 'I think someone's hiding the truth.'

Thirty

Finn sat on a low stool in his living room, with hands smeared with oil as he worked on the vintage Harley frame spread out before him. It was a stripped-down rebuild and something to keep his hands busy when his head wouldn't shut up.

The stereo played an old Springsteen track, the vinyl crackling like campfire wood. The needle skipped. But he didn't fix it.

Taryn hadn't called. Not that she was supposed to. And not that he could have called her if he wanted to.

But still…

One month and only a couple of short text messages.

And, yeah, he missed her.

Didn't mean anything. When it should have meant nothing. Come on, it was only three days after weeks of bickering with each other.

It just meant the house was quieter. The beer went untouched. And the shadows didn't talk back.

He reached for a wrench, twisted it down, listening to the click of steel on steel. The bike didn't complain. Unlike the paperwork piling up in his inbox back in the Batcave.

The quarry had stayed quiet with the one-month shutdown, and the illegal surveillance still ongoing. Stone had even bought extra cameras for Romy to continue filming her documentary.

There'd been three smaller busts: branded calves moved on false tags. One rogue contractor in Katherine skimming the sales. And another stock agent trying to retire early by accepting kickbacks for allowing a lesser grade of stock to pass through.

But the big one? The operation behind the operation?

That was hibernating like a grizzly bear, waiting for spring to come before that beast started stealing stock again. Only this time, his team was ready to pounce.

Finn wiped his hands on an old rag and stood, stretching his back. He reached for a soda from the fridge and was halfway to cracking the can open when he heard an engine. Too fast, and unfamiliar.

He dumped the can on the kitchen bench, grabbed the shotgun from behind the fridge, and slipped into his boots by the back door.

He took the long way round, cutting behind the water tank, hugging the shadows, with his eyes locked on the erratic swing of headlights cutting across his front yard.

Sliding on the gravel it was enough to spot the mismatched tail-light.

It was Red's ute.

Grady *Red* Galloway, the elusive Stock Agent he'd been chasing for a year. It had taken over eight months just to put a face to the title, that was linked to three deaths and millions of dollars in stolen livestock.

So why the hell would that red-bearded bastard be barrelling onto Finn's property in the dark?

Through the long grass, he held his shotgun raised and ready. If Red was stupid enough to come here, he'd get a very different kind of welcome.

'Finn!' It was Brodie.

Finn lowered his shotgun as he stepped into the light. 'What's wrong?'

Brodie turned.

Finn stopped cold.

The kid was covered in blood. Limping, with his left arm hanging uselessly at his side, the shoulder lower than it should be as if dislocated, with blood dripping from his fingertips.

'Help!' Brodie gasped, a fragile kid with chest heaving, and

eyes wide with terror, stumbled towards him. 'It's Lydia—she's dying!'

Through the open driver's door he spotted a body slumped on the passenger side.

Finn cut across the bonnet, his boots kicking up gravel. Blood slicked the door handle, his grip slipping as he opened the door.

The smell hit first.

Blood and diesel, with the tick of the engine the only sound.

Lydia was half-sprawled across the passenger seat. Blood soaked her shirt, matted in her hair, and pooled into the footwell. It was too much blood.

Her chest barely rose, with shallow, stuttering gasps, like each one might be her last.

Finn checked her pulse. 'Brodie. Open the back of the troopy. *Now.*'

Finn slid an arm under Lydia's legs and lifted her off the seat. She was limp as if boneless.

'Clear out the ropes, unroll that spare swag in the back for me to lay Lydia down,' he barked out to Brodie. 'Then grab the towels off the line. We need to slow down the bleeding.'

Brodie limped into motion, wrenching open the troopy's rear door with his good arm. He half-fell into the back, dragging the ropes aside and unrolling the mattress, to limp away for the threadbare towels waving from the verandah.

Finn laid Lydia down in the back. 'Hang in there, Lydia. It's going to be okay.'

She let out a small, pitiful sound like a whimper that didn't reach her throat.

Brodie returned, clutching a bundle of old towels. 'Here, Finn.' The wince on his face gave him away. His left arm hung low, while more blood trickled steadily from a gash at his temple. The kid was barely on his feet, but he was still trying.

Finn didn't waste time in the race against the clock as each pump of Lydia's heartbeat was slowing down.

'Get in. Keep pressure here.' He guided Brodie's trembling hand over the worst of Lydia's wounds, just below her ribs that had to be broken, with signs of internal bleeding. 'Don't let go, you hear me? You let go, she bleeds out.'

Brodie's eyes widened as tears and sweat streaked through the dirt and blood covering his face.

Finn ripped another towel into strips and wrapped a strip tight around Brodie's head to stem the bleeding from the deep gash. He then fashioned a makeshift sling for that wrecked arm.

The kid cried out, biting down hard on the pain as Finn secured his arm.

'I'm so sorry, Finn. It—'

'Mate, tell me on the way. Just get in, hold onto her tightly, and both of you stay with me.' He slammed the back door shut, leapt into the driver's seat, and gunned the engine before peeling off in a cloud of red dust.

The troopy tore down the dirt road, gravel spraying out from behind the tyres, as the engine howled through every gear.

Finn flicked on the radio sitting on his dashboard and barked into the mic. *'This is Sergeant Wilde on route to Elsie Creek Hospital. Two patients—one critical. ETA ten minutes. Have a trauma team on standby. Over.'*

Comms got the message.

He tossed the radio aside, then slapped the magnet-mounted LED light onto the roof—red and blue strobes bright enough to scatter kangaroos for miles. The siren was already screaming under the dash, just a few short bursts to clear any other critters thinking about crossing the road, because this was an express ride to town.

He glanced in the rear-view mirror. 'What the hell happened, Brodie? You should've gone to the hospital.'

'I wanted to. I was going to—'

'It was my idea.' Lydia's voice was barely more than a breath.

Finn almost missed it and turned off the siren. But he left

the red and blue strobe lights flashing against the gum trees, painting twisted trunks in bursts of colour, casting long, jumping shadows across the dirt. On a deserted outback road, it looked like the bush itself was pulsing with alarm.

Again, he checked the mirror.

Lydia was staring up at the troopy ceiling, her mouth moving with effort. 'I was giving Brodie a driving lesson.'

Brodie was barely sixteen and had yet to get his driver's permit.

'Where?'

'Back road. Doing a fence check,' answered Brodie. 'That's when we saw them loading cattle.'

'Who?'

Brodie swallowed hard, glancing down at Lydia with tears in his old eyes.

It was Lydia who spoke. 'Red and Two-bob Bob. But Red had told me earlier he was going to be away for a few days, last-minute job…'

Brodie jumped in, voice cracking. 'Red saw us. He came after us. We tried to get away, but I'm not good at driving, I—'

'RED RAMMED US!' Lydia bellowed, using whatever energy she had to say it loud and clear. '*Red's ute hit the side of my car while trying to make us stop. He hit us so hard we rolled into the gully.*' She whimpered, the tears trickling down her cheeks to mix with the blood matted in her hair. 'Brodie hit his head.'

'I'm okay. I'm just worried about you.' But even Brodie's voice was cracking from the fear and the pain.

Finn's hands gripped the wheel tighter. 'Where?' he snapped. 'What road? What paddock?'

Brodie seemed somewhat dazed, the blood now seeping through the bandage on his head.

'Don't faint on me now, kid. Keep talking to me, Brodie. I need you both to stay awake, so talk to me. Where did this happen? Where did Red run you off the road?'

'Um…' The kid thumped his bad arm, to wake himself up.

He shut his eyes to not scream, but when he opened them, they were clear.

The ballsy little bastard.

'It was just this side of Boab's Bend,' Brodie said, his voice clear now. 'Along the far southern paddock of Warraga Downs. We were checking their back border fence because Lydia said the owners were away on some last-minute holiday in Darwin.'

'What was Red doing out there? And why would he chase you?'

'Red was there,' she said in between pants for breath, that Finn strained to hear her. 'With Two-bob Bob. They had a— had a—'

'A truck,' butted in Brodie, hiding his pain as he spoke.

'What kind of truck?'

'A big one. Not a road train. But it was a livestock truck. Dusty green, canvas tarp over the back. They'd already corralled the cattle and were ready to load. The fence was cut, too. And they were on the wrong side of the fence, Finn,' pleaded Brodie. 'They were stealing cattle. Plain as day.'

Finn's grip on the wheel went white-knuckled. The quarry. The freight. It was happening again.

Had Taryn released her report? Giving Bob and Red the go-ahead to start lifting stock again?

Or was it just an opportunistic theft based on dumb luck and an open gate while the owners were away?

'How did you end up with Red's ute?' Finn asked.

'I took it, after I hit him... I think I killed him,' confessed Brodie, as his head heavily dropped to his chest.

'What?'

'Red pulled Lydia out of the car, and he was screaming at her. I had to drag myself out through the passenger side. I could hear Lydia's screams and Red's shouts, so I grabbed the first thing I could find. A stick. And I hit him.'

'Did you see him get back up?'

Brodie shook his head. 'I thought he was going to kill Lydia, Finn. I couldn't let him hurt her. I had to do something.'

Aw, hell. 'What was Red saying to you, Lydia?'

'I told him I knew… That I was talking to the police and knew he was stealing livestock. I saw him stealing those cattle at Warraga Downs. Red-handed.'

The betrayal must have been the final straw for Red to lose it like that.

'I thought Red was going to kill you, Lydia.' The kid clung to the only person in the world who had ever loved him. The woman who'd stood beside him in court and fought to get him out of his parent's house. She'd helped cover the cigarette burns on his arms and gave him a job, clothes, and a purpose while teaching him how to read and write.

And now she was bleeding out in the back of Finn's troopy, and there was nothing poor Brodie or Finn could do to stop it.

Still, she lifted a shaking hand to cradle his cheek. Just like a mother would. 'It's okay,' she murmured. 'You did good, Brodie. Finn's taking us to the hospital. He'll look after you now.'

She turned her head slightly, catching Finn's eye in the mirror. 'It was self-defence, Finn. Brodie only did it to protect me.'

'I'm sorry, Lydia,' Brodie whispered. 'I didn't know what else to do. He was going to hurt you—' His voice hitched. 'I killed Red. I stole his ute. I should've—'

The kid looked like his universe was caving in.

And maybe it was.

'You did the right thing.' But Finn's words felt hollow.

He saw it now.

This—*all* of this—was his fault.

Again, her eyes found his in the rear-view mirror, glassy and full of something deeper than pain. 'You'll watch over him, won't you? No matter what happens next, you'll stand by my boy?'

Finn couldn't speak.

Brodie was looking at a manslaughter charge. Car theft. And who knows what other charges would show once the dust had settled—but right now they were both in trouble. Even though Lydia was bleeding out in the back of his troopy, she was still trying to protect the boy like she always did. Trying to make Finn keep his word, as if making it her last handover.

It only made Finn press the accelerator harder, forcing the troopy to roar through the night. She was not dying in the back of his car.

Brodie sat beside her, trembling with adrenaline now, struggling to keep his hand pressed against her wound. How cruel was this world for a boy who'd finally found a life filled with hope, and now it was about to be snatched away from him.

'Trust in Finn.' Her voice was paper-thin. 'You're safe with him. Always were.' Again, she glanced up at Finn.

Finn didn't answer, he just nodded once and made that silent promise.

When the floodlights of Elsie Creek Hospital snapped into view.

Thank God.

By the main doors, the hospital staff stood with a stretcher, ready to move.

Finn braked hard, yanking the troopy to a stop just shy of the front doors, and jumped out. *'We've got a critical bleed on the female, Lydia Galloway, aged 51. And a secondary concussion with a shoulder trauma on Brodie Cross, minor, 16 and under my care!'*

He threw open the back doors.

The nurses and the doctor moved fast—three around Lydia, one helping Brodie.

As they lifted her onto the stretcher, Lydia reached out blindly with her fingers, grasping for Brodie.

She found his hand and gripped it tight as if scared of

letting go. 'You're safe now, sweetheart. You're no longer that boy anymore, but a man I'm so proud of. You're a good man and don't you ever forget that, no matter what happens.'

Brodie broke into full sobs as the nurses pulled him back.

But Finn was there, holding the kid upright as Lydia was wheeled inside, and the emergency doors closed behind her.

Thirty-one

Finn sat in the chair by the window with his elbows resting on his knees, the silent radio clipped to his police vest. The curtain on the window was half drawn, giving him an outside slice of the night sky—deep, black, and wide as the land itself.

The last time he'd been in this room, it had been to see Bree. She'd just had a baby girl. Little Charlie Riggs, who had hair like her mother.

It was supposed to have been a good day. But all it'd done was remind him of everything he'd lost. Of Liam. A child he never got to watch grow into a man.

And now here he was again. Same hospital. Same ache in his chest. Different kid.

Finn's fingers curled tight around the cup of coffee he couldn't drink as he watched over Brodie just lying there, stitched up, bandaged, and drugged into silence, where he hoped the nightmares would never find him.

Yet Finn sat. And waited, watching over the boy.

Because once upon a time, someone had sat like this for him. Back when the hours stretched longer than they should, between midnight and dawn—when the world got too quiet and the weight of everything got louder and he was a kid who'd run out of luck. Wearing cuts and bruises that did little to hide his scars, you needed someone watching over you in times like that. He knew that.

Back then, it was Drew.

Not Commissioner Bannon. Just a cop named Constable Andrew Bannon, who didn't know one end of a horse from the other, wearing city boots that got stuck in the mud. He'd sat by Finn's bed after that mustering accident, asking the dumbest questions, while spending half his downtime scribbling in one of those dog-eared, mail-order word puzzle books, like he was cracking codes instead of killing time.

And yet... he'd stayed. Watching over a kid in a hospital bed. More than once.

Finn had never said thank you to Drew. Not for the pardon. Not for the second chance. Not for just being there when a sixteen-year-old boy didn't have anyone else. But for making a dumb deal that Finn would teach Drew how to spot the signs of a good steer in exchange for helping out the local troublemaker.

That stupid deal had saved his life.

And now?

Now he was watching over a kid the same age he'd been. A kid also with cigarette burns on his arms—just like the ones Finn had hidden beneath the complex ink that covered his arms and chest that hid his history. But it didn't erase it.

From the moment they'd met, Finn had recognised the same haunted look in Brodie's aged eyes. He got it.

Finn also knew that Brodie would wake up soon. And when he did, the kid would swing one of two ways—he would fall apart, or get angry.

Finn knew that fork in the road. Hell, he'd taken both paths, and still ended up in prison.

So what made Finn think he was the right man to keep this kid on the rails?

But he'd promised Lydia. And promises meant something to a man trying to outrun the wreckage of his own life.

Brodie needed someone. They'd knocked him out just to reset his shoulder, and now he had an IV in one arm, the other strapped tight in a sling.

The tough little bastard had driven with a dislocated shoulder. Bleeding. Scared out of his mind, just to get to Finn. And even then, not once had he complained. All he'd cared about was Lydia. Getting her help. Keeping her alive.

That took guts most grown men never had.

Sadly, he hadn't said a word since.

But Finn hadn't moved either and wasn't planning on it. Not when the nurse checked Brodie's vitals. Or when Marcus radioed in with updates from the crime scene at Boab's Bend. He didn't even move when the doctor finally came and told him Lydia was critical, but stable. For now.

Red had disappeared. Two-bob Bob as well. Which meant, at least, that Brodie hadn't killed Red.

According to Amara and Porter, who were first onsite, the blood found at the crime scene had been a mess. Lydia's ute had rolled a few times to stop, face down behind a tree in an old irrigation ditch.

As for the alleged stock theft?

Well, they'd made it look like it hadn't happened. Yet, when Cowboy Craig showed up, he'd found the tracks back to where the fence had been neatly patched, with tyre tracks leading away from the gully, as a mob of cattle casually stood around chewing their cud, while watching the show.

But Finn knew better.

Come daylight, the brand checks would start. And the property owner, rushing back from Darwin, would know exactly what was missing. Because prime stock didn't just wander off in the dark. Everyone knew that.

In the meantime, Marcus had set up roadblocks across the southern and northern highway corridor. While Craig and Porter were in the Hellhound checking back trails. They were casting the net wide—but it might not be wide enough.

Finn knew Bob had Red, who'd be crippled with guilt… or stuck with a blinding headache. Holed up somewhere close, licking his wounds, buying time, waiting to hear if Lydia survived.

And in this town?

News never stayed quiet for long.

Not when Finn had stormed into the hospital with Brodie and Lydia's blood on his shirt, barking into his radio and phone like a one-man taskforce to get everyone on the job.

Half the other rooms were filled with patients, locals

who'd peered out into the corridor to see what was going on. People who knew someone… who knew *everyone*. It wouldn't take long, and word would fly across that invisible outback telegraph line, where Red would wait for word before his next move.

But where would the bastard go?

The roads to Katherine and Darwin were boxed in. The small bush hospital was the only one within cooee. And if Red's wounds were bad enough, he would've been kicked out the front door in a drive-by of the hospital, because no one wanted to be associated with a stock thief in cattle country.

No, if Red needed patching up, Bob would take him somewhere quiet.

Hidden.

And there was only one place left that made sense…

The quarry.

The same bloody quarry they'd had under surveillance this past month. The one Stone and Romy swore hadn't seen movement in days.

And the kicker?

Their trucks were still there. Tagged and being watched — thanks to the tracking units Amara and Finn had tucked behind wheel wells and under the chassis lines.

But the truck they'd used tonight? That one wasn't even on their radar.

As to how the crime of stock theft happened. Hmm…

Lydia, being the neighbourly person, had said the owner was out of town, and she'd swing past the southern paddock to check the back fence during Brodie's driving lesson.

And Red? He must have overheard Lydia on the phone about the owner being out of town—but not all of her plans. Or Red asked her what was new in town. Something so simple that maybe even Lydia hadn't realised what she'd said.

It wasn't hard to picture the rest of the story…

Bob the ringer, showing up with Red, handing out

business cards under the banner of SW Rural Contracting. Asking if they needed any fencing or mustering done, to scope out the place under the guise of needing a gig.

Only this time, they didn't find a new client to rip off later. They'd found payday. An empty station, with a livestock truck sitting in the shed with the keys tucked behind the visor—like they always were. Along with a fence line that backed straight onto a dirt road with cattle nosing through the gaps, reaching for the tall weeds on the roadside.

Easy pickings.

They just hadn't expected Lydia to be out there with Brodie behind the wheel.

Finn rubbed a hand over his jaw. He wasn't letting them go that easy. No way in hell was he done with Red and Bob. Who were still out there, starting from the wrong side of the highway. Hours away from the quarry. But both fugitives were locals, they'd know how to cut through the scrub, using the dark to their advantage.

But prepping his team to storm the quarry in the dark?

Suicide.

Just the mere mention of the quarry over the radios could also blow their cover. Finn and his team had told no one. They didn't even have it on paper, because as Finn had explained to his team, their surveillance was illegal. Inadmissible in court. And Izzy had warned them it was enough to have their entire case thrown out should they dare to make an arrest.

No, what Finn needed were his maps. The old kind. The ones that showed every bore trail, river cut, cattle path and gully. All the information he'd collected from Bree, Cowboy Craig, Stone, even Porter, and lots of other cattlemen, hunters, and stockmen who'd shared with Finn. He could then see their escape plan, and all the other paths that'd lead to one place...

The quarry.

What he'd kill for his maps and—

Click.

The door that led to the corridor eased open with a whoosh.

Tanisha stood there with hair wrapped high in a satin scarf, wearing silky pyjamas covered in bright pink flamingos, holding a thermal coffee jug in one hand and his old canvas bag he kept in the office in the other.

'Well,' she said, 'would you look at this place?'

Finn just stared at a lot of silky, loud, pink pyjamas. She was even wearing a matching pink coat, sprinkled with cat fur, and green cactus-shaped slippers peeking out from under the hem.

A far cry from the woman who usually wore the Territory's navy-blue police uniform.

With one generous hip, Tanisha pushed the door closed and sashayed inside with all that silk whispering against silk, as her cactus slippers slapped softly against the lino.

She was the loudest and brightest thing in the quietest room.

'Don't start,' she smirked, setting down the bag with a thud. 'It was this or the matching unicorn set. But the glitter has gotten into the seams making it too itchy to wear to bed, although it's great for cocktail hour.'

Her eyes landed on Brodie and softened. 'Aw, poor baby. Curled up like a little kitten.'

She glanced at Finn again and held out the cup. 'Amara called. Said you might need a coffee, and every map you had lying around in the Batcave.' She nodded at the bag on the floor.

'Thank you.' Finn took the cup, the rich coffee aroma warming.

Tanisha raised her chin. 'Now, mister. Marcus said you'll have a plan, and I quote, *to box those bastards in.*'

Thirty-two

Daylight was only a slither of soft mushroom pink stretching over the horizon as the jet touched down with a low hum. Dust kicked up in spirals across the simple airstrip, settling against the wire fence, before the jet had come to a stop.

Taryn greeted the dawn as she descended the jet's stairs, only this time in her jeans and T-shirt, not a pencil skirt and suit.

Waiting at the bottom, arms crossed like a border guard who'd been cheated out of a sleep-in, stood Mickey in his grease-stained grey coveralls. Squinting at her like an aged Popeye, swatting at a fly with his matching grey hand towel.

'Bloody hell,' he muttered. 'What is it with you friggin' Feds, always gotta land before coffee hour?'

Taryn offered him a smile. 'Morning, Mickey. So it's common to have jets land at this airstrip, huh?'

'Nah…' He narrowed his eyes at the sleek high-powered jet. 'The last time one of you lot landed in one of these things was maybe a year back?' Mickey scratched behind his ear. 'Round the same time that there Stock Squad made their first case, like it was official, or somethin'. That Commissioner fella—yeah? The one Stone called *Big Daddy* something or other. Him. He came in one of these things.'

'The Federal Agricultural Commissioner, Drew Bannon?' She stood dead still.

'Yeah, him. Flew in like he owned the place. Handin' out police badges and slappin' backs of the Stock Squad at the end of the tarmac, by the cop shop there. Only thing missin' was a bunch of babies for him to kiss.'

'What were you doing?'

'Helping his snooty assistant load boxes onto the jet.'

'What boxes?'

'Y'know?'

'No.'

'Look, lady, I'm not your tour guide here to share the gossip-what-not, either. What's with the twenty questions?'

'I need to know.'

'Yeah, like I need to know how to get you gone so I can get goin' with my day.'

'I'll buy you a beer, like I do for your brother, Billy.'

'Well, then…' He sniffed, wiping down the front of his grey coveralls as if wearing a tie.

'What did those boxes look like?'

'Y'know, simple brown ones. Same size as them nappy boxes we send up to the communities—only colder.'

'Colder?'

'Yeah.' He nodded. 'Like they'd been sittin' next to an aircon all day. But they weren't, which was odd, y'know.'

'If it was a year ago, how come you remember them now?'

'Coz they were labelled as conference packs for NT Tourism or some rubbish. All of 'em had these little flags on the side that said they were brochures for some conference. How the heck they got out here, I dunno.' Mickey gave a snort of disapproval. 'If it's one thing we don't need is more flamin' tourists makin' a mess of everythin'.'

'So, you don't like strangers.'

'Tourists, holiday-makers, camera-clacking yahoos with their caravans blocking the roads and parking spaces.'

'I'm not a tourist.'

'Whatever. I didn't want them near the place. And that's why I remember them boxes and that jet. It was real sleek, with two normal commercial pilots. Not military, like you've got there.' Mickey squinted at the jet on the runway, the crew doing ground checks in military uniform, preparing to leave.

'I believe you. But are you sure it was the Commissioner?'

'I may be old, but I got a memory on me like an elephant—

even for junk I don't wanna remember.'

'Uh-huh.'

'I remember coz that bloke came off that jet wearing a full flamin' suit. You know the whole jacket and tie thingy. Do you know how rare it is to see a necktie round 'ere.'

'I'd imagine so.' It was a culture shock going from the land of boots, jeans and long-sleeved shirts and hats to a city full of men in suits with hands softer than hers.

'I asked his assistant who the suit was, and he told me he was some commissioner for agriculture. Made sense he'd come out here. Thought it was election time meself, it's the only time them pollies do a drive through, y'know.'

'So, what else do you remember? About the boxes?'

'Well… Then me and his snobby assistant—who couldn't read right—he asked for the boxes.'

'He's an assistant to the Commissioner. I'm sure he could read.'

'Nah, I meant he had trouble pronouncing the name.' Mickey paused to scratch the back of his head. 'Come to think of it, we both did.'

Her pulse skipped.

Plain boxes. Cold to the touch. Labelled with flags.

Taryn also had a copy of the Commissioner's travel entries. All his dates and logs of every visit, every flight he'd ever made these past three years. And not once, anywhere, did it say that the Federal Agricultural Commissioner had ever physically visited Elsie Creek!

All his calendar meetings for the Stock Squad had been done by pre-booked video link. Even the ones he'd secretly held with Amara were noted.

'Mickey, *mate*, do you think you'd have the paperwork somewhere?'

Mickey jutted out his ruddy jaw. 'It'll cost ya another beer to look at a man's privates, y'know? I don't show my books to just anyone. Specially an auditor, like you.'

From her workbag, she dragged out her badge to order him, but changed her mind, slipping her federal badge into the back pocket of her jeans instead. Billy, Porter, and even Cowboy Craig had told her how best to handle the grouch. As the common enemy she shared with Stone, the more you pushed someone like Mickey, the more likely he'd tell her to get nicked.

'Tell you what, how about a flick through your folders, and a lift to the pub in that nifty buggy of yours that you use to tow planes around, and I'll pay you a carton of beer for your troubles?' She'd seen Mickey zipping into town and back on it, even waving at her once on her way to work. Big smiles, laughing at his joke of making her walk the long paddock the first time she'd arrived, just over six weeks ago.

'You're on.' Mickey opened the door to his office, with a wall of folders along one side and a service counter running down the centre. He pulled a bulky binder from the shelf. 'You flick through that lot, while I make sure that jet of yours has finished messin' up my airstrip.'

'Done.' She dumped her bag on the floor inside Mickey's office. 'Hey, Mickey?'

'What?' He caught the door and scowled at her, either from the light, the need for glasses, her, or it was just his personality. She suspected it was the latter.

'How come you don't let Stone land his helicopter here? He does have a badge.'

Mickey gave a gruff chuckle. 'Because if I did, I'd have every bloody muster chopper turning this airstrip into a dust bowl. That's why the publican, God, bought that paddock out the back of the pub. Coz most of them station choppers only come into town for a grog run at the pub. If it's an emergency, they'll head to the hospital.'

He jabbed a finger toward the far end of the tarmac, where the red cross glowed brightly on the roof from the spotlights. Just like *Strong Arm of the Law*, the retro mural painted on the roof of the police station, lit up by the floodlights still blazing.

It was that early.

Taryn ducked back into Mickey's office. The folder he'd pulled out, sat fat and overstuffed on the long counter, with a whopping big radio set up at the end, beside a half-drunk coffee and a wooden stool.

She flipped open the binder and began digging through handwritten logs and carbon copy dockets, trying to remember the exact timeline from her own notes.

The *Rough Stock* case…

That was it, their first case.

She dragged out her notebook and flicked back over her notes to the first interview and her finger paused on a diary scan of Amara's notes: *Morning tea with the Commissioner – buy new shirt for Stone!*

She'd missed it.

But it had a date!

Flicking through Mickey's folder again, there it was…

Same date. Same week.

A delivery docket in Mickey's folder:

Delivered by Temp Roicks Pty Ltd.
Signed by SW.
Booked through Merc Topski Inc.

Well audit me sideways!

It was two names from her list of ghost companies.

Temp Roicks Pty Ltd held the quarry, where they'd set up holding yards with access to the airstrip. But according to the date on Mickey's docket, they hadn't officially secured the quarry land at that stage.

But the one booking flights in and out of the country through backwater airstrips was Merc Topski, a registered international livestock exporter.

Only now, she had a direct link between the two fake companies, with the Commissioner on board, passing through this small outback town.

Was Drew really that much of a bastard? Shaking hands with Finn and his team, congratulating them for their first win as the newly formed Stock Squad—while literally loading stolen livestock genetic material onto a flight right in front of them?

Arsehole.

The jet roared back to life, powering through its take-off, making the office windows shake.

Soon after, Mickey came back inside, grinning like a kid. 'That'll wake the dead.'

'Mickey, have you still got the flight records from this date?' She held up the folder.

He squinted at the page. 'Yeah...' He groaned as he bent down to rummage through the bottom cupboards.

Taryn snapped a photo of the docket, her lips pressing into a thin line to stop herself from laughing like a loon, or hopping on one leg with hope.

But, come on. This was it.

Proof.

It was worthy of that dorky dance. Because she had a stack of witnesses who could testify that Commissioner Andrew Bannon was in Elsie Creek, shaking hands with the Stock Squad, using a jet booked by an illegal company.

Taryn also had enough paperwork to recognise Drew's assistant's signature, who probably had no idea what his boss was up to.

It was so typical of a career bureaucrat like Drew to not get his hands dirty, letting other people collect parcels and pilfer livestock.

But she needed to play this right, and deliver all this news straight to the Stock Squad without tipping off a single soul.

Its why stealth had been paramount these past two days, using her two-day travel time as Taryn's excuse to vanish off-grid from Canberra like a departmental ninja.

Instead, she drove straight to her parents house.

There, it'd been a two-day tag-team with her father at her side, as they rifled through files, shell companies, financial reports and falsified permits.

Honestly? It was the best daddy-daughter bonding time they'd had in years. Nothing said *I love you Dad*, like co-authoring a take-down of federal-level corruption over coffee, and some criminally good cookies, to build the bones of a genuine case.

And when her mum came home and spotted the manic gleam in both their eyes, she cracked open the emergency champagne and practically demanded a victory speech.

Taryn gave them one—just not the one she'd planned.

Mid-toast, mid-sobbing ugly cry, she blurted out: *I'm pregnant.*

Her mum froze mid-pour, corked the bottle, and set it aside without a word while her dad pulled her into a hug and handed her a box of tissues. Both offering to support her. Whatever she chose.

As a kid, moving all the time, she didn't have close friends. She'd only had her parents. When her mum offered nappy-changing duties and full coverage of school holidays, then her dad promised summer beach trips, awkwardly muttering something about building sandcastles and learning to surf, it had her blubbering about how scared she was, and all the stuff they never really got to do with her—all the things she'd secretly wished for as a kid but never said aloud.

But now, she got it.

They hadn't been absent to be cruel. They were working their arses off, not just to provide her with a good education, but the best damn life lessons a kid could absorb. And honestly, what kid gets to see three presidents, a sultan or two, and the Queen before she's had her braces removed?

They hadn't just worked for their careers. They loved their jobs. And Taryn knew that, because she loved her job, too.

Well, at least, she used to...

After sitting back in Canberra this past month, buried in policy, while dodging office politics, water-cooler gossip, and second-guessing her life choices, it had her wondering.

But these last two days—working with her dad, building something real, getting justice for her family and for the Stock Squad, it reminded her that this work could make a difference.

She understood now what Finn was doing. What it cost

him, and why he kept going. And she was going to do her best to help him, too.

She just didn't quite know how to tell him about the other part yet. Because *Hey Finn, quick sidebar—you knocked up the auditor and here's my PowerPoint presentation* probably wasn't the most professional way to start a debrief.

Honestly, if she could write it on a sticky note and slap it to his troopy's dash, then run, she would. Which might suit someone like Finn Wilde. The most emotionally repressed man north of Alice Springs. You know, classic romance vibes.

Which was wild, considering she first came to Elsie Creek with a five-step plan for dismantling the Stock Squad—and somehow ended up emotionally free-falling for one of its most damaged members.

She had a plan for confronting Finn about the job. She had bullet points, strategy, and a tight little speech in her audit folder.

But this other thing?

She was absolutely, terrifyingly, winging it.

And she hated winging it.

Taryn shook her head like she could physically rattle the feelings loose. She straightened her jacket, mentally filing her baby-daddy dilemma under *panic later*.

Because right now? Drew Bannon was on top of the pile, to finally give her cousin the justice she deserved.

And she had a plan.

Step one: grab a room at the pub. Dump her gear. Pay Mickey his beer—if you could buy beer this early in the morning.

Step two: grab coffee and carbs from the food van by the train station. A decaf for herself, and a double shot for Finn, because he liked to drink mud. And enough sausage rolls, savoury pastries and sprinkle-topped cakes to feed a hungry police station.

Step three: say hello to Cecil the water buffalo on her way to waltzing into the police station with a smile, some sugar, and a stack of files. And the cutest stash of cat toys she'd ever laid eyes on. Feathers, glitter, tiny plush cactuses that squeaked when you poked them, all for Tanisha's felines.

Honestly, Taryn should have known she was pregnant the second she started going full *Aunt of the Year* over cat accessories. She'd practically cooed at a damn feather on a stick.

Hormones.

Yes, the struggle was real.

And so too was walking into the Batcave like it was any other day.

Because the one thing no one expected this morning was her.

What she didn't expect?

Was how fast that plan was about to fall apart.

Thirty-three

Maps, files, scribbled notes, including a satellite photo of the quarry, were spread across Brodie's hospital tray like a lost section of a war room. Finn crouched over them, eyes flicking from his phone screen to the mess of maps in front of him, then back to his phone's screen:

Taryn Hayes

Her name stared back at him, his finger hovering over the dial button.

He wanted to call her. Hell, he *needed* to. Not just for her report. She was the only one who could read his notes and make him see what he'd missed. He had the ground tools, and had laid the foundation, while Taryn had the knack of filling in the gaps and giving it a polish for the bigger picture. It was like he'd start the sentence, and she'd finish it as they both worked to finish the same job.

But he didn't hit that call button.

Instead, he ran his hand through his hair and let the biro clatter to the floor.

He scooped it up, a grin tugging at the corner of his mouth at the memory of Taryn casually mentioning that her childhood babysitters had taught her how to take down a teddy bear with a ballpoint pen.

A pen.

Of course she'd weaponise her office supplies.

Damn, he missed her.

He sniffed to get back to work in the hospital room that

smelled of antiseptic. His blood encrusted shirt only added to the aroma. But he didn't want to leave, so he wore his police vest to disguise it.

The radio chatter had silenced now, only highlighting Brodie's shallow breathing.

Then it came…

A deep, echoing roar, that was low and fast.

Finn stiffened.

Jet.

It wasn't a sound you often heard in Elsie Creek—not unless someone important was landing. He crossed to the window, parting the vertical blinds with two fingers.

The sky was salmon-pink with the kind of outback dawn that made you feel like the world held its breath between heat and dark. And there, in the distance, a sleek shape tore across the horizon heading north in the wakening blue.

He stared for a moment, gut tightening. Could it be…Her?

Taryn?

Nah.

He shook it off.

Turning from the window, Finn moved to where his laptop sat open, among his maps, and manila folders with scrawled notes. On the floor his open duffel bag held more rolls of maps and files.

A plan was forming. One he hoped to execute at first light, when he was calling a meeting with the squad.

They'd strike the quarry.

But he couldn't leave Brodie yet. He'd made a promise to watch over the kid, to keep him safe. And Finn needed to be here when the boy woke up.

He glanced back at the bed.

Brodie shifted with a rustle of sheets. A breath hitching, shallow and uncertain, then came the confused panic.

Finn was beside him in seconds. 'You're alright, mate. You're safe.'

Brodie blinked blearily with his brow furrowed. 'Lydia?'

'Still fighting,' Finn said gently. 'Same as you.'

The kid's eyes darted around the room like he wasn't sure if any of it was real.

Finn pushed open the door, and hollered into the corridor, *'Oi! He's awake in here!'*

A nurse called back, 'Be there in a sec!'

Finn returned to Brodie's bedside. 'You need water?'

Brodie gave a slow, shaky nod as he tried to sit up, only to wince, as if remembering he'd hurt his shoulder.

'Whoa up there, mate. These things come loaded.' Finn hit the button to raise the mechanical bed. He wasn't about to fluff any pillows, but he'd make sure the kid didn't fall out of bed.

Finn reached for the cup and straw sitting on the ledge. He held it steady while Brodie drank, like he hadn't had a drop of water in days.

'There we go,' Finn murmured. 'Doc will be here soon.' He then leaned in and whispered, 'I'll smuggle in a stash of iced coffees and lollies later.'

That earned him the faintest flicker of a smile as the kid sagged back against the pillows, jaw clenched like he was fighting the pain.

He then checked out the room, which held nothing, not even a TV, not that they got television reception out here. The frown forming across his deeply tanned forehead said it all. Being stuck staring at four walls was going to drive a kid like Brodie nuts.

Finn reached into the duffel bag and pulled out the puzzle book that was dog-eared and sun-faded, like it had been through a dozen dry seasons. 'I found this shoved in the bottom of my bag. Forgot it was there, to be honest. Figured it'd help, as it kept me sane when I was stuck in hospital once—well, as sane as I can get.'

Brodie lifted his chin with curiosity. Hopefully, it'd take his mind off his worries for a moment or two. And the boy was also learning to read and write, so it wouldn't hurt to do something fun with letters.

'I was your age when I copped a horn to the ribs on a

muster. Thought I'd go mad staring at the ceiling.' He hesitated, surprised at how it had caught him off guard, even after all this time, when he mentioned the name, 'Drew was the town's cop where I was, and he dropped off a book just like this. Said it was good for the brain. Strategic thinking, pattern recognition, that kind of thing.'

Finn cleared his throat. 'Didn't believe him, of course. Thought he was just trying to keep me quiet. But it turned out, he wasn't wrong.'

He flipped to one of the half-finished pages and ran a finger along the jagged trail of circled letters. 'You start seeing how things link. Words hidden backwards, sideways, diagonal. Patterns you'd miss if you weren't looking. And once you get the hang of it, I reckon your brain stops feeling like a busted fence post for a bit.'

Brodie gave him a sidelong glance as if Finn was some ancient dinosaur, handing a teenager a paper and pen, when they were all about handheld phones and video games.

But Brodie wasn't your ordinary teenager.

'And if you get bored, you can find all the rude words.'

Brodie gave a quick flicker of a grin, a spark in his old eyes where the worry was heavy.

Finn leaned back against the wall beside his bed. 'Look, don't stress about all the rest. Besides, that's not how the law works. You protected Lydia. You did what no one else could.'

'Yeah, but—'

'*But* don't say anything to Marcus or anyone in the NT Police, not unless I'm with you. Look, we haven't found Red, so as far we know Red isn't dead. And forget saying you stole Red's ute. Yeah?' Finn waited for the kid to nod, it was small, even if his old eyes weren't so sure. 'And don't worry about the licence thing. I'll spin it a bit. Worst case, we'll say the bull was driving.'

That got the faintest huff of a grin from Brodie, which he took as a good sign. That's if Red was still alive. If not, then they'd have a whole gun-barrel of trouble to deal with then.

'I've already told Izzy to come and back you up.' Finn then

added, straight-faced, 'Heard you've got a crush on her.'

Didn't the kid go redder than a road train's tail-light, dragging the hospital sheet up to his chin like it could hide the burn. 'Isobel Callahan is the best criminal lawyer in the Territory,' he muttered, all stiff and defensive.

Finn bit back a grin. 'That she is. Scary when she wants to be. Might even bill you extra if you keep blushing like that.'

Brodie groaned and hid his face behind his palm.

'Yeah,' Finn said, smirking, 'you're gonna be just fine, mate.'

The door creaked.

Finn turned as a doctor, with tablet in hand and a stethoscope looped casually around his neck, entered the room, looking like he'd just walked off a magazine cover and into a bush clinic.

Dr Stewart Mannen.

The Hot Doc, according to Tanisha. Who'd nearly tripped over her own cactus slippers when she'd realised this doctor was on shift. She'd wanted to volunteer and stay all night.

Pfft.

'How's Lydia?' Finn knew Brodie would want to know the same.

'She's stable. Still critical, I'm afraid.' Dr Mannen checked the IV, then adjusted something on the monitor.

'Can I see her?' Brodie's voice was hoarse, barely more than a rasp.

'Let me check on you first, before we decide.' The doctor checked Brodie's head wound, peeling back the dressing with practised care.

The jagged line of eight black stitches ran just below Brodie's hairline, swollen and angry looking, but clean. No infection.

The doctor checked Brodie's shoulder full of angry purple and blue bruising.

Brodie winced, eyes flicking shut for a second. 'Hurts less than it did last night,' he muttered. And for a kid who used to endure torture from his parents, that said more than any pain scale ever could.

Finn's jaw tightened, with his hands curling into fists at his sides. The kind of tension that came from knowing—really knowing—what it meant when a kid downplayed pain like that. 'His pain?'

'You'll feel that for a while,' the doctor said, gently pressing along Brodie's collarbone. 'Luckily no broken bones. But your ligaments are going to scream at you for a week. Your neck muscles, too, due to a slight whiplash from the vehicle rollover.' He then flicked a pen light to check Brodie's eyes. 'You have a moderate concussion, but you're coherent, responsive, and no swelling, which are always good signs.'

'Can you give Brodie something for the pain, to take the edge off it.' Because the kid might be playing tough, but he was hurting. 'Just nothing addictive...' It's how his mother got hooked.

Brodie nodded.

Finn also knew Brodie's parents were addicts too, so the kid steered clear of anything to do with drugs, scared he'd end up like them.

Dr Mannen jotted down some notes as he spoke. 'We'll keep Brodie on light painkillers—nothing that'll fuzz him out. He needs to rest. And to drink plenty of water.'

Brodie adjusted his legs under the sheets, trying to get comfortable. Moving slower than usual, but still moving.

'What I need is to pee. And I'm starving.'

Finn smirked. 'I'll take that as a good sign.'

Dr Mannen chuckled. 'Once you've eaten and had a shower, Brodie, I'll tell the nurse to take you to see Lydia. But I will warn you, she's still critical, and it might be confronting. That said... I think she'd like knowing you're close.'

Finn gave a sharp nod. 'Thanks, Doc. Call me if there's any change, yeah?'

'Will do. And maybe you can go home and change, too.' The doc nodded at Finn's shirt, splattered with blood.

'Just wanted to make sure...' Finn rubbed the back of his neck, not wanting to say that he'd been watching over

Brodie's bed, without sounding like he was babysitting the boy who was practically a man.

'Are you taking over Brodie's care?' the doctor asked quietly.

'I am. Until Lydia wakes up and tells us what to do.' Finn didn't look at Brodie when he said it. But he meant it.

Brodie, already pale, clenched the edge of the sheet.

That was the thing about this kid, he'd already learned not to ask for anything from anyone. He'd sadly learned a hard lesson, that being wanted came with terms and conditions that weren't always favourable.

But now…

Someone else was also choosing him, too. His small circle was growing.

Brodie didn't say a word—just reached out and grabbed the word puzzle book. His fingers curled tight around it like it was the only thing anchoring him. That if someone like Finn was willing to give Brodie a go, he might give Finn's book a go, too.

Finn didn't call attention to it. He just pulled a pen from his police vest and passed it over.

Brodie took it.

And then the radio crackled to life.

It was Tanisha: '*All units, be advised: public disturbance escalating at the Elsie Creek Hotel. Requesting immediate response. Locals are gathered—agitated and aggressive.*' Then it was like she'd leaned into the microphone and said, '*Listen, guys, the stockmen are calling for Red's head.*'

Dr Mannen's brows lifted. 'I didn't think the pub opened this early.'

Finn looked back at Brodie. The stockmen adored Lydia. And they hated cattle thieves.

'No one's opened the stockyards today.' Brodie's voice cracked. 'Not since…'

Dammit. It was a lynch mob about to tear this town apart.

Thirty-four

Taryn stood in the pub's front doorway, blinking at a wall of broad shoulders and wide-brimmed hats, with voices that rumbled like thunder across a storm front. Packed with wall-to-wall stockmen, drovers, ringers, station hands, even truck drivers—and it wasn't even 7 a.m.

She recognised a few faces from the food van's queue by the train station, men who'd nodded at her over lukewarm coffee and bacon rolls. Now they stood shoulder to shoulder, boots scuffing the floorboards, as the tension in the air thickened it could've cracked glass.

'Back in my day, we'd have chained rustlers to a micky bull and let the Territory sort him out...' muttered one guy to a huddled crew of hats.

'Strap 'em to an ant mound and pour a tin of black treacle over the top. Let him feel every bloody bite,' said another man, two rows back.

'Red knew exactly what he was doing. Turned on his own. On Lydia. That's why she's in the hospital,' grunted a third group.

Taryn muscled through the wall of testosterone and tension, her suitcase doing the heavy lifting against men in long-sleeved shirts, deep suntans, and assorted wide-brimmed hats. 'Excuse me. Move... I swear, if one more elbow hits this case—'

The crowd reluctantly shifted, like she was a fly interrupting a cattle sale.

A pair of cattle dogs lounged beneath a corner table, tongues lolling, eyes half-lidded like they were unimpressed by the lot of them. One gave a single thump of its tail as she passed, the only welcome she got from all these blokes in boots.

But the tension coming off this lot of hotheads, it was like something was about to snap. And soon.

Behind the bar stood Mean-Rene. Beside her stood Billy, dressed like an old jazz player, his fedora tilted low as he hooked a thumb under his suspenders and hitched them higher on his shoulder.

'You've opened early,' Taryn said to Billy, dumping her case down with a thud.

Billy nodded. 'What are you doing back?'

'I'd like to get another room…' But did they have any with this many people in town?

Taryn's eyes swept the front bar again, then locked onto the one person who wasn't panicking.

Samantha.

The publican, who the locals called *God*.

Amara said the woman was smarter than she ever let on. Silently standing at the back of the room, casually sipping her coffee like this happened every day of the week.

'Watch my case.' Taryn made her way over. 'What's going on?'

'Red and Two-bob Bob were caught stealing cattle from Warraga Downs.' Samantha gave a slow nod at the crowd. 'And there's nothing this mob hates more than someone stealing cattle.'

'I can see that. But the anger?'

'That's because Lydia and young Brodie were the ones who caught Red and Bob in the act. But then Red rammed his ute into Lydia's car to stop them.'

'Are they okay?'

'Lydia is in the ICU, and we're waiting on news. Brodie got pretty banged up, too. Poor kid's been through hell, that one…' Samantha sipped on her coffee, as if to swallow her emotions, while keeping a watchful eye on the room. 'And with no Lydia or Brodie around, there was no one to open the stockyards this morning.'

'So you opened the pub instead?'

'I've got a special licence for emergencies,' Samantha added. 'I use it during floods, bushfires, or cyclones on Christmas Day. We don't have a town hall for them to share their grievances, so they come here.' She nodded at the crowded room.

Taryn's brow lifted. 'You're making money off this?'

Samantha smiled, slow and unapologetic. 'I do have a business to run. But a large per cent of today's sales are going straight to Lydia and Brodie, should they need anything. There are a few hats going around if you want to add to the cause.'

Samantha then leaned over and said with a seriousness Taryn had never seen in the publican, 'You'd better cross your fingers that Lydia makes it or there will be no holding this mob back.'

'Why?'

Samantha looked out over the room of grumbling men and their coiled fists. 'You do know what this is, don't you?'

Taryn arched an eyebrow.

'It's not just a pub full of angry stockmen. It's a bedside vigil. For her. For Lydia.'

'Is this normal? Remember I'm from the outside.' And Taryn felt every bit the outsider.

'Lydia's not just the clerk—she's the mother of the stockyards. She's been there thirty-five years and never took a sick day. Through heatwaves and floods, Lydia is the one they all see first thing in the morning. She's that voice on the radio telling them where to go, who to sign off with, and what to do. She's that warm, motherly voice in a place full of blokes who don't know how to ask for help. The one who holds their secrets, handing them their stock cheques, while she pats their hands when they're too proud to cry. She'll scold them when they've mucked up with their missus, and then tell them exactly how to fix it. And I'd bet she's told over half the men in this room what to buy their wives for Christmas.'

Samantha's voice softened, but it didn't waver. 'Lydia has a thing for making leather goods. And she's probably made leather belts and muster-ready radio holsters for every man in this room. She's fixed more buttons on their shirts and patched more barbed-wire tears on their jeans, than anyone would dare count.

'You see, Red didn't *just* betray Lydia. He betrayed *all* of them.' Samantha tipped her chin toward the crowd. 'They trusted him because *she* did. And Red hurt Brodie, too—and that boy,' she said with a glare loaded with such absolute fire it made Taryn step back, 'has already been through hell. And if Lydia dies? You'll have a lynch mob on your hands before the sun's fully up.'

'They need someone to speak to them,' Taryn implored. 'It's your place.'

Samantha peered over the room, arms folded, reading the crowd the way some people read weather patterns—like she already knew which way the wind would turn. 'If I stand up now, it'll stop being a legal matter. This room? Sure, it'll listen to me. But that's not how this should go down.'

'Why not?' Taryn scrutinised the young publican.

'The police need to show they can handle this. Because if they can't, then everything we're holding together out here— the law, the processes, and the peace—starts looking optional. And that's a terrible idea in a place that is considered the last frontier, where lawlessness can thrive in the wilderness, and where rules are easily forgotten.'

Taryn realised then… Samantha wasn't just a player at the table. Not even the dealer.

She was *the house*.

The one who set the rules, where those house rules mattered, because the house *always* won.

In Elsie Creek, the mayor might wear the sash—but Samantha wore its dusty crown, pouring the beer, holding a kind of quiet-queen energy that kept the game honest… all while cleverly letting everyone think it was their idea to play.

Samantha was protecting the town for the good of its

people. No wonder they called her God.

'Just so you know, you're the only badge left in town. The rest are out on a manhunt. So, I suggest you tell them that there's a better way to handle this than spilling blood on my floor built for beer, boots, and mateship—not revenge.'

'Me?' WTF!

Samantha just raised an eyebrow at her, like ordering Taryn to do what had to be done.

Annoyingly, the young publican was right.

'Don't get me banned from my beer if I do this.' Taryn had no choice. She nodded at the publican, who only grinned at her.

Taryn had never talked down an angry mob of stockmen before. But she'd walked into boardrooms with a badge, a warrant, and zero patience.

She'd made plenty of arrests with a speech to match—enough to watch those smug suits speed-dial their lawyers, while the office girls looked ready to cry, and some pimply kid by the copier turned so pale his zits passed for freckles.

Her mother once told her the trick to commanding a room full of men in uniform was to speak like you owned the mission, not just the paperwork. That it didn't matter if they wore brass buttons or dusty jeans and stockmen's hats—men were still men. Prone to pride, and generally allergic to being told what to do by a woman.

And right now, this room didn't need a speech from a cop like Finn—who didn't do speeches and would level people with a stare that said *don't make me talk*.

Lord help her...

She took a deep breath and marched straight to the bar—because of course the bar was the stage—and, without a word, climbed on top, praying she didn't stack on the way up and face plant into someone's dusty boot.

A few heads turned. Someone muttered. Probably wondering if she was there to confiscate their beer or worse, shut the pub!

Wouldn't that start a riot.

'Well, here goes nothing…'

Taryn pulled in a breath, shoved two fingers into her mouth, and whistled so piercingly sharp it cut through the conversations like a knife.

The pub fell quiet. A chair scraped. One of the muster dogs sat up alert, tail thumping, like it knew things were about to change.

But all eyes were on her.

She scanned the crowd, offering them a dry smile. 'Ladies. Gentlemen. Stockmen. Sleepwalkers. And whoever left their saddle outside—your horse is currently blocking a Hilux.'

A few chuckles gave her a foothold with their attention.

Taryn then reached into her pocket for her badge and snapped it into place on the hip of her jeans with a crisp flick. 'I know some of you have heard of me. The Fed.'

She raised a brow, letting the silence ride for a beat.

'Look, I'm not here to ban you from your beer or tell you how to brand a beast. I'm here because I've seen what this town stands for. What it fights for. And this—' she gestured around the room of gathered hats, 'is something worth fighting for. The people in this town. And that includes you lot.'

She made eye contact with the hard men who lived weathered lives in a pub that was this outback town's parliament of power. The hallowed front bar that was thick with tension as if the walls were waiting for permission to breathe.

'I'm so sorry about Lydia and Brodie. I truly am,' she said with a hand to her heart. 'I get that this town, you, have all suffered a blow. But this,' she said with her hand sweeping over the room. 'This isn't justice. And I'm sure Lydia would only want the best for all of us.'

'What would Brodie say?' she asked, then huffed. 'Actually, knowing teenagers, he'd probably mutter something sarcastic and pretend not to care. But he *would* care. Because Brodie knows what this place is made of.'

The bar filled with silence now. Real silence.

'I may be that outsider, but what I've seen of this town? It's something rare. Something layered with this incredible ingrained community spirit. Like the red dust doesn't come off easy, but it gets into everything and somehow it makes you stronger. You look after each other in ways I've never seen before. Not in city offices or federal buildings. Not even in families that say they're *close*.'

That earned her a few quiet nods.

'You build things here. You fix things. You carry pain with your heads high, and you don't ask for help until someone's handing you a cold beer and a fresh bandage for a wound you didn't even know was showing. But that mate beside you, willing to give you a hand, and you them? That's not weakness. That's the great Aussie spirit and something to be proud of. So if you want to honour Lydia, do it by being who she believed you are—good men, who don't need to raise a fist to prove they care. And if you want to help? Great. Then help.'

She pointed toward the front doors. 'Let's start by getting those stockyards open. That's what Lydia would want—trucks moving, cattle sorted, and all that yard dust back in the air where it belongs. So, who usually helps when Lydia goes away on holiday?'

A voice shouted from the back: 'Bree!'

'Call her!' someone else shouted.

'Only if you've got some cupcakes,' said another, 'she'll drag the baby with her, no sweat.'

Laughter rippled through the room like relief cracking at the tension.

Taryn grinned. 'You heard 'em. Someone call Bree and order a double batch of cupcakes for her, and someone to help her with the baby.'

Baby.

Nope, not the time!

She forcefully put her hands on her hips, and not on her belly. With her badge catching the pub's light, she refocused on the crowd. 'If any of you have any information, sightings, or whispers? Please report it to Tanisha at the station. And if you're the type who doesn't want to dob in a mate… there's a confidential tip line for that too. No need for names. Just your truths.'

She eyed the room one last time with a lot of them nodding back at her.

'Now, let's get those stockyard gates open. And let's show Lydia we've got this covered until she's back behind that desk, bossing everyone around with a cup of coffee and clipboard in hand.'

A few cheers rose as the crowd started to scatter.

She jumped down, heart thudding like she'd just mustered a thousand head on foot. As laughter, along with the scuff of boots and a renewed purpose, filled the pub behind her.

She didn't see him — not until he was there.

Finn.

Tall, dust-worn, eyes locked on hers like she was the only damn thing that mattered in the entire world. His hand wrapped around her wrist, and without a word, he pulled her into the small storeroom behind the bar. The door swung shut behind them with a thud.

'What are y—'

But the words never landed.

Because Finn kissed her.

No hesitation. No build-up.

Just one hand sliding to her nape, the other curving around her waist like he'd done a thousand times in her dreams and wasn't letting go again.

He kissed her like he'd waited too damn long and wasn't about to waste another second with words. It was a kiss that was full of heat — wild, outback heat — and something deeper. Like *home*.

Taryn had no hope of resisting. She simply melted. Completely. Into their kiss.

Their boots were toe-to-toe, as her heart thudded against his chest, her hands fisting into his shirt like it was the only thing keeping her upright.

He wasn't just kissing her—he was *claiming* her in a way that made time blur, and everything she was feeling made sense.

By the time they broke apart, her lungs were burning, her lips tingling, and her brain was off traipsing somewhere halfway down the hallway.

'Well,' she whispered, breathless. 'That was…'

'Hello,' he murmured close. 'It's about time you showed up.'

Thirty-five

Finn didn't give Taryn a choice. He just shoved her suitcase into the back of the troopy, like it was always meant to be there, like she was. Didn't say she had to stay with him, he just wasn't letting her argue about it.

She was here. That was enough. For now.

He'd gone to the pub, ready to knock heads because he didn't do speeches. He didn't do crowds or calming words. That was Marcus's job, and Finn was happy to back them up. But the Elsie Creek Police weren't even close to making it back into town before this pub exploded.

But the moment he'd stepped inside the bar, the fight drained right out of him.

Because there she was…

Taryn. Standing on the bar like it was her battleground. In jeans that clung like memory, with her hair clipped back in that no-nonsense way that had him itching to set it free.

And the whole bloody town, who'd been spoiling for violence, had quieted.

For her.

He couldn't breathe for a second.

She'd been gone a month. No calls. Nothing. Just radio silence reduced to short sharp text messages, because they couldn't let anyone know. It'd destroy the case they were building and wreck everything.

So, he'd told himself it didn't matter. Told himself he was fine. Kept busy. And stayed focused.

But seeing her—

Damn, didn't it hit him like a dust storm to the chest. The noise of the crowd faded, and all he heard was her voice—

low, calm, anchoring.

And he'd just stood there. Every nerve ending reaching for her like the month apart hadn't happened.

It wasn't just that he'd missed her.

It was the way his body *knew her*. Along with that ache in his chest that said, *there you are.*

He hadn't realised how hollow he'd felt until she filled his space.

So when she'd climbed down off the bar, and when her boots hit the floor and she'd turned —

He didn't think. Didn't speak.

He'd just reached for her and dragged her somewhere behind a closed door and kissed her. Because if he'd tried to say anything to her, beyond hello, he would've ruined it.

But that kiss…

When he should've been thinking about work and the town, he was thinking about her lips, and the way they'd crashed into his like they'd both been holding their breath for weeks. How her mouth had tasted like sugar and defiance. And how she'd looked at him afterward, like maybe she didn't regret it.

That was the part he couldn't shake, that moment that kept playing over in his head.

Soon after, she'd made him take her to the food van at the train station, muttering something about reinforcements, and came back armed with coffees and breakfast rolls like she was preparing for a siege.

'Your cup of mud.' Taryn handed him a takeaway cup inside the troopy. 'Drink it.'

He didn't argue as she talked the entire drive to the police station. Her familiar scent, her voice, her place on the passenger seat—all belonging.

What didn't belong was Taryn talking about the weather. How miserable Canberra was with chilly rain and grey clouds. And how the clouds were rolling in early and maybe they'd get rain by the weekend.

She didn't give a damn about rain or weather. That was

the first clue.

Then she started on about the glittery cactus-shaped cat toys she'd bought for Tanisha—clue number two.

And then her retelling of her boss's weird story about wrestling crocodiles the size of ten bathtubs, being told around the water cooler that it nearly choked some intern chewing on a jelly snake. Three strikes.

Taryn Hayes was stalling. Like it was any other morning where she hadn't just dropped into town and stolen his breath.

He knew her well enough to spot the dodge. She didn't do nice. Not like this.

Sass-talk, yes.

Small talk? No chance. They'd never bothered with small talk. Not from the moment they'd met.

So when they pulled into the car park behind the police station, he cut the engine and waited.

Taryn reached for the coffee tray.

But he put his hand on hers, to make her pause.

'It's not like you to beat around a patch of spinifex like this, Fed,' he said, low. 'What's going on?'

Her inhale was staggered, as if hesitating.

'Must be big.'

'It is.'

Her whole demeanour shifted, as that quick, razor-sharp confidence of hers faded into something quieter.

And in the pit of his guts, Finn felt it like a warning. Especially when she looked at him like he only had a few weeks to live. 'It's Drew,' she whispered. 'It's all Drew.'

He didn't move. Didn't blink. But everything inside him dropped like a steer caught off-guard, with its legs yanked out from under it.

'The stock theft?' His voice was hoarse, already knowing the answer.

She nodded. 'It's bigger than just here. It's nationwide, Finn. Drew used your first Gaps File report and turned all your research into a how-to guide to steal livestock. Every weakness you flagged within the industry, he used it as a blueprint to build an illegal empire.'

Finn stared at the dashboard's cracked trim and the old sticker peeling off near the vent. The troopy had taken hits before. So had he. But this one…

'The man who gave me a second chance,' he murmured. 'The man who told me to build this squad…'

'Used it to cover his tracks, he was—'

'Say it.' He braced himself, already guessing it.

She shook her head like she couldn't.

So he said it instead. 'He set me up to fail.'

Wasn't that the ultimate kick in the guts. Enough to force the air out of his lungs, while struggling for the strength to breathe again—and only then he heaved in fire.

She gave his hand a squeeze. 'I'm so sorry, Finn.'

'That's not what I need to hear. Give me something.' He needed that lifeline.

She nodded at him like she understood. 'I have more than enough to bury that bastard for life.'

He swallowed down the heat to listen beyond his raging pulse. 'How?'

'I've spent the past two days going through everything with my father, and we've connected the dots. We found legal proof of how Drew buried it in shell companies, fake contractors, cryogenic shipments, including his use of livestock routes. The Commissioner wasn't helping the Stock Squad, Finn. He was helping himself. The worst of it is…'

'Go on.'

'He's been in Elsie Creek and used that airstrip.' She pointed to the airport that sat beyond the mesh fence. 'Drew shook hands with the Stock Squad, giving your team their badges, while he had his assistant loading boxes filled with cryogenic canisters onto his jet. Arsehole.'

Finn's hands curled around the steering wheel, knuckles tight and white. His jaw clenched, his eyes locked on the windscreen like it might give him a different point of view, to take back all those years of loyalty and blind faith he'd given to his mentor, Drew.

'He used me,' Finn said, his voice rough. 'I defended him. Trusted him. And all this time… he was gutting this country's prime stock from the inside out.' He pressed the heel of his hand to his chest, like maybe if he pushed hard enough, he could stop the hollow tearing him apart.

Her hand curled around his arm, her thumb brushing the crook of his elbow. 'I'm so sorry.'

He didn't speak. He couldn't even move as the silence in the cab filled with a pressure in the air that made it hard to breathe, as the words echoed in his head, like static through a busted radio. *He used me. Built his illegal empire on my second chance. Making me the frontman for the system he was stealing from.*

It clawed at him like barbed wire lashed across his back.

Come on. Why this? When Finn had spent his entire life crawling out of gutters.

A drunk for a father who'd taught him pain and fear.

A badge ripped from his chest the second he'd earned it.

A son he'd buried.

A wife he'd lost.

Leaving him with no family, only fists in prison where every inch he'd ever gained, he'd bled for.

And just when he thought he'd found a place to build something that mattered, when the Stock Squad felt like a second chance, *this*.

If the stockmen in this town were ready to lynch Red and Two-bob Bob for stolen cattle, what would they do to him, the bloke who'd unknowingly handed the keys to the kingdom to *his boss!*

He thought of Lydia. And of Brodie. Of Craig, Amara, Stone, Romy, Porter, and Izzy—all of them. How could he face any of them? The walking punchline of a twisted con.

Finn didn't realise he was shaking until he felt her hand, steady and warm, resting on his forearm.

'You need to tell them.' His voice cracked, like every word had scraped past the bruised edges of what was left of him.

'The team look at me like I've built something solid. I can't be the one to take that from them. But you… You're the outsider. The Fed. You're the one who came to find the truth.'

And damn, didn't she find that truth.

A bitter twist of a smile ghosted across his face. 'That's why they'll listen. Because you were the enemy. And now, it's time for you to deliver.'

The line hit hard at how that wheel had turned.

Taryn stared at him with wide eyes. Because they both knew he wasn't wrong.

She'd been the enemy who had come to dismantle them. And now, she might be the only one who could hold them together.

Thirty-six

Finn stood at the back of the room. Didn't feel like he had the right to sit at the table—not anymore.

He'd done that before. Right at the very start of all this. Back when Drew had walked into prison wearing that suit and a smug smile, laying down a federal pardon in front of Finn, who'd been chained up like a dog.

Should've known it came with a price.

Nothing's free, mate.

Especially when you give an ex-con a badge and a budget.

Taryn stood at the front now, where he used to stand. Badge clipped, files in hand. Facing his team, with the glow from the widescreen shining like a halo around her.

They were all there, Craig and Izzy, Romy and Stone, Amara and Porter, taking up space at the round table that held his maps, sipping coffee and spreading pastry crumbs. While Finn held up the back wall, not because they'd pushed him there, but because he didn't feel he deserved a seat anymore.

'*Everlight Energy Solutions* was the start of everything…' Taryn was finally giving that PowerPoint presentation she'd once threatened him with as a joke, only now each dot point was just another nail sticking into his spine.

'Everlight bought land, all strategically set in places that were high value areas for livestock across the country. They installed a few solar panels and cleverly collected federal grants. And as we all know, there was no energy being generated. It was a front that Izzy figured out.' She nodded to Izzy seated at the table beside her husband, Cowboy Craig. 'And it's what got Meghan Forrester killed.' Taryn's voice faltered for the first time as she announced, 'Meghan was my cousin.'

A heavy quietness settled across the room on that revelation that Finn had never shared with the team.

Stone sat back, wiping his mouth, to stop speaking. Amara blinked, then gave a sympathetic look to Izzy and then to Taryn. Craig slid his arm around his wife's shoulders and whispered something, but Izzy didn't flinch. But her knuckles whitened around the coffee cup in her hands.

Finn saw it.

Saw the tight line of Izzy's jaw, where the pain was buried deep, but not forgotten.

Meghan Forrester's murder may have been solved in the eyes of the law. Renzo had done it. Izzy had seen it.

But Renzo had died before he could stand trial.

And Finn knew without a doubt just from Taryn's stance, that she had worked out the connection—because that woman only came to this town to seek justice for her cousin.

And with no fanfare, Taryn announced, 'The guy behind it all is the Federal Agricultural Commissioner, Andrew Bannon. He's the man who wrote the grant applications and is the face behind Everlight Energy Solutions.'

It was like someone had pulled the plug on the entire room. Even the air felt stunned.

'Big Daddy is the bad guy?' Stone let out a low whistle.

Taryn nodded.

Craig just muttered, 'Well, I'll be damned.'

Finn knew it'd hit Amara the hardest. She'd backed this squad like gospel, believing in Drew, the job, the badge—*him*.

And now?

Amara sat frozen, eyes fixed on the table, her thoughts probably spiralling, trying to retrace every conversation she'd ever had with Drew. All those so-called secret check-ins, all those quiet meetings she thought were routine. When she finally told him—*only after Taryn caught it*—and told her to report it to the correct chain of command.

Only now, Finn could see the truth dawning in her eyes…

Drew hadn't been guiding her, he'd been recruiting Amara, to wedge her out from under Finn's shadow without her even realising it.

Slowly, Amara turned to face Finn. Guilt and a raw, wordless apology filled her eyes, that gutted him more than anything Taryn had said.

Finn held her gaze from across the room and gave the smallest shake of his head — *No. You didn't do this.*

And in that moment, he knew she understood.

The bad part was that Amara now knew the sting of being betrayed by someone you trusted.

Beside her, Porter squeezed her hand, while murmuring something only she could hear. Whatever it was, it worked. Her jaw loosened. Her shoulders came down. And for the first time since Taryn had dropped the bomb, Amara breathed.

Thank you, Porter.

'How did you work that out?' Izzy asked, shifting in her seat.

'It started when I found a sealed juvenile file that linked Drew directly to Renzo,' started Taryn. 'Drew had buried Renzo's charges when he was fifteen and brought him into a so-called rural mentor program.'

Aw hell no! Finn's gut clenched at the word: Mentor.

'From our research, we found Drew used Renzo to do his dirty work. Paid him for it, too. And I've got the bank trail to prove it.' Taryn clicked through an assortment of images, early criminal photos of Renzo, the juvenile file, and Renzo's bank account, one they didn't know about — but Taryn did.

She clicked to another screen and up came another face they all knew.

'Renzo's co-offender in Izzy's kidnapping, Dane *DC* Carter, was killed in Darwin prison last year while on remand. His killer?'

Finn had been hedging his bets it was Red who'd arranged that one.

'Another one of Drew's boys. Another juvenile from that

same mentor program.' Again, Taryn showed pictures of a prisoner, from a juvenile to an adult with files linked to Drew's name.

'The money?' Izzy asked.

'Was paid to his mother's account, who is raising his son.' And she showed bank accounts, and surveillance photos of a boy and his grandmother.

'And Renzo?' Izzy's eyes widened as if watching a horror movie. 'What about the car accident that killed Renzo?'

'The driver, who smashed into that prisoner transport, killing Renzo and those two prison guards, was also part of Drew's mentor program. But this one,' Taryn said, clicking to another set of images of a stranger, from his juvie record to a man. 'He had terminal cancer. Drew gave his family a payout, claiming it was from some bogus insurance company. They had no idea. But it clearly demonstrates a pattern. With Renzo and Dane Carter's deaths, they were just pawns in Drew's game, and he likes to clear his board of any loose ends.'

Dead men don't talk, they all knew that. Finn especially.

Taryn then looked at the team. 'Drew kept up the juvenile mentor program because it made the perfect recruitment pool, but he tailored it to their individual needs, as if preying on their weak spots. Playing the long game, better than any chess master to build his own crew on call. He'd pay their debts. Buy their loyalty. And erase their records. Only to call in those favours when he needed to.'

The words hit Finn like a steel boot to the ribs, making his heart drop hard, turning it into something ugly.

He'd fought his way out of hell more than once—only to find the devil wore a badge, offering him a hangman's rope and calling it a pardon.

And the worst part?

Finn wasn't the first. But he also wasn't just a pawn who'd helped Drew build that playing board—he'd become the poster boy for a federal con job.

Taryn clicked to the next slide. 'When the Stock Squad shut down Everlight, Drew didn't fight it, because he didn't need it anymore. He had the money. So he stopped, blocked, and deleted all connections to Everlight. And then went about setting up a different kind of operation, doing the same thing that Finn suspected with Everlight, creating way stations, like they have at the quarry.'

She circled a logo on the screen—*Stokemir PC Inc.* 'This is an international export company. It's new and looks clean on the surface. But that's where all the funds stolen by Everlight Energy Solutions went.'

Izzy murmured. 'All of it?'

'Yep. It's where Drew laundered the money to fund his entire operation—the planes, leases, transport, even bribes.' Taryn clicked the remote again. A new slide appeared: company logos, email headers, wire transfers. There were so many of them, it was doing Finn's head in.

'But how did it all work?' asked Romy.

'Red did the scouting, targeting the bloodlines, looking for prime herds and exotic species that would fetch top dollar on the international markets. Red would also take Bob with him, as if recommending him as a contractor for these cattle stations. Bob told people he had a vet technician on call, and someone to manage the logistics.'

Which just confirmed Finn's suspicions of how Red and Bob had tried to steal stock at Warraga Downs last night.

'That tech guy,' Taryn added, tapping the screen, 'was Bastion. And the reason I know this is that the emails all go through one company *M.T. Spiker Co.* It's registered to an empty shed just outside Dublin, South Australia—home to one of the country's busiest saleyards, where stock rolls through by the thousands. Making it the perfect place to hide in plain sight.'

Taryn clicked to the next slide. 'Officially, M.T. Spiker Co. sells fencing gear, vet supplies, stockfeed... real salt-of-the-earth feed store kind of vibe. Only the website's full of stock photos. The phone rings out to a cheerful robot, and the shed is so empty it echoes. But the email? That's definitely manned.'

Izzy raised an eyebrow. 'Let me guess—payments in split invoices, off-brand suppliers with government-sounding names? Like Everlight's paperwork.'

'Bingo. And half the ABNs link back to shell companies all headquartered at other strategic stock centres across the country.' Taryn tapped on the table where his team sat.

'Sounds like the livestock industry's version of Monopoly,' muttered Stone without any of the smart-arse humour he was known for.

'Except the only thing that gets passed around is stolen genetic material and fake waybills.'

Across the room, Finn didn't say a word. He'd been to those stockyards, even stopping at that shed Taryn flashed on the screen. Back when he thought he was laying the groundwork for something clean, flagging it in the first Gaps File as a potential quarantine site. A base for a southern stock squad. And that mongrel had turned it into a *shopfront for thieves.*

'And through M.T. Spiker Co,' continued Taryn, clicking through a series of emails, 'Red and Bob would get emailed tasks or requests overseen by Drew. Everything from livestock orders, to digging up dirt on people they could exploit to become potential truck drivers, like Tooley—the guy who had a clean record, two kids and a crippling mortgage.'

Craig leaned forward, his brow creasing. 'What about Sawyer Dixby? Is he SW?'

Taryn shook her head. 'SW Rural Contracting is Bob's. His real name is Samuel Ward. The red pickup Sawyer drove was leased under Bob's company. Even though it's under the parent company of *Temp Roicks Pty Ltd*, which owns the quarry, it's Bob who's in charge of that area.'

'I knew Bob was related to the Dixbys, I just didn't realise he'd be helping Sawyer,' said Craig.

'Well, from what we saw in the paper trail, Bob was Sawyer's cousin, and he knew that the overseer needed to stay hidden. Based on the emails, Red knew Sawyer had a debt and was desperate for a way to make money. Only Red used that to control him. And, maybe out of guilt for the obvious manipulations, Bob got his cousin, Sawyer, what he called...' She flicked down through her notes and said, 'the red yank-tank.'

'The Ram?' Porter asked.

She nodded, holding up one of her files. 'I found the paperwork for it, even the receipts for tools that Bob got for his cousin to help him find those missing deeds out at Dixby Downs station.'

'Did they kill Sawyer?' Porter asked, who was the same as Craig, both men had always wondered if it wasn't murder, when they'd first found Sawyer's dusty grave.

'I don't know.' She gave a shrug.

Amara asked Taryn, 'And the quarry?'

'The quarry was always their backup if Dixby Downs was ever shut down. Because of the logistics, Dixby Downs suited them better, until the paperwork went through on the quarry.'

Taryn clicked again and showed more documents, linking them to companies and places. 'And just in case the quarry got too hot? This past month they've been prepping the paperwork for Noonamah Rise. Another remote rural NT holdings that is still connected to the same logistics web.'

Finn's stomach turned. Was that where Red and Bob were hiding out now?

'So how are they moving stock?' Stone asked, 'The road trains, the gear? How do they get it in and out without raising flags?'

'*Corkspite M. Group*. They order the trucks. Handle all the land logistics. Their invoices are legit—on paper. Again, registered for feed, grain and livestock logistics, useful for moving bulk goods. And I've found, through interstate data, that their trucks are always in the area the *same days* stock thefts are reported. But here's the kicker...'

She paused, forcing Finn to prepare for another kick in the guts from this PowerPoint presentation.

'I suspect it's the same trailer swap scheme, just like that truck you busted on the Spinifex Highway. Good stock swapped out for second-rate stock. Or the truck shows up light.' Taryn looked at the team and said with a layer of heaviness, 'And it's not just here, guys. This is happening in three other states: Western Australia, South Australia, and Queensland.'

The murmur, and the shoes shuffling under the table, demonstrated the enormity of the situation all being laid out before them. Each screen. Each new layer. It was like swallowing broken glass.

'As for the high-value hauls, the specialised stock like those elite equestrian horses, crocodiles, banteng, the rodeo bulls… Those are taken purely for frozen genetic material and shifted up north to those way stations—like Dane Carter's property he'd sold to Everlight, then Dixby Downs, and now the quarry.' She clicked to a map on the screen. 'Excluding Everlight's property, Dixby Downs and the quarry have airstrips, where they use chartered jets to carry those cryogenic containers inside simple cardboard boxes. Every shipment has customs paperwork filed through *Merc Topski*. A registered international livestock exporter, that gives the impression that it's Eastern European, but it's a front for offshore transfers with lots of legitimate looking paperwork wearing a fake Customs rubber stamp.'

She then paused, putting down that clicker that was going to give Finn nightmares every time he heard it. And how she looked at him didn't help either.

'It was all in your Gaps File, Finn. All of it. You just didn't know the names of the companies, but you had it all there, on the wall in your home.'

'What's with all those company names?' Stone muttered at the table. 'They sound like someone shook a Scrabble bag and made-up those names and logos.'

And that's when it clicked—the right kind of click…

The pattern.

'Have you got a list of those company names?' Finn

demanded, standing now a few inches off the wall. 'Just the names.'

'Sure.' Taryn swiped through her laptop, then clicked to an image on the screen behind her, where the logos vanished and were replaced by a list of names, some he hadn't seen before:

> *STOKEMIR PC*
> *M.T. SPIKER CO*
> *MERC TOPSKI*
> *CORKSPITE M*
> *SPICK METRO*
> *SPERTICK NOM*
> *KROMIC SPET*
> *PRISCOM TEK*
> *K PERSCO TIM*
> *P STORM KICE*
> *TK. SPICER MO*

'*That mongrel*—' The expletives rolled into one as Finn stalked to the whiteboard, grabbed a marker, and scrawled two words in big block capitals:

PRIME STOCK

Finn's chest heaved, nearly driving his finger through the wall as he pointed at those letters. 'They're all anagrams. Every single one of those company names spells the same thing—*Prime Stock*.'

It was another word game.

All those years of scribbling inside those damn word puzzle books, Finn saw Drew's pattern—the man who loved those books and had introduced them to Finn, just like he'd done with Brodie only this morning.

But now the words felt like gravel tearing at his throat. 'Drew's not hiding behind the names. He's laughing at us. Right in our bloody faces. Every company name is just another way of saying what he's stealing: *Prime Stock.*'

The anger coiled low in his gut, rising sharp behind his ribs at this insult.

He turned to face the team. The ones who'd followed him. Trusted him. And now he had to force the words out. 'I'm sorry. Not just for missing it, but for dragging you all into this. I thought I was building something good. Turns out I was handing Drew the tools instead.'

His jaw tightened as he looked each one of them in the eye. 'If you want to walk, I'll understand. I won't stop you… But right now, I need you. All of you. Because I know exactly how to bring that mongrel down. And this time, we take everything with him.'

As the silence stretched, he didn't blame them for being cautious. If he were in their position, he'd have bolted for that door too.

Then footsteps.

Taryn crossed the room, stood beside him and faced the team. 'Having interviewed you all individually, I know you joined Finn because you believe in the mission. You stayed because you believe in the man… And you were right to.'

She gazed at Finn and somehow her voice softened. 'This is the guy who rebuilt his life, who took a broken system and used it to protect what matters. Who gave this town a team worth trusting. So, if he's standing, I'm standing. And I'll do whatever it takes to help this team, and you, Finn.'

Finn didn't speak. Couldn't. Not with that knot in his throat.

Amara was already pushing her coffee aside with a determined nod, lighting up her trusty tablet. 'Ready when you are, sir.'

Porter leaned back in his chair with a nod. 'The Hellhound is fully fuelled to stir up the dust.'

Craig cracked his knuckles, lips twitching into a half-smile. 'Point the way, Finn, you know I'll always have your back, mate.'

'You'll need someone to make this work legal, if you're

going to take this prick down,' said Izzy, dragging over all of Taryn's paperwork. 'I want him to pay for what he did to Meghan.'

Taryn nodded at Izzy

Stone muttered, 'You know me, I'm always up to party, Bossman.'

Romy nodded, squirming in her seat as if full of nervous energy. 'Tell me what I'm shooting at—'

They all looked at her.

'With my cameras, obviously.' She shrugged, sheepishly. 'But I'll fly whatever drone you need to make it happen.'

They were in. All of them.

And that knot in Finn's chest… loosened. Just a little.

His voice, when it came, was low and gruff. And very Finn. 'Well? What are you waiting for? An invitation?'

And the ultimate plan to bring down the Commissioner began.

Thirty-seven

At the quarry, the air was thick with heat, as the scent of dry grass and dust tickled Taryn's nose, when her stomach rumbled, again.

She ignored it. Even though she'd already thrown up breakfast, twice, there was no room for queasiness now—not when Finn was one step away from either justice or a breakdown.

After everything he'd learned about Drew, the lies layered over years of trust, Finn needed something solid to hold on to. Not another secret curled in her tummy that might tip him off the edge.

He needed a win. And she'd do everything she could to help him get it. So, she'd give him this instead. The mission.

From their high ridge lookout over the quarry's main compound, the team laid low in various areas. Some beneath camo netting, gear prepped, with their comms on a closed loop. All in a position to watch for dust kicking up along the main entry points.

Porter's voice crackled through the radio. 'I've got a visual on the target vehicle. It's them. Stolen Warraga Downs truck—two on board.'

Finn shifted beside her, his binoculars fixed on the vehicle and all but snarled over the radio, 'It's them. Hold your positions.'

A full-sized stock truck—not a road train, but big enough to turn heads in the city—roared into the quarry. Its faded green sides were dented and sun-aged, with a heavy tarp stretched over the livestock bay for shade.

Bob was driving, with Red slumped in the passenger seat,

head bandaged, looking like the lucky loser of a crocodile-wrestling contest

Bob didn't waste time. Before the dust had settled, he'd leapt from the truck, then disappeared inside the demountable. Before the front door had even swung shut, he burst back out, carrying a duffel bag with clothes hanging from the zip.

'Everyone, watch for their freight,' Taryn said over the comms. Because they didn't just need Bob and Red. They needed Drew. And the cargo.

That was the stuff to seal the deal.

They watched Bob toss his duffel bag into the truck's cab where Red hardly moved. Bob reversed the truck toward a ragged stack of hay bales. There, Bob started digging through straw like a farm kid after Easter eggs.

And then he hit something.

Tugged.

And out came a blue tarp.

Underneath it—boxes.

Just like Tooley and Mickey had said. Plain cardboard boxes with brown tape, light enough to lift, with small flags on the sides labelled *Conference Pack*.

'Oh, perfect,' Taryn said under her breath, as she zoomed in on Romy's drone feed on her laptop. 'As Mickey, the master of all things grumpy would say, *those criminal masterminds of the Territory are about to be undone by a haystack full of flamin' tourist pamphlets in nappy boxes.*'

She blinked.

Nappy boxes.

Nappies.

Was that word going to haunt her for the next two years? When she didn't even know how to change one, let alone know what a nappy box looked like.

And now here they were, her first visual cue to impending motherhood, came from a smuggling ring hiding stolen prime stock genetic material in what looked like baby bulk buys.

Fan-tastic.

'If any of those boxes say *NT Tourism*, I'm putting it in my audit report under *Reasons I Deserve a Pay Rise, a Desk, and a Pack of Barbecue Shapes*.'

'You're spiralling,' muttered Finn, beside her.

'I'm just adapting,' Taryn shot back. 'It's a skill. You should try it sometime.'

Finn's mouth twitched. Just barely.

She exhaled heavily. The fear, the nausea, the need for sardines, and the what-ifs—still there. But quieter now, as she focused on the target. Even if it meant taking down this mess one dodgy nappy box at a time.

She scrolled back to her laptop, watching the live satellite map stutter and refresh. 'Inbound jet is twenty minutes out,' she said. 'Quarry landing site is hot. It's all happening, peoples.'

Her fingers flew across the keyboard, switching between feeds from the drones, comms, body cams, flight paths. 'You might want to warn Romy to keep her drones below the radar ceiling, Sergeant. We need them for eyes on, but we can't spook that other jet's approach. And tell Stone to stay tucked in below that escarpment.'

Finn's jaw clenched. 'Listen, Fed, we've been watching this place for a month. Thanks to Romy's motion cams, that are normally set up to catch crocodile nests and swamp buffalo, we've repurposed them for this.'

'I thought those were just for documentaries.'

'They are. But they also pick up human movement. We wired half of them into the quarry's light towers.' He gestured toward her screen. 'Craig's got Romy's GoPro. Porter's got his vest cam, and Romy will have her drone footage. If this goes to court, we'll have every angle covered.'

Taryn arched a brow. 'What is this? A sting or an outback fashion show? You've got more cameras on this than the paparazzi barging in on a red-carpet event in Milan.'

Finn gave her a look. Clearly unimpressed.

She grinned. 'Go on. Say you missed me.'

He snorted. 'Like a busted boot misses a bindi-eye seed.'

'Charming,' she drawled. 'Please, don't get all emotional on me now.'

'Just focus, Fed.'

'I'm trying. But you haven't even made me a coffee that tastes like mud since I got back. Clearly, something's missing in my life.'

His mouth twitched. Not a smile—but close.

'You're terrible at affection.'

'And you're still talking.'

'You're welcome.'

Finn narrowed his eyes, the corner of his mouth fighting the need to curl. 'Keep it up and I'll put you on car wash duty at the police station. That's every vehicle. Including Craig's horse truck.'

Taryn gasped, hand over heart. 'You monster. Those things haven't seen water since water was invented.'

Finn just shook his head and muttered, 'See, this is why I drink my coffee alone.'

She grinned, her eyes flicking to the incoming radar image of the jet.

Then something clicked.

All humour dropped as she watched Bob ease the truck toward the airstrip to wait for that jet. 'Wait... Something's not right.'

'What now?'

'Why would Drew fly into the hot zone? He's smarter than that.' On her laptop, she pulled up the Ag School conference site and crosschecked the speaker's schedule, including the emails she had access too. Her breath caught. 'Look... Drew has cancelled the speech he was meant to give this afternoon.'

They needed to know where the head snake in a suit was at all times. And she'd spent all morning combing Drew's emails, confirming that Bob and Red were headed to the quarry to meet the jet.

Finn had the plan in place. All she'd done was back it up with flight logs and digital proof—like he'd started the sentence, and she finished it. Not to show off, but because she liked having the last word. And he let her.

She'd never had a partner so in sync. It felt like he was someone she'd worked closely with for years, not someone she hadn't seen in a month

'And?'

'Look at the time stamp on his email.' She tapped frantically, pulling up the time-stamped files. 'First one's from Bob at 10:47 last night. That's two hours *after* you got Lydia and Brodie to the hospital.'

She read aloud:

> FROM: sw@mtspiker.com.au
> TO: ops@mtspiker.com.au
> SUBJECT: need pickup
> did look-see with Red, found warraga empty.
> took truck, were lining up a dozen fats when
> it went to hell.
> red got clocked hard. bleeding bad.
> no ute, no way out.
> town's after us. highway's blocked. cops
> looking.
> not leaving him.
> this is the plan, yeah? quarry run.
> send the jet.
> —bob
> Sent: 10:47pm, Wednesday

'Then Red follows up with his email an hour later, threatening Drew.'

Finn frowned and leaned in closer to her laptop screen to read the email:

> FROM: red@mtspiker.com.au
> TO: ops@mtspiker.com.au
> SUBJECT: Confirm your end
> Don't think you can block me by not
> answering your phone.

You'd better have that jet lined up, Drew!
This is the out you promised.
My wife is in hospital with some kid from the
yards. She saw too much, told me she's
been talking to the cops.
I've got nothing left in this town.
And you know what I know.
Don't make me say it twice.
—R
Sent: 11:58pm, Wednesday

'Then it takes Drew almost six hours to respond, and that's when he books the jet from Adelaide to Darwin. Around the same time, he sends this.' She brought up email three:

FROM: ops@mtspiker.com.au
TO: red@mtspiker.com.au,
sw@mtspiker.com.au
SUBJECT: Re: Confirm your end
Jet is on track.
Be there with the last load.
D.
Sent: 5:17am, Thursday

Finn shrugged. 'He delayed his response, making Red sweat it out. Drew would do that. Or he was asleep. It was midnight.'

Taryn shook her head. 'Drew would've had an alert set for emails from Bob or Red. Those two made him too much money. And we both know Drew is the kind of man who keeps at least three backup plans especially for times that feel like chaos.' Especially after a message like Bob's.

She looked at Finn. 'Drew never said he'd be on that jet. He just confirmed it was coming. When I crosschecked the bookings,' she said, tapping on her laptop, 'I found something else.'

'What?'

'A second manifest, logged by the shell company Stokemir PC. That's the bank Drew hides behind. This one's inbound from Canberra to Darwin. Look...' She spun her screen towards him. 'The time stamp matches Drew cancelling his speech at the ag conference. Minutes after Bob's first email came through.'

She met Finn's eyes.

Finn didn't need to say it. They both knew what it was.

Drew's running.

'Would Drew have an escape kit?'

'Yeah,' Finn muttered. 'Passport, cash, burner phone... maybe even a fake ID.'

Taryn frowned. 'Where would Drew stash it? Somewhere discreet? Not his house.'

'No.' Finn shook his head. 'Drew's smarter than that. He wouldn't use post office boxes, that's too obvious and too traceable. He would've just bought a nondescript car and paid for long-term parking. Somewhere public, out of the way, with 24-hour access to drive through, grab what he needed out of the boot, and then keep moving. Like an airport.'

They stared at each other, trying to work out if Drew had the time to fly back to Canberra and get on that other jet? Or was Drew on the jet coming from Adelaide?

'What I don't get is why Darwin?' she murmured. 'Both jets are headed there. If he's escaping, why not disappear from somewhere bigger, like Sydney or Melbourne?'

'Because Darwin's the perfect exit point. Always has been.' Finn took over her laptop and brought up a map of Darwin. 'It's remote. Quiet. With lots of international traffic, and not just tourists. There are plenty of private hangars that run flights to the Indigenous communities, islands, deserts, and mine sites. There are FIFO locker services, and long-term car parks no one monitors—especially with miners coming and going 24/7. Perfect for someone like Drew to walk right through without even getting near a security camera.'

'Among his many fishing stories, my boss called Darwin

the gateway to Asia.'

'And for good reason. You don't need to vanish in a big city. You vanish in a city so small and forgotten that no one's watching.' He looked at her. 'And around here? The NT's so small, half the Federal jobs are covered by local cops playing dress-up for the Commonwealth.'

'Would Drew know this?'

Finn nodded. 'He's been in and out of Darwin plenty of times to fly overseas. I'm sure he'd know every loophole in the system. After all, it's where he'd sent all that high-end stolen stock, like the equestrian horses, to get their genetic material to smuggle out of the country. He didn't keep that livestock down south, he had them all brought up here.'

'I've got his flight logs for the past three years.' She tapped at her laptop. 'Might be worth checking how often he dropped into Darwin. And if he's rented out any long-term car parks under his bogus company names.'

'Yeah, well, if he's as rich as you say, Drew wouldn't have just one exit plan. He'd have a dozen. Some stashed in capital cities. Some offshore. All of them quiet.'

'Seriously?'

He glanced at her. 'Drew wouldn't run. He'd tighten his tie, smile for the cameras… and vanish in a fancy suit like it was all part of the schedule.'

'Well, then, we'd better ruin his schedule, huh?'

Stone's voice cut in over comms: 'A jet has just been picked up on my radar… I've got eyes on it. Circling. Pilot hasn't dropped his landing gear yet.'

Taryn's mouth thinned. 'That's not Drew's ride in—it's his backup. He's not on that plane. He's sending someone else in to collect the freight, and to clean up loose ends. You said those names, what were they? The only others who knew about this quarry?'

'Clancy and the pilot.' Finn's brow tightened.

She tapped her screen again. 'I bet Drew's split the trail. A smuggler's trick. Leave one flight obvious, and let the real one vanish in the noise.' Her mind reeled. 'Just like there's nothing on paper about Drew ever visiting Elsie Creek.'

Finn looked at her as the weight of it sat heavy in the space between them.

Drew might already be gone.

Or he was still coming.

'Do I have time to text Marcus? He'd have the contacts to send someone to Darwin airport, to watch for that other plane.' She could only hope.

Finn nodded. 'I'll be fifty-fifty… Drew's either on that jet, or halfway to a beach with clean boots and cold beer.'

'Let's make a bet…' Taryn smirked as she sent the message to Marcus, who was busy coordinating from the Batcave, with Izzy helping him draft warrants, prepare charges, and trawl through her files for anything they could use to make legal arrests. 'If I'm right, which I am, we'll find Drew on the other jet, you'll be learning how to make real coffee. The kind that doesn't taste like river sludge. Oh, and you'll be wearing an apron for the tutorial.'

'Apron?'

'And a new kettle that whistles. Maybe a new gas cooker for the troopy, too. We're doing this properly, Sergeant.'

Finn grunted. 'Fine. But if I'm right… you're giving Cecil a bath.'

'Absolutely *not!*'

'You made a bet.'

'Cecil is a water buffalo who tried to eat my hair.'

'He likes your perfume.'

'He hunts me with his big wet nose and flower crown like some snorting Valentine's Day mascot who got the date wrong.'

Finn smirked. 'Cecil likes you, and he deserves a spa day.'

'First, I never expected the words *spa day* to ever come from your mouth.' Taryn groaned. 'Second, he's a water buffalo, not a bridesmaid.'

'Still counts. Bet's a bet, lady.' He held out his hand.

'Fine.' She shook it.

Below, the quarry jet cut through the sky like a scalpel. Its shadow streaked across the cracked basin as it dropped toward the compacted earth, aiming for the rough runway where Red and Bob waited for their escape.

Finn held her hand a second longer than seemed necessary.

Taryn felt the spark dart up her spine like a live wire. The words were there, right on the tip of her tongue, ready to be said.

Then Taryn's phone buzzed.

She flicked it open, her eyes flaring at the news.

'Not more bad news.' Finn groaned.

'The second jet from Canberra, it landed in Darwin. *Empty.* Drew was never on that jet.'

Finn looked at her. Then they both turned to watch the jet circling the quarry's runway. 'We're on.'

Thirty-eight

If this went right—if they bagged Drew on this incoming jet—Finn was calling for deck chairs and a barbecue out back of the police station, just to watch Taryn scrub down Cecil. That water buffalo would love it. And something with a lot of bubbles. Tanisha would be all over that, whipping up cocktails loaded with edible glitter, and ordering Porter to play DJ for the day. Come on, they needed something good to come out of this. Something to laugh about, for once.

But first, they had to finish it.

The wind stirred up the dust across the clearing as the jet roared overhead—sleek, low, and moving faster than anything that should've been landing in the outback.

The stolen Warraga truck spilled shade across the edge of the pad. Red was slumped against the bull bar, while Bob paced like a caged dog, clutching that duffel bag like it held the keys to salvation.

Finn crouched behind the scrub, comms clipped tight to his mouth. 'Stone, where's the pilot going to load?'

Stone's voice crackled back, low, 'The jet will taxi to them. That's why Red's out of the cab, best place for the handoff.'

'Will the pilot kill the engine?'

'Has to. For that type of jet, the strip's too short for a hot load-out. The pilot will shut down to secure the cargo and save fuel, considering this is an outpost.'

'Making them sitting ducks.' Finn nodded to himself. 'Copy that. We wait for the engine to cut and for the pilot to step out and help load. That's our window… We box them in. Taryn and I will storm the jet. Porter, you're the fastest, hit the stairs from the left. Amara and Craig take Red and Bob at the truck and watch for runners. You see movement, shut it down.'

He glanced skyward. 'Romy, you're our eyes. Call out anything we miss. Use the drone to track escape paths, and don't let anyone disappear into the scrub.'

'Copy that,' replied Romy as a low thud of rotor blades kicked off and rolled through the comms.

'Stone, you come in behind the jet, but make sure you're under the radar so he can't spot you and take off. Your mission is to block their path. Make sure no one leaves on that airstrip.' Finn peered across the clearing. They were ready.

The jet hit the makeshift runway with a hard bounce and kept rolling, dust blooming in its wake.

Taryn crouched low beside him. 'We should move in closer now that the plane's on the ground. That long grass will cover us.'

Finn nodded as he spoke over the comms. 'Team, use the scrub for cover. Stay low. And wait for the pilot to get out. Stone, that'll be your call.'

And with that, the squad inched forward like ghosts, with hearts pounding under the sun.

The jet taxied, then came to a slow stop. A few moments later, the door hissed open. Steps unfolded and a heavy-set male, wearing sunglasses too big for his face, stepped out to wave Red and Bob forward.

'Hey, Clancy, glad you could make it.' Bob called out.

That raised Finn's eyebrows. So, the only other two who knew about the quarry, was the pilot on that jet — and Drew.

Finn remembered the day the squad first got their badges, waiting for Drew to climb off another similar jet, where heat waves washed over the tarmac. That day, Finn had been so damned proud of his team, because they'd earned it.

And Drew had stood there in his tailored suit, shaking hands, patting backs — while his assistant hauled those boxes full of stolen genetic material behind him. Heading for Singapore for some BS conference, Drew had said. Couldn't stay long, he'd said. Even though Amara had done morning tea, bought Stone a new shirt, and polished the cutlery like she was meeting the king.

Singapore, my arse.

That bastard was already shipping product, using their squad send-off as bloody cover.

Even with the rage now coiling like a tight fist, back then Finn hadn't thought twice—because he'd trusted the bastard, who'd been poisoning the whole system.

So no, that smug prick wasn't out on the dirt. Drew would be sitting pretty inside that jet, with feet up, laptop open, and probably smiling at how well the plan was going while getting ready to tear strips off Red for causing this mess as soon as they climbed onboard that jet.

Finn's jaw locked tight enough to ache, as if to hold back the fire roaring up his throat.

Not yet.

He'd waited this long.

He could wait one more minute.

They'd wait for the pilot. Then he'd drag Drew off that jet and choke him with the same polished rope the mongrel once called *a pardon*.

'I look better than you lot.' Clancy, the big guy, trotted down the stairs to unclip one of the jet's cargo hatches. 'Where's the stash?'

'In the back of the truck,' said Bob.

'Give us a hand. Red, you can't get on board bleeding like that, mate. Drew'll spit at the cleaning bill.'

'Don't give a shit.' Red pushed off the truck and started limping. 'While I'm at it, I'll give that mongrel a mouthful.'

'They're loading…' Finn itched to move, anger driving him now.

'We wait for the pilot.' Taryn gripped his wrist. 'You said it's Stone's call. He'll know when it's time.'

She was close. Too close. The press of her shoulder against his, the heat of her breath in the still air that filled with the enticing scent he'd missed. She was the only thing keeping him steady, preventing his rage from ripping through everything.

But then in the meekest, softest voice he'd ever heard her use, she whispered, 'I'm sorry. I'm such a chicken, but in case this goes sideways... you should know—' She swallowed. 'I'm pregnant.'

It didn't hit like a bomb. It hit like silence.

A deafening slap right across his jawbone.

Finn spun to face her, to see if she was joking.

She wasn't.

Pregnant?!

The word echoed through him like bootsteps stomping down an empty hallway.

And all he could do was stare at her.

Then Stone's voice sliced through the comms: 'Engines down... *Pilot's out. Go!'*

Taryn sprinted. Fast. Handgun up, badge glinting. Breaking cover first—*without him!*

It only took a moment before Finn chased after her. Snapping back into the mission. And away from the thing he suddenly couldn't stop thinking about. *Pregnant?*

Craig peeled down the passenger side of the truck, rifle up.

Amara swept left, flanking the truck. *'Federal Police!'* she shouted with her handgun perfectly poised. *'Hands where I can see them!'*

Red groaned. Bleeding, his shirt soaked in sweat, he dropped to his knees.

Bob dropped his bag and bolted straight for the jet.

'Bob's heading for the plane!' Romy's voice snapped through comms as the helicopter roared overhead.

Bob reached the stairs. Hand out on the rail to climb for the plane.

When Porter's warning cracked like thunder, as he pressed the gun's barrel into the back of Bob's head. *'One more step and you'll be eating through a tube for the rest of your life, if you're lucky.'*

Bob's hands flew up. 'Don't shoot!'

Porter pushed Bob hard against the stairwell, cuffed him, then dragged him back to kneel beside Red at the front of the truck.

Finn got a bead on the guy they called Clancy, who'd ducked out from the plane's cargo hatch.

Big and calm, Clancy carried himself like he already knew who he was supposed to kill and where to bury them. His jacket bulged just enough to confirm he wasn't carrying a boarding pass—he was packing.

Finn didn't hesitate, his gun raised, ready to roll. 'Drop the weapon. Now.'

Clancy gave Finn a slow once-over. Sizing him up like this was round one of a fight he'd already counted on himself to win.

Finn didn't flinch. He never flinched. Not in prison. Not in the yards. Not when guards ran betting pools on how many rounds he'd last without making a sound.

And not now.

Taryn shifted left, her gun's sights locked. 'Don't test us.'

Still nothing.

Then, behind the goon, a second figure stepped out from the jet's underbelly. Older. Wiry. Hands already up.

'Pilot!' he prattled like a panicked teen. *'I'm just the pilot! I'm not part of this, I swear!'*

That tiny beat of distraction? It's all Finn needed.

He surged forward, catching Clancy's wrist mid-draw—just as that weapon cleared the jacket's fabric—and twisted. A tight, brutal move he didn't need to think about because he'd done it a hundred times before, sometimes for justice, and sometimes just to breathe another night, inhaling concrete and cold steel bars.

Finn slammed Clancy's back into the side of the plane. Then let loose a crack to his ribs followed by a clock to the mouth.

The gun hit the tarmac with a heavy clatter.

Finn barely registered it.

Not when he was dancing along that edge now, barely one

breath away from making it personal and letting all that fury free.

He could've hit Clancy again. Oh, he wanted to. All that frustrated rage inside needed an out. 'Do you wanna dance with the devil?' He said with an evil edge to his voice and a sneer that promised he'd dance to their deaths if he had to.

Clancy raised his arms, fingers wide, with his wrist swollen and lip bleeding, but the whites of his eyes showed his fear. 'I surrender, okay. Take it easy, okay.'

But Finn wanted to hit him again.

Hell yeah, he wanted to.

But he didn't.

Instead, he shoved the guy down, slapped the cuffs on hard, and forced his breathing to level out. In. Out.

Don't lose it now.

And when he looked up—

Taryn was there, covering him. Her eyes steady, gun still raised, legs braced like she'd hold the whole damn plane back if she had to.

She'd seen him almost let his rage bleed through his self-control.

But what got him the most was she wasn't scared of him, knowing full well what he was capable of. She just gave him the smallest nod, like she understood the war still going on behind his ribs and still stood beside him. Again, proving she was tougher than he'd given her credit for.

When Stone's chopper swept low behind them, blades roaring like a warning from the gods, and effectively blocked the jet.

'I have the pilot.' Taryn dragged the cuffed pilot to Amara, who then took him to kneel on the tarmac beside Red. 'Call out who's secure?'

'I've got Red… You mongrel thief.' The normally calm and casual cowboy was pissed. Craig yanked the flexi-cuffs tight, giving a grim nod—the kind a stockman gives when he's caught someone who'd broken their cattleman's code.

Dried blood had trickled down Red's face to blend into his

long red beard. The wound from Brodie's blow still seeped beneath the rough, hastily wrapped bandage.

But no one showed him any pity. Not when every ringer who'd ever passed through the Elsie Creek Stockyards adored Lydia, especially Craig who was close to her.

On his knees, Red twisted his torso as he tried to fight the cuffs, the sun, and no doubt the ache from his head wound. 'Wait! Lydia? Is she—'

Craig gripped Red's shirt front, his snarl bared teeth. 'You don't get to say her name. And you sure as hell don't get to ask.'

Red collapsed back onto his knees, head down, defeated.

Finn didn't say a word. Didn't need to. Craig would have the satisfaction of Red's arrest. And he needed it.

They all did.

'Bob's down, too.' Porter forced Bob to kneel on the tarmac beside Red.

'Second male from the jet, Clancy, secured.' Finn dropped the goon down beside the pilot, as the crims lined up along the tarmac, kneeling under the sun.

He turned to look for Taryn.

She was already heading for the jet's stairs, gun drawn. 'I'm going in.'

'I'll back you.' Porter was fast as he took the steps two at a time to quickly catch up, to give her the support she needed.

That left the truck.

Finn flicked a signal to Amara.

No words needed.

She'd been shadowing him for over eighteen months now. The perfect apprentice, who was sharp, steady, and always two steps ahead when it counted.

They moved, one on each side, with boots light on the tarmac, side-arms raised, and every sense alert. Finn took the driver's side, Amara the passenger's, flanking the vehicle.

As the helicopter fell silent, and the rotor's dust wash settled, Finn reached the back first, and raised a fist for Amara to pause.

They just had to be sure they had everyone.

As she aimed her gun at the back canopy, he peeled back the canvas flap.

No bodies.

No shooters.

Among the bale of feed hay and scattered tools, stood a pile of ordinary brown cardboard boxes. There were no address labels, just a strip of brown tape sealing the lid, and a faded sticker that read: *Conference Pack—NT Tourism*.

He drew his knife from his belt, and with a sharp flick, he slashed the box clean down the seam.

Inside… cryogenic canisters.

Four of them. Nestled tight within the moulded foam, where each silver cylinder stood upright—sealed, sweating, and still cold enough to burn. The box was lined with thermal packaging, the kind used for vet vials or lab-grade samples.

And yet, outside, it was nothing special. Just a brown cardboard box, sealed with cheap tape. The kind of box no one looked at twice.

Even its label: *Conference Pack—NT Tourism*, was harmless. Exactly the sort of thing that passed through airstrips and depots without question.

Thirteen boxes sat on that truck.

A baker's dozen of clean-cut brown packages, taped up and labelled like conference crap, holding…

Fifty-two tanks.

Holding more than ten road trains of breathing assets. With no hooves. No mess. Just pure genetically pristine bloodlines, frozen and ready to stock a national stud program.

Worth millions.

Who knows how many more boxes had already disappeared overseas before today.

Finn reached into the box and gripped the metal. Even through his gloves, the chill bit down like dry ice. He hauled a silver canister free. It was about the size of a small welder's gas bottle, but sleeker, and polished to a sterile sheen like it belonged in a lab, not a stockyard.

Frost clung to the nozzle, with mist bleeding off the collar in slow, icy tendrils. A yellow hazard triangle warned of extreme cold. Another sticker read: *Cryogenic Liquid. Handle With Care.*

Finn didn't need the warning symbols to tell him what would happen if this stuff thawed. And it sure as hell didn't belong in a cardboard box.

It'd been one year of chasing ghosts, ever since they'd learned what happened to that rodeo bull, Wraith's Wrath, from the Rough Stock case—it all came down to this. A box.

'And they call this a white-collar crime.' He could just hear Taryn, the queen of corporate crime, sassing him with: *Still think my suits and heels are overdressed for the outback?*

But this was the payload. The proof.

They finally had something they could use.

His gloved fingers brushed the frost off the lid. The canister was still cold, the metal sweating in the heat, the seal intact. He hefted it high to check the sides and the base. 'Judging by the weight and frost line, we've got a few weeks left before this lot defrosts into worthless sludge,' he muttered.

'I read somewhere that under correct storage conditions, genetic material like this can stay viable for decades—thirty, forty years, easy.' Amara counted the boxes beside him, using her phone to record everything. 'Long enough to build world-class bloodlines from scratch, and no one would ever know the difference.'

'This isn't just stock theft and selling it to the highest bidder,' Finn said, holding the canister. 'It's rewriting the future of this nation's stock industry.' He exhaled slowly at the weight of it all.

'You know what else they could hide in this?' Amara's tone was edged with fury. 'Disease. Mutation. Anything. And they left it tucked under hay bales like it was fertiliser.'

'You're right.' Finn's jaw tightened. 'Drew didn't just steal stock and the genetic material. He put this country's entire livestock industry at risk. Biosecurity, trade, reputation... all of it.'

He hoped like hell Taryn had that prick down on his knees, with a bloody nose, and whatever kind of justice the lady wanted to dish out. He'd back her, before he pushed her aside to have his go. Gently, of course, after all she was—

Dammit.

Get back in the game.

If Taryn could stay focused, in that jet, breathing the same air as Drew bloody Bannon, then so could he.

He clicked his mic. 'We've got product. I'm guessing it's their last haul.' But also a haul that seemed to be tracking on time, considering the condition of the canisters.

He could hear noises from inside the jet, someone opening doors and turning it out like a drug raid.

Porter was at the top of the stairs, peering inside the jet's cabin, while their four captives remained handcuffed, on their knees, being watched over by Craig and Stone.

Taryn appeared in the jet's open doorway, the wind tugging her hair. 'He's not here... Drew is not on board.'

Thirty-nine

The tarmac at Darwin International Airport shimmered under floodlights, with the heat still clinging to the concrete long after the sun had set. Another jet screamed overhead—military. Flashing like a streak of light and flame, it vanished over the Top End's sprawling suburbia like a shooting star across the black night sky.

Most folks forgot that the airport shared its runway with the RAAF base, who actually owned it. And on nights like tonight suburbia just had to deal with it, as three military jets launched one after another, cutting ahead of commercial traffic and stacking the airspace like it was theirs to own. Because it was.

Commissioner Andrew Bannon squinted skyward as the third fighter jet tore across the night sky, banking sharply above the runway. A blazing stream trailed behind it like a roman candle on steroids, brilliant and volatile, punching through barriers like it owned the sky.

The sound hit seconds later with a low, violent roar that dragged behind the jet like a late guest, rolling into his back and out through his chest. It always came like that, delayed and dominant.

Drew didn't flinch. Because he rather liked it. The theatrics. The precision. The kind of firepower that bent airspace and made every other aircraft sit and wait—including his own jet, which sat grounded, while the boys in grey showed off.

But damn if they weren't magnificent to watch from his unhindered view on the airstrip.

Drew checked his watch again.

Clancy was late.

Another member of Drew's mentorship scheme. Quick with his fists, slow with his reasoning, but useful in situations where subtlety was optional.

Drew never expected brilliance from his boys. Only results.

And if not, he always had a backup plan, or three.

That's how it always worked, building contingencies since his first years in the sticks. Recruiting smart kids, the angry ones, the broken ones. Moulding them. Positioning them in case he needed them.

Some, like Finn Wilde, had exceeded all his expectations.

The scruffy boy who'd taught him everything he knew about cattle, back when Drew was just a city-born probationary constable, dumped in the outback by a bitter recruiter with a grudge. That's what started his first plots for revenge.

Finn had been his first real asset. Like a son, once. Bright, loyal—raw. Then he'd fallen, just as Drew knew he would.

Perfect, really.

That boy had been born for a redemption arc, and Drew, of course, had been the hero to drag Finn out of that savage little pit, dress him up with a badge, put a bit of fire back into his spine, and sent him striding into the wild like a good little errand boy.

And Finn thought he'd built the Stock Squad.

Please.

Finn was just a tool—a sharp one, sure—but still a tool. And tools were effective, until they weren't. Like Finn, who wasn't playing the game the way he was meant to. And Red had gotten lazy enough to attract Finn's attention.

So now it was time to tap another one of the boys on the shoulder—Clancy.

It was all part of his final play.

Of course, he would not run like Red, reeking of failure and desperation. No, Drew Bannon did not run. He walked. Head high, suit tailored to precision, pockets full, and future assured.

It was all part of being well-prepared.

The second Bob's email came through—panicked, clumsy, and laced with the story of a blood trail—Drew knew it was time to go. Red's little domestic disaster had only accelerated the inevitable. Idiot.

If there was any doubt that someone had been watching the operation before, they sure as hell would be watching now.

So Drew did what he always did—moved first.

His mentor once told him: *Always plan your exits before your entries. Basic politics 101.*

And so, he followed the plan.

Within minutes, he'd cancelled his speech, packed his case, booked a jet under a clean shell company, and was in a taxi to the airport.

He'd left a miserably wet and rainy Adelaide just past midnight, with the winter rain biting through his coat, creating the kind of cold that clung to your bones.

He then landed in Darwin at 4:15 in the morning.

Under a warm tropical sky, filled with stars, and no one around to bother him, it gave him the perfect cover to strip off his heavy coat and find his car in the long-term FIFO parking bay, where it sat untouched.

Inside the boot was his exit plan: passport, cash, burner phone, and an invaluable collection of government-cleared travel documents. All quietly approved and never dated, just waiting for him to choose the country.

Half an hour later, he'd checked into a hotel to play tourist, ordered breakfast and coffee. Unpacked first—because he always unpacked first. Then dressed in some luxury resort wear starting with an unbuttoned linen shirt, designer slides, and tailored swim shorts sharp enough to pass for dress shorts, the kind he'd seen worn by Bond, as played by Craig, in *Skyfall*. The perfect attire for a man sitting poolside while committing international crime, sending emails to Clancy and the pilot to prep the jet out of Adelaide. Then he sent another email to log the empty Canberra flight, purely as a distraction in case anyone was watching.

And finally—to Red.

Letting that bastard sweat had been fun. Because no one threatened Drew Bannon and got away with it.

All of it done with coffee in hand, poolside. Just another FIFO exec, or a southern tourist dodging winter. No one gave him a second glance.

And now he waited under the cover of darkness for the quarry jet to arrive.

Only the RAAF held things up, with their fighter jets clogging the sky with noise.

Just a minor inconvenience, really. Nothing more.

He glanced at his watch. Again. Almost 8pm.

The cargo came first, and he wasn't leaving without it. That much was non-negotiable. Not after everything it had taken to collect, preserve, and move covertly across state borders, under fake names and falsified manifests. The product was too valuable. It was the kind of freight that could sink a nation's trade economy—if ever exposed.

Again, he checked his watch.

A breeze carried the acrid tang of turbine exhaust fumes across the airfield, offering no relief from the heat and sweat as it curled beneath his collar where he stood ready to climb on board his waiting jet.

But only once the quarry shipment had arrived.

He wouldn't touch it. That's what he paid others for.

Like Clancy, who he'd sent to collect the boxes with the extra duty of permanently releasing Red and Bob from the fold. Along with a little torching of the stolen truck and everything else remaining at the quarry, to destroy all evidence. And then the pilot, being handsomely paid to keep quiet—especially with that little bit of blackmail of him flying high from a cocaine-party spree—would fly Clancy up to Darwin to offload the boxes to Drew's waiting jet. No witnesses. No loose ends. Goodbye Elsie Creek.

And then Drew would step aboard jet number two, take

the boxes, and vanish.

Now all he needed was Clancy's jet from the quarry to land.

A flicker of movement caught his eye across the tarmac.

Surprisingly, the quarry's jet had arrived without him noticing. Quietly slipping in-between cargo holds as the floodlights poured over it, followed by the soft hiss of its undercarriage settling.

The hatch opened away from him.

He squinted. The way the two jets were positioned, and the angle of the floodlights, it kept the disembarking crew in silhouette. Just a few figures who seamlessly transferred the freight, box by box, from that aircraft to his.

One of the ground crew, carrying a clipboard, gave a wave, as he exited Drew's jet. 'Cargo transfer is complete. You're clear to board.'

'It's about time.' Drew dabbed at the sweat on his brow with a pressed handkerchief. He tucked it neatly into the breast pocket of his tailored suit. In his bespoke boots, with his crocodile-leather briefcase tucked under one arm, he dragged his carry-on across the tarmac to the second aircraft.

He didn't look back as he climbed on board.

'We're already behind schedule. So, let's leave now, please,' he instructed the pilot, while the co-pilot, seated with his back to him in the cockpit, busily flicked the switches in preparation for take-off.

'*Cabin crew, prepare for immediate departure.*' The head pilot's voice carried over the cabin's speakers.

The door sealed shut behind him.

Inside, cool air greeted him, along with grey leather seats, silence, and a hint of jet fuel. It was the scent of polished power. Exactly how he liked it.

Drew barely glanced at the boxes, stacked among the seats. That would wait. First, he strapped into his seat.

Soon, the lights of Darwin flickered beyond the windows as they raced down the runway. The jet lifted. Levelled. And then banked left for the open seas. He could be in Bali in two hours. Singapore in four. Anywhere but here.

Once the jet had levelled out, Drew loosened his tie, undid his top button, then unbuckled his seatbelt, and moved down the aisle to where the boxes, marked *Conference Pack—NT Tourism*, took up space.

What a joke.

He broke the simple taped seal on one of the boxes.

A hush of cold mist slipped free, curling like breath into the cabin's still air. Inside, the sleek, silver cryogenic canisters rested in their foam cradles.

Drew pulled on his custom-made leather gloves. He wasn't about to lose skin, even over a million dollars' worth of embryos.

He then lifted one canister with care, both hands beneath it as if cradling a child. Only better…

A silver vessel that wasn't just valuable, it was reproductive power. Elite bloodlines. Genetic superiority. Potential livestock that could outbreed, outlast, and outprice anything else on the market.

And with that came power and control as the source. Where access would be sold to the highest bidder.

It wasn't just payday, these canisters were pure profit.

But this also represented so much more. This is what he'd be remembered for, not a badge or a title passed down by some short-lived government. But something he'd done that would last. Something that would outlive them all. The world called it livestock. Drew called it his legacy.

And then—*click*.

There was a bright flash in his eyes.

He staggered back, blinded.

'Smile, Drew.' It was Taryn Hayes. The federal auditor he'd sent to destroy the Stock Squad. With phone in hand, badge at her hip. Smiling like a woman who'd just won a Christmas ham at some pub's meat raffle.

And beside her—Finn Wilde, tall and silent. Holding a pair of handcuffs, wearing a death glare that said: *Run, and I'll make sure you never walk again.*

Forty

'Andrew Bannon.' Finn stepped in closer with his cuffs clenched so tight in his fist his knuckles had gone bone white. Now beyond angry, his every breath was an inner fight to not snap and dish out the punishment this bastard deserved.

And yet…

Just her presence. Taryn's. Steady and silent beside him, was enough to calm him some.

Didn't stop his voice from sounding loaded with lethal heat. 'You are under arrest for conspiracy to commit murder and livestock fraud, illegally trafficking in biological specimens, obstruction of justice, fraud, and the unlawful use of Commonwealth funds.'

He caught Drew's wrist, and locked on the first cuff. Cold and clean. In the front purely for transport. If he had his way, he'd cuff him in the back.

'You do not have to say or do anything—'

'Finn—'

'Don't.'

The second cuff snapped into place.

'—but anything you say or do may be used as evidence. Do you understand?'

'I gave you that badge,' Drew sneered. 'I gave you a second chance. You think they'll listen to you over *me*?'

Finn cinched the cuffs tighter.

'You're making a terrible mistake.' Drew looked at Taryn, desperate now. 'You don't know what you're doing—'

'Actually,' she said, flipping her phone around to show him she was recording, 'we know exactly what we're doing.

But do keep talking. It's great for evidence.'

'How?' Drew barked, eyes flicking around the cabin. 'How the hell did you get on this jet?'

Finn gave a grim smile. Not that he felt like smiling.

Between him and Taryn, they'd built the plan in the kind of shorthand where he'd start a thought, and she'd finish it, leaving the rest of the team scratching their heads. But they understood each other enough to know this plan would work—even if he hadn't had a second to wrap his mind around their *other* issue. Let alone talk in private.

Not when he didn't do speeches.

So he nodded at Taryn, the lady who enjoyed having the last word, to lead this conversation.

'You were expecting product, not people,' Taryn said, with that wicked little grin of hers. 'Clancy gave us just enough. And the pilot? He spilled the rest of the story. I told Finn he could pass as Clancy, with his build—which he did. Obviously.' She rolled her eyes for a dramatic pause. 'All I did was swap shirts and cap with the Darwin ground crew. Who, by the way, were all local Territory and Federal Police helping us load your precious cargo. And the man flying this jet?' She pointed to the closed door of the cockpit. 'Also, a Fed. And the one who flew the jet in from the quarry? That was our guy, Stone. You remember him? The Stock Squad's part-time pilot and crocodile wrangler. The one who calls you *Big Daddy*.'

Drew's eyes flicked from Taryn to the cockpit's closed door, then back to Finn, as his mind tried to comprehend the impossible. 'You don't have a warrant for this jet.'

'But we do. It was Finn who cracked the code on the naming pattern for your shell companies.' She patted Finn's shoulder like he was the hero of the day.

But he didn't feel like a hero.

'*Prime stock*,' Finn growled with his brow low. The fury still simmered beneath the surface and pressed against his rib cage, looking for an escape.

But she did it again. That simple pat on his shoulder, just in time to tame the beast within.

Drew turned to Finn. 'You worked it out... You always did like those word puzzles.'

Finn's hand flexed at his side. 'Yeah, they were finally good for something. I passed one down to this broken kid, only this morning at the hospital. Same age as I was when you gave me one of those books. Pretending that being a mentor meant something, when it was only a cover to recruit pawns.'

Drew's mouth curled into a sneer. 'You don't have jurisdiction here. We're already in international airspace.'

'Oh, boy.' Taryn shook her head, grinning like she was about to teach a toddler how magnets worked. 'Isn't your compass way off. And I thought men knew directions.' She nodded towards the small window. 'We're still in Australian airspace, piloted by Federal Police who'd make sure we were. And we're still technically on your property, which was legally listed on the arrest warrants—so says our legal consultant, Izzy, who *you* tried to have killed.'

She then held up her phone again and leaned in closer to Drew. 'Also, thanks for opening a box on camera. Already in the cloud.' She smiled brightly up at her phone. 'Now, smile for the selfie, Drew. My dad's gonna love this one.'

Click.

Drew flinched at the camera flash.

'Sit down, Drew.' Finn remained gruff, even as he tried not to smirk.

'I made you,' Drew hissed with desperation, as he was shoved back into his seat. 'I built this team.'

Finn leaned in. Clicked in the seatbelt, then tugged it real tight. His face was close enough for Drew to feel the heat behind the words. 'Yeah... And then we rebuilt it—*without* you.' He glared at the snake in a suit. 'Get comfortable. We're going home.'

Drew shifted in his seat. Buckled in, cuffed. Still smug. Still breathing. Both optional if Taryn left them alone for a second.

Finn dropped into the seat opposite the man who'd once

handed him a pardon and a badge. He stared at Drew with everything he wanted to say, as the level of heated betrayal knotted behind his ribs. 'You used me. You—'

'Finn.' Taryn's voice, soft but firm, came from just behind Drew's shoulder. 'Careful… Less said, the better.'

She was right.

He exhaled heavily, and looked away.

She was already on her laptop, legs crossed like she was sitting in a cafe, and not a prisoner transport.

She winked when she caught him watching, then went back to work.

Finn ran a hand down his face. They hadn't had a single moment. Not once since the quarry sting where the truth detonated between them. And now, there was still no room to breathe.

He was emotionally landlocked, trapped in a jet, cuffed to the past—while the future was growing in the seat behind Drew.

Already this flight home felt long.

Finn couldn't sit. Not with Drew. Not this time.

He stood, leaning against the cabin's bulkhead, arms crossed. Silently watching his prisoner.

He'd stood like this once before…

Back in prison, where he'd been the prisoner, staring down at Drew who'd laid out a pardon like bait.

Finn hadn't sat then. Didn't feel like he'd earned it.

Again, he'd stood in the Batcave, when Taryn's PowerPoint presentation showed his betrayal. He couldn't sit at the table, not with his own crew—not when he was the fool who'd brought Drew into their world.

But this was different.

Now he stood because Drew didn't deserve to share that space. Because the man who had once loomed over him figuratively, now sat, literally cuffed and cornered.

Taryn sat behind Drew, laptop open, already working through the paperwork they'd need by touchdown.

Only then he'd realised her silence was deliberate.

With her phone balanced on the armrest beside her, it was still recording. Strategically placed just out of Drew's line of sight.

Damn, she's good.

Because she knew Finn didn't do interrogation rooms.

Not after prison. Not after being the one cuffed, stared at and judged.

He preferred crime scenes, paddocks, the back of a ute, and places where he could breathe away from four brick walls, a door, and a ticking clock.

And she got that. Without the need to push or suggest a formal statement. She just set it up. Quietly. For him. Once he'd calmed down, of course.

Again, there was that shorthand they'd built across dust, road maps, and close calls.

But there was another question that needed to be asked. The one that twisted low in his guts: *Was he good enough for her?*

Finn honestly didn't know if he deserved her, either.

Taryn had come back for justice, not for him, but for her family, who had bled because of what Drew had had done to her cousin, Meghan.

And now? With everything shifting beneath their boots: a baby, his team on trial, and his boss in handcuffs—what kind of future could he even promise Taryn, when he didn't even know if he still had a job?

After a long stretch of silence, Finn spoke the one question that had never stopped circling... 'Why?'

Drew sat back, staring past Finn, like it was all playing out on a screen only he could see.

'I was the Federal Agricultural Commissioner. I read the reports. Took the calls. Saw the families sinking under the red tape. Being forced to complete mandatory carbon reports while they battle floods, drought, and fires—with the banks breathing down their necks setting crippling mortgage rates, and the creation of new taxes, while livestock is dying or drowning in paddocks. And they get no support. Only more paperwork and empty promises from the government that had been elected to help them.'

Drew sighed, all dramatic flair, and kept talking. 'I've watched foreign investors gut this country. They mine our minerals, take our resources, and walk away without paying a cent in taxes. They're not buying cattle or sheep stations to run stock. They're tearing up prime farmland for failed solar schemes and carbon offset credits. And there are now more foreign investors who own our precious water resources than actual farmers, and most of it goes straight into fracking for overseas companies. Prime grazing land is being sacrificed so the cities can keep their smart homes lit, while forgetting who the hell feeds them. And our government? Doesn't lift a finger—except to vote in another pay rise and now, backflip on a promise to block American beef imports. Imports! Into the second-largest beef exporter on the damn planet. And you want to paint me as the villain?'

He didn't say it in anger. Not even bitterness.

And that was the worst part—because every damn word of it was real. The country was being gutted while the government smiled for the cameras.

'And yet you were in a position to fix at least some of it,' Finn said, his voice like dry gravel. 'But instead, you chose to rip off the farmers and landowners who trusted you. So stop playing politician and say the real reason why you did this.' He glared at Drew, daring him to finally tell the truth.

'I told myself I was preserving something,' continued Drew, lifting his chin in defiance. 'I was the one holding the line when no one else would. And when the system fails completely—which it will—I'll be the one to help replace it. I tried to keep families on their cattle stations and crop farms. I swear I did. I've helped pay their bills, put fuel into their generators, and built a supply chain that actually worked, and wasn't controlled by the supermarket giants. Sure, I profited. But so did everyone else. You weren't chasing villains, Finn. You were dismantling the only thing keeping the Australian livestock industry alive for Australians.'

Yet Finn saw it—Drew didn't think he was the villain. Drew actually thought he was fixing a broken system. One backdoor deal at a time.

'And what about the farmers you stole stock from? How were you making their lives better?'

Drew lifted his hands, the chain of his cuffs clinked, as he loosened his tie, opening his crisp shirt wider as if really getting it off his chest.

The man always did like a podium, and Finn also knew Drew liked to fill in stretched out silences with words. But for once, the politician didn't have an answer for that.

Finn's jaw twitched. 'And you used my Gaps File to do it.'

Drew didn't even flinch. 'You needed a purpose, so I gave you one.'

Finn stepped forward. 'No. You gave me a lie.'

The plane dipped. A subtle shift, but Finn felt it in his chest. Landing prep.

Drew stared at the cuffs around his wrists. 'You wouldn't understand,' he muttered. 'You still believe the law can fix things. Please. It's as broken as the government is. Pretending they're defending the people, when they're only there for the corporations lining their pockets. And I—'

'No. You're not a hero, Drew. You didn't save anything. All you did was exploit the system, bleed it dry, then called it *help* so you could sleep at night.' Finn glared at the man, his mentor of over twenty-years.

Stone's voice crackled over the speaker. 'Prepare for landing, peoples, we're home.'

'That was quick,' said Taryn.

'Stone told me Darwin to Elsie Creek, in a jet like this, takes less than twenty.'

Enough time for Drew to open one of his boxes and get arrested.

To confess.

And fall.

The drone of the engines hummed low as the wheels kissed the runway with a low bounce, enough to rattle the boxes occupying the spare seats.

The jet rolled to a stop, as the hum of the engine slowed. Out the window, the sky lit up in flashing red and blue from every police vehicle in town, lining the Elsie Creek airstrip.

He turned to Drew. 'Time to go.'

Drew looked down at his cuffed wrists, then out the window as if looking for a rescue or some sort of applause.

The only audience was a scowling Mickey. Waiting in his grease-stained, grey coveralls, with his arms crossed like he owned the runway. Which, technically, he might do.

Stone opened the hatch, and the steps hissed down, winking at the Commissioner. 'Hello, Big Daddy, welcome home.'

Outside, Marcus, the OIC, Tanisha, their ACPO, and the rest of Elsie Creek's tiny NT police force were waiting.

And at the base of the stairs stood the Stock Squad.

Craig. Izzy. Amara and Porter, with Stone rushing to Romy's side. All wearing their badges and vests.

They didn't wear a uniform that matched. Wearing different boots, vests, hats and histories. They weren't trained the same, but they all had unique skills and personalities that may clash—but when united, they were a force.

And this was more than just another arrest, because this might be *the last one* they ever did together as a team, in the same place where Drew had once handed them their badges and shook their hands at the start.

After what Drew had done to them, they were going to finish this right.

Finn's boots hit the tarmac like a punctuation. He turned back to face Taryn, her hand firmly around Drew's arm.

She didn't gloat. Didn't smile. With badge gleaming at her hip, she escorted Drew down the steps to face the squad he'd betrayed.

'You built them.' Finn said to Drew. 'Look at them. See what you could have been proud of.' He gripped Drew's shoulder and shook him. 'LOOK AT THEM!'

Drew raised his head. Yet, the once-pompous prick,

couldn't even look them in the eye. He was done.

Then Izzy stepped forward and her hand swung back, unleashing a mighty wallop.

Whack! The crack echoed across the tarmac.

Drew's head snapped to the side, wincing at the sting from the lawyer who usually fought with her pen, not her fists. 'What was that for?'

Izzy stared him down, her voice tight with fury. 'That was for daring to shake my hand. For lying to my face about Everlight. And for pretending you were sorry, when *you* tried to have me *killed*.'

She then swung again, hitting his other cheek with a *crack!* 'And that was for Meghan.'

Izzy didn't wait for a reaction. She just stepped back in line beside Craig and gave Finn a quiet nod.

Finn's heart may still be heavy, but something in him finally stilled. Justice wasn't perfect. But it was done.

Drew stood handcuffed in his fancy suit, his tie askew, with his pride unravelling. The man who had once handed out badges and shaken hands, was now the one in chains. The team he'd sent to catch criminals had caught him instead.

It had come full circle.

A man who once held the country's agricultural industry in his palm was being led away by Marcus, flanked by two NT uniforms. All done without any media to tape his long walk across the floodlit airstrip.

Stone muttered to the team, 'There goes Big Daddy and his walk of shame.'

Craig snorted.

Amara huffed a laugh.

Even Romy cracked a smile, with her chin tucked low.

But it didn't lift the weight. Not completely.

Because now, as the flashing lights were turned off and the police vehicles drove away, they stood there…

One ex-con who'd become a federal sergeant.

One federal inspector.

One Northern Territory senior constable.

One South Australian constable.

One lawyer.

One cowboy and stock inspector.

One crocodile wrangler and pilot.

One videographer.

And one tiny outback town.

None of them were sure if they'd still have their jobs tomorrow. Well, except Porter and Taryn.

Yet, Taryn stood beside Finn, while Izzy watched the paperwork literally walk away, with Craig's hand resting lightly on her hip. Stone held Romy's hand, and Porter slung his arm around Amara's shoulders. All standing side-by-side as a team.

It was done.

But would they still be the Stock Squad tomorrow?

Forty-one

Finn leaned against the open doorway, hands deep in the pockets of yesterday's jeans. Before him, pale but alert, Lydia was propped up slightly in the hospital bed.

Nearby sat Brodie. Curled up like a border collie in the chair, one arm flopped across his middle. The many colours of his bruises highlighted by the fluorescent lights.

'Well, it's about time you showed up.' Lydia even smiled.

'Been busy.' Finn dragged the chair to the other side of the bed to watch over the pair. Sitting slowly, every joint in his spine groaned like a stockwhip uncoiling after a long day's muster. He rested his arms on his knees, worried he'd never get up again.

'Go on, I want an update. We both deserve to know,' she demanded.

'Well, deemed flight risks, bail was refused and Red and Bob are being transported to Darwin prison this afternoon.' They were only waiting on medical clearance to move Red's arse.

'So Red's...' Brodie swallowed.

'Fine. Just a bunch of stitches.' Pity he never got to give them to Red himself.

Brodie's whole body sagged with relief.

Lydia squeezed his hand. Then asked Finn, 'The charges?'

'It's close to eighty charges and counting, just on stock theft alone.' That raised some eyebrows.

'And the rest?'

'Vehicle theft, fraud, assault, deadly intent with use of a vehicle, domestic violence and murder.'

Lydia's eyes flared wider. 'But I'm—'

'Of Sawyer Dixby.'

'The missing overseer? Seery?'

Finn nodded. Thanks to the tag-team interrogation of Taryn playing good cop, while Finn glared from the open doorway, Bob spilled first, and fast.

According to the gospel of Bob, he was going to rescue his cousin from Porter and Craig, who were closing in on Seery during that manhunt across Dixby Downs in the Hellhound.

After what Seery had done to Porter and Amara, he would have gone for attempted murder, assaulting police officers and everything else they could think of for what that prick had done to his team members.

Except Red knew that Seery would talk. Without a doubt.

So when Seery thought he was getting help, Red had picked the spot that even Bob never saw — the bulldust pit of death.

Red shot out the tyre of the quad bike, causing Seery to lose control. When the bike hit the bulldust and sank hard, pinning him beneath it, Red refused to let Bob out of the passenger seat to help his cousin. Instead, he slammed his fist into Bob, warned him he'd kill him too, and drove off, leaving Seery to drown in the dust.

'Do you want to see him?' Finn asked Lydia.

'I'd rather get a restraining order and frame it above the kettle.' Lydia gave a short huff over the man she'd once promised to grow old with. She straightened out her sheets, fussing over them like she did for others, but now it was her turn. 'I loved him, you know.'

Finn looked up, while young Brodie winced as if feeling her pain.

'And he loved me. But he didn't love all of me. Red didn't like that I was smart. That I could run numbers faster, and read a beast better, than half the agents on the books.'

'Is that why you only called yourself a clerk? And not the boss lady? Because we all know you're a lot smarter than you let on.'

She gave a sly shrug. 'My fault, really. I let Red think I was smaller than I was. Didn't want to shame the man by outranking him in the eyes of his mates. You know, every few years the stockyard's lease is offered to me, I've always said no.'

'Who owns the stockyards?' Somebody had to be making money on the place. And Finn knew Tanisha and Porter would love to know. 'I know it's a trust.'

'Um…' Lydia hesitated.

'God, does,' replied Brodie.

'You're not old enough to know the publican,' scolded Lydia.

The kid grinned. 'I'm not allowed in the front bar of her pub, either. But I do know Samantha owns the place. She just doesn't tell anyone. Let's them all think it's Lydia, who doesn't tell anyone, and so Red acts like he does.' Brodie grimaced. 'Sorry, Lydia. For the crack over Red.'

But she shooed it away.

'I've never seen Samantha near the place,' mumbled Finn.

'She doesn't visit,' said Lydia. 'I go and see her at the pub if I have an issue. Other than that, Samantha never interferes. She's the perfect business partner, really.'

'But she does visit.' Brodie grinned like he was sitting on the secret of the century. 'All the time.'

'When?'

'Samantha brings me over a hot meal, some sweets from the kitchen, and a few scratched soda cans she reckons she can't sell in the pub. But there's nothing wrong with 'em.'

'When?'

'Late at night, on Train Days. When the yards are full of stock, we'll sit on the rails, chat, and eat. That's how I know. She asks me about the stock numbers. And she's real good with numbers. Samantha even taught me a trick or two on workin' stuff out in my head.' Brodie tapped the side of his temple.

'You've always been good with numbers.'

'Thanks to Samantha.'

'Are you saying the publican gives you private maths

lessons?' Finn arched an eyebrow at the kid, who he knew was getting tips from Izzy to help him read and write. But this?

'Yeah.' Again, Brodie nodded, with that cheesy grin shining under his bruises. 'Samantha scratches the figures out in the yard's dirt like some schoolteacher—just prettier. Only she explains it all in beer and bush stuff. Like how many jerry cans you need to fuel a road train from town to Darwin. Or how many litres fit in a water tank for a couple hundred head? Or how to work out the time and distance on a roll of barbed wire to fence a yard. That sort of maths. Stuff I can see and use.'

'Where? When?' demanded Lydia.

'All under the floodlights with the cattle watchin' on, while I'm scoffin' tucker like a crow on the rail on Train Days.'

'Is that why you'll hold back on some of your maths assignments?'

'Only the tough ones, coz Samantha helps me understand them.'

Finn wiped away the grin. 'Damn, Brodie. Don't let the other stockmen hear that—they'll either get jealous, or they'll all be lining up for maths lessons in the bulldust from God herself.'

Brodie then leaned closer, his voice dropping as if sharing a secret with Lydia. 'I know Samantha doesn't like to interfere. But she told me that as the boss you can make it bigger, hire more staff. You've been doing it for thirty-five years, and that you're doing a great job. And if God is saying that, I'm agreeing.'

Lydia lay back, sinking into her pillow, and closed her eyes for a moment. 'She's a clever young woman, that one, and I don't think she's even made thirty, you know...'

'She's not that old, is she?' Brodie's nose wrinkled.

Finn shrugged. 'I was brought up to never ask a lady's age.'

'Good response.' Lydia nodded. 'Samantha first offered me the lease over six years ago, when the old manager retired, and every year since. But I always said no…'

'Because you didn't think you could? When we can all see you're doing it now,' said Brodie.

'Because…' Lydia paused.

'Of Red,' said Finn, blunt as ever.

She dropped her head, eyes closed. 'Samantha was very clear on that, said it had to be in my name only, not Red's. Like she knew…'

When she opened her eyes again, they were clearer than Finn had seen in weeks.

'But here I am, at fifty-one,' she said, lifting her chin. 'And Samantha is right. I am the manager, and I'm hiring more staff. That if I want to take a holiday, I will. If I want to spend two weeks making leather belts, I will. And if I want to create a workshop in my back shed at home, and paint the kitchen yellow, while blasting Dolly Parton while I do it, I will.'

Brodie gave her a pained side glance. 'Dolly who?'

'Behave, you.' Lydia playfully swatted at him. 'And when we leave here, you're gonna pack your bag and move in home with me, young man. Just like we always talked about. I can finally give you that spare room so you can be with family. And you've always been like a son to me. So I'm giving you a home, Brodie Cross. Because I've got no one else, just you…'

Brodie sat back, his eyes wide and glassy. 'What's the catch?'

Finn nodded at the kid for asking, it's what he'd do, because things rarely came for free. Especially after what he'd just been through with his mentor.

'You're not going back into the yards, not while I'm running them.'

'But it's my job.' Brodie winced through the pain as he sat higher in his chair.

'Not anymore. You're getting promoted.' She reached over, even if she flinched, to grab his good hand, like a queen giving out royal decrees. 'You've got a head for numbers. You smashed that word puzzle book of Finn's in record time.'

'Really?' Finn raised his eyebrows at the kid.

Brodie shrugged, holding up the book, covered in doodles.

'I'll have to get you a new one, then.' And for the right reasons, too.

'Brodie might be busy, because he'll be learning the family business. You're not that kid in the gutter anymore, Brodie. So no more ripped jeans and boots with the soles hanging off. You deserve better. You always have. And I'm sorry I let Red stop me from doing anything sooner.'

'It's okay, I didn't mind the yards.'

'You'll still be at the yards, my boy, but learning the office, working your way to running the auctions, which I know you'll be good at. And I know you love the auctions. There's a lot more to the place than shovelling dung all day, and it's time you take that next step.'

The grin on Brodie's face said it all. The kid was speechless, with his eyes glistening like all of his Christmases had come at once.

And for an uneducated kid like Brodie, who never thought he'd get far in life, beyond being a low-hand in the stockyards, he deserved it.

But then Lydia turned to Finn, and the fire in her eyes hadn't faded.

Was it too late to bolt for the door?

'You're a good man, Finn Wilde. But you live like you're waiting for something to disappear.'

'Excuse me?'

Lydia folded her hands neat as a pin over her lap. 'Your house looks like you're still in prison, like you're expecting to be sent away again. But you've well and truly earned your place in this town. You don't need to have Craig and Stone give you that *in* with the locals anymore, because everyone already respects you. So move in properly, will ya. Buy yourself a couch. A table. Hell, get a rug. And some coffee mugs without cracks in them, and a coffee machine where it's impossible for you to make coffee that tastes like—'

'Mud?' Instantly thinking of Taryn. That pang of everything about her hitting his chest, because they still hadn't talked.

'Yeah.' Lydia's eyes narrowed at Finn. 'You like her, don't you?'

'Who?' Finn wiped a hand over his scruffy chin that hadn't seen a razor in days.

'The woman who makes your stance loosen a little. Who gives you that tiny spark in your eyes, like that smile is going to happen, but doesn't. And you know why?' She arched an eyebrow at him. 'Because you're not letting Taryn in. Or anyone else, really.'

His mouth opened, but her finger wagged at him, effectively cutting him off.

'Where is she? I heard Taryn came back, and talked down the lynch mob in the pub. Is that true?'

Finn nodded. It's where he'd last kissed her, when he wouldn't let words get in the way.

'Why did Taryn come back?'

'For Drew. For her family… And now she's leaving.'

'When?'

He glanced at his watch. 'In about ten minutes.' He didn't do goodbyes, never could, and coming to visit Lydia seemed the best excuse to not watch Taryn leave.

'But Taryn only just got here.'

'She's heading back to Canberra.' They were using the same jet they'd commandeered to bring Drew in from Darwin, with Taryn escorting him to an off-site federal prison where Drew would be held until trial, with no chance of bumping into anyone from his mentor program.

'She's going home…' And from there, they'd coordinate the next wave—using Drew's own emails, call logs, and Drew's phone.

The Fed had already given Drew's PC and phone to Finn, telling him: *The bastard used your file as his how-to. You might as well use what he left behind as the roadmap to take them all down.*

Finn hadn't smiled—even though he wanted to kiss her, because damn, it felt like she'd just handed him the keys to his dream Harley.

Every name, every meeting, every shell company—it was all there. And now they were going to burn it down, one contact at a time. Giving him the chance to make up for what Drew had done.

Payback was already in motion, with quiet calls to people he trusted in small towns. Nothing official. Not yet. Just eyes and ears on the ground. The kind of justice that moved slow, struck hard, and ended with everyone in cuffs.

Sure, he could talk about work with her. But *the baby*?

That was the bit he couldn't touch.

And yet with Taryn leaving, it felt like the end of something he hadn't even had a chance to start.

'Why is she leaving so soon?' Lydia asked.

'Work. Taryn's been offered a promotion. I heard her talking to her boss about it in the Batcave...' The woman was going places, especially after this bust. Although they were doing their best to keep it quiet for now, only the trusted were called.

Taryn didn't need someone like Finn holding her back.

Not when she'd been working nonstop, helping the rest of the team push through the mountain of arrest charges, and the ton of paperwork that came with arresting Drew and his local crew. They'd been at it all night, taking turns to make tea, with no coffee for her. He'd even muttered decaf during a brief lull between them, right before they were interrupted.

Finn was the first to hit the food van when it opened. Not for bacon—anything but bacon, as the only other clue he had about her pregnancy, in a conversation that needed to happen, but never did.

He'd done his best to keep an eye on her, making sure she had the good chair, with plenty of water on hand. He just didn't get too close to her, thinking he might break her, or ruin what they had.

Even now, Finn didn't move. He couldn't.

Taryn was leaving...

And he still hadn't told her how he felt. Or even discussed her pregnancy to find out what she wanted.

'She's going places. Taryn doesn't need someone like me slowing her down.'

He didn't say it for the sympathy.

Hell, he didn't even mean to say it out loud. It just came out. But it was the truth.

She was leaving.

And he hadn't told her a damn thing.

Not about the house that he'd always wanted as a home — where maybe… he wanted her to stay. There. With him. Before he'd even known she was pregnant, because he'd never dared entertain the thought.

And now? When he didn't even know if he had a permanent job, what kind of future could he offer her? Especially when she was pregnant.

After all, he'd failed his own family in the past…

He'd been that kid who couldn't watch over his baby sister. The kid who'd made promises to his mother that'd he give her a better future. And as a man, he'd built a family of his own, then left them behind when he took that undercover job. The one that ruined everything.

He didn't blame Bree for coming back to Elsie Creek Station, to be with her family, her grandfather. It'd always been her home.

While Finn had none. He was so used to being alone that he'd never realised at the time he did. He had a wife, Bree. And a boy, Liam. And yet he'd let them go, like he'd always done.

Now, all he had was an empty house that needed a paint job and a Harley in pieces on the living room floor.

Lydia was right, it was like a prison. Because he'd had everything stripped from him once before, leaving him with nothing but a cell. And ever since, he'd been bracing for the moment it'd all be taken from him again.

And Drew had done just that, with what he'd done to the Stock Squad, his dream job.

Yeah, he was a man full of regret. That was him. Pain walking.

Lydia shifted in the bed, then said softly, 'I know why you came here, Finn. To watch over your boy.'

Was it that obvious that he always drove that back road to the stockyards? The one where the small country church came into view. Where he'd think of his little boy, Liam, thinking that'd be the last time anyone would call him dad.

His throat tightened, making him swallow hard.

'And maybe you're that big brother to Brodie. Lord knows, he needs one.'

'I dunno, I think the boy can do better than me.' Considering what his mentor had done to him.

'Stop that.' She swatted his hand. No wonder she earned her name as the mother of the stockyards. 'You see truth. And you care, I know you do. It's a strength you rarely show people. But you also do more. What you did here in this town? Catching Red. Stopping Bob. Bringing Drew down?' She exhaled a slow and proud sigh, with a hint of pain, as if staying strong for him. 'You didn't just start a Stock Squad, you protected what we are, our livestock industry, and our way of life.'

Finn dropped his head, with his shoulders so heavy, he couldn't look at her or Brodie, let alone himself.

But still she kept going, leaning over to hold his hand the way his mother used to—before the valium dulled her, before his father ran that red light, causing the five-car pile-up with the truck that left him alone in the world.

Maybe that's why it had been so easy for someone like Drew to slide in and fill that gap.

Lydia's hand squeezed hard, dragging him out of his thoughts. 'You gave this town hope, Finn. You gave them something to believe in again, like the way a good father looks after his family…'

He wiped a hand over his mouth. *Christ*.

'And now, I believe it's your turn to do something good for you.'

Forty-two

'Why do I have to coax the water buffalo off the tarmac?' With a hand on her hip, Taryn scowled at the breathing boulder, standing butt-centre in the middle of the airstrip. Red ribbons and wildflowers twisted around his horns like it was some outback version of Oktoberfest—minus the beer, but full of attitude.

Chalk scrawled across his hide read:

LYDIA IS GONNA BE OKAY!

On the other side, it read:

COPPAS GOT THEM DUFFERS!

Mickey, in his grease-stained coveralls, flicked at a fly with his hand towel. 'Well, you see, we've just started becoming friends, Cecil and I. So I can't start pushin' boundaries while still in the fragile stages of our friendship, just coz *you* say so.'

'He's blocking *your* runway.'

'Yeah. Only coz you're the one who wants to leave, like a flamin' tourist does, and I don't like tourists.'

'Oh, really? I'd never have guessed it.' Taryn rolled her eyes, overtired and moody, so of course she had less restraint with the sass.

'Or maybe Cecil's gotten all snooty you're leaving, and that's him protesting like the Vegan does.' He scratched at his ruddy chin. 'Come to think of it, he is a vegan, you know.'

'What?'

'And you two bonded, right?'

'I did not bond with a buffalo.' But Cecil was blocking the middle of the tarmac sniffing at their jet.

'You gave him flowers.'

'I fed him flowers, so he didn't lick me or do that heavy breathing in my ear, when he'd follow me to work like a labrador. Your brother told me that trick.'

'But Billy didn't tell you that all it takes is one flower, and you're Cecil's friend for life.' Mickey gave a wicked grin.

'Nooo.' Her eyes widened. 'Did I get tricked into doing some unknown tribal marriage thingy to a buffalo?'

'Got the memory of an elephant, that one.' The grumpy old man winked, the kind of wink you'd never trust. Like that grin.

It was enough for her to take a step back. 'How did Cecil get in here? You have a fence.'

'He's one of 'em flaming Houdini buffaloes. Opens gates, doors, fridges too. I could never keep Cecil out. He likes to eat the wildflowers, and I reckon he licks the dew off the tarmac, like one big tongue scraper.'

'Great.' Taryn grimaced. 'And what does Cecil use to floss? The windscreen wipers off a plane?'

She pinched the bridge of her nose.

It wasn't the sleep deprivation. And it wasn't the ridiculousness of chasing livestock off a small town's runway. It was everything else.

Because she was leaving this town with all its quirks, this job, and that hint of a life that had somehow crawled under her skin and settled in like it belonged there.

And Finn Wilde hadn't said a word.

She'd accepted that, because Finn didn't say goodbye. They'd been here before.

He also didn't want complications in his life right now. Not her, or the baby.

Which was fair, too.

She hadn't exactly dropped the news gently. She'd hit him with it, mid-sting, mid-murder investigation, and mid-mentor-betrayed-him take-down, which kind of demolished everything he'd valued.

She had no right to judge Finn, not when she hadn't even fully processed it yet, when denial had been doing a bang-up job about it all.

But she wasn't running. Not this time.

She had a plan.

She'd rewritten her report, top to bottom. The one Drew had tried to manipulate. And she was going to take it straight to the top, even if she had to walk it into Parliament House herself; she would. The Stock Squad deserved permanent funding, and she would damn well make it happen.

So what if it cost her the promotion, and even if it cost her a second chance at whatever she may have with Finn and this town, it had to be done.

Besides, she had money saved, she had holidays accrued, because she never took them. Long service leave, too. Yes, she was a career cop who really had no life outside of the office. She also had maternity entitlements in a folder she'd updated the other day, even while struggling with denial, because she was that type of person.

She had spreadsheets.

Backup plans.

PowerPoint slides she could weaponise for court.

She could do this.

And she had her parents' support.

Even if her mother would probably start interviewing ex-SAS soldiers for nanny duties by lunchtime. The same type of nannies who'd taught Taryn how to disarm a grown man using nothing but a shoelace and a ballpoint pen before she could spell kindergarten. And yes, the teddy had been a worthy opponent, who had to be re-stitched so many times, her father was worried she'd need therapy.

Her father? Oh, he didn't get off that easily. No, her father would already be tinkering in the garage designing a baby-sized Kevlar. Possibly a GPS chip to subtly insert at birth. And some sort of satellite-linked pram defence system, just in case someone tried to cut the line at the baby clinic, or park, or wherever it is that prams filled with children congregated.

Yes, they were terrifying.

And yes, she loved them.

Especially when she was terrified herself. Her. A mother.

But Finn Wilde?

She hadn't planned on him, either. And that look he'd give her when he thought she wasn't watching. Or the way they moved together in sync, like they'd trained for years in a language only they knew. No, she most certainly had not meant to fall for a man who left behind more coffee cups than conversations.

But having a baby?

And giving the Stock Squad a permanent future?

That was the kind of long-term plan she could hold on to.

It was the perfect medicine to forget a man like Finn Wilde.

Or so she told herself. And would keep telling herself, too.

She glanced at her watch. Ten minutes until wheels-up. Everyone had already been chased away after their goodbyes—except the buffalo—with their hugs and their *please come backs*.

Drew was already shackled on board like a taipan in transit. Right where he damn well belonged. Bound for a high-security institution under Commonwealth order, where they sent the nightmares in neckties and the big fish to rot.

From there she was hoping to go home, shower, and face dive into a bowl of whatever unholy combo of carbs and sugar her hormones had decided was gourmet this week.

Probably Milo, straight from the tin, with mashed potatoes and a mango sorbet. Separately, she hoped.

But no promises.

Oh, and a big block of cheese she wasn't planning to slice.

And maybe with some macaroni. And caramel sauce.

'Mickey, you need to move the buffalo.' And she needed food, sleep, and to plan doctor visits.

'How?' Mickey flicked another fly off his elbow, utterly unbothered by the chaos.

'Try psychic suggestion? Bribery and corruption? That always works.'

'Aren't you a cop?' He grinned at her, with that one-eyed squint like Popeye but without the corn pipe.

'I've got half a croissant on the plane. Or some cheesy chips and a box of gummy bears. One of them might work.'

And that's when she saw him.

Out of the corner of her eye, over by the hospital. Finn Wilde.

Running.

Taryn froze on the outside, while inside her heart did something weird in her chest.

Not panic. Not quite.

Okay, there was some panic pounding in her chest because big, rugged, emotionally elusive Finn—was running across an airstrip like a man with a purpose.

And holy hell, the things that did to her body, mind and soul.

'What's he doing?' she whispered.

Mickey squinted. 'Did he forget something on the plane? Or does he wanna smack around the prisoner some more, like Izzy did?'

Finn skidded to a stop right in front of her, his eyes locked on hers. 'Mickey, go make yourself useful somewhere else.'

'Righto. I'll just... pet the buffalo then.' Mickey shuffled a whole two steps, maybe four, only to lean against Cecil, where both man and flower-wearing beast stayed glued to the drama like it was prime-time telly.

Taryn folded her arms, bracing for something... Sarcasm? An apology? Or more grunty silence?

But Finn took a step closer.

Then another.

And then—he spoke. 'I never wanted this... Not the squad, the house or this job. Not after my boy.'

Her breath hitched at his personal heartache, putting protective hands over her own belly.

'I came to Elsie Creek to watch over a grave. Because I was

a ghost when I got here.' His eyes filled with hurt as he spoke. 'And then you showed up with your spreadsheets and rules. Your rants about my coffee tasting like mud, with your need to always have the last word. And yet you got under my skin so fast, and so much deeper than anyone has before.'

Taryn swallowed hard, trapped by the open vulnerability in his eyes.

'I didn't see it coming,' he said, taking another step closer. 'Not when I didn't want to feel again. And yet you've somehow made me want everything.'

He paused to take a breath or two.

There was no way she was going to interrupt and ruin this. Not a chance.

'I'm scared, Taryn.'

Holy mother of mayhem!

'Because you're not just strong,' he said. 'You're going somewhere and you don't need anyone. While I've spent my whole life thinking I wasn't worth staying for.'

Then he looked at her like she was the only thing left in a world worth chasing. Like he saw past the sass she wore like armour, and past the humour that hid the loneliness.

He saw the parts she didn't even know how to name. The bite that kept people at arm's length, so they never got close enough to bother her when she left. Because she was the one who *always* left. Each new posting, every new embassy transfer, she'd learned to pack fast, settle quicker, and never get too attached. Goodbyes always came before hellos.

And now here she was, getting ready for another departure, another rotation, falling into the same old rhythm.

Only this time, Finn was standing there, more stubborn than the buffalo blocking the runway.

And for the first time, she didn't want to swerve.

Somehow, the more he unburdened, the more she unfolded herself, as if opening to let him in.

'I'm...' He rubbed the back of his head as if trying to find the words, from a man who didn't do speeches. 'If you go to Canberra, I'll follow. I'll climb on this jet with you, right now, and sit beside you. I'll sleep on the floor at your place, whatever you want. Because I want to be there for you, for the baby, and whatever future you'll let me have… I don't need to read a map to know I'm meant to be with you, Taryn. I just need you to say you want me there, too.'

Taryn stared. Unsure where her voice went, of if she could remember the English language.

Nearby, Mickey sniffed as he wiped his eyes with the same towel he used to clean aeroplane parts. Even Cecil snorted like he approved.

Finn stepped in closer, to gently tuck a stray hair behind her ear. 'I'm here, Taryn. I'm not going anywhere, not unless it's with you.'

That was it. That was all it took. Speech over, it was now the real Finn— the man of action, whose deeds and silence spoke more than any words ever would. And with one hand curled at her waist, the other found her jaw. His thumb traced just beneath her cheekbone like it had every right to be there. And then…

He unapologetically kissed her.

Giving her the kind of kiss that wasn't asking for forgiveness or permission, but it told her everything he hadn't been able to say.

It was a kiss that didn't hesitate as it found its way into her heart like he always had, without warning and without a doubt. Fierce, unshakable and impossible Finn.

And when she caught her breath, she knew.

It was him.

It had always been him.

Sliding her arms up his shoulders, she kissed him back like she'd been waiting a lifetime to kiss him. Like her body had tuned into his frequency from the very first moment he'd given her that sideways glance across the Batcave, the day she'd arrived. The one full of his bad attitude, while she was covered in dust, having walked the long way around the airport, with a buffalo breathing heavily behind her—who was still breathing heavily, now.

Only this time her hands fisted his shirt, as she softened into him like a surrender as she kissed him.

There was no question now.

No games.

No pretending this was casual anymore.

Because this was the kind of kiss you planned your whole future around, where you talked about generations of family. It changed everything, because nothing else mattered but them. Him and her. And the baby made three.

He finally pulled back, just enough to look at her. 'So, I'll take that as a yes?'

A smile curled slowly across her lips, which still tasted of him. 'I should warn you… my parents aren't normal.'

Finn gently pressed his forehead to hers and smiled. 'Good. Neither am I.'

Forty-three

Six months later

Finn's boots echoed softly down the corridor, this time unshackled and with no guards flanking him. The air in this place was still cold. And it still smelled like bleach, rust, and bad decisions. But this time… he got to leave.

The prison guards nodded as he passed. Some even smiled.

They knew who he was now. They'd read the headlines: *Ex-Con Leads Rural Raids on Cattle Crime.*

He didn't need their approval. But he could see that he'd earned their respect.

The interview room was the same. Still grey and grim, buzzing with bad fluorescent lighting in the place where the VIPs would go.

But the man sitting at the table? He wasn't a VIP. Not anymore.

The ex-commissioner, Andrew Bannon, didn't have a suit. No fancy tie. Just that prison orange that made you look ill.

Finn didn't shake his hand. Didn't sit either, he just looked at him.

Drew raised a brow. 'Still not much of a talker, eh?'

Finn shrugged.

'You look well,' Drew offered.

Finn glanced around the walls, then back at Drew. 'Better than the last time I was in one of these kinda places.'

From his back pocket, Finn dragged out a small booklet and dropped it onto the table with a soft thud. Word puzzles. 'Saw this and thought I'd drop one in, and give you an update.'

Drew raised an eyebrow. 'To gloat?'

Finn had considered telling him it was all done, and why Drew was now out of solitary, because all the arrests had been made. But then shook his head. 'I came to say thanks for the chance. And for nearly ruining everything that matters to me.'

Drew winced but said nothing.

'The Stock Squad stuck. We've got permanent funding now, and we're expanding interstate after using your playbook to dismantle your operations on a national scale. Guess who's managing the budget?'

Drew shrugged.

Finn's voice softened. 'Taryn.'

'She stayed?'

'Hell yeah.' Finn's grin grew full of pride. 'She stayed and married me.' He held up his left hand, flashing the new wedding band. Why wait, he'd told her. Life didn't.

Surprisingly, Taryn hadn't blinked when he'd asked her. Coming from a military family, fast marriages were a tradition. Her parents had done it. So had her grandparents.

She hadn't said yes for the baby, or for the sake of appearances. She said yes because she knew exactly what she wanted. And so did he.

As a wedding gift, his new father-in-law helped Finn buy a real coffee machine, complete with man-to-man coffee-making lessons. No more drinking mud. Where coffee had become a quiet ritual, that was part science and art for Finn.

But he still refused to wear the apron, despite Taryn's old bet she'd made back in the trenches before she'd dropped the pregnancy bomb.

But there were a couple of aprons hanging in the house, a couch, fresh paint on the walls holding some of his favourite framed maps. And he was building a child-proof cabinet for his records. They even had a new dining suite, and the spare room was now a nursery, with his Harleys living outside in the shed. His house was finally a home.

Drew chuckled as he leaned back in his chair, the chains around his wrists clinked. 'Never thought you'd settle.'

'Me neither.' Finn looked him square in the eyes. 'Didn't think I deserved it. But it turns out… I was wrong.'

Drew just gave a nod.

'Just so you know, I'm aware you didn't put me in this place, but you got me out. You got me that pardon, even if it was for all the wrong reasons. And it's only because you gave me that pardon, that I haven't done any payback.'

Finn then leaned over, fists on the table, his voice low for the guards to not overhear. 'You see, you're in my playground now, Drew. In here it's a small world, where I've got the kind of respect, and owed favours, from people you could never buy because they've only got time. But me, I've got a town that backs me. A job that means something. And a future with a family, and a kid who'll probably ride before they walk.'

He stood back, sizing up the man who looked older. Greyer. And so much smaller now.

'You gave me a chance by giving me that pardon, so you'll have my protection until the final sentencing, where they'll put you in the big house with the bigger boys, because we know you're never getting out. So, I'm not coming back for updates. Don't send me any Christmas cards. Don't call. And don't bother asking me to top up your bank to bribe the prisoners or guards. You are, and will be, completely on your own. A forgotten someone I'll never bother to remember, and I'll never tell my children about you. And your legacy will never exist.'

He walked to the door, then paused to peer over his shoulder. 'You were right about one thing, though.'

'What's that?'

'I still prefer to stand. And I still don't like giving speeches. I let my work, and my actions, do the talking for me.' And he let the door clang shut behind him with that heavy shudder of steel. Leaving his former mentor sitting there broken and already forgotten.

Finn had somewhere better to be now, he had a future to

walk into. One that he'd never believed he'd earn—a future filled with love.

Love. It still scared the hell out of him.

But he wasn't in chains anymore. Not even the hidden ones he used to wear on the inside.

Now?

He had a new wife and a baby on the way. A found family made of good friends who always had his back. A job that meant something. And a home that was both real and permanent.

He'd heard someone say that you're lucky if you get to fall in love once. They never mentioned how many different kinds of love there are to experience in that one lifetime. Or how right it could feel when you finally let yourself have it— and felt that you deserved it.

But the love of a good woman? That was something else entirely.

That was the kind of love that was all about sharing the silence, where she looked at him like he was worth it. It was the kind that slowed down your heart, that made the world feel safe enough, as their love grew.

And so did her belly.

Because life didn't stay still. It moved. Changed. And sometimes it got to slow down in the best possible ways to take in the open air and outback sunrises.

It was Elsie Creek.

That dusty little nowhere postcode, with a water buffalo for a traffic hazard, and a reduced speed sign that only Cecil ignored.

Finn shook his head, smirking to himself as he made his way through the maze of corridors and steel doors.

Bloody town.

Elsie Creek did something to a person. It took in the rough and the worn-out, the ones with nowhere else to go, and gave them a home in the dust.

It didn't ask questions. It just took you as you were.

Sure, it had its fair share of stickybeaks and serial

gossipers. But it also had something rarer—real, rural spirit. The kind where everyone knew everyone, but still gave you space.

And when things went belly up? You wouldn't find a faster helping hand in the country—with the occasional lynch mob, sure. But also, a clever young woman who ran the pub like an outback parliament, wielding a quiet-queen energy, to tame that wild town.

No, Finn didn't need to say it aloud. That town was different. It was special.

That nowhere postcode?

It was his now. Permanently. And he was damned proud to say so.

Elsie Creek was the kind of place where the road ran long and flat, perfect for cruising on his Harley with his wife on the back, and the engine loud enough to drown out every doubt in his head.

A place with no fences. No phone towers. Just a big sky—like they were cruising through a painting that hadn't dried yet, under colours too pristine and wild to explain.

And for anyone who didn't respect the land? The outback had a way of biting back. And it did…

The clang of the main prison doors echoed behind him.

He smirked as he checked his phone.

A text from Taryn:

> *When can we go home? I'm done shopping.*
> *Mum can get us a jet.*

Finn texted back:

> *On my way now. Let's go home, baby.*

And he stepped into the sunshine, a free man ready to face his future, who was more than ready to go home.

For there was nowhere else like Elsie Creek. It might be just a speck on the map—one that Google kept misplacing—

but it was on *his* map.

It was part of his marked territory.

A spot in the Northern Territory, known as Australia's final frontier, where the cattle and crocodiles outnumbered the people. Where the outback's sunburnt dust carried its stories while also keeping her secrets, and it's where the lucky ones found something rarer than gold — they found love...

And called it home.

THE END.

For now...

WANT ONE MORE RIDE
WITH THE STOCK SQUAD?

See what happens next in the
Exclusive Bonus Epilogue

Free!

Plus behind-the-scenes goodies & more

Simply go to: https://melarowe.com/stock-squad-xtras/

Want more from the Elsie Creek World?

Binge-read the bestsellers found in:

- *The Elsie Creek Series*
- *The Station Duology*
- *The Stockmen Series*
- *The Stock Squad*

Find them at your favourite online bookstore.

AUTHOR'S NOTE

(Which is more of a letter to you!)

Turning off the porch light at the end of a long, dusty, unforgettable journey...

Well, that's exactly what this moment feels like.

This book marks the end of *Prime Stock*, the closing chapter of the *Stock Squad Series*, and maybe the end of the *Elsie Creek Series*, too.

A series that's taken us through cattle yards and crocodile-filled creek crossings, wild rides in cyclonic skies, and the crackle of campfires filled with starry skies and stories. Where cattle stations were reborn, stock squads were formed, crimes were solved, families were found, and where so many hearts were mended in the most unexpected places.

Elsie Creek was never just a place.

It was dust and diesel.

Teacups and front bar beers.

And how it held a quiet strength along with layers of outback stubbornness, cleverly wrapped in an ancient landscape that kept her secrets and her stories — if you dared to look.

And you did.

So thank you for walking its red dirt roads alongside me.

For waving back at Cecil and admiring his flowers.

Maybe even ordering that last beer at the pub.

Most of all, for loving these characters as much as I have.

The series may be ending here—but the outback never sleeps. She's always waiting...

Rough. Fierce. Kind.

And full of stories.

So let this be your final wave from the pub's front doors, where Cecil gives you that last nod as you turn towards the open road where the sun sinks beyond the never-ending horizon.

Just know that even if you're leaving this town, you will always have a place in Elsie Creek—right alongside me.

With all my thanks,

A. ROWE

ABOUT THE AUTHOR

Mel A. Rowe is a bestselling author who writes romantic escapes for readers who crave emotionally rich stories with heart, hope, and hard-won happily ever afters.

Taking ordinary characters on extraordinary journeys, Mel's stories travel from remote outback towns to quiet streets tinged with magic and myth—blending banter, found family drama, and twists that linger long after the final page.

Living in Australia's Northern Territory, Mel enjoys random outback road trips, fumbling with her camera, annoying her family with her bad singing, and making new friends in the middle of nowhere—except for water buffalos. She's been chased by a few.

Find Mel at

MelAROWE.com

Also by MEL A ROWE

ELSIE CREEK SERIES:
The Art of Dust
Diamond in the Dust
Caked in Dust
Xmas Dust
Muster in the Dust
Rolled in Dust
Written in Dust
Doctoring Dust
Buffalo Dust

OASIS OF THE OUTBACK DUOLOGY:
The Station, Volume One
The Station, Volume Two

THE STOCKMEN SERIES:
Stockman's Sandstorm
Stockman's Stowaway
Stockman's Stormcloud
Stockman's Showdown

THE STOCK SQUAD:
Rough Stock
Cold Stock
Wild Stock
Prime Stock

STANDALONE STORIES:
Avoiding the Pity Party
Unplanned Party
The Football Whisperer
Winter's Walk
Run Beautiful Run
The Sister Trip
Forget Forever

For more visit MelAROWE.com

A week later, Lucy sat at the kitchen table, staring at her laptop while gulping down a second cup of coffee. She had been awake for several hours working on an application that stubbornly refused to back up.

"You're up early."

Lucy jolted, nearly spilling her coffee. The house had been silent, and she had been so engrossed in her work that she hadn't heard Abbey pad into the kitchen.

Abbey didn't seem to notice Lucy's surprise. She stifled a yawn and headed straight for the coffee machine. "Love the formal attire. Is that what all project managers are wearing?"

Lucy smirked, glancing down at her emoji-covered flannel pajamas. "Don't you know, this is all the rage?" She stood up and stretched out her back. "And it's Systems Administrator Manager."

Abbey swatted the air. "That's too techie for me."

Lucy rolled her eyes. She didn't care what Abbey called it; she was glad to be done with the migration project and rewarded with a promotion. The promotion came with a raise, bigger projects to manage, and the opportunity to work from home three days a week. Finally, it felt like she was settling into this new life.

"Now that you'll be home more, I'm going to bug you about helping me build the website for the business." Abbey started the coffee machine. "I don't understand that side of things at all."

Lucy carried her mug to the kitchen sink, debating whether to have a third cup of coffee. "I'll help as much as possible, but I'm not a website developer. Also, just because I'm home doesn't mean I'm not working. I have my own things to do and want to spend my free time with Kaylee."

"I know; I'm just excited to get this business up and running. Maeve quit her job to make this happen. I haven't given up anything— yet."

Lucy smiled at her sister. "Trust me, before you know it, you'll give up sleep stressing about everything. This business is about to be your baby. You'll lose a lot of blood, sweat, and tears, but it will be amazing."

Abbey was in the process of building a travel business with her old boss, Maeve. They had met years ago when Abbey worked in the travel industry before she decided staying at home full-time was more important for Lola. Maeve wanted to start a company creating travel experiences around Europe. She offered a job to Abbey, begging her to help build the dream with her.

"I'm also going to push you to join the PTA with me," Abbey added. "Trust me, after tomorrow's festivities, you'll be begging me."

Lucy glanced up to the ceiling. "I highly doubt that. I'm helping you tomorrow as a favor."

"The PTA is a great place to meet people," Abbey told her. "How else are you going to make friends?"

Lucy gave her sister a look. "I have you; what more do I need?"

Abbey carried her mug from under the coffee machine to the counter. Opening the fridge, she pulled out the milk and twisted the top off. "Lucy, you live here now. Don't you want to become part of the community? You know, make friends, go out and socialize, build a support group? You need more than just me."

Lucy rinsed out her mug and set it on the dishrack before picking up a towel to dry her hands. "Support for what? Single, working moms?"

"Yes. It's nice to have like-minded friends." Abbey stirred her coffee and set the milk back into the refrigerator. "You're more than just a project manager and a mom. It's okay to have a social life, mingle and gossip with the ladies occasionally. That's all I'm saying. I mean, I didn't have many friends growing up; it's nice to have some good people in my life."

"You didn't have friends?" Lucy spat, tossing the towel onto the counter. "You were so popular. You were always going out."

Abbey stared down into her coffee. "It wasn't as if I could bring anyone home."

"Well, no, you definitely wouldn't have done that," Lucy scoffed, heading back to her place at the table. "You spent so much time at other people's houses, though; surely you had a good group of friends."

Abbey chuckled awkwardly. "It wasn't because they were my friends. I invited myself places and practically forced them to let me in. In fairness, many parents didn't want me hanging around their kids, and some refused to let me in their homes."

Lucy's gut twisted; she hoped Abbey's childhood had been better than hers; clearly, that was not the case.

"I used to tell kids I was adopted." Abbey hung her head. "I said my real parents died in a fire, and mom was an aunt who had taken me in."

"Did they believe you?" Lucy asked softly.

Abbey shrugged. "Who knows, but I was able to hang out with people more once I played the victim."

A burst of anger ran through Lucy. Abbey didn't need to *play* a victim; they both were victims.

"Everyone called her a drunk and a whore," Abbey's voice dropped. "They called you that too. I'm sorry I never stood up for you."

Lucy huffed out a laugh. "I can stand up for myself, Abbey, and I don't blame you one bit. You did what you had to do to survive. Besides, Mom *was* a drunk, but she wasn't a whore. However, I wasn't a drunk, but I was probably a whore, so they got things mostly right."

"Don't say that, Lucy," Abbey chastised. "All those people just liked the sound of their voice."

They both fell silent as they heard footsteps descending the stairs.

"Morning," Kaylee shuffled into the room, yawning and scratching her head. "Working from home today?"

"Yes, starting today, I get to work from home three days a week," Lucy replied, smiling. "Some projects may require me to go in more often, but I have a light load this week."

Kaylee fingered through the boxes of cereal lining a shelf. "Good. So, you're still helping with the Halloween Disco, right?"

A swarm of butterflies took flight in her stomach, slamming against her insides as if eager to break free. The simple thought of being in the same room with Aidan set her nerves on edge.

"Umm, yes, Sweetie." Lucy gulped, her throat suddenly feeling parched.

Kaylee's face lit up. "Oh, good. I was afraid you would back out for some reason."

Kaylee pulled a box of Frosted Shreddies from the shelf and popped open the lid.

As much as Lucy wished she could back out, seeing the look on Kaylee's face was priceless. Her daughter still wanted her to show up for things. There was a brief period, however short it may have been, when Lucy wanted *her* mother to show up for the school plays and concerts or show any interest in her child's life. Her mother always had an excuse to be absent.

Kaylee shoved a handful of Shreddies into her mouth while pulling down a bowl to pour a generous amount into. "I can't wait for you to meet Chloe, Hanna, Eve, and my teacher. Well, I guess you already met him, but he's so cool, Mom."

Lucy's face flushed.

"Oh, she's met your teacher, all right," Abbey teased.

Daggers flew from Lucy's eyes.

"What does that mean?" Kaylee scooped a spoonful of cereal into her mouth.

"Nothing," Lucy said flatly, quickly changing the subject. "Let's go shopping after school."

Kaylee's eyes lit up. "Halloween costumes?"

Lucy nodded and wiggled her eyebrows up and down. "Maybe we'll get some hot chocolate and dinner."

Kaylee gave the thumbs up. "Best day ever."

Lucy's heart continued to hammer in her chest as she

turned back to her laptop. The words on the monitor blurred together, and she longed to be sucked into the screen if only to avoid another awkward encounter with Aidan.

Since their unexpected meeting last week, Lucy couldn't get Aidan off her mind. She constantly pictured those piercing blue eyes, the dark brown hair that begged her fingers to run through it, and his sexy half-smile, half-smirk. And, of course, that accent; she could listen to him talk all day long.

Although she didn't want an awkward encounter, she couldn't deny her desire to see Aidan again. Maybe she wouldn't be caught off guard if she was ready and knew seeing him was inevitable. Perhaps one planned meeting would erase the mystery and finally free him from the entanglement of her thoughts. Everything would be okay if she could keep her composure and not act like a squirming child.

If only she hadn't been so careless that night. She shouldn't have gone home with him. It had been fun to flirt, to feel sexy, but she should have stopped at that. Of course, never in a million years would she have imagined Aidan would turn out to be her daughter's teacher. That tidbit of information would have changed everything.

"See you after school, Mom." Kaylee hugged her quickly, pulling her back to the present.

"Have a good day."

Once the girls were gone, Lucy focused on work. She couldn't let thoughts of Aidan distract her any longer. Tomorrow, she would face him again; this time, she would be better prepared.